MW00953433

Raves \ _____ ~~....~...an Novels

Obsession Wears Opals
                    "Passion and adventure seamlessly blend as
Bernard stirs a tale steeped in intrigue and secrets, keeping pages turning and
interest high."   *RT BookReviews*

"Renee Bernard has redefined what makes a hero and heroine heroic"
                                        Tin Ong, GoodReads

Passion Wears Pearls
"Chemistry between the characters sparks and crackles with a vibrant energy
that shivers up your spine keeping you on the edge of your seat well into the
night."   *Veiled Secret Reviews*

"Renee Bernard hits another one out of the park!"
                                    Lindsey Ross, GoodReads

Ecstasy Wears Emeralds

"Sensuality fills the pages."   *Publishers Weekly*

"Level of emotional force that makes sure you cannot put this book down!...Ms.
Bernard skillfully weaves a tale of love and learning, friendship and betrayal to
lead you down a merry path..."
                                    Veiled Secret Reviews

Seduction Wears Sapphires

"An amazing read, I enjoyed it immensely...Ashe and Caroline are wonderful
characters that made me fall in love with them from the beginning of the story."
Night Owl Reviews

"A fine book, well crafted, well researched, and an entertaining romantic
novel...Historical romance fans will be delighted, I have no doubt."
                                        The Book Binge

"What a refreshing new take on two people who from first sight are determined
to detest each other...I was immediately engrossed with the fiery, witty dialogue
and the curiosity of how this couple, who loathed each other upon their meeting,
would come full circle to a beautifully shared love in the end."
Fiction Vixen

Continued—

Revenge Wears Rubies

"Sensuality fairly steams from Bernard's writing. This luscious tale will enthrall you. Enjoy!" –Sabrina Jeffries, *New York Times* bestselling author

"If you're a fan of spicy hot romances mixed with a bit of intrigue and set in Victorian London, don't miss this one!"   *The Romance Dish*

"Galen's journey from emotional cripple to ability to love is a captivating, erotic romance."   *Fresh Fiction*

More praise for the "grand mistress of sensual, scorching romance"*
"Sinfully sexy. . . Wickedly witty, sublimely sensual. . . Renee Bernard dazzles readers . . . Clever, sensual, and superb."   *Booklist*

"Scorcher! Bernard debuts with an erotic romance that delivers not only a high degree of sensuality but a strong plotline and a cast of memorable characters. She's sure to find a place alongside Robin Schone, Pam Rosenthal, and Thea Devine." –*RT BookReviews

"Very hot romance. Readers who enjoy an excellent, sizzling Victorian story are going to thoroughly enjoy this one." –Romance Reviews Today
"Shiverlicious! A captivating plot, charismatic characters, and sexy, tingle-worthy romance. . . Fantastic!"   *Joyfully Reviewed*

"Crowd-pleasing."   *Publishers Weekly*

"[This] steamy historical romance is [a] great debut for this new author. . . Filled with steamy and erotic scenes. . . The plot is solid and the ending holds many surprises . . . Tantalizing."   *Fresh Fiction*

The Jaded Gentleman Titles by Renee Bernard

REVENGE WEARS RUBIES
SEDUCTION WEARS SAPPHIRES
ECSTASY WEARS EMERALDS
PASSION WEARS PEARLS
OBSESSION WEARS OPALS

The Mistress Trilogy by Renee Bernard

A LADY'S PLEASURE
MADAME'S DECEPTION
A ROGUE'S GAME

Off World Chronicles by Robin Geoffreys

TREASON'S HEART

A Story from The Eternity Gambit©
Comic Book

AZRAEL'S GIRL

**

www.reneebernardauthor.com
www.Facebook.com/ReneeBernardAuthor
Twitter.com/ReneeBernard

**

Listen to Renee Bernard on BlogTalk Radio! "Canned Laughter and Coffee" is a live weekly Internet radio program interviewing current popular romance authors hosted by Renee Bernard. Professionally produced by COS Productions as part of their Readers Entertainment lineup, this program gives readers a chance to "meet" their favorite authors and find new must-reads through an informal chat and the opportunity to hear the craziness behind the scenes of the romance industry. Visit www.readersentertainment.com and just click on Readers Entertainment Radio! Or tune in online on Tuesday nights at 8:30pm EST to listen live!

Desire

Wears

Diamonds

✦

RENEE BERNARD

This is a work of fiction. Names, characters, places, and incidents either are the product of the author's imagination or are used fictitiously, and any resemblance to actual persons, living or dead, business establishments, events, or locales is entirely coincidental.

*This book is dedicated to Anne Elizabeth. She knows a warrior's heart and I am
confident that Michael would find a welcome respite at her table.
He is a quiet soldier, Anne, and like you, a gentle soul.
I love you, Sister-Friend.*

*And to Geoff and the girls. You are my life. Thank you for making it an
adventure.*

*And finally, to my Beloved Readers.
This one is literally written for you. Every note from you, every kind review and
post fueled my desire to write a better book. And you inspired me to keep going.
This book is Yours.*

Acknowledgments

If there's been a theme to these last few months, I'm going to say it was about friends. I gained so many new incredible friends and was blessed to keep the great ones I already had, to the point that I overheard myself boasting that I'd achieved a Mark-Twainian (I made that up but I hope it comes across...) level of success. I have an inner circle of trusted souls that have given me new confidence—as if life were still a high school cafeteria and I finally found my peeps. (Did I say that right? Can you tell I'm thrilled to be at the nerd and geek table? Is it okay that at my age I just used the word peeps for the first time?) In any case, to the Universe, I want to say thank you for my friends. (But of course, Universe, if you want to throw in a lottery win for good measure, I would never complain.)

Every once in a while, you get lucky and your agent, who is brilliant and supportive, also turns out to be a great friend and the brother you never knew you were missing. I want to thank Eric Ruben for his patience, his kindness, his humor and of course, for the most glamorous client/agent dinner I've ever experienced. I am spoiled forever.

I want to thank Lindsey Ross, for being my muse and sister-friend. More than a reader, I have to say that without her amazing support and personal encouragement, there's no telling where I would be today. Lindsey made me feel like a rock star, which if you'll refer back to the first paragraph of these acknowledgements, is an incredible accomplishment. If nothing else ever came, I'd count myself a lucky woman for the friendship we share.

I have to thank Ian Parton for his guidance on British military history and the details that can make or break a historical romance (which means if anything in this fictional work related to British military history is broken, it's my fault—not his!) And special thanks are given to Juanita Decur, for being my historical period costuming muse and at the end of the day, my friend. And to Megan Bamford, for making the world seem cozier and more wonderful by just being herself. Not only is she assisting me in my quest for unofficial Aussiehood, she bought me an English Title and made me a Lady (a feat my mother is still amazed at and that the DMV will have to contend with when I renew my driver's license and insist it goes on there!) A trip to Brisbane is on my list of life goals and I'm determined to get there!

I want to also thank Lisa Watson. She is my lost twin sister and my only regret is that I somehow didn't find her until just recently. Lisa, if I didn't believe in serendipity and the amazing blessings that can come from turning right instead of left, you're the living example that it's all true and that all things are possible. I love you.

And of course, I have to thank my mom. Because despite the craziness, she still takes all my calls and laughs with me until we cry. You were my first best friend and you are the gold standard by which all others will forever be measured.

I used to be respectable and chaste and stable,
but who can stand in this strong wind
and remember those things?
Love has taken away my practices
And filled me with poetry.

—RUMI

PROLOGUE

Bengal, India
1857

There were some things in the articles of war and codes of military honor that never translate into battle. Michael Rutherford had tried hard not to think about it too much. He wanted to believe in officers and gentlemen and the almost religious requirements of the British military to establish order amidst chaos. As if the way a man packed his kit or laced his shoes could alter the course of a battle or change the world…

But that was the tall lanky boy who had joined the army so many years before. That was the naïve son of a gameskeeper who had thought to head out into the world to make his fortunes and find his way. He'd longed for the dark green jacket of the light infantry where his skills with a rifle would win him fame.

And he might have achieved it, if…

If he hadn't been pulled from the line after a bit of exhibition shooting arranged by the unit leaders where he'd astonished them all and struck a glass marble from atop a rose at over a hundred and fifty yards without damaging a single petal. If a British general hadn't decided to take him on as his personal attendant and guard. If he hadn't saved the man's life twice and guaranteed that the man's continued desire to stay alive hinged on Michael's presence, transforming him into the world's biggest rabbit's foot.

He'd existed in a twilight of rank, more servant than soldier, and all bodyguard for a man he'd genuinely despised for his icy manners and arrogance. But loyal Englishmen didn't think of a commander's character when they accepted his orders or pulled the trigger. Obedience and loyalty were tied inextricably together and by the time the man he'd become had looked up,

Michael Rutherford was convinced that he was as far from honor as a man looking up at the moon.

He'd experienced the worst that war could offer and realized that fear was a weapon all its own. He'd noted how the Englishmen claimed civility and demeaned the natives but then acted with a savagery that belied their humanity.

Even to the last…

It was a remote province and a small village but because the general's position had been threatened, Michael had obediently taken the rifle he was handed, accepted his orders and made his way to high ground. Under the cover of the skirmish and chaos of the fighting, he'd shot the targets he was directed to shoot, protected his fellow soldiers, and then fired at will until there was nothing to aim at. By the time the dust had cleared and reason had returned, there wasn't a part of his soul that wasn't broken.

We've lost India. We cannot hold it. Not like this. They'll drive us to the sea, just you wait. And I'll drink the waves in with relief, God help me.

The battle was won and the local puppet raj and authorities were pleased to see peace restored. Michael was alone in his convictions. That night, the officers drank to victory and Michael watched their shadows on the walls—elongated and grotesque. He stared at the tricks of the light until the other men forgot that he was there on the verandah.

And then he overheard the general, drunkenly whispering to one of the lieutenants. "I should put him down for a medal but Rutherford's a villain. He has the conscience of a tiger but there's no better man for the work…"

"What work?" the man had asked.

The general's smile was as warm as a crocodile's. "Did you know that Rutherford can shoot the flame off of a candle at five hundred paces?"

The lieutenant nodded, his expression uncertain. "An asset in the field."

"I've given him use of my new rifle and the benefits have been extraordinary. An American Sharps rifle in the hands of a skilled marksman is a thing of beauty, sir. But in the hands of a common thug," the general leaned in dramatically lowering his voice, "it is savage perfection."

Lieutenant Hall frowned. "Or murder…"

The British did not hold to ungentlemanly tactics in the field. Long range silent and stealthy war did not suit their ideals. Long range shooting from cover was for hobbyists and hunters and even the dark green coated light infantry deployed in units for all to see, their rifles gleaming in the sun. The general alluded to something unheard of and something that Michael instinctively knew the other officers would not believe.

The British Army did not use assassins.

But Michael knew better.

Rutherford's a villain.

He'd waited until the drunken festivities had finally broken up and then dutifully appeared as if he was conveniently arriving at the right moment to escort the general back to his quarters.

"Damn it, Rutherford," the man complained. "How can anyone as big as you are be that bleeding quiet?"

Michael shrugged, but held his tongue. He knew better than to actually answer the man. General Timsworth wasn't interested in any stories of how Michael had acquired his skills and Michael wasn't keen on revealing anything so personal to a man he genuinely hated.

Once they reached the house the general had commandeered, Michael wasted no time. He made sure the servants were seeing to the general's personal comforts while he headed directly into the office and began drafting what he needed. As soon as he was finished, he tucked the man's field desk under his arm and headed up the stairs to find the general alone.

"What the devil!" General Timsworth growled. "I didn't summon you, man! See to the grounds and be sure to tell the guard that if they so much as let a mouse in here to disturb my sleep, I'll hang them up by their thumbs! You're dismissed for the night!"

"Sign these and I'll go." Michael held out the orders he'd drafted.

"What the hell?" Timsworth took the sheet from him begrudgingly and then stared at the page. "Release from service? Are you mad?"

"Sign it and I'll be on my way." Michael set the small portable writing desk next to him. "Your official seal and stamps are there as well."

"I'll call for the guards and you'll be on your way to a hanging you insubordinate animal!"

Michael didn't blink. "Good riddance to a common thug then. I shall naturally have to confess all before I am executed. Which would have been discounted as lies if you hadn't bragged *in detail* to your men about my abilities and how pleased you are with the results."

"I didn't—" Timsworth's protest died fast as the cloud of alcohol lifted slightly and made him wonder just what he had boasted at tonight's party. Timsworth groaned and readjusted his nightshirt. "War stories over brandies. They'll think it bluster and have forgotten it before dawn."

"Let me go and I'll say nothing. I'll take it all to my grave. But if I stay, you'll have to kill me because the next time I get a weapon in my hands, I can't say for certain which direction I'll be pointing it in."

"That's mutiny! You're a dare to threaten me? A renegade who thinks to dictate terms and stroll away from his duties? You have the stones to deal with your commanding officer like this?"

Michael marveled that he couldn't feel his own heart beating. "My commanding officer? Technically, I'm not officially in the army, thanks to your machinations. Remember? You removed me from the ranks and have listed me as a valet on every pay voucher. So much for my chance at a pension, eh?"

Already dead. I'm already gone.

"You're paid well enough and..." Timsworth's color drained from his face. "I spared you from the dangers of the common rank and file. You've enjoyed a privileged stay abroad as my personal attaché, have you not?"

A stay abroad? Why does the man feel compelled to make it sound like he's taken me on some exotic tour for which I should be grateful? Stupid git.

"As your privileged attaché, I've seen enough to make a report of my own to end your illustrious military career. Let me go. A drum head trial will only draw attention to the matter and make your statements at the dinner seem all too true. But you can tell them you dismissed me for insubordination, or gave me leave to return to England, or—I don't care what you tell them. But I'll take that signed paper stating I served you well and without fault for all these years and that I'm no longer in your employ."

"This." Timsworth held up the paper with a sneer. "This is not an official document by any stretch of the imagination, Rutherford. Who do you think will be fooled by some handwritten scrawl you force me to sign under duress? And who exactly will care enough to ask for it before they mistake you for a deserter and put a bullet into your head?"

"I doubt that anyone will have the time to search for one man…not in the months ahead."

"Why? What can possibly lie ahead to spare your pathetic life?"

He can't see it. The Sepoys are increasingly angry and we've marginalized them into a corner…we're outnumbered and spread thin with a civilian population of our own that we cannot protect. And he's got us shooting children without a thought to the ramifications. These new rumors of the pig grease are simply an excuse for it all to go wrong.

"Sign it, general, and we shall call it an even trade. My life or death doesn't matter, right?" Michael took one step closer, allowing his commanding officer to truly appreciate the physical differences between them. At a breath short of seven feet, he towered over the average height and weight of the older man, a force to be reckoned with. "You see, I don't expect to survive long on my own in India; which means I have nothing to lose."

"One does not simply walk away from the British Army and the East India Company because they wish to. I'll forget this conversation and put in a word for you to see that you attain a position with the—"

"This isn't a request for a transfer. If you have to, put my name in the casualty lists and be done with it." Michael didn't move a muscle, and waited for the inevitable.

He didn't have to wait long.

Timsworth's arrogant ice broke and his hands began to shake, marring his signature but it was still legible. "Useless. Dishonorable waste of a man! Scribble does not change the facts. You're a demon, Rutherford."

"No." Michael gifted him with a crocodile smile of his own.

But I'll be damned if I'll linger in Hell and play soldier for the devil.

CHAPTER ONE

London
May 1860

Michael Rutherford leaned his head against the carved molding that framed one of the windows in Dr. Rowan West's study. The eclectic clutter and cozy colors behind him soothed his spirits. Dr. West's haven worked its subtle magic on all the men of the Jaded whenever they came. It was a casual sanctuary that had kept them close and provided a place for them to talk, plan or relax and kept the brotherly bonds between them tight.

At the moment though it was allowing Michael to hide from the festivities of all his friends below. Darius Thorne had finally wed the lovely Miss Isabel Penleigh in a quiet ceremony that was sure to set off a firestorm of scandal. It had been weeks since the ink had dried on Miss Penleigh's first marriage's annulment, but the plan for a quick wedding to Darius had been thwarted by her parents. In a cruel move, Lord and Lady Penleigh had sued Netherton and claimed that Isabel was not in her right mind when she left her "dear husband" and that if Lord Netherton intended to keep her dowry, he would have to keep his wife as well.

They'd have been in the court for months or years if the villain Netherton hadn't finally broken his silence privately to her parents about the illegitimacy of the marriage, his bigamy and his disinterest in regaining Isabel's hand. They'd agreed not to expose him to the law in exchange for her dowry, or whatever was left of it after he'd paid off a few debts.

It was an uglier end than Thorne had hoped and a terrible betrayal of her parents to coldly collect their daughter's dowry and then promptly to disown her outright for her "unsightly" condition and her wretched choice of a man with a profession and not a drop of blue blood.

From what Michael could see, neither the bride nor the groom's happiness had dimmed in the slightest despite the storm of disapproval around them.

Apparently love made even the cleverest men refuse to see the dangers. *Another wedding...*

Darius's face had shone with triumph as he recited his vows and Michael begrudged him none of it. He was glad for all his friends to have made their way back to their lives. It wasn't resentment that drove him away from the revelries.

It was an uneasy sense that there was a dark force in motion that would rather see the Jaded at funerals than flowery celebrations of tender future joys. The Jackal was still out there. The fire at the Thistle was solid proof that he'd underestimated the danger and it had shaken his confidence in his ability to keep his friends safe. Then Darius had told them that he'd uncovered the presence of a third party who believed that whatever mystic item they'd spirited out of India must remain in their hands.

Their fate was now supposedly controlled by an ancient prophecy and keeping the sacred treasure out of the Jackal's hands was more than a game of fortune—losing to the Jackal would be the end of all of them and all that they loved.

Nothing but enemies of the worst kind—the kind I can't see.

Came close to seeing the bastard in that fire though. Hell, he was close enough to touch in that smoky stairwell.

Michael shoved away the memory. He'd lost a lot of sleep wondering how differently it would have turned out if he'd been at the head of their group when they'd met the Jackal face to face. His fingers clenched around empty air in his frustration.

"You're not up here moping, are you?" Rowan's voice interrupted.

"I'm not a child to pout in corners." Michael's back stiffened and his face grew hot with the realization that he'd protested a little too loudly. He looked exactly like a toddler hiding in the drapery, and he knew it. "I have a headache."

"I'll get you something for it then."

Michael turned and waved him off. "There's no need. It will pass."

Rowan crossed his arms as he sat on the edge of his desk. "Your absence was noted. Couldn't you at least *pretend* to be happy for them?"

"I *am* happy for them. I am happy for all of you. I am brimming with joy."

"I can tell. You look like a man on the edge of a giddy collapse," Rowan said dryly. "Perhaps if you smiled, it would come across better. But then, it is *your* turn next even if you do try to hide from it."

Michael crossed his arms. "If you're implying that I'm somehow slated to get married next, you're daft."

"Careful, Rutherford. Every bachelor who ever makes a proclamation of his determination to die alone invariably brings down the wrath of Aphrodite herself and lives to take it back." Rowan crossed his arms to mirror his friend's stance. "Ask any of us, if you don't believe me."

"Leave me be. I can't help but feel as if we're making a mistake, sitting back on our heels and pretending that nothing is wrong. And this public show of—" Michael sighed. "By all means, go enjoy the party, Rowan, but I...I can't."

"It was months between incidents last time—"

"Why?" Michael cut him off. "Why so long between every attempt? Is he baiting us? It takes veins of ice to demonstrate that kind of patience, wouldn't you say?"

"I wouldn't know. I may have many faults but excessive patience is one I may have skipped, Rutherford." Rowan dropped his arms, yielding the fight. "Which is what brings me in here to find you, friend. The wedding party? Remember? Darius has been desperate to marry his Isabel for weeks now and if not for the legal tangle, this happy day would have occurred over two months ago."

"Damn it, Rowan. Why hasn't the Jackal snapped at our heels yet?"

"You yourself agreed that after that fire, Darius probably wasn't the only one requiring time to recover. Perhaps we were lucky and the man has succumbed to pneumonia." Rowan stood to head over to the side table and pour himself a drink. "And we're not sitting back on our heels. Galen, Ashe and I are having all our stones discreetly evaluated by different London jewelers and in small lots to avoid raising too many questions. Even Darius has suggested that Josiah's pearls be weighed to see if any of them are false and have something hidden at their center. We'll find the "diamond in disguise"."

Michael closed his eyes against the pounding at his temples. Ever since he and his friends had escaped from a dungeon in India, a prophecy involving the gems they had tucked into their pockets from their insane host's treasury had haunted their every step. Over time, they'd learned that they were actually the guardians of a mystic 'diamond in disguise' but in order to keep it safe, first they needed to identify it. Each man of the Jaded held a different stash of stones after a casual ceremony where they'd divided the gems they'd taken by color. Galen had taken the rubies; Rowan, the emeralds; Ashe, sapphires; Josiah had taken the pearls; Darius, opals, and Michael had ended up with the diamonds. As a result, it was Michael's cache that was exempt from scrutiny. They'd all agreed a diamond disguised as a diamond was a bit redundant.

Michael shook his head, opening his eyes. "And then what? You see? Even when we figure out which of your gemstones is the ever elusive sacred treasure, we still have the Jackal at our heels and I don't like running."

Rowan took a small sip of his brandy before answering. "We could bury all the remaining treasure somewhere impossible for the Jackal to ever find and…"

"And spend the rest of our lives fending him off," Michael supplied. "It's a nightmare I'm not willing to entertain. We'll need to face him and end this."

"True. But the answer on how to make that happen won't come any easier while we hide in closets or with you forbidding any of us to leave our homes without bodyguards." Rowan poured another drink for his friend. "We're taking every precaution we can, Rutherford."

"I don't see you hiring those extra footmen I asked you to," Michael said with a growl.

"I'm a lowly physician, Michael. I'm not expected to have a large household and it's not as if the house isn't open to anyone seeking medical attention which means it's open for anyone to do their worst if—" Rowan caught himself and stopped. "I'll get another man on staff if you get one, Rutherford."

Michael smiled. It was a ridiculous notion and an easy point to forfeit. Michael was a giant of a man, a few inches shy of seven feet in height, muscular and well-balanced in his athletic form. He lacked the thick neck of a brawler but there was no mistaking his power. And as the Jaded all knew, for all his massive size, Michael Rutherford possessed the grace of a cat, forever startling them with his talent for entering rooms unnoticed or appearing where he was least expected.

Michael Rutherford was the last man on earth who appeared to need a bodyguard.

"I don't think footmen are the answer," Michael conceded. "You're easy to rattle, old friend."

Rowan's eyes widened in surprise. "Is this a sense of humor I detect? Were you having a go at me, Michael?"

Michael shrugged, his expression sobering out of habit. "I have always had a sense of humor. I'm just more selective in my jollier moments. And today, I'm afraid, isn't one of them."

"When is a better moment? Hell, it occurred to me that I've never really seen you laugh, Rutherford."

Michael folded his arms and gave Rowan his most intimidating look. "I laugh."

Rowan took a seat behind the desk. "All right. I'll take your word for it. You laugh. What next then for the Jackal? Besides finding the treasure…"

"The Jackal sees us as the aggressor and blames us for the fire at the Thistle. Unless he's had an epiphany in the intervening weeks since it happens, it means he knows nothing of the third party that Darius uncovered."

"Let's hope so."

"So we must put ourselves in the Jackal's shoes. He is in a two party fight and his opponent has demonstrated a willingness to use deadly force." Michael's voice took on a low measured cadence, as his imagination took hold. "He is outnumbered and every blow he strikes is either deflected or ineffective. If he weren't frustrated and furious before, he is now. The gunshot at the Thistle proves it." Michael unconsciously reached up to touch the faint scar on his cheekbone from the Jackal's missed shot.

"Yes," Rowan echoed again, this time more softly as he respectfully took in the strategic turns of a soldier's mind.

"He may regret firing his pistol because he'll never again be able to show the white flag to draw us out. Even if—even if we were stupid enough to start that fire, he might worry that he gave away too much in his rage. Subtle attacks didn't drive us to ground, and his one and only attempt to meet us in the open nearly ended in his demise…"

"And some of us with him," Rowan added.

"It just reinforces his impression that we are an unpredictable enemy," Michael said and took the large chair across from Rowan as he began to relax into the conversation.

"Very well," Rowan took another sip from his drink before he continued, "the Jackal thinks we are arsonists as well as jewel thieves. Lovely!"

"If I were the Jackal, I wouldn't be accepting anymore of your invitations. It could never be public enough to suit."

"So we're back to waiting for him to make his next move."

Michael closed his eyes. "If I were the Jackal…"

"Go on."

"My best weapon is my anonymity."

Rowan grimaced. "If you know you still have it. It was close quarters in that stairwell according to your accounts. What if he fears you got a good look?"

Michael shook his head, his eyes still closed in concentration. "No. That fear has long been dispelled. If we'd identified him, we'd have already been on his doorstep. It's been a few weeks and no one has come calling. He's decided we were all as blind as he was in that smoky hellhole."

Michael opened his eyes.

Rowan became very still. "I can see it in your face. Finish your thought."

"If I were the Jackal, it's no more games. When I'd gotten the soot out of my system, I'd come after you one by one until I had what I wanted or until every one of the Jaded were dead."

"Does he have our membership in hand then?"

Michael nodded. "Half of us, at best. Blackwell is known to him; and you. Not Darius, I suspect, though with he and Isabel temporarily taking up residence with Ashe and Caroline, it wouldn't take a genius to make the connection. Josiah might also be on his list of possible suspects but his impairment may have saved him the Jackal's surety and slowed his hand."

"How? Is it possible that he is morally sound enough not to attack a blind man?" Rowan asked in astonishment.

Michael sighed. "No. I don't think the man has a single moral restraint. But Josiah's attendance at our informal meetings has been sporadic at best and his public appearances recently were even more rare. Hastings is an elusive ghost and I've sent Eleanor a letter to privately ask her to see that nothing changes on that front."

"He'd be furious if he knew you'd asked his new bride to keep a tight hold on his leash." Rowan's tone was raw with disapproval. "You overstep, Rutherford."

"Hastings is the most vulnerable man in our circle, Rowan. You want me to see things through the Jackal's eyes?" Michael leaned forward, the intensity of his gaze frightening to behold. "I want to teach the Jaded a lesson about fear. I want you to give me what I want. And I want you to be sorry that you didn't give it to me the first time I asked. So I'm going to slit the throat of the weakest among you and make sure each and every one of you watches so that the next time I ask, you're on your knees."

"You...are a very scary man sometimes, Rutherford."

Michael tried not to wince. "Not fit for parties then?" Michael said, a shadow of mirth flitting across his features. "Should I just go?"

"There's no escape for you, friend. Even if the devil is at the door, life must go on."

Life must go on. Even if I'm the devil in that metaphor?

Already their lives had changed so much since they'd returned to England. Michael conceded that Rowan was probably right. He took the glass he was offered from his friend's hand. "I'll toast the happy couple from here."

"Michael, may I ask you something?"

"Of course."

"Of all of us, I'd say you've said the least. About India."

"What is there to say? It was a slender slice of hell." Michael's throat closed before he added quickly. "In that dungeon."

"I'm still amazed we survived all of it," Rowan said.

"We were lucky to only lose one man," Michael said with a sigh.

"Two."

"Pardon?"

"Two men. John died just after we'd escaped but there was another man at the beginning, remember?"

"My god, I'd forgotten him completely!" Michael stiffened in embarrassment and stood in a rush. "Damn it!"

"We'd exchanged names in the pitch dark and barely sat down before they dragged him out! It's not as if we had any time to bond with the fellow..."

"That's no excuse!" Michael kicked the desk and grimaced at the pain.

Rowan held up a hand as if to stop him, but didn't approach his friend. "Hell, it happened so quickly. They took him out never to return. Darius said the guard muttered something about a bird for execution and we knew—"

"They were going to kill him. Some kind of example probably to entertain the locals." Michael ran a hand through his thick hair. "Sterling."

"Sterling," Rowan repeated. "Sterling…what was his last name again?"

"Porter, wasn't it? Yes, it was Sterling Porter." Michael's hands fisted at his sides. "Damn it! How could I have blocked the man from reckoning?"

He walked back over to the windows to stare down at the street below. *How was that possible?*

Hell, I've been so caught up in everything. In survival and then in escaping, in getting back to England and keeping them all safe from Jackals and prophecies, knife wielding assassins, poisoners and burning buildings…

But to have forgotten one of our own? Even if we only knew him for an hour, it doesn't seem right. It's as if I've allowed him to be die twice…

"You're wallowing in guilt over there, Rutherford."

"Are you a mind reader now, Doctor West?"

"Michael, please. We couldn't see our fingers in front of our faces for the first stretch. We never saw his face and there wasn't a lot of conversation to be had. He was gone before we'd even had time to accept what was happening and we all pushed him from our minds to avoid thinking of the worst."

"You're probably right."

"Probably?" Rowan shook his head. "Hell, *I'd* forgotten him, too! It was Darius who corrected me when I said something of it a few days ago; about how lucky we were all six of us to overcome so much. So you're not alone in this, Michael."

"Sterling Porter." Michael set his drink down and rebuttoned his coat. "No, I am not alone, but I have something to do."

"What do you intend?"

"To track down his family and offer my condolences." Michael squared his shoulders. "It won't be much but at least they'll know where he fell."

"Not today, Michael. It's Darius's wedding day," Rowan said quietly.

Michael held his breath, wanting to argue, wanting to tell his friend that he ached to escape the confines of the house and not sit by in awkward isolation at the celebration. But Rowan was right.

"Of course. Time enough afterward." Michael let out a long sigh. "We should get back downstairs. I don't want to miss the wedding toasts and the send off."

But I'll be on it before nightfall no matter what and begin the search for his family.

There's been enough waiting.

It's time to take action.

* * *

"It's a lovely menu, Mrs. Dorsett," Grace said quietly as she handed the paper back to the cook. "Thank you."

"As you wish." Mrs. Dorsett's expression remained stony and Grace did her best to ignore it. She'd been running her brother's household for nearly seven years but her gentle nature didn't lend itself to authority. In the first year, she'd once begged her older brother to release Mrs. Dorsett but he'd laughed at her childish request and merely pointed out that he liked the woman's cooking. And then he'd added that until she had proven to be as invaluable as the cook, she would need to accept the charitable nature of her position.

She'd learned her lesson and never complained again.

She'd acquired a steadier hand and uncovered the real reason for Mrs. Dorsett's foothold. It was her brother's need to keep up social appearances by employing a cook—even if that servant had the education and bearing of a badger. Appearances were everything.

Our father's lesson to my brother, I fear. Though I wonder what lesson I took from all those years of invisibility...

Her brother had brought her to London at seventeen years of age after their father had remarried and indicated that he had no place for another woman in the house. His new wife was the widow of a country squire and had no desire to share her position with another woman—even the quiet and odd daughter of her new lord and master. The flimsy excuse that Grace could find a rich husband in Town had been accepted without argument. No one really believed that Grace was going to take London by storm without a title, dowry or any chance at a debut but no one had spoken up when they'd packed her off to the city with her meager belongings.

Of course, if any of them had bothered to ask, she'd have assured them that she had no desire to marry. Grace hated nearly every aspect of the confined and careful life of an English woman; but she knew better than to reveal it. As Mrs. Dorsett retreated, she began to write all the weekly expenses into the house's journal in her neat careful hand. She knew to the half-penny where the budgets were allocated. Over time, she had added a woman's touch and turned a dreary dark house into a light, cheerful and elegant home.

Once the ledger was up to date, she set the accounts aside and took a deep breath of relief. She fingered the buttons of her blouse's high collar at her throat and leaned back in her chair. The house was in order, the chores in hand, the menu set and she had the afternoon to herself and a few precious hours to do exactly as she wished.

A few precious hours to escape...

A new story she'd been working on with savage pirates and an underwater kingdom beckoned her back to the pages she'd hidden away. She'd been up until two in the morning wrestling with krakens and trying to decide if her heroine's prayers for rescue should be answered in this installment, or the next chapter.

Grace eagerly unlocked the large hidden drawer underneath the rose painted surface of her ladies desk and pulled out the well worn leather bound notebook that was her one secret source of solace in the world.

Respectable ladies did not write nonsensical stories and outrageous tales for the working class. Respectable women did not entertain naked tribes of cannibals and leagues of wizards in their heads. Respectable women had no notions of murders and mysteries and would turn their noses up at the very suggestion that there was entertainment to be had with harrowing encounters with dashing highwaymen or in the discovery of secret societies of vampyres.

Yet Grace did not write tame poetry or weak prose. Her soul's fabric was not suited to dainty fairy tales. And no one who knew her had any idea...

Her older brother simply thought her a strange creature with no gift for social situations and Grace had allowed it. After all, it meant that her interior landscape was her very own to manage and it allowed her to plot her path out of the stifling cage she occupied. So long as her brother believed she was only scribbling away in some kind of girlish journal, Grace was free to do as she wished.

She pulled out the linen wrist covers she'd made to protect her sleeves from getting ink stains and settled in with a sigh of blissful surrender, dipping her favorite pen into a heavy glass inkwell at the ready.

Their tridents gleamed in the silvery depths as they cut off Captain Martin's escape. "Poseidon will have your bones to atone for this trespass!" cried the—

Grace's hand froze when the jarring sound of the front door's bell rang out.

She had to bite her lip to keep from crying out in disappointment at the interruption but there was nothing to be done for it. It was a small house and the crisp click of Mrs. Dorsett's heels on the wooden floors downstairs as she moved to answer the door was unmistakable.

Grace held her breath for a moment, hoping that whoever it was, might have business that the ever-efficient Mrs. Dorsett could manage without spoiling the—

"Right this way, sir." Mrs. Dorsett's sharp voice carried up the stairs through the floors and Grace's head tipped back with a sigh as she relinquished the breath she'd been holding. But disappointment at the interruption was almost immediately replaced by a stronger emotion.

Shock.

A male caller? Did she say 'sir'?

The low rumble of a man's voice in reply to Mrs. Dorsett made her sit up a little straighter, her curiosity completely piqued. Grace put away her tools and her writing as quick as a cat, locking her things away and made a rushed inventory of the sitting room to make sure that it was presentable.

She stood, her nerves jangling, and smoothed out her skirts just in time as Mrs. Dorsett rapped on the door and then opened it before Grace could answer her.

"A man to see you," Mrs. Dorsett stated flatly and then turned before she'd even shown the gentleman in, as if the intrusion of a visitor was her least concern, much less the rituals it might require or the impropriety of leaving her mistress alone with a strange man.

Grace bit her lip to keep from groaning aloud at the bungled social niceties but the sight of the tallest man she had ever seen *ducking under* the doorframe to enter her sitting room ended her ability to protest.

Indeed the sight of a very handsome and very large man in a simple dark suit with his hands gripping his hat in front of him shyly dwarfing her ended every intelligent impulse or thought she had hoped to have to make up for Mrs. Dorsett's failings.

Dear God. He's so...impossible!

"I was not expecting any callers, sir." She swallowed and prayed as hard as she ever had in her life that the heat she felt in her cheeks was miraculously invisible. For here was not only an unexpected male caller but one that not even her own overworked imagination could have conjured. Thick black curls streaked with white in a salt and pepper effect offset the beauty of rugged masculine features, a square jaw and the gentle light of his eyes. Despite the white touches in his dark hair, he was not old but a man in his prime. He was broad and lean and appeared as solid and unyielding as any bronze statue in a park—except this chiseled wonder was standing in her sitting room. She curtsied slightly, at a loss for how one proceeded when demigods came to call. "I am Grace Porter."

"You're…" His voice trailed off, his expression reflecting genuine misery as his hat suffered from his white-knuckled hold in its brim. Pale grey blue eyes the color of a winter sky darted from hers as he took in the room. "I should have thought this through past the front door," he said softly.

Grace blinked. "Is it a visit or a tactical siege?"

It was his turn to look at her in surprise. "A visit, I hope." He replied as if asking if such a thing were acceptable.

Her next impression was that the man was undoubtedly the shyest human in the British Isles with the set of his shoulders and tentative stance. *Why he looks like he's getting ready to run from a fire breathing dragon!* Grace warmed to the knowledge, courage flooding through her. "Then I should tell you that you are welcome. Would you care to take a seat?"

He shook his head. "I don't think I should."

"It *is* the first step of a social visit," she offered. "Sitting. Or so I'm led to believe…"

He shook his head again, openly eyeing the delicate legs of the chairs, all carved to resemble bamboo and birds. "It may be but I don't think your furniture will survive the attempt."

Grace tried to see the room from his vantage point. It did look a bit dainty. "Perhaps it's a wicked custom to give a woman's dull life a bit of humor to see gentlemen attempting to navigate through our gauntlets of glass trinkets and silk pillows."

"That sounds like a frighteningly real possibility," he replied. "Please pardon my manners," he said, his cheeks reddening. "I am…ill-suited to…drawing rooms on my best days but this visit is particularly challenging. It's a lovely room but I won't linger long."

Grace's stomach fluttered with butterflies at the effect of his presence. *This is ridiculous and if I don't stop staring at him, he'll declare me an idiot and there's an end to it.* "I'll accept the compliment and the brevity of your intended stay, if only to try to save your hat." She bit her lower lip. "I'm sure it's stopped breathing by now if you care to release it."

He smiled shyly and relaxed his grip slightly on his cap. "There. A life spared."

"Well, that's one thing set right. But I'm probably the one to apologize for a lack of manners." She straightened her back, doing her best to compose herself and channel a more serene countenance. "I have the habit myself of speaking first without thinking although I don't recommend it to anyone for its consequences. But let's ignore the rules and stand, shall we? Even so, you'll need to provide your name if we're to make another start. Don't you think so?"

He nodded, becoming instantly more somber. "I am Michael Rutherford. I…I met your brother, Sterling, in India."

Grace nodded, pleased that he was in the right house after all but mortified anew at her candor with an associate of her brother. Sterling hated wit in a woman and had complained more than once that she had the decorum of a dairymaid. Then again, she didn't expect her brother to allow him to call again so it hardly mattered. "Oh! Well, I'm afraid, Sterling's not here. I don't expect him home until the evening, Mr. Rutherford."

"What?"

Something in the way Mr. Rutherford asked the question made her heart skip a beat. He hadn't asked it as if he wasn't sure of his hearing. Instead he was suddenly looking at her as if her sanity were in doubt.

"He's at his office at the Company, near the East India Trading Docks. There was a shipment from the Congo that required his attention, he said. Are you unwell, Mr. Rutherford?"

He barely moved, his reply soft and careful. "Sterling Porter. Is at his office."

"He is." She clasped her hands together, unwilling to let trembling fingers betray how unsettling it was to be at the center of Michael Rutherford's keen study.

"Your brother. Your brother who was in Bengal in 1857 is in London. Your brother, Sterling."

"As I said. But Sterling speaks so rarely of his time in India that..." Grace caught her breath. "I'm sure he'll be glad to hear that an acquaintance stopped by to—"

"No!" Mr. Rutherford blurted out, only to hold up a hand as if to make amends. "I mean, I would rather surprise him, if I can. It was—such an amazing experience and I know he has fond memories of our time together. Please, don't tell him I called."

"Don't tell him?" Grace put a hand against her heart, taken with the unexpected turns in the conversation. "What a perfectly mysterious thing to ask!"

"No great mystery, I assure you." His gaze never left hers and Grace tipped her head to one side to study the puzzle he presented. He appeared as sincere as a vicar on Sunday but there was something stern and desperate in his face. And the writer in her was enrapt at the idea that he was caught in some heroic conundrum.

"Please, Miss Porter."

It was the way he said "please" that did it. Grace had to bite the inside of her cheek to keep from smiling at the impossible bubble of rebellion rising up from her toes. A man she did not know was asking her to conspire to keep secrets from her brother and despite all logic, she couldn't think of a single reason to say no. "He hates surprises."

Mr. Rutherford held his ground. "Most men do."

She smiled at the wicked admission of their conspiracy. "Very well. If as you say, there is a bond between you, then I wouldn't wish to be the one to spoil your reunion."

"You are too kind, Miss Porter." He took a firm step backward and then bowed awkwardly, his eyes never leaving her face. "May I call here again?"

Her mouth fell open in shock. "You could if..." It was a lovely bit of irony. Normally, it would be Sterling who would forbid it but since the call was a secret and Mr. Rutherford only wished to return to surprise her brother—there was no chance for a refusal. Grace managed to nod mutely in assent.

"Thank you." He straightened and turned without another word, ducking out the doorway and showing himself out of the house with quiet footsteps on the stairs.

Grace stood where he'd left her until she heard the front door open and close as he exited to the street outside and then she sat back down at her desk a few seconds before her knees turned to rubber.

I should make Captain Martin a good deal taller, I think...

CHAPTER TWO

Michael Rutherford was running.

He'd been so relieved and surprised when his Bow Street runner had quickly uncovered a London address for Mr. Sterling Porter and indicated that his sister was in residence. He'd rushed over there, sure of finding some version of a plain spinster with black crepe-draped portraits of her dead brother in the front hall. He'd braced himself to deliver the grim confirmation of a man's passing and wasted no time in stopping off cards or making appointments.

After all, social graces weren't his forté.

But now...

Michael moved away from the house as quickly as he could, every instinct warning him that the last thing he wanted was to be caught in the open if Sterling returned home early.

Sterling Porter was alive.

Which meant one thing.

Sterling Porter was the Jackal.

Damn. Damn. Damn.

It all made sense but he'd never seen it coming. Only a man who'd been there would have had knowledge of what they'd taken but the dark—something as primal as the dark had kept them from him all this time. He'd never seen the faces of the Jaded and he'd left them there too quickly to learn much about them. Probably because he hadn't expected them to survive, much less return to England with the treasure that Sterling must have been after all along.

How Sterling had escaped was a greater mystery to Michael but one he set aside for the moment.

He started to hail a hackney cab and then dropped his arm because at the moment, he had no idea where he should go first. His head was spinning with revelations tangled up with the image of a diminutive woman with pale skin and hair the color of rose gold pulled back in a plain chignon. The delicate creature who had nearly made him forget his purpose with her surprising references to sieges and the labyrinth presented by sitting room furniture.

Miss Grace Porter was a complication he couldn't afford—and couldn't afford to ignore. Like any tactician, he knew better than to disregard her presence. A cunning part of him he wasn't proud of pointed out that she might also be his only avenue into the Jackal's lair.

Hell, that was…what the hell was that?

If he'd felt oversized and clumsy before meeting her, he felt like an ogre at the first sight of those bright clear blue eyes peering up at him. She was a stunning beauty with strong features. Even more compelling, there was something about her that snagged and held his imagination. Without artifice or the customary feminine fluttering that women adapted, a terrible habit that mystified and troubled him, Miss Grace Porter had faced him with unique directness. She'd generously ignored his rudeness and ham-fisted pleasantries and then kept him off balance with the turns of her quick mind.

He wasn't sure there was a recovery to be made after he'd abruptly ended the exchange and fled the house. But he'd secured her agreement to allow him back. It was a weak cast to try to give him more options to reapproach the Jackal, but there was a small part of his brain that had argued that it was the most unnecessary and inappropriate question a man could ask when he was hoping to come back and ultimately kill the woman's brother.

How does that go? May I call on you again, Miss Porter? I'd like to murder your brother some time before Sunday and I was hoping you'd extend an invitation to tea to allow it…

Michael groaned aloud at the jarring reality of where a single "social call" had led him. Not that he was going to kill Sterling…well, not…by Sunday.

And not over a tea tray in his parlor.

Either way I'm the demon who's come to her door—and there's no taking it back now.

Damn.

✳ ✳ ✳

"What happened to your hat, sir? It's a mash!" Mrs. Clay fussed sweetly. "My goodness gracious!"

"I—I must have sat on it," he offered lamely. Michael scuffed the wet and mud off his boots as best he could, leery of tracking it into the interior of the well-kept inn he lived in. Mrs. Clay ran a tight ship at the Grove but for the life of him, he couldn't see how she managed it so sweetly. She bustled and hovered and without a single cross word, had everyone in her employ cheerfully doing her bidding, competing to please her.

She shook her head and held out her hand. "Give it here, sir. Let me have a try at mending it and if not, I'll ask Tally to give it a proper burial in the side yard, with all the honors due it. Not that I'll have the maids sing hymns or wrap it in a flag but hand it over, Mr. Rutherford."

He reluctantly held it out to her, not because he had a sentimental attachment to the damn thing but because he had no other and the weather required one. He also knew his landlady well enough to know he was about to give her a great amount of happiness. "Mrs. Clay, would you be kind enough to pick me out a new hat? I have no eye for it but I beg you, something simple and dark. No…decorations, please."

Her eyes lit up and she clapped her hands together, further smashing the remnants of his damaged cover without a blink to her ample bosom. "Oh, Mr. Rutherford! What a joy! I can't remember the last time I got to buy a man a hat! Mr. Clay, God rest his soul, always let me pick out all his things for I swear that man had no sense of it. I do miss some of his bolder attempts at selecting a waistcoat though, and…" She stopped herself and stepped back.

"Just write down the haberdashery you prefer and give it to Tally when he's up with your dinner and I'll see to it right away."

He nodded gratefully and turned to head upstairs but then stopped. "Mrs. Clay?"

"Yes?"

"Thank you."

She blushed and straightened her apron. "It's just a hat, Mr. Rutherford!"

"As you say." He retreated up the stairs, through the first floor sitting room and to his apartment door, unlocking it with a sigh. It was a unique sanctuary, with its oversized bed custom made for him so that his feet or arms didn't overhang the edges, and sturdy furniture more suited to a hunting lodge than a city inn. The room was nearly devoid of decorative objects, other than the few that Mrs. Clay had added, but it boasted a beautiful large rough stone fireplace and a mantel where he'd put his penny novels and favorite books held in place by a rusted counterweight and a plain wooden box that held various odds and ends.

With the ingrained habits of a military man, there was a place for everything and everything was in its place. He hung his coat on its hook and set his boots next to the fireplace grate to dry. In the top drawer of his dresser, next to his shaving kit and personal items, Michael retrieved a locked steel box and tucked it under one arm. Then in his wardrobe arranged with his meager selections by weight and season, he located the small hidden compartment against the back where he'd put the key to his desk.

Ever since his careless mishandling of his notes had led to near disaster when Josiah's Eleanor had bumped into him before the terrible fire at the Thistle, Michael had started locking away his diary and notes. Caution had gripped him ever since—caution and a growing sense of guilt; guilt that it had been his idea to start encoded exchanges with the Jackal, taunting him into a nearly tragic meeting at the gambling house.

They'd survived the fire—just barely. And none of his friends had ever hinted that he held him accountable for the mess. But it didn't matter. Michael wasn't the kind of man who required someone else to point out his faults. He kept too close a watch on them himself.

Without wasting any time, Michael sat at his desk, unlocked his papers and began penning notes to all the men of the Jaded to summon them for a meeting, grimly conveying the urgency and avoiding the subject at hand for security's sake. He was cautious by nature and didn't want any misdirected notes to give anyone an idea of what he'd discovered.

Normally, they'd have met at Rowan's but one simple thing made Michael alter their routine and draw his friends to the Grove—he didn't want them to be too predictable.

Well, that and he didn't want to go back out in the cold spring rain without a good cap.

* * *

Sterling Porter leaned back in the small uncomfortable confines of the hired hackney as it made its way through the streets of London from the East India Trading Company's docks. It was later than usual but he'd warned his sister that with his new responsibilities his hours were harder to predict.

Not that it affected his expectations of a hot dinner and orderly house.

Grace was generally useless but subservient enough to suit him and she made no demands on his resources. He'd resisted her arrival years before but later decided it helped him to have her in hand. His house was run the way he wished without argument and she was an improvement over a wife who would complain about his lengthy absences and travels; or interfere with his plans with endless questions.

Grace was strange and awkward, despite her beauty. She was always scribbling in her journals, although on what subjects Sterling couldn't imagine. She almost never left the house, had no acquaintances he could name as significant and had no interests beyond the books in her small bedroom or maintaining the walled garden. He had once speculated if Town would change her, but Sterling scoffed at his own anxiety on that account.

He'd dutifully included her in a few small social gatherings after she'd first arrived on his doorstep but it had led to nothing but embarrassment. When Grace did speak, the questions she posed to his friends were always ridiculous or shockingly odd. The turns of her mind boggled him. Sterling had no sense of humor when it came to these matters and no desire to have it known that his sister was "off" or even worse, a "free-thinker" or radical. Better to keep her home and out of sight than asserting her bizarre opinions on the mythology of clouds or asking how sailors made scrimshaw to colleagues and peers he was attempting to impress.

He blamed his father for her lack of education and polish, but wasn't surprised at it. Their father had convinced her that she was plain and Sterling saw no benefit in correcting his little sister's lack of vanity. She'd had some schooling and a few tutors and was literate enough for a woman but Sterling hated the echoes of his country childhood and it was hard to look at her and see anything else. He'd long since determined to have as little to do with his past as possible. His father's idea of success was a year with a good crop where his grain mill business thrived and he could swagger about the village and have the other men tip their hats when he passed by.

Fat small-minded fool!

Sterling knew he was meant for better things and had driven himself ruthlessly to achieve his goals. From a menial job as a clerk, he'd slowly clawed his way up through the ranks—but not very far.

Not nearly far enough to suit him.

Sterling had always made the most of every position and every connection, no matter how seemingly inconsequential. If there were leverage to be gained, he'd found it and sniffed out any hint of business that might prove profitable. From the first, he had invested his meager earnings into small deals until he'd made a name for himself for uncovering good opportunities. Both within the Company and without, Sterling had brokered business relationships and made the most of every chance. He'd saved enough money to get a taste for the finer things, but greater chances to prove his worth and advance in the company eluded him.

At least, they had until the fateful day he'd been assigned to reorganize the reports from a remote province in Bengal. In a forgotten file, Sterling had uncovered an opened missive from the appointee there that spoke of a mythic treasure. A raj had made casual mention of a sacred treasure, a diamond whose beauty and power would make any other look like a worthless pebble in comparison. The raj wished to give it to the Queen of England in exchange for one of her daughters' hand in marriage.

It was the most ridiculous offer and claim imaginable. And other reports from the area confirmed that the local raj was known to be mentally erratic, so no one had paid the ridiculous letter any mind and his mention of a treasure was lost.

Except that it then had Sterling's full attention.

It made no difference to him if the man were a raving lunatic. It was the diamond he was after and after several weeks poring over other obscure reports in the archives of the Company, he found another reference to a "sacred treasure" and some snippet of a ridiculous prophecy that alluded to foreign hands holding the treasure and taking it far away so that the stone could fulfill its destiny.

And in his mind the dream and quest had fallen into place. He would present himself as the preordained foreigner to the raj and take possession of this treasure. The East India Trading Company would simply be the agency through which it passed, but if the diamond were as spectacular as promised…Then the Queen would have her gift and Sterling would be rewarded with a knighthood and a fortune for bringing it to her. He would become *Sir* Sterling Porter and every trace of his humble beginnings would be erased.

He'd campaigned tirelessly for the resources to make his journey and won a monetary advance from his superiors to travel to India. And then nothing had gone according to plan.

The carriage pulled to a stop and interrupted his thoughts. He paid the driver what was owed and climbed down unassisted. His cheer dissipated a little as he opened his own front door. A true gentleman had a servant waiting to open doors and take his coat and hat. For a moment, he wondered if he should task Grace with greeting him.

No, better not. Grace is the acting lady of the house and it wouldn't do to have a neighbor call and find her at the door bobbing curtsies. Not after he'd been asked about the golden haired scullery maid seen scrubbing the front steps last spring. Still one would think that without being asked she'd have the common sense to greet the brother who clothes and feeds her and generously sees to her welfare—

"Welcome home," Grace said as she came down the stairs, unknowingly underlining his thoughts. "I've held dinner and Mrs. Dorsett made certain to—"

"Damn it, Grace." He dropped his satchel on the small table and began shrugging out of his overcoat. "It isn't *holding* dinner. How many times do I have to tell you that dinner is served *on time* when I arrive in the evening?"

"Of course."

"I'll eat in my study tonight." He held out his coat and scarf to her. "Have her serve me there."

"Of course."

Sterling turned to go but something made him slowly swing back to assess his sister. She was meek enough, but there was a flush of color on her cheeks and a brightness to her eyes that made him wonder if he'd missed a step.

She almost looked...*Happy?*

"Grace?" He folded his arms. "Did you have a pleasant day?"

Her eyes widened for a split second but then she answered sweetly. "You are so kind to ask! I had a lovely day. The weather was uncooperative so I was able to finish the accounts for the monthly budget along with the menus and then invented my very own furniture polish using that orange oil that Mrs. Saunders recommended. But I added a touch of—"

"Oh, for god's sake!" Sterling shook his head in disgust and retreated to the sanctuary of his office, unwilling to be bored to tears by the trifles of her day's domestic triumphs.

And missed the mischievous grin on his younger sister's face.

CHAPTER THREE

There was a long moment of shocked silence after Michael spoke as each of the Jaded tried to absorb his words.

"He was…one of us?" Rowan asked from his chair. "You're certain?"

"Why did it never occur to any of us that he wasn't dead?" Galen asked.

Darius readjusted his wire-rimmed glasses. "Seriously? Perhaps because death seemed the most likely fate when the guards hauled him out of that dungeon never to return? Perhaps because we couldn't think of a reason for him *not* to be dead?"

"At the Thistle," Josiah said. "In the stairwell, remember? He said, 'We meet again' and something about being 'old friends'."

"I remarked about it at the time," Michael said, then walked to the study's window and looked out into the night. "And then forgot it all like a fool in the days that followed."

"It was a vague clue at best," Ashe noted. "The bigger hint was that the bastard appeared to know far too much about what happened to us in Bengal."

"Sterling!" Darius sighed. "We've had a ghost on our heels all this time."

"I say we make him a ghost in earnest and sleep in peace tonight!" Ashe grumbled.

Rowan rubbed his temples with a sigh. "No one's arguing that he's not a deadly enemy of us all, but I'm not sure I can…plot a cold blooded murder."

"It's not murder. It's justice!" The hatred in Ashe's voice was as sharp as steel, and just as unyielding. "My first born lost because of his poisons and very nearly, my Caroline! What's to discuss?"

All of them except Michael exchanged looks. Months and weeks of hating a nebulous foe had culminated in this. Their enemy now had a name and was literally within their reach but like Shakespeare's Hamlet the men were learning that even a sense of righteous vengeance couldn't erase all of a man's morals—or his reluctance to personally "do the deed".

Darius touched his friend's shoulder. "The authorities wouldn't agree and I don't want to see you hanged for such a worthless man's life, Ashe. We have no solid proof of his involvement in anything that's happened to us. Not one shred that we could hold up in a court of a law as a shield to protect us if this goes wrong."

"Darius is right. It's our word against his. I don't think a failed mugging, the random confessions of a murderer who then killed himself, hearsay, and a blind man's recounting of faceless burglars and an assault on his night watchman along with," Galen leaned back with a wry grin as he continued, "Oh, yes! How can I forget? Our involvement in a gambling house fire and the odd belief that we've been featured in an ancient Hindu prophecy; is going to sway a jury or persuade anyone of anything. Hell, it all just sounds like one of those bad penny novels that Michael enjoys!"

"Hey!" Michael stiffened. "Leave off a man's books!"

"Hey!" Josiah protested with a laugh. "And I resent being characterized as a blind man!"

"My apologies to you both. I should never judge a book by its presentation and for a man wearing tinted spectacles at night and using a cane, you can see how one might make the mistake," Galen countered archly. "What were we talking about again?"

Josiah tipped his head back against the cushions of his chair with a smile. "God, I love these meetings."

"He's here in London! Where *exactly* in London?" Ashe pressed.

Michael crossed his arms defensively. "He is here in London. And I'm not giving you his home address, Blackwell. For reasons that should be obvious, I'm not telling any of you any more until I'm ready."

"No more secret messages in the papers, no more worrying about where he is or how to draw him out," Ashe said. "You found him and I say we move quickly before whatever advantage we have evaporates."

"We still don't know why he wants this sacred treasure or if he's ultimately the one behind what's happened. If you move too fast, Ashe, you could end up forfeiting everything," Darius calmly stated. "The Jackal may be on a leash and we'd be no better off."

"He's right." Galen took a sip from his lemon water. "But then, Thorne's always right."

"Gentlemen," Michael said, turning back to face his friends. "There is no chance of the scales not balancing. But I need you to trust me. I need you to back off while I assess the situation and determine the best course of action. Penny novel or not, we're finally in a position to hold the reins and steer the plot in our direction."

Ashe's ice blue eyes narrowed. "It's not a question of trust, Rutherford. But I don't want to hang back and see this snake slink off again!"

"I won't let him escape," Michael said, his voice like hot stones falling on a drum. "And when the time comes, I'll be the one to end him and I'll act *alone*."

Silence descended again and Michael went on.

"You have your lives now and families to protect." He straightened his shoulders, imposing his full height and daring them to argue that he wasn't the man for the job. "Besides, I'm already engaged in this. I say we limit our exposure to one man. There's no need for the rest of you to step in. I have this well in hand. If I need help, I'll ask but not unless it's absolutely necessary."

"Wait!" Ashe wasn't backing down. "You cannot suddenly think to pretend that we are not in this together already."

"No. We are in it together. But these next few miles will probably end in bloodshed and I'm the one who has the Jackal in my sights." Michael took a deep slow breath and then let it out carefully. "I'm the only one here who knows what it is to kill a man."

"As a soldier, yes, but..." Rowan came around to sit on the edge of his desk. "Surely this is different."

Michael shook his head. "The only difference will be that this time I might enjoy pulling the trigger."

They held their collective breath and Ashe sat down slowly.

"Damn," Darius whispered. "You always did know how to get in the last word."

"I have him in my sights. And I *never* miss." Michael went on. "Never."

"Then that settles it." Galen set his drink down. "We leave it to Rutherford to come up with a plan on how best to take care of the Jackal. Darius goes off on his honeymoon tomorrow as planned and we hold here. We stand with Michael and offer whatever help he requires and for now, we keep out of the way."

Every man nodded his assent except Ashe, his eyes still locked onto Michael's unflinching gaze. "Swear to me that no matter what happens, Michael, you'll do whatever it takes and my Caroline will be safe."

"I swear it, Ashe."

Ashe nodded. "Then I'm content to stand by. For now."

Michael sighed. It was all he could have hoped for, considering that Ashe more than any of them, had experienced the worst of the Jackal's schemes. His beloved Caroline had nearly died and suffered a brutal miscarriage after ingesting poison meant for Ashe. Even now, her health was fragile and she was confined to bed during this new pregnancy. They all knew that Ashe lived every day in mortal terror of losing his incomparable American in childbirth. It made him more volatile and none could argue that Ashe wouldn't be better off a hundred miles from London and whatever was about to unfold.

But no one was going to move Ashe an inch in his current state of mind.

So the compromise was victory from Michael's vantage point.

Hell, if I can keep all of them at a safe distance then no matter what happens, I'll have kept all my promises to the Jaded.

Because this wasn't the first vow he'd made to his friends.

In the dark of a dungeon in Bengal, Michael Rutherford had sworn to protect his friends and make whatever sacrifice was asked to get them home and restored to their lives.

The group visibly relaxed, returning to their favorite spots in Michael's apartment, refilling their glasses and settling in to talk about the turns of fate and try to make sense of ancient prophecies or the more enticing mysteries of how best to please a new wife. Each of them was convinced that they had landed the most beautiful woman in the world and had converted, like most affirmed bachelors, into fanatical husbands.

Michael knew better than to enter the lighter turns of the conversation. He retreated to the window seat and let out a quiet sigh. He was the last bachelor standing and with the dark days ahead, he had no intention of altering that fact. But for now, he also had no intention of mentioning to his friends the wrinkle in the cloth that was Grace Porter.

She's irrelevant.

Michael's brow furrowed as the thought failed to carry any conviction, especially weighed against a restless afternoon where she'd invaded every moment he'd had—even as he'd fought to focus on the Jackal alone.

Does she know her brother is a foul excuse for a human being? Could any one with a look that clear be untouched by the horror of it? If she is in it, then she's just one more element to watch. And if she isn't...

If I move carefully, could I accomplish my goals without bruising her spirit?

Michael closed his eyes, shutting out the rise and fall of conversation behind him. He'd accepted a commission of murder to protect men he held as dear as brothers, and lied to those same men about how much he would enjoy the task.

No pleasure in it. But if she is an innocent in all of this—if I can't manage it gracefully, I'll swing from the gallows for it and forever be known as a demon—especially to her. But if I take my time and can hold Ashe back long enough to let me find my way through, perhaps I can save her...

If not myself.

CHAPTER FOUR

In the days that followed, Michael immediately hired a Bow Street runner to track Porter's movements and began to gather intelligence like a general planning a battle. If there was ground to be lost, Michael wanted it to be to Sterling's disadvantage so he wasted no time. Normally, he'd have done all of it himself but since he'd been to Sterling's house, he had no faith that Grace would keep his visit a secret. She was the Jackal's sister and her loyalties would probably lie with him. If she betrayed that he'd called, his height was bound to be mentioned. No one ever failed to mention how tall he was, even to him—as if Michael Rutherford were miraculously unaware of his condition.

Except Grace Porter.

She said nothing of it and I'm so used to hearing some tired remark, I missed it entirely.

Michael's hand stilled, hovering above the notes he'd been making in his small leather covered pad as he leaned back against the carriage seat. He'd hired the hackney for the day and ordered the driver to simply wait on the shaded lane indirectly across from Porter's home. It was a good spot to make his covert observations shielded from view and out of the weather.

Michael looked again at his handwritten notes and considered how very different Grace was from every woman he knew. Grace had calmly addressed him as if giant rude men invaded her sitting room most ordinary days. She reminded him of Lady Winters, the first woman to break into the Jaded's small circle and the first person he'd ever met who was more stubborn than Galen Hawke, now Lord Winters.

I wasn't as miserable today in Grace's drawing room as I was in the Haley's but this was different. I should have asked more questions when I had the chance. I let the situation derail me and it's hard to think of what to say while Miss Grace Porter is looking at you.

Michael pushed the thought away, unwilling to let the memory of Grace's charms distract him from the task at hand. If she'd told Sterling about him, a description would be a natural inclusion in that conversation. It might be the one detail that betrayed him if he spied Michael personally lurking around the docks or outside the East India Trading Company's buildings.

Instead since his discovery of the Jackal, he'd done what he could to watch the house from a safe distance and added his own observations to his hired man's. The house itself was small but on the end of a desirable street for anyone up and coming and the adjacent square was once considered extremely fashionable. Michael sketched out what he could remember of the interior and the layout of the narrow house from his brief view, noting as many details as he could.

He'd also confirmed that there was only one live-in servant to speak of. The sour faced woman he'd met was their cook and an indifferent housekeeper. They took another girl on as maid for a day or two a week, but nothing steady. He saw no sign of Grace leaving for calls and no visitors came to the house for tea or afternoon conversations.

It bothered him to think of her without friends.

She's too young to be so isolated.

The runner had added the news that Sterling hired hackneyed carriages to get to work if the weather was foul, but would walk the first legs of the journey if the day were nicer. Even so, he would hire a cab for the last of his commute so that he always arrived by carriage.

The one story that sealed Michael's instincts about Mr. Porter's identity had been a nearly off-hand notation. "Man was laid up for a few weeks since sometime in January. Grocer said it was all quiet and half-orders for a while. Something about pneumonia. Though he's back to work now apparently."

Pneumonia? Or a good lungful or two of smoke, more likely.

"I wonder how he explained to his sister about the singed holes in his coat or the stench of the soot," he asked aloud.

He jolted upright as the very object of his daydreams suddenly come out of the side ally in a plain brown day dress holding a small basket, as if slipping out to do some shopping. She looked even prettier than he remembered. She would be about twenty-four years of age. At thirty-one, she made him feel ancient.

She should be married with a house of her own.

She was overworked, as far as Michael could see. The same grocer who'd gossiped about Sterling's mysterious illness had also shared his opinions about the "lady of the house" as well as the Porter's cook. Mrs. Dorsett was not liked in the neighborhood and unpopular with the tradesmen for her sharp tongue and haughty manners. But Miss Porter was the subject of great speculation. She'd been seen scrubbing the front steps and doing the work of a scullery maid, but her gentle manners and ladylike demeanor were much admired on Baker Street. "Never a cross word! Remembered my little one was ill and made a lovely dolly for her with a lace and satin dress," the grocer had stated. "She still has it, sir! Tattered now but as precious as gold to my sweet girl."

Michael watched Grace for a few seconds and something about her manner caught his eye. She looked guiltily over her shoulder back at the house before adjusting her bonnet to shield more of her face.

Where are you off to, Miss Porter? And why so worried that someone will see you?

He pushed forward and adjusted his own coat. If she were walking a short way, then the carriage trailing her would be obvious, but if she hired a cab and he was on foot, he could lose her. Michael took a deep breath and decided to split the difference. He waited until she was away and then he climbed out of the carriage, quickly ordering the coachman to follow at a discreet distance.

As she moved through the city it was hard not to speculate on her destination. They passed the grocer's markets and the streets with the ladies' shops closest to her home. If she meant to pick up something ordinarily on a woman's list, Michael was fairly certain there was no need to look so guilty.

Did the quiet and reserved Miss Porter have a lover?

An unexpected wrinkle, but nothing to spoil our plans.

He ignored an odd bubble of irritation at the idea of Grace Porter meeting a man for a clandestine or heated exchange. It was an irrational reaction and Michael pushed it away. After all, what did he care if she had a dozen secret lovers?

Still, Michael wasn't going to leave anything to chance. Whatever her business, he didn't want to allow any blind spots to complicate matters. She might be running an errand for the Jackal.

He kept out of her sight, grateful for the natural shield of a lady's bonnet that interfered with Grace's peripheral vision. But Michael began to close the distance as the turns she took led them away from the more polished streets and avenues of the city and more toward the poorer end of the city. Jackal's sister or no, Michael was not going to allow anything to happen to a woman alone.

He watched with some trepidation as the pedestrian trade looked rougher and rougher as she went. Her pace was determined and unflagging so he disregarded the notion that she might be lost.

He'd have slowed to add to the buffer between them when the sidewalk narrowed but he didn't like the way one of the street urchins began to mirror her steps. He adjusted the buttons of his own coat and changed his course to parallel the young boy. Her basket had the thief's complete attention so it was fairly easy to form a plan. He would trip the boy and then duck into the next alley to ensure that if she turned around there'd be nothing to alarm her. But when he saw the flash of a sharp blade in the boy's hand, his instincts were alerted to the danger and Michael reacted only as a protector.

He grabbed the boy's wrist and lifted him with a twist that demanded that he either drop the knife or forfeit the bones in his arm.

The boy kicked out with his thin little legs, his dirty face highlighted by wide eyes as he experienced unplanned flight. The knife fell away and Michael noted that it was an expensive weapon, engraved in silver with a shaped ivory handle—probably a prize from a gentleman's boot.

"Heave off," he whispered. "I'm not going to hurt you, you little snipe."

The boy was disarmed and diverted, and Michael was about to just let him go but instead of surrendering the child transformed into a hellcat of teeth and claws.

"Oy!" the boy screamed. "Get off it!"

It would have been laughable except the boy's boot squarely connected with Michael's testicles and everything imploded in a white shattering pain that felt as if someone had hammered iron spikes into his hip bones and up into his spinal cord. His hands went numb and he released his charge who did him no favors by crashing into Grace as she was starting to turn around at all the commotion.

Cunning little animal!

Mortified to be seen, he was powerless to do little more than watch as her basket was upended and sheets of paper flew up around her to be blown into the street. Grace screamed and then did the most surprising thing of all and something he would never have anticipated.

She blindly dove after the chaotic flurry of parchment into the street, and for Michael everything slowed. He last thing he remembered was the sound of an approaching carriage as he lunged to grab her coat and yank her backward.

Only to lose his footing and then the world was all horse's hooves and carriage wheels.

And darkness. And one last thought…

There you have it. Getting hit by a carriage doesn't even come close to taking a shot between the legs.

Lesson learned.

CHAPTER FIVE

Grace squeaked as someone grabbed her firmly from behind by her collar and
yanked her off her feet. But as her backside connected with the dirty sidewalk,
her squeak became a scream as her rescuer slipped and took her place and the
phaeton's back wheel struck him down. She heard the sound of the driver's
whip driving the horses on and in numb horror realized that the carriage's
handler had no intention of stopping to see who he'd murdered.

She lurched forward again, to wave off the next carriage and prevent
her good Samaritan from being struck again. She knelt next to him and gasped
in surprise.

It's Mr. Rutherford! My god! There's a way to surprise Sterling with a
reunion! I've caused his friend to be injured and...I'll be caught out for sure!

Another bystander stepped down to help her pull her savior from the
muddy street and onto the sidewalk, but got nowhere for her hero was a bit
heavier than the average bloke. "Please!" she pleaded to another group of
gentlemen passing along. "Please help me to move him!"

They complied, a bit reluctantly, but Grace ignored their lack of
manners, openly grateful for their charity. It took three men to lift him and she
guiltily scrambled behind them to pick up what pages she could while they
achieved the pitiful sanctuary of the cobbled stone walkway and dropped their
unconscious burden.

"He's probably done for, if you ask me, miss." One of the men said as
he placed a white silk handkerchief under his nose. "Unless you know him, I'd
say brush off your skirts and clear off!"

Grace stood, glaring at the man. "Feel free to apply that wisdom to
yourself, sir! Brush off your skirts and be on your way!" She shoved the

muddy pages into her basket and knelt anxiously at Michael's side, paying no further attention to the insulted men who withdrew with growls about insolent women and suicidal fools. "Mr. Rutherford," she said softly. There was a small trickle of blood from a cut at his hairline and at the sight of it, terror crystallized inside her chest.

Oh, god. He did this saving me and I was—I was blindly chasing after a chapter about a band of cursed pirates and undead mermen!

"Mr. Rutherford," she tried again, tentatively patting his cheek to try to rouse him. "Sir?"

"Shall I send for help, miss?" a woman stopped to ask. "Is he dead?"

"No! I mean, I don't..." She sat up a bit straighter and prayed he wasn't. "I need a cab."

"I'll hail one for you," the woman offered and left Grace to attend to her charge.

"Don't worry, sir. I'll get you to a hospital and all will be well," she told him softly. Mr. Rutherford opened his eyes at that exact moment and made her yelp in surprise yet again. "Mr. Rutherford!"

"No hospitals," he said calmly. "I am perfectly fine."

Grace pressed a hand against her forehead, relief making her dizzy for a moment. "No offense, Mr. Rutherford, but men who've been struck by carriages do not get to argue that they are in perfect health. At least, not while they are lying on their backs outside of a tobacco shop."

He lifted his head, a groan slipping past his teeth and proving her point. "Then I'll sit up."

"Please, sir." She held his arm, helping him up as best she could. "Perhaps I should not have staked my argument on your...physical position."

"Cab, miss?" the driver called down from his perch, having stopped at the hail.

"Yes!" she said, just as Mr. Rutherford was barking, "No!"

Grace looked up at him and might have been swayed, but the small trickle of blood on his head became a rivulet that trailed down the side of his face. "Yes. We are most definitely in need of a carriage."

"I am *not* going to a hospital, Miss Porter."

"Then accompany me home and you can take the carriage wherever you'd like afterward." She'd have said anything to get him inside the cab, a vague plan coalescing inside her head about convincing him to see reason once he was off his feet.

Several pedestrians moved past them and Grace held her breath.

"Fine. We'll get you home safely," he conceded then looked up at the driver. "The lady will give you her address and then we'll go on from there."

The driver touched his hat with an odd smile. "As you wish, sir."

The driver helped Mr. Rutherford to his feet and Grace gathered up her basket to stand next to them, only to be bemused as she realized that Mr. Rutherford was holding his hand out to her to act the gentleman and help her inside the waiting cab. As if it were perfectly normal for bruised and bleeding men to adhere to social courtesies.

She eyed him suspiciously. "You're not going to bolt once I'm wedged in there with my skirts, are you?"

His jaw tightened, but his expression was hard to interpret. "On my honor, I won't make a run for it."

Grace took his hand and climbed up then true to his word, he followed her. If she'd been cavalier about the man's physical size and presence before; there was no escaping his dimensions now. The springs on the carriage protested a bit as he shakily ascended into a space that was meant to hold only two passengers and inserted himself as carefully as he could onto the seat next to her.

There was not an inch to spare. He made a great effort not to infringe on her skirts or her person, but it was in vain. By the time he landed, the length of his thigh was harbored up against hers, the outside of his hip touching hers and only by twisting his upper torso at great cost to his comfort did he avoid practically taking her into his arms.

Layers of crinoline and petticoats did little to shield her from the heat of his flesh and even with his hands politely holding the handle and door frame to keep his weight from shifting against her, it was a delightful crush.

In countless stories, she'd written of great passion or unrequited love, all fueled by her own guess at the subject since she'd never so much as held hands with a man she wasn't related to and only once witnessed an impolite kiss between her father's assistant and a farmer's daughter behind the market wall. It was all supposition and borrowed descriptions from ladies magazines and books; with a salacious dash of what she hoped was a man's frankness if he had explored the fictional world of the dreadfuls.

But there was nothing fictional about the erratic beating of her heart and the curl of an electric spiral of tension coming to life between her hip bones arcing all the way up to the crown of her head. "Well!" she exclaimed, aware that she was three shades of pink at the discovery of the wicked confines of a hackney cab when shared with Mr. Rutherford.

"Well?" he asked.

"I'd say the odds of a quick escape are beyond us both now." She started to laugh and then covered her mouth with a gloved hand, mortified. "I'm so sorry! That was terribly forward!"

"You did say that you tend to speak your mind," he said. He pounded a fist on the roof to signal the driver to move off. "Nothing rude in that, Miss Porter. If you ask me, it's a charming weapon that disarms more than it wounds." He averted his face and watched the traffic as it passed.

Grace's mouth fell open at the compliment, stunned into a brief silence—but only briefly before curiosity reasserted itself. "I should thank you, Mr. Rutherford, for stopping me from…falling."

"It was instinct, Miss Porter. I'm only wishing I hadn't tripped over my own feet in the attempt."

"I still can't believe you were there." She looked away from him, nervously. *Does he wonder why I was there? He's a friend of my brother's and if he mentions it to Sterling when he sees him...God help me, it's a tangle.*

"May I ask you to tell me?" he asked.

"Tell you what?"

"I know what *I* was trying to save when I fell into the street. But what were you trying to save, Miss Porter?"

Grace's grip on the seat tightened. "I...would rather not say, Mr. Rutherford."

His eyes dropped to her basket where the edge of a rumpled sheet of paper was visible and she shifted to push it further under her skirts. She'd have told him it was rubbish but then her sanity would be in doubt. After all, who dove into the street without looking after rubbish?

"Not even a half-hearted attempt at a lie?" he asked. "I'm quite gullible."

She smiled shaking her head. "I'm not saying I'm not capable of deception, sir. But with you, Mr. Rutherford, I find I am at a loss. I owe you my life so I will begin by repaying you with total honesty."

"So, the papers are...?" he pressed gently.

"None of your concern." Grace held her breath and bravely awaited his disapproval.

"You are a woman of mystery, Miss Porter."

She felt a flutter of a warm spasm of pleasure inside her chest at the words. "What a lovely thing to say!"

"Is it?" Mr. Rutherford asked in shock. "Are you sure?"

She shrugged. "Well, it sounds better than..." Grace caught herself, wishing the man didn't have a talent for making her act like a giddy schoolgirl. The carriage rocked as one of the wheels struck a deep hole in the road and Michael's face took on a gray tinge. She stiffened her back and attempted to redirect the conversation. "We should divert the driver and get you to a hospital, Mr. Rutherford."

"Absolutely not. I promise I'll see a physician, if that will content you."

"It barely satisfies but I don't know you well enough to bully you one way or the other, sir."

"You bullied me into this carriage."

"That was a feat, wasn't it?"

"It was. I can't remember the last time I was bullied into anything, Miss Porter."

"I will refrain from abusing my powers if I can."

He smiled back at her and for Grace, the world faded away. Suddenly the reality that Mr. Rutherford was taking up over half of the small space in the hansom cab's interior; that his feet were by necessity tucked under her skirts; that every time she inhaled she was treated to a heady mix of the scent of his skin and a hint of cinnamon and musk. *His soap? Or the herbs his wife adds to his laundry…*

"It's oddly comforting to be ordered about," he admitted. "Too many years in the army are to blame I suspect."

Before she could ask him any one of the dozen questions that leapt into her mind, the carriage came to a halt and her worst nightmare unfolded.

Michael felt the familiar carriage he'd hired to spy on the woman sitting next to him pull to a stop and everything instantly changed.

"Please," she whispered, reaching across to catch his hand, anxiously looking into his eyes. "Please don't tell him…anything! I beg you!"

Before he could respond or even comprehend who it was he was not telling whatever it was he wasn't supposed to say, a man was pounding on the carriage door, his angry face peering in at her through the window. "Mrs. Dorsett said you'd gone for errands but I don't recall you needing a carriage to—Who is this man?"

Shit. There goes the high ground!

Grace opened the door, feigning outrage. "Sterling! How can you be so rude?" She climbed down unassisted before Michael could stop her. "Mr.

Rutherford was kind enough to see me home after I had a bit of a mishap while shopping. I tripped and would have fallen into traffic if not for his effort to save my life!"

"Mr. Rutherford?" Sterling asked, his angry expression giving way to confusion. "How gallant of the gentleman!"

"I was looking at ribbons for a new bonnet and—well, I know the details of my days bore you, but yes, thank goodness for Mr. Rutherford! I know he'd hoped to surprise you but I'm afraid I spoiled things for him."

"To surprise me? Had he?" Sterling took a measured step back, his gaze firmly locked on Michael, his curiosity unmistakable. "I'm sorry. How is it that the gallant Mr. Rutherford wished to surprise me?"

"He'd come by to call on you a few days ago...but there was an incident, as I said, and...I think his ribs are broken..."

"To call on *me*? You said nothing of it, Grace." Sterling's brow furrowed as he tried to take in the jumble of facts.

"At my request," Michael answered quickly, not fond of the way Grace's face was losing color. "I wished to give you a pleasant surprise." He was virtually trapped inside the carriage, wincing as he shifted forward on the seat, doing his best to ignore the glassy sharp pain in his side. Good manners dictated that he climb down for introductions, but Grace was still blocking the doorway and made no sign of moving.

"To what purpose?" Sterling asked.

"To reacquaint himself naturally!" she said. "You've met before but...as I said, he is injured so—"

"*Naturally*?" Sterling looked at her in astonishment. "Is it possible for me to have forgotten such an acquaintance?"

"From India." Grace glanced back at Michael, biting her lower lip. "Is that not what you said, Mr. Rutherford?"

"Yes. In India, briefly." Michael kept his tone as light as he could, his hand on the carriage door as he braced himself. "I was in the army and hired out by the East India Trading Company."

Sterling's eyes shifted back to Michael. "I don't recall a Mr. Rutherford but I never really paid much attention to the men in the lower ranks."

Grace gasped at the insult. "Sterling!"

"No offense taken," Michael said. "Unlike some, I've never pretended to be a gentleman."

Grace gasped again but Michael couldn't take it back. Nor did he wish to after seeing how the words had hit their mark as Sterling's composure faltered.

The bastard's all about show and pretense.

Sterling recovered and smiled. "A man of such sharp wit is generally unforgettable, Mr. Rutherford, yet I'm still having difficulty placing you. Tell me again how this surprise was to be engineered and how you are in a carriage with my younger sister?"

Grace's agitation was keenly evident as she continued to block her brother's path. "Please, Sterling! Mr. Rutherford has been nothing short of heroic! He saved my life, at great risk to his own only to be rewarded by us keeping him from seeking out a doctor!"

"Such a dramatic act! What dangers are leaping out of bonnet shops that I'm not aware of?"

"I fell into the street in front of a carriage and he pulled me back, just in time." She turned shyly back toward Michael, her cheeks flushing a deeper shade of pink. "I felt the breeze from the turning carriage wheels against my face. It was—terrifying!"

Michael's eyes widened a little in surprise as her tone expressed more delight than fear at the recounting. Apparently Miss Grace Porter was not a woman who shied from adventures. *Damn. She's more appealing at every turn.*

"What a great coincidence that he was there!" Sterling crossed his arms. "What street was it again?"

"Sterling!" She protested then continued her voice dropping to a softer plea. "Please, brother. Surely this is a conversation that can wait for a better time!"

"How horrible of me. I don't wish to seem ungracious. Come inside and I'll send for a doctor and we'll—"

"Don't trouble yourself on my behalf," Michael cut him off. There was no way he was going to allow himself to be dosed with laudanum and become defenseless under Sterling's roof. He forced himself to sit up straighter, gritting his teeth against the pain. "Forgive me if I keep my seat but I'll take Miss Porter's advice and take the carriage on to see my own physician."

Broken. I don't need Rowan to tell me I've broken a few ribs.

"Perhaps my brother's suggestion is the wiser course, Mr. Rutherford!" Grace protested, turning back to plead her case through the carriage window. "You are clearly in pain, sir! Please! Stay!"

Michael shook his head. He didn't know if Sterling really recognized him but he didn't want to linger and find out before he was confident of being able to stand on his own two feet. "I should go. I've disrupted the day enough."

"Not at all," Sterling said. "Even if I'm not clear on the course of events, I'm grateful for your actions. Mr. Rutherford, you must allow me to repay you for your bravery."

Michael was grateful for the shield of the carriage door to hide the involuntary fisting of his hands in frustration. "No payment is necessary."

Sterling went on. "A humble show of thanks. Come to dinner Sunday next. We can reminisce about our adventures in India and truly reacquaint ourselves."

Grace's head popped up, surprise framing her expression. "D-dinner?"

"What say you?"

Hell, no! I say I'd rather eat dinner with a viper!

Caught. He was caught. Whatever vague plan he'd been working on had evaporated the instant he'd fallen under that blasted carriage wheel. He was caught in his lie to Grace. Logic and the rules of polite society dictated that he should happily accept an invitation to "reacquaint" himself with Mr. Sterling Porter. One look at Miss Grace Porter and it was a jumbled mess in his mind, her strange guilt at being on Oxford Street and the lies and secrets she was enlisting him to keep—whatever they might be.

He cleared his throat. "I would hate to impose—"

"No imposition!" Sterling smiled again and Michael felt a bubble of bile rising in is throat. "I insist. Grace would be in attendance and I'm sure, she would be hurt if you refused."

Trapped like a fly in amber. Damn it!

"How can I refuse?" Michael said then looked to Grace. "Dinner. Sunday next."

"Let's say eight o'clock?" Sterling added.

If she'd protested, Michael would have had his excuse to withdraw from the invitation, but Grace looked up into his eyes, a strange flash of anxiety in their blue depths, adding to the puzzle.

"Yes." Michael said, a man in a trance.

"Sunday next, Mr. Rutherford." Sterling clapped his hands and broke the connection between the pair.

Michael touched his forehead out of habit, reaching for the brim of a hat that wasn't there, and was rewarded with a shard of hot glass stabbing into his side. But the pain was nothing. He'd have endured anything and kept the smile on his face rather than reveal weakness to his archenemy. He knocked on the carriage ceiling to signal the driver and the horses pulled away into the lane and spared him the sight of a Sterling Porter's crocodile smiles.

Game is bloody on now.

Surprise.

CHAPTER SIX

"You've broken at least two ribs, Rutherford." Rowan announced as he felt as gingerly as he could along Michael's side to explore the damage done. "Are you spitting up any blood? Does it particularly hurt anywhere else?"

Michael bit his lip to keep from saying anything too sarcastic. "I've not punctured anything if that's what you're asking and it hurts like the devil when I breathe. Please just wrap it as tightly as you can and let's call it good."

Rowan smiled but pulled out the bandages he would need along with a pair of good scissors to cut the cloth. "Why are all my friends such terrible patients?"

Michael ignored him.

Rowan slowly lifted Michael's arm to hold it away from his body while he started the wrap. "It's badly bruised. You'll have a blueberry pie under your armpit before morning. The cut on your head is incidental and I don't see the need for any stitches but you may have another scar to add to your lovely countenance."

"I don't care." Michael reached up to touch his head and regretted it as the pain from his ribs sliced up his spine. "Damn! Well, at least my balls have stopped throbbing."

"I'm not going to ask. But I'll leave you something for the pain." Rowan eyed his bag. "I brought a new mixture that is said not to be addictive if—"

"No. There's no need. Now is not the time to be groggy or slow-witted."

"Is this part of your plan? Did the Jackal do this?"

"No. A four in hand. But…the situation may have moved things along."

"Tell me."

"She was there."

"She?"

"The Jackal has a younger sister." Michael reached up to run his hand through is hair out of habit and winced in regret at the gesture, instantly dropping his arm back to where Rowan had held it. "And don't look at me like that."

"Any other man, I'd be more worried. But let's have it."

"She'd stumbled into the path of a carriage and I pulled her back. She's proclaimed me a hero and her brother has invited me back for dinner Sunday next." Michael stood to retrieve his shirt. "He is eager to *discuss* our adventures together in India."

"My god! It's a nightmare!" Rowan shook his head slowly. "This is insane, Rutherford. You can't play parlor games with this man."

"I'll do what I have to. It's the meeting we meant to have weeks ago only this time, it's better. We risk only one of us. One way or another, he'll reveal himself. He's too frustrated to pass up his chance and too overconfident not to make his threats and when he does, he'll tell me what we need to know. Hell, I've already determined so much more of him than we'd ever hoped."

"And if he's more clever then you give him credit for and keeps his cards close to his chest? Then what?"

"Then I'm the one who'll take advantage of the chance. His sister has been kind and if I'm a good guest then perhaps I'll get invited back again. Maybe I can find a way to search his study for clues or uncover an advantage to give us the lever we need to push this son of a bitch into the sea."

"A good guest?"

"Leave it, Rowan."

"All he has to do is express disapproval at what he'll term an "unacceptable suitor" and you're on the wrong side of that door. Game over."

"We'll see. I'm not there as a suitor. I'm a family friend who saved his sister's life and has a connection to the East India's fighting forces. If he presses me, perhaps I am looking for a position as a bodyguard."

"You're putting yourself in harm's way, Michael. He's already got his suspicions. My god, this could twist on you so fast! One moment you're having tea in his parlor and the next thing, he'll be burying you in his back garden."

"No. He kills me without a word? And gains what? Proof that he's a murderer? I go missing and all you have to do is call the police. He'll swing for it and it's done." Michael stood slowly to test his mobility. Rowan's expert wrap had eased much of the pain but he knew he wasn't going to be running up any stairs anytime soon.

Rowan began to repack his doctor's kit. "Unless the Jackal has handlers and we're facing the next battle blindly without you."

"Whatever I learn as I go, I'll convey it to you as quickly as I can, so there's less of a chance of me taking any "revelations" with me. Just don't share any details with the others until it's necessary. I'm not giving up on this. For the first time, we have an advantage that Sterling doesn't have."

"And *exactly* what advantage is that?"

"He's the one playing by the rules. I don't have to."

Rowan shook his head and relatched his case as it closed. "Michael. If this game is being played indoors and over dinner tables, I'm worried that you don't even know all the rules. And when you don't know all the rules…"

"It's easier to be defeated," Michael finished the thought. Rowan had a point. He could hardly boast about his skills in good society. His friendship with the Jaded had brought him into the outskirts of more than one gathering but Michael Rutherford was no polished player. "I know enough to wipe the mud off of my boots. It's a simple dinner inside the man's home. If I use the wrong fork, I hardly think it matters but if it goes beyond that and I'm forced to jig before the Queen of England, I'll ask Ashe to give me a quick tutorial on waltzing."

Rowan smiled. "What I wouldn't give to see his face when you ask him!"

Michael ignored the jest. "How long until I'm healed?"

"At least a month but that would be if you rested, avoided strain and took to leisurely hobbies like reading." Rowan picked up his coat. "See how wise I am not to even suggest it?"

"Very funny." Michael began buttoning his shirt. "And since I have no intentions of taking to my bed?"

Rowan shrugged. "Hard to say. Six weeks? Two months? Are you going to hurl yourself under any more carriages?"

"You are the worst doctor in London," Michael said with a growl. "I'll be better in a fortnight and that's an end to it."

Rowan stepped back, tipping his head to one side as if studying a great mystery. "Anyone else, I'd say I knew better, but I swear, Rutherford, you do have a knack for surprises."

"Let's hope so." Michael stretched, testing his mobility a bit. "For all our sakes."

A knock at the door interrupted them, and Michael moved to answer it, opening it to find young Miss Maggie Beecham standing there sweetly holding out a hat box. Mrs. Clay had hired her a few weeks before to help at the Grove but already it was clear that she'd become like a daughter to the landlady and had a good disposition for the inn. She was a rescued "soiled dove" he suspected, but Michael was not the kind of man to judge a person by their past. He simply liked her for her honest sweetness and the way she had already learned to use her hands to talk to Tally, Mrs. Clay's deaf son.

"I believe this is yours, Mr. Rutherford," Maggie said. "Although Mrs. Clay said I'm to make you open it immediately and voice an opinion in my hearing."

"I see." He dubiously took the box, forced to open the door a bit wider so that Rowan could enjoy the show. "Can't you just tell her I liked it?"

Maggie crossed her arms, as threatening as a spitting kitten. "You listen here, sir! She's pacing in her rooms over it and all soft at the thought of disappointing her 'dear giant' as she calls you." She wrinkled her nose and tapped her foot. "It's a hat! Don't you be difficult or I'll..." Her bravado faltered and her eyes threatened tears.

"For god sakes, open it, Michael!" Rowan chimed in wryly. "The girl means business!"

Michael untied the cord and unceremoniously dropped the box on the floor to pull out a black wool felted hat. He'd expected more of a working man's cap but his eyes widened as he beheld a fine gentleman's topper with a satin black band around the crown. It was bound to make his simple clothes look a bit shabbier in comparison but at that moment, with the heft of it in his fingers, he was in awe.

"Well?" Maggie asked anxiously.

"I am—speechless. Please tell Mrs. Clay that it is the finest thing I've ever owned and I'm..." Michael had to swallow an odd lump at his throat, "flattered that she sees me as worthy of it."

Truth was, it was the first gift he'd received in his lifetime. Even if it was on his accounts for payment, it was the sentiment behind it that made it precious to him.

"There! That wasn't so hard now, was it?" Maggie was all smiles. She curtsied and retreated back down the stairs to make her report.

Michael closed the door only to be faced with the sight of Dr. Rowan West staring at him as if he'd grown horns. "What?"

Rowan shook his head. "All this time. How have I always seen you as a hardened warrior when all along...you are just as human as the rest of us, Rutherford."

"The broken ribs weren't a more substantial clue?" Michael jibed. "Rowan, you really are the worst doctor in London."

"Good thing my wife is a physician," Rowan countered. "I'll send her to attend you next time you decide to hurl yourself under a carriage to save a damsel in distress. Although I warn you, Gayle is fearless enough to tell you the things I'm not."

"And what is that?" Michael asked.

"That you're in danger, Rutherford. And that love makes a man blind."

"Love? Do not mistake me getting misty over a hat for some crush on a housemaid to—"

"Not Maggie, Rutherford!" Rowan cut him off. "I'm saying between your ties here at the Grove, Mrs. Clay, Tally, all of them, even the Jaded; you have as much to lose as any of us and aren't you the one who is constantly warning us about needing to protect our blind sides?"

"I don't need a lecture on this subject, West. I've seen to the Grove's security."

"You're deliberately misunderstanding me, friend."

"I'm not." Michael held his ground. "I'm telling you that no one I care for will be lost. We've made it this far, Rowan, and I won't drop my guard now."

"And what if *you* are on our list of people we're not willing to lose, Rutherford?"

"I promise you that if I can find a way to survive this mess, I will. Will that suffice?"

Rowan sighed and gathered his bag and coat to leave. "No, but who am I to argue?"

Michael caught his arm for a moment. "You're a trusted friend, Rowan, and a good man. No matter what lies ahead, you'll always be the touchstone that they lean on. I hope you know how much I trust in that."

"Michael." Rowan pulled his arm free. "If you don't live through this, I'll kill you myself."

He was gone before Michael could think of a clever reply. He looked back down at the hat in his hand and felt the icy brush of fear trail down his spine. He would talk to Mrs. Clay about adding another man to the watch, but the Grove wasn't his only weak point.

Not anymore.

Because when he'd seen Mrs. Clay's gift his first real thought had been that a certain pert little beauty might think him handsome if he wore it to dinner on Sunday…

Damn.

* * *

Grace closed and locked the door to her bedroom and leaned against it, hands splayed as if to keep out the strange chaos of the day. The twists and turns of the afternoon had left her reeling and then Sterling's strange behavior after Mr. Rutherford had left had added to her anxiety.

After his initial anger at her unconventional and unchaperoned return in a carriage with a strange man, Sterling had been practically gleeful after the verbal sparring with Mr. Rutherford had ended. Giddy as a boy on Christmas, he'd left her on the steps and whistled as he went into the house and then shut himself up in his study without explanation.

Grace had waited in her first floor sitting room, jumping at every sound, convinced that at any moment he would return to his senses and the scathing lectures about her stupidity would begin. Or the interrogation about where she was and what she was up to before she'd fallen into the street.

She composed her lies, rehearsing them in her head until she was dizzy with it.

But Sterling never bothered to emerge until dinner and Grace had then endured the strangest meal of her life. In near silence, her brother simply sat in his chair, eating with the zeal of a starving man breaking a fast, pausing only to grin at her like a man enjoying a fabulous jest.

"You…are in a good mood tonight."

"And why not?" he said with a laugh. "My luck has finally changed! Thanks to my darling sister!"

The endearment was unfamiliar sounding but Grace managed a nod. "Your luck has changed you say? How so?"

He'd shrugged his shoulders. "Don't you trouble your pretty little head about it! It's all in hand." He'd returned to his food with relish and Grace had abandoned conversation. She knew better than to poke a sleeping tiger.

It must have been a quick meal but even afterward she couldn't remember a longer evening. Sterling had left the table without another word and Grace had helped Mrs. Dorsett clear the dishes before numbly heading up to her room to hide.

She shook her head and stepped from the door. *Perhaps he is just happy to see his friend, Mr. Rutherford. But he didn't seem happy at first. In any case, I should be grateful for the distraction and the reprieve.*

Shouldn't I?

She crossed the room to retrieve her basket where she'd tucked it under her bed. She sat at her vanity and began to lay out the damaged and torn pages, her hands shaking. Grace tried to reorder them, copying out one of the pages that had been torn and realizing which sections were missing entirely. All in all, the story was largely intact and Grace began to recover her work. She hated the sight of her tattered parchment and had to wipe her face to clear away the frustrated tears at the precious hours of work she'd lost.

Not to mention the income.

She'd a steady demand for her colorful stories from a publisher and while the money was modest, Grace had the luxury of saving every tuppence she'd made from her work. The secret income was hers to hoard and she had every intention of doing so until she had enough—enough to leave her brother's house and make her own way in the world.

But that dream had nearly come crashing to an end today, an end almost as grisly as the one she imagined for herself if Mr. Rutherford hadn't intervened. If her brother had pressed for details of her errands or if Mr. Rutherford had corrected her lies in front of him, Grace shuddered at the consequences.

She leaned back in her chair, ignoring the ache in her shoulders, and closed her eyes. It was all so tenuous. The publisher had made it clear that there was no shortage of eager writers to fill their pamphlets and that any drop in quality or professionalism would be noted.

And of course, they didn't realize that the author was a woman. Grace had presented herself as a lowly clerical assistant to the eccentric Mr. A.R. Crimson, a slightly mad artist who (beyond his penny novels and serial chapters) only communicated with the outside world via notes and letters and was never seen publicly. It was pure invention and as it turned out, a very convenient one.

But it was a flimsy illusion her brother could destroy with one word as her closest male relative and legal guardian.

My fate rests in the hands of a total stranger. And yet strangely enough, Mr. Rutherford and I have done nothing but keep each other's secrets from our first meeting.

Mr. Rutherford's appeal was potent and extremely distracting.

She leaned forward to study her reflection for a moment but saw nothing beyond the ordinary. Her hair was a reddish-blonde, a common enough hue, though she was grateful it was thick enough to hold a curl. Two blue eyes; a decent nose, a touch long and sprinkled with unfashionable freckles; good cheekbones but her cheeks seemed too chubby to her critical eyes. Her lips were… Grace squinted as she pouted at herself to try to make them more bow-shaped and succeeded in making herself laugh.

The inventory of her physical attributes was at an end.

"I do not look mysterious, at all!" she sighed. She frowned at the notion, disappointed. She didn't really want her face to betray the inner workings of fairy kingdoms and blood-thirsty ghosts but it appealed to a shielded part of her soul that Mr. Rutherford alone could see something in her that others couldn't.

Her brow furrowed. He'd encouraged her where her brother would have expressed curt disapproval and even complimented her on her stubborn refusal to tell him about her pages. He'd stumbled onto her greatest secret without realizing it and nothing was certain. Sunday loomed in her mind, the blade of a guillotine above her neck.

If her strange alliance held, then an escape from Sterling was still possible. But if Mr. Rutherford made any reference to her awkward accident on Oxford Street, she'd better be ready with a good lie or two or Sterling would drive her out of the house and onto the streets.

Grace smiled at the oddly liberating thought of selling gruesome pamphlets by A.R. Crimson from a little cart along the streets. *What song would I call as I walked down the lanes? "Grim entertainment to make you swoon, come for your pages, come!"?*

She pulled out a fresh sheet of paper and by sheer habit, began to write down the images and ideas that bloomed inside her head of a vendor of mysteries who sold cursed stories to deserving victims. She penned "The Merchant of Death" and then let her imagination ramble and roam where it wished only to realize that most of her thoughts still centered on a certain tall man with salt and pepper curls. Without hesitation, she pulled out her diary and through the written word, she described the strange fire that had blazed through her as Mr. Rutherford had been pressed so closely against her in the carriage; she relived the terror of seeing him fall into the street and narrated her defiance in attempting to shield him from Sterling's aggression.

He is better than any hero, she decided. Mr. Rutherford was beyond ideal but even he was probably a man of the age and would be as scandalized as her brother if he realized her true intent. His admiration would dissipate like smoke.

For all the swooning and passionate undertones in her stories, Grace was not a woman prone to romantic notions. When she was thirteen, her father had informed her very coldly that the reason he had spent any money on her education was that he had no illusions of her flowering into any great beauty.

"You'll make your way by your wits, Grace. Or not at all."

He'd followed the dire announcement with a lengthy speech on her potential future as a governess, tutor, teacher or lady's secretary if the fates were kind. Grace didn't recall the rest of his words exactly but that was because her mind had wandered back to the grisly turns of a book she'd been reading on gladiators and the Roman coliseum.

It wasn't that she was a disrespectful girl. But once you agree with your father that your life will probably hold little beyond the corralling of other people's children or being a glorified servant, there is really no point in dwelling on the finer details of your future misery.

It was such a strange compulsion; to slip away into daydreams powered by her love of books and her need to scribble down her stories. Grace knew the limitations of her meager education, despite her father's complaints of the cost and had never aspired to write great fiction. She'd feared for a long time that she really was simply odd and that the workings of her mind might be a sign of illness. But since the obsession was her only consolation, Grace had abandoned worry and embraced it.

With her foolish stories, Grace had survived all the years of her father's icy disregard, her stepmother's cruelty and an unwanted daughter's exile to London to finally fulfill her destiny and prove that her father's investment in her education hadn't been a waste—she was a glorified servant at last!

Time slipped away from reckoning as she patched and repaired the story, and then began a new tale. Instead of a bloody confrontation with underwater mutants for Captain Martin, her hero would be sold into slavery and bought by the beautiful and deadly Princess of Atlantis who was fascinated by his very tall male human form... She wrote into the night until she fell asleep with her head on her desk...and fell into the strong arms of Michael Rutherford.

CHAPTER SEVEN

The following afternoon, Grace returned to Oxford Street to complete her errand but this time she hired a carriage to avoid the crowded walk and any chance of mishaps. She had never before missed an appointment and was nervous at the breech. She asked the driver to wait and then walked past the tobacconist shop to enter a green painted door with a simple plaque next to it that read, "S&Y Publishing".

Up a narrow staircase, she climbed carefully avoiding touching the banister or walls for fear of soiling her beige kid gloves. The grime and disrepair of the hallway would have given anyone pause, but Grace was too familiar with her path to pay it too much attention. At the top of the stairs, she went inside the first door, painted the same repulsive green as the one on the street, and squared her shoulders to face whatever lay ahead.

"Mr. Pollson, good day!" she said brightly.

"It is, but I expected you yesterday," he said with his usual surly bite. "Did he forget us then?"

"Not at all! I'd come as promised and was set upon by a pickpocket downstairs!" She gave him a stern look of disapproval, her best imitation of Mrs. Dorsett. "Ruffians, sir! My employer was furious to think of it!"

Mr. Pollson stood too quickly from his cluttered desk, an avalanche of scraps of paper and unbound pages sliding onto the floor. He merely stepped over the mess to come around to address her. "The tobacco shop downstairs said there was a commotion but I...had no idea, miss. I hope Mr. Crimson's work was not stolen!"

Grace shook her head, accepting that his concern wouldn't be for her safety. "No, thank goodness! But nearly so! The pages were a muddy shambles, I can tell you that, after the ruffian tore them from my hands. We spent the night repairing them. Even so, Mr. Crimson bade me come again to ensure that his commitment is made."

"Good, good, good! You have the next installment there?" he asked, eyeing her basket.

"Yes, sir." Grace dutifully handed the pages over.

"Is Mr. Crimson pleased with them?"

"Yes. He is…very pleased. He said he thought you'd like the twist with Poseidon's Curse, something about a reflection of the opium trade. It's all quite gruesome."

"Good, good, good!" The man's eyes lit up. "Ah! The man has a gift for gore, if you ask me!"

"They're selling well then?"

"Why? What has he heard?" His expression became a bit more closed off, as he shrugged. "They go well enough. Sales can always be better in these hard times. Hard, hard times! You remind Mr. Crimson that times are *very* hard! We pay good money and don't burden him with complaints when pamphlets don't move, do we?"

"No. He is very grateful for the arrangement."

"As he should be! There's a hundred more to take his place if he don't like it!"

"Mr. Crimson has expressed no complaint, sir! In fact, he told me this morning how pleased he is—with the quality of your establishment."

The man's countenance relaxed. "Here's the payment for this then." He held out a thin envelope.

Ten glorious pounds!

"Ten is very generous, sir."

"It's fifteen! You tell him to keep those installments coming regularly and include more stories of that band of undead gypsies if he knows what's good for him. We reward loyalty here at Sigley and Yardling, Printers Extraordinaire!"

She took the envelope from him, enrapt at the idea of her newfound wealth. Without thinking she unbuttoned her blouse at her collarbone and slipped the sealed envelope inside, before putting herself to rights.

"Miss!" Mr. Pollson exclaimed in shock.

"Oh!" Grace blushed, although perfectly aware that the glimpse of her throat probably wasn't as much of a scandal as the tantalizing idea that the payment was now nestled in the scandalous region above her cleavage. *What a bother!* "I apologize, Mr. Pollson, but my employer would be furious if I misplaced his payment and since I missed our appointment yesterday due to pickpockets outside your door…"

"Y-yes…very practical of you," he said. "You are…" Mr. Pollson sat back down slowly. "Quite fearless."

"Why, thank you, sir!" Grace beamed and fought off the urge to curtsey she was so pleased at his words. "Well, I should be back to Mr. Crimson. He will be waiting, you know."

"Waiting." Mr. Pollson waved his hand in dismissal, his expression a man already distracted by his nest of papers. "Go, yes, and remember to remind him that where the body count is high—"

"Readers sigh," she finished dutifully. "Good day, Mr. Pollson."

Grace retreated, her footsteps light on the stairs going down to her waiting carriage. The sun shone and with fifteen pounds in her chemise, she almost forgot her troubles.

Almost.

She had four days before Mr. Rutherford's return and before the dreaded Sunday dinner. If this were her last payment from Mr. Pollson, then she would have saved nearly three hundred pounds over time. It wasn't a fortune by any means, but she'd decided that it was enough. Enough to make a start if Sterling threw her from the house; and even if he stripped her of her pen name, Grace was determined that another aspiring male author could be invented in a pinch. It might be a while before the new man found a publisher, but she'd managed it once. Surely another editor would see the same promise that Mr. Pollson had spied!

And if not—Grace did her best to smile as the streets of London passed outside her window. *Then I can fulfill my destiny as a servant, and scribble tales by candlelight for maids and footmen! I would be content with that.*

✳ ✳ ✳

When she got home, Mrs. Dorsett was waiting for her with a note in hand. "It's a dinner party, is it?"

"On Sunday, but there is only one guest so I don't think we'll be going to too much trouble," Grace said, removing her bonnet. "Something simple, yes?"

"Not according to Mr. Porter!" Mrs. Dorsett waved around the paper in vindication. "You'd think a Duke was popping in for a meal by the looks of this menu!"

"Oh, dear," Grace said, calmly holding out her hand. "May I see it please?"

Mrs. Dorsett shoved it toward her. "I ain't no fancy chef! Never made claim to it so if this guest is too high and mighty to eat a good hearty fare, I'll be taking Sunday off!"

Grace sighed. Sterling wanted servants but he was not generous enough with their wages to hire more qualified staff. She'd been making due with Mrs. Dorsett for years and patching the gaps where she could with day maids and an occasional gardener. "You are a very good cook, Mrs. Dorsett, and I'm sure we'll come up with a compromise between…oh!"

Grace glanced at the list and was immediately aware of the cause of Mrs. Dorsett's mood. *Five courses on menu cards? Jellies and tarts? A poêlée for the sweetbreads? And what in the world is this bit about lobster ragout? My god, it's two weeks budget for one meal and—where would she and I begin to prepare this?*

"You see? You see, then!" Mrs. Dorsett tapped her foot impatiently. "If that is the menu then it's Sunday off!"

"I will speak to my brother and amend the menu." Grace folded the offensive note and firmly tucked it into her skirt pocket. "I need you on Sunday, Mrs. Dorsett, so as usual, please plan on taking Saturday afternoon as your own."

"Am I to serve, too?" the woman asked, her lips pressed into a thin pinched line.

"I'll send a note to the agency and see about an extra hand or two for the day. I'm sure Sterling will approve considering…" *Considering it's obvious he wishes to make a very good impression on Mr. Rutherford.*

"As you wish."

Grace made her way up the stairs and did her best to quickly tackle the bulk of the work. She wrote the note to the agency for a kitchen maid and a footman for Sunday and sent it off before she approached the rest of her chores. The second floor bedrooms were straightened and dusted, the laundry pulled for the morning's labor, and first floor sitting room was dusted and aired. Even as she pounded the pillows on the settee, she smiled to think of Mr. Rutherford's refusal to risk taking a seat.

Then she moved down the hall to her brother's private study and office. Sterling's sanctuary was her least favorite room in the house. It was the most opulent and garishly appointed space, with shelves of "treasures" Sterling had collected from all over the world. He had a penchant for religious figurines and small portraits with eyes that met your gaze no matter where you stood in the room. It was a disconcerting feeling to be so coldly watched by dozens of eyes and they had secretly inspired more than one of her ghost stories.

She made quick work of the dusting, stopping only to stick her tongue out at a particularly ugly statuette of a fat man whose turban was in the midst of transforming into a snake. He smirked at her with a brass grin nonplussed. "Enjoy the jest, horrid thing," she whispered. "I'm betting you wouldn't be so content if you knew how quickly you'd end up in the rubbish bin if I had my say in the matter."

"Grace!" Sterling exclaimed from the doorway. "Tell me you are not *talking* to my artwork!"

She wheeled around, instantly anxious. "Of course not!"

Sterling crossed his arms. "Then who were you addressing just then?"

She folded her hands in front of her. "I was merely speaking my thoughts aloud, brother."

"A horrible habit you will break instantly!" he announced as he came into the room. "Bad enough that you speak your mind when there are human beings in the room, sister, much less nattering away like a lunatic!"

"As bad as that? I'll refrain from thinking aloud." She tried to tease him out of his dark mood. "But the houseplants will be so disappointed to miss our chats."

"Grace!" His eyes darkened with fury. He moved to take a seat behind his desk before making one impatient gesture toward the chair across from him. "Sit."

"Yes." She dutifully perched on the upholstery and waited expectantly, trying to ignore the taste of dread that flooded her mouth. "You look displeased."

He shook his head. "I want to talk to you about this upcoming dinner."

"Of course. It was very generous of you to—"

"You'll wear your best gown and you'll make an effort to limit your comments to the most innocuous and inoffensive topics allowed." Her brother pulled his pipe from a carved wooden box on the desktop and began to light it. "I want you to be as agreeable and appealing as humanly possible."

Grace blinked a few times, unwilling to trust her ears. "My best gown? Is Mr. Rutherford...is he truly a good friend then that you're so anxious to—"

"What he is to me is none of your concern," Sterling said firmly. The match in his fingers flared as it caught, creating a fleeting distortion of his features in its light. "You'll be on your best behavior, Grace, and strive not to disappoint or embarrass me."

She nodded. "I always do. But *appealing?* I'm not sure I understand what you're asking."

He rolled his eyes. "What did I ever do to deserve you?"

She bit the inside of her cheek to keep from giving him a witty answer and instead held her place and her tongue.

Sterling cleared his throat and tried again. "This evening is very important to me. For once, do as you are told. Behave."

"Yes."

"I won't keep you from your duties any longer." He said dismissively and then leaned back in his chair, drawing on his pipe.

She stood slowly. "I've spoken to Mrs. Dorsett about the menu and amended it for presentation and for economy. I've arranged to have two extra servants to make things run more smoothly and to allow for a good impression." She let out a slow breath to steady her nerves. "Rather than just behaving like a lady, I hope my brother is wise enough to allow me to act like one and organize the social details as I see fit."

His gaze narrowed but he finally nodded. "By all means."

She left at his concession, turning on her heels and departing with as much dignity as she could muster. Her confusion about Mr. Rutherford's return was coalescing into a strange storm but there was no remedy for it.

Sterling's reversal toward Mr. Rutherford was hard to explain. She wanted to believe it was a genuine invitation based on gratitude for his heroic actions or even an open interest in rekindling a friendship. But something wasn't right.

Agreeable and appealing? Is he playing matchmaker? Is that even possible after years of echoing my father's sentiments on my utter unsuitability?

No answers came to her. Her own physical reaction to Mr. Rutherford and weakness for his compliments only muddied her internal debate. She'd wear her best gown on Sunday and make an effort to stay quiet. She'd do her best to appease her brother and keep Mr. Rutherford's respect. But one thing was certain.

She'd be prepared for the worst and have her savings pinned inside her clothes in case she needed to make a run for it.

CHAPTER EIGHT

Michael, Galen and Ashe all stared at the odd shaped stone on the table between them. The size of a walnut, it was a pale red thing, almost pink in cast, and Michael tipped his head to one side to see if another angle would help improve its appearance. "Seriously? This is it?"

Galen leaned back. "The jeweler said it appeared to be a dyed stone. Wasn't that the whole point of the quest? To find a gem that might be disguised to mask its true nature?"

"Is it a diamond then?" Ashe asked. "Is it *the* diamond?"

"Darius will be back from his honeymoon in a week." Galen said. "I'd say he probably knows some kind of test to—"

The impact of one of the fireplace andirons crashing down on top of the stone sent Ashe wheeling backwards from his chair onto the floor and Galen leapt up to avoid the worst of the corresponding mess.

"Rutherford! What the hell!?"

"What? I'm done wasting time and I don't have a week to wait." Michael lifted the ornate and heavy tool and shrugged at the sight of a pulverized pile of pink glass-like crystals. "I'd say it's definitely not a diamond."

The door to the library crashed open as Godwin came through with two younger footmen on his heels, all of them armed with medieval weapons they'd grabbed from a suit of armor in the hallway. "Sir! Are you...all right?"

Michael guiltily hid the andiron behind his back. "Sorry, Godwin."

"An experiment gone wrong," Ashe chuckled as he stood up, brushing off his pants. "No harm done."

The footmen retreated as Godwin entered the fray, his brow furrowed with disapproval. "The table might disagree with your assessment, Mr. Blackwell!"

Galen took one slow step away from Michael, clearly trying not to smile as he subtly indicated who the culprit might be. "Rutherford was just demonstrating his knowledge of gems."

Ashe mirrored Lord Winter's guilty move away from Michael, enjoying the mirth of the moment and deliberately put his hands behind his back like a contrite schoolboy. "Mr. Rutherford is *very* enthusiastic about gem quality."

Michael shot them both a dark look of his own that promised retribution, but for now, it was Godwin he addressed. "I will see the table repaired or replaced, Mr. Godwin and naturally, it won't happen again."

"See that it does not!" Mr. Godwin said, finally setting aside his mace. "I will advise Mrs. Clark the cause of the mess so that there are no misunderstandings below stairs and ask that *all of you* refrain from murdering any more of the furniture."

"Yes, sir." All three men answered dutifully and then miraculously managed to keep themselves from laughing until the butler had retreated.

"God! That's a story to tell!" Ashe sat back down in his chair, with a wry grin. "I swear I thought he was going to send us all to bed without supper!"

"Enjoy your fun, Blackwell, but when Mrs. Clark has a word with your wife, I doubt I'll be invited back," Michael said as he replaced the andiron.

Ashe laughed. "As if you would care! You blanche white every time you get within a hundred yards of feminine company!"

"Enough!" Michael crossed his arms. "Since we've established that that wasn't the diamond in question, let's shift back to the obvious question."

"All right," Galen straightened his shoulders and gave Blackwell a quelling look. They all respected Michael's dislike of society and shy nature but Galen knew him better and suspected that Ashe had hit a nerve. "We've done with the opening entertainment. Let's hear it."

"Yes," Ashe said as he retook his seat. "Is the obvious question something along the lines of what are we going to do now that we're out of ideas about this blasted diamond?"

"No." Galen stood and went to the sideboard to pour himself a cup of tea. "The diamond is probably under our noses, much like a certain villain was. No, the real question is why do you not have a week to wait, Rutherford?"

Michael held his breath as the last of Ashe's playful demeanor evaporated instantly. Ashe leaned forward on the cushions. "Something has happened with the Jackal."

"Not yet." Michael held up his hands defensively. "And I am *not* out of ideas."

"I'll cling to the promise of that 'yet'."

"Stop nagging the man!" Galen said over his shoulder. "I mentioned it only because I wanted to be sure that all was well. Rutherford has already earned our trust so stop hovering like a rag lady over a rubbish bin."

Ashe waved him off. "What is *yet* to happen within the week?"

Michael sighed. "My first face to face meeting with the Jackal if you must know."

"Hell! That's something, isn't it?" A new quiet seized the room and the spring light through the windows that moments before had seemed bright, now felt devoid of warmth.

Michael nodded. "It is."

Galen set his tea down. "It's faster than I imagined it."

"It's faster than I'd planned," Michael conceded. "But it's also not what you're imagining, your lordship. No pistols at dawn."

Galen made a face. "I hate it when you address me like that, but you're doing it like a master tactician to distract me. It won't work, friend. You may as well tell us all of it."

"It's a dinner. I'm invited to a meal at his home."

"You'll not eat a bite without tasting your death if he's still got any more poisoners in his employ!" Ashe barked. "You've lost your mind."

"I'm too large for him to carry my body from his house undetected and you can dance at his hanging, gentlemen." Michael moved to pour himself a stiff drink. "I'm safe enough."

"Would you like one of us to stand by?" Galen offered. "I could even acquire an invitation to join you."

"No," Michael said. "It's exactly what I wish to avoid. It's not an ambush. It's a first foray into finding out where we stand."

"I hate this," Ashe growled. "If it isn't an ambush, it should be."

Michael ignored him and stepped back to take his leave. "If you find the "diamond in disguise", please send word to me right away. Otherwise, I'll leave you gentlemen in peace."

"In peace? Are you serious?" Ashe closed his eyes and stretched out his legs, a grown man's imitation of a pout. "I need a stiff drink. And I'd be peaceful if I had an end to this interminable waiting and—"

"He's gone, Blackwell." Galen picked up his cup and returned to his chair.

"What?" Ashe sat up in astonishment. "I didn't hear the door!"

"It's Rutherford. When do you ever hear the door when it's Rutherford?" Galen smiled as he shook his head in admiration. "The size of an elephant and the grace of a housecat. It's terrifying, really."

Ashe lowered his face into his hands, his façade of control giving way. "Terrifying," he echoed softly and then went on in a tight whisper, "God, what isn't? Welcome to my world. Kill him, Rutherford, and let me sleep at night. Kill the bastard."

Galen said nothing, politely averting his gaze to look out the window on a beautiful spring day that reflected nothing of his friend's despair. Ashe's young American wife was upstairs still confined to her bed for weeks yet to await the birth of their child. He needn't ask to know that her health was still precarious. All the Jaded knew it. The Jackal had tried to poison Blackwell and his beloved bride had suffered in his place and nearly died. Now, she was expecting a baby in late July and where the most robust woman could be lost, his defiant Caroline was treading on unsteady feet. Ashe's fear was palpable, and every man understood him. The risk of losing the women they worshipped to a horrible end in childbirth—it was not to be imagined, much less endured.

But Ashe was staring into that dark unforgiving precipice and Galen's throat closed at the cruel threat. It was a phantom that Ashe couldn't name or fight.

But the Jackal...

Blackwell had seized on the notion of this enemy and Galen suspected that it was easier to hate and empower the Jackal like an evil talisman that if destroyed, could guarantee the safety of his Caroline—yes, that belief was easier to hold to than to yield to blind Providence without complaint and trust that an invisible god would bring her through it.

He didn't judge Ashe for it. Ashe was the quickest to laugh and the first to urge the Jaded to enjoy whatever life was left to them. He'd overheard Darius Thorne defending him once, when Rowan had disapproved of his rakish ways. Darius had said, "Ashe is open hearted, West. Watch him and you'll see. He doesn't give his loyalty or his love in measured amounts."

So, Galen guessed the man didn't hate in half measures either.

"Rutherford has it in hand," Galen said carefully. "And if you doubt it, just remember the fate of that stone and be grateful your name isn't Sterling Porter."

✳ ✳ ✳

Michael accepted the cut crystal glass filled with wine from Sterling's hand and waited for his host to fill his own from the same decanter before he risked a small taste. Despite all his bravado, he had no wish to die in a useless demonstration before he'd achieved any of his goals for the night.

The Sunday evening dinner was unfolding slowly as Michael waited warily for Sterling to make his move, doing his best to test for weaknesses without any direct confrontations as the genteel presence of Grace Porter in an off the shoulder evening gown with a spray of orange lilies in her hair held him in check.

As far as Michael was concerned, it was exhausting.

He'd braced for a barrage of personal questions that had yet to come. So far, not one breath of India, not one hint of their shared past or the threats to the Jaded's future… Instead, Sterling Porter had dominated all conversation to the turn of the seasons and to regale them with colorful stories of the East India Trading Company's efforts to curb piracy and secure more Asian trade routes.

Sterling wore a red silk brocade vest with silver buttons and Michael began to wonder what kind of man he was really facing. Porter was younger than he'd imagined, in his late-thirties, with fair coloring like his sister. Where Grace evoked an ivory cameo with her long classical features, Sterling looked far more earthly with dark shadows under his eyes. He was lanky and slight, a touch too pale even by English standards which hinted that his health was not necessarily good. But his expression betrayed a feral intelligence and a keen wit.

The Jackal was a man, but what sort of man, Michael still didn't know. A petty bureaucrat? A clerk with aspirations? Middle class, yes. But it was clear that Sterling Porter believed he was meant for better things. All the reports of his runners bore out in the man's every gesture and word. *Ambitious prick, aren't you?*

Michael had worn one of his better coats and a complimentary gray muslin waistcoat that Mrs. Clay had assured him was extremely flattering, but one look at his host and he knew he was underdressed for the occasion.

The man's a popinjay! Ashe would have a thing to say about his overdone cravat and then ask me why I haven't shoved this crystal glass down his throat. Damn it! I'm getting nowhere and Grace…

Grace was far more distracting than he'd accounted for. It was the current fashion to display a woman's bare shoulders and throat in the evening and Michael was confident he'd seen his share of necks—but this was apparently different. Why, he wasn't sure, but the sight of the naked curve of her shoulders and the elegant lines of her collarbone and the barest glimpse of the rise of her breasts was driving him mad. Instead of tracking Sterling's every word or studying the man for any sign of treachery, he kept glancing at Grace Porter and wondering how he could politely beg her to put on a shawl.

Or ask her why she wasn't talking.

She was far too quiet. Sterling barely had time to draw breath, much less eat, in between his speeches and if Grace even looked as if she might have something to say, her brother cut her off.

"Of course, Grace has no opinion on the matter," Sterling said in between bites of veal. "She knows as much of pirates as a sparrow does of parsnips."

Michael should have left it. After all, letting Sterling blather on was the wiser course if he wanted to learn anything of the man's mind. But wisdom slipped from his grasp as he noticed the color in her cheeks darkening at her brother's dismissive comment.

"Is that certain, Miss Porter?" Michael asked her directly. "I don't think an opinion requires direct experience, don't you agree?"

She beamed at him. "If it did, I should think that most of the House of Lords would be mute. Or most men for that matter!"

"Grace!" Sterling dropped his fork. "What a thing to say!"

The joy in her eyes dimmed and Grace bit her lower lip. "A poor jest. I apologize."

"Not a poor jest," Michael set his glass down as carefully as he could. "And why apologize for being clever? A smart man I know once told me that intelligence was never offensive where ignorance always is." He looked directly at Sterling and decided he'd had enough of polite games. "Pity that so few who are stupid ever think to make amends for the pain they inflict on others."

Sterling's gaze narrowed and Michael looked at him openly defiant. "A pity."

"But I'm a plain spoken man, as you know," Michael said calmly. "Pirates or parsnips, it's all the same to me."

"Is it?" Sterling asked. "Tell me, Mr. Rutherford, what work do you do? What is your profession now?"

At last. Here we are.

"As I was seventeen years a soldier, I apply what talents I can as a consultant to businesses and individuals for their security. I'm told I have a good eye for spotting potential weaknesses and averting crime."

"Interesting," Sterling said. "But looking at you, I'd say to avert a crime all you would have to do is be present. I can't think of a burglar anywhere stupid enough to try to walk around a guard of your stature."

"I'm not a guard and if it were that simple, I'd be happily unemployed."

"And where do you reside, Mr. Rutherford?" Sterling went on amiably. "Does your business provide a good living?"

"I do well enough," Michael answered, caution flaring at the sickening idea of Sterling Porter strolling into the Grove uninvited. "Not as well as you, if the home you have here is any sign of your fortunes."

It was an easy bit of false flattery and he was rewarded with a strange flash of emotion in Sterling's eyes. Either it was triumph or suspicion, but before Michael could weigh it out, Sterling reached for the decanter to refill his glass.

"I have just had a grand idea, Mr. Rutherford." Sterling grinned as if they were the best of friends. "One that Grace is sure to approve."

Grace looked up in surprise. "Would I?"

"Grace is often confined to the house and has few chances for social events. There's a ball coming up in less than a fortnight in early June hosted by a friend of ours, a Mr. Rand Bascombe. Why don't you join us? He is an acquaintance through associates at the Company." Red wine sloshed over the edge of Sterling's glass unheeded, a crimson stain spreading out on the white linen tablecloth. "Rand is back from a miserable expedition to India that reaped nothing but death. Bad luck with fevers through his party and apparently, an inability to look at a compass to keep from going in circles."

Michael kept his expression neutral. "All that and he's still in the mood for a party?"

Sterling laughed. "His new wife may have tipped the scales. Apparently she's so thrilled to have her husband back she's willing to overlook the circumstances—and why not?" Sterling smiled, a wicked icy show of teeth. "I warned him it was a stupid idea to stomp about over there. But then, you must know. That region is no place for little men or small dreams."

"No."

"Do you know Mr. Bascombe, sir?" Sterling asked.

Michael shook his head. "By reputation only." What Michael did know was from the squat villain's involvement in the East India's first clumsy attempts to flush out the Jaded and from his assault on Lady Winters. Bascombe was a toady of a man and Galen Hawke loathed him so much he'd once said that if Rand Bascombe were on fire, he wouldn't hesitate to add kindling. *If I'm not careful, I'll have to worry about holding Galen back if he catches Bascombe's scent…or this could become a real brawl.*

Sterling held up his wine. "I'd love to introduce you to him."

"I see." Except he didn't. He didn't see how walking into Sterling's larger circle of acquaintances in the East India Trading Company would be courageous or suicidal. *Probably a bit of both.* "I don't think his wife would thank you for an extra guest considering the circumstances."

"There isn't a hostess in London who complains when a bachelor is added to her party." Sterling took another healthy swallow from his glass. "Isn't that true, Grace? Wouldn't you enjoy it if Mr. Rutherford accompanied you to a ball? Shall I include you in the evening, dear sister?"

To her credit, Grace Porter looked as shocked and unsure of the notion as Michael felt; but there was something in the turn of the conversation that didn't sit well with him. Sterling was charmingly bullying her into attending Bascombe's or into submitting to Michael's company. Either way, Michael was off balance.

Grace blinked and then finally cleared her throat. "Pardon?"

"I'm not the best choice of escort for a formal party and I think your sister is struggling to diplomatically say as much." Michael let out a slow careful breath. "Grace is too kind to admit her aversion to the notion."

Sterling laughed. "If she's hesitant, I don't think you're the source of her fears. Is he?"

"No." Grace pushed the pastry on her plate from one side to the other, a woman struggling to appear disinterested in the topic at hand. "He would be an excellent choice of escort to any occasion. And it's not fear. I can think of eight things far more terrifying than a ball!" She looked up directly at Michael. "Be at ease, Mr. Rutherford. I am *never* included on my brother's outings and he's teasing you with the threat of waltzing. You are safe, sir. Now, please, Sterling, I beg you! Leave the subject!"

"It's true," Sterling sighed. "You are safe. She doesn't even own a ball gown."

A man would have to be blind not to see the stinging agony of Sterling's insult as it flashed in her blue eyes before she busied with refilling her water glass. The pain in Michael's ribs failed to compare with the knife-like blow to his midsection at the sight of Grace Porter's struggle not to cry at the dinner table. Michael's hands fisted on his lap under the tablecloth in frustration. *Just when I think I cannot dislike you more Sterling Porter...*

"Well!" Sterling went on with friendly smile that didn't quite warm his eyes, "All your country fears are laid to rest as Mr. Rutherford has spared me the cost of getting you one, Grace! Now I really am in his debt."

To control his emotions, Michael did his best not to look at Grace. "I look forward to meeting your friend Mr. Bascombe and hearing about his adventures. But I won't consider attending without her."

Sterling smiled. "What a delightful surprise!"

Grace put her fingertips over her lips. "M-Mr. Rutherford! I can't—"

"There! It is a nice change for you, Grace. Not that you'll be taking any turns on the floor—"

"And I'll dance with her." Michael spoke without thinking. "That is, if the lady will allow it."

Grace's mouth fell open and Michael had to swallow hard to ignore the fiery impulse to cheer in triumph. It was the most ridiculous thing he'd ever said but in that moment, Michael Rutherford didn't care. All he cared about was that Grace Porter was not going to be left behind. And that when Grace Porter's eyes shone, it made his chest ache to say something comforting and kind to her or more—to reach for her, to touch her, to draw her against him and shield her from the sharp edges of the world.

"Of course, she'll allow it," Sterling answered for her. "Just mind you wear good shoes and watch your toes."

"It will be a night to remember," Michael said and then impulsively decided to test the waters. "Bascombe and I can compare notes about Bengal and perhaps I can help him see where he went wrong. I could improve his chances if he intends another attempt."

The effect on Sterling Porter was immediate. His good humor evaporated and his expression became haughty with fury. "There is nothing there for him to find!" Uncertainty crept into his eyes and he stood abruptly. "I think that's enough for one night. I hate to cut things short but my head is raging."

"I don't understand." Grace stood, forcing Michael to follow suit. "Sterling. Are you sure? I set out the port and cigars if you—"

"Our delightful evening is at an end." Sterling stepped back. "I can walk you out, Mr. Rutherford."

Michael nodded then gave Grace an apologetic look. "It was lovely, Miss Porter. I enjoyed the parsnips *and* the pirates and look forward to seeing you at the dance."

She radiated happiness and curtsied gracefully. "Thank you."

He bowed and followed Sterling out and down the stairs. As the man lumbered with his fury down the steps, Michael eyed the center of his back and contemplated the irony of being within inches of the Jaded's enemy.

One little push and we could save ourselves the trouble...

He didn't know why Sterling would bring Bascombe into things and if they were rivals for the same treasure, then why in god's name would Sterling risk another player on the field? What was his game?

By the time they'd safely reached the ground floor foyer, it was a relief to have the temptation gone. Sterling in his haste had forgotten to signal the footman so they were alone to retrieve Michael's coat and hat. Normally, Michael would have readily taken care of the matter himself as he always did but the awkward frustration on Sterling's face was priceless.

The dinner. The crystal. That horrible jelly molded entrée... There should be a man here to fuss over my departure and hand me my hat and it's killing him that there isn't.

Michael deliberately folded his hands in front of him and waited on the last step, instinctively adding to his superior height to give him a better advantage.

"Bascombe..." Sterling stopped. "I should apologize. Bascombe has long been a thorn in my side. I'm a practical man where Bascombe's a dreamer. He is convinced there is a great treasure yet to be discovered in India, a forgotten treasure room."

"Treasure rooms are rarely forgotten."

"Yes. Exactly." One of the lamps were lit but the shadows were distorted by an arrangement of flowers on the table next to it and Sterling's face looked mottled by the play of light and dark across his features. "Tradition and superstition would hold back a starving populace for only so long once a ruler fell. You see, I heard stories of a small raj in the jungles of India who was quite mad. In fact, he eventually became so insane that he insisted on marrying a statue of a local goddess. Can you imagine it? Five wives and forty concubines and he replaces them all with a life size stone carving with painted lips and arms like an octopus."

"Did he really?" Michael asked, genuinely intrigued. He'd heard rumors of the raj's madness or how things had come to a head but this—this was a confirmation he'd never have guessed at. "What sacrilege!" he whispered.

"Sacrilege," Sterling echoed. "And beyond. They say it was the wedding night that did it. The groom wished to take things literally and his people decided they'd had enough. The palace forces were drawn away with a revolt in the village and then a second band of rebels stormed the palace with torches and machetes, setting off stolen explosives and destroying much of the building."

And set the Jaded free in the process when the south wall blew out and exposed us to fresh air for the first time in months...

"A good precaution to draw the guards away," Michael said. "But I doubt they would have stopped them if he'd violated their goddess."

"The villagers didn't ask where they stood on the matter. The road to the palace was paved with the blood and body parts of the raj's soldiers, his servants, his wives and children."

Michael pushed the images away, sorting through the memories of a black chaotic night full of smoke and screams. "And the raj?"

Sterling shrugged. "I heard a few versions of his murder but there was a consistent detail about disposing of his body in a latrine trench. Hell, I'll bet they're pissing on his bones as we speak."

"Mr. Porter," Michael said, refolding his hands politely. "Why am I going to a ball at Bascombe's?"

"You mean, besides your obvious tendencies toward chivalry and a weakness where it comes to my sister?" Sterling asked. "Does it matter?"

It mattered. But something held him in check.

Play the game.

"I look forward to the party." Michael stepped down off the final riser. "Was there anything else?"

"I'll need your address, Rutherford. To send the invitation, naturally." Sterling crossed his arms, smiling innocently like a scorpion.

"I'm at the Grove on King Street."

"Is it a hotel?" Sterling asked in astonishment.

"It's a simple inn. I have no home of my own and prefer the company of strangers." Michael lied with what he hoped was an indifferent tone. "The rent is low enough but it is a respectable address."

"You live in an inn?" Sterling asked again. "I would never have guessed it, Rutherford."

Michael smiled. "I'll take that as a compliment and be on my way—except..."

"Except what?"

"My hat and coat?"

"Damn it!" Sterling stepped back to cross the hall and open a narrow closet by the door. "Footman—useless sod!"

Michael held his ground, enjoying the small petty victory of watching Sterling Porter, the Jackal and arch nemesis of the Jaded, wrestle with his coat and retrieve his hat to personally deliver them into his guest's hands like a common servant. Michael had never given a fig for the rules of class or the myriad of protocol that stifled an Englishman's existence. But this! This was a moment not to be squandered.

"Thank you, Mr. Porter. It was a very interesting evening. Please give my compliments to your sister." He bowed and made his way into the dark night, every nerve ending on alert to an ambush or unforeseen twist. He didn't underestimate his enemy. But now that he knew Sterling better, it was a powerful temptation to do exactly that.

Sterling slammed the door to his study behind him and threw another small log onto the fire. The fireplace poker was cool and heavy in his hands and he gripped it until his knuckles turned white.

He's one of them. I'm sure of it. I was almost sure when he was in the carriage but when he walked in and ducked under the doorway... Smoke or no smoke in the fire at the Thistle, Sterling had the impression that the one in the back of that stairwell had been as big as a horse. *There can't be many men of his size...and the coincidence of his arrival and the way he'd shadowed Grace...he's one of them. His familiarity with Bengal and the mad raj, the knowledge of Bascombe and his quest. Curse that dungeon's darkness! I'd have had all of them and saved myself all this choking effort and mess.*

He thinks to get close and draw me out once he's learned my weaknesses.

But Rutherford's the one who is about to get a lesson in weakness.

Once I saw the way he was looking at Grace—my God, I couldn't have planned it better. As odd as she is, she's caught his fancy. What a miracle!

All I need do now is let nature take its course and when the time is right, that treasure is as good as mine!

If they have it...

Doubt was the enemy that had relentlessly shadowed him for years. *The raj was mad and if he was deluded enough to marry a rock might he not also be insane enough to call a piece of horse manure a diamond? Could I have been wrong all along? If Rutherford is part of it or has a fortune, then why live like a nomad when he could be a king?*

Sterling poured himself a generous glass of tawny port and took several slow deep breaths. "No," he spoke aloud to the portraits and figurines that surrounded him in a silent chorus. "It's real and almost in my hands. No more scraping together the means to threaten or blackmail those elusive and cowardly Jaded idiots. No more missteps and foolish alliances! I'll have it before the Season is over and all of this will have been worth it!"

All this time, praying for one single foothold and I have it.

And I have my dear sister to thank for it.

He tossed the amber liquid down his throat, ungenteel gulps soothing the icy knot in his stomach. "And if Grace is the price I pay, I shall count it a bargain!"

CHAPTER NINE

Michael climbed out of the carriage behind Ashe, like a man walking to the scaffold. He'd vowed to walk through fire to achieve his goal and so he couldn't turn back. But if Ashe had offered him the choice of a burning pit instead of crossing through the doors ahead, Michael was fairly certain he'd cheerfully opt to imitate a human torch.

"I have clothes," Michael repeated uselessly. "I have an evening coat."

"You need a better one," Ashe said as he reached the door. He turned back and rewarded his friend with a wry grin. "Don't deprive me of my fun. Besides, you said it yourself. If it went beyond a simple dinner, you'd let me help you."

"I hate Rowan for telling you that."

Ashe opened the door with a flourish. "No, you don't. Come, Rutherford, face your fears."

Michael squared his shoulders and walked in the shop, removing his hat as he accepted his fate.

"Welcome to Anthony's!" The tailor was a diminutive man with a shock of dark curls on his head. He spoke with an Italian flair and he eyed his newest client with the quiet excitement of an explorer spying a vast unconquered coastline. "I see what you had alluded to, Mr. Blackwell. Mr. Rutherford, if I may be so bold as to state the obvious, you are—remarkably tall!"

"Am I?" Michael asked, pretending shock. "I had no idea!"

Ashe rolled his eyes. "Yes, I'd say that's enough of that. He's ridiculously tall. The question is, Mr. Antonelli, can we dress him so that he looks like a ridiculously tall *gentleman*?"

Mr. Antonelli clapped his hands together. "Of course! So striking and so noble! Beyond his height, his coloring alone is bound to give the ladies pause, and with those strong broad shoulders, narrow waist and such nice lines--"

Michael's brow furrowed. He'd never given his physical appearance much thought, except for the advantages his size might give him in a bar fight or a battle. But to have a man waxing poetic about his coloring and figure was very awkward and he credited it to the shopkeeper's desire to flatter and make a sale. Michael crossed his arms and gave Ashe a cutting look. "You're enjoying this too much."

Ashe took a chair by the raised dais, cheerfully settling in for the hours ahead. "I never denied how much I was looking forward to this. But," he took mercy on his friend and hailed the tailor, "Mr. Antonelli, Mr. Rutherford is a modest man. Please. We must not tell him how handsome he is, sir. He's insufferable enough as it is."

"Right," Michael shook his head. "This from a popinjay!"

"Gentlemen! Peace!" Mr. Antonelli pulled out his measuring tape. "Let us see what we can do for you, Mr. Rutherford."

"He needs everything from the skin out. He has a social season ahead of him and he must be ready for anything. An evening coat and suit, plus something more formal for special occasions and for god's sake, at least, two afternoon coats and a morning coat and something for every day that doesn't make him look like he's about to commandeer a tannery."

Michael started to protest but held back the impulse. It was easier to give in than point out to Blackwell that he was not going to spend his time changing clothes and worrying about the color of his waistcoats. It was one ball and perhaps one or two casual meetings beyond that—and his business would be concluded.

"Your best quality and finest cloths, sir." Blackwell located a sample book and began flipping through the plates. "But nothing too ostentatious or garish. No decorative buttons or ornate cuffs. We'll keep it understated and elegant. This one. This. Six of these shirts in that linen there. Clean lines. We want nothing but clean lines in the cut. Rutherford doesn't need ruffles. Make him a falcon in a room full of overdone pigeons, Antonelli."

Michael shook his head. "You're a bit imperious over there, Ashe."

Ashe smiled. "I forgot myself. And of course, I apologize, Mr. Antonelli. Where are my manners?"

"A generous customer is *never* a rude customer." The tailor smiled. "But Mr. Rutherford is kind to defend me." Mr. Antonelli measured and made his notations, climbing up on a small stepladder to address Michael's shoulders and back. "Please turn to face me, sir."

Michael turned to see that he and the petite tailor were almost eye-to-eye. "My father used to say that you could put silk on a donkey, but it would still be an a—"

"Language, Rutherford!" Ashe did his best imitation of Michael's northern accent.

"There are no ladies present," Michael stated flatly.

"No, but you better break that habit now. Nothing chills a woman's blood faster than a vulgar man." Ashe stretched out his legs. "In my wilder days, even I knew to address every woman like a duchess…"

"Before bedding them like whores," Michael grumbled under his breath. "Thank God for your American!"

"What was that?" Ashe asked, his gaze narrowing dangerously.

"I believe I said I was glad your wilder days are behind you." Michael shifted to address the tailor. "Please don't ask him about his wife, Mr. Antonelli. He starts reciting dusty poetry and it is hard for a bachelor to bear."

"Never!" Ashe protested weakly. "I have never recited poetry."

Mr. Antonelli smiled. "My wife still loves poetry. But I will spare you a recitation of the classics, Mr. Rutherford, if you will but stand straight and lift your arms."

Michael did his best to comply, wincing a little as his ribs protested.

"You're wearing bandages?" Mr. Antonelli asked. "Are you injured, sir?"

Ashe sat up straighter. "What was that?"

"Broken ribs. I fell a couple of weeks back. It's nothing." Michael continued to hold still. "Nice to know that Dr. West doesn't give *every* confidence away."

Mr. Antonelli dutifully returned to his measurements and then climbed down to begin to pull fabrics in the next room. Ashe took advantage of the opportunity for them to speak privately. "Here." Ashe held out a folded paper.

"What is it?"

"Galen sent it. Lady Winters has sketched out the layout of Bascombe's house. She was a guest there when she first arrived in London and apparently," Ashe said as he raised one eyebrow, "she was intimate with the back corridors and secret doors in the stupid badger's residence."

Michael took the paper and tucked it into his pocket. "It may come in handy. Please tell Galen to give her my thanks but to please stop involving his wife in this…business."

Ashe smiled. "You'd better ask the sun to stop rising while you're at it. A wife is not part of a man's life, Rutherford. She *is* his life."

Michael sighed. "Very well. It was a stupid thing to say so I'll withdraw the request."

"When you're a married man, you'll learn the way of it."

Michael took one firm step back. "I am *not* marrying and I am *not* learning the way of it. Don't think for one moment to paint me with that brush. The rest of you have fallen into it and I wish you nothing but happiness with your lovely wives, but do not make the mistake of trying to recruit me into the ranks."

"Careful. If you protest too much, the universe has a way of grinding lessons into your skull and I should know!" Ashe raised his hands in surrender. "Don't kill the messenger, Rutherford."

"I won't. It's just…"

"What is it?" Ashe asked.

Heat lashed up his face and Michael hated the humiliating taste of shame and embarrassment that filled him. "I will *never* marry and the reasons are obvious so stop taunting me and let's just get this over with."

He turned his back on Ashe, effectively ending the conversation as Mr. Antonelli returned with his arms full of fabric bolts.

"No browns for you, Mr. Rutherford," the tailor sighed. "Only lovely midnight blues and then the greys and blacks the evenings require. You inspire me, sir! With your height, you will soar!"

Michael rolled his eyes. Apparently Ashe's falcon reference had stuck in the man's mind. "Feet on the ground, if you please."

Ashe circled the shop, fingering fabrics and making a few more selections while the tailor began the more precise and labor intensive measurements he would need. Rutherford's words echoed in his head and presented a new puzzle.

The man would never marry and the reasons were "obvious"?

Ashe glanced over at his friend who was grimly submitting to Antonelli's attentions and muttered comments. There was no obvious impediment to marriage that Ashe could see. The man was beyond hale and hearty. He was also, undeniably, inclined toward female company. Ashe would have thought no less of him if it were otherwise but Blackwell's instincts told him that any man who transformed into a shy tower of awkward movement whenever a woman was present was *not* unaffected.

Hell, the saying is still waters run deep…not cold.

So if the man was attracted to women, possessed a sizable secret fortune, had all his working parts and was upright and breathing; what was the "obvious" barrier to seeking a wife?

Ashe waited for revelations to come, but there was no flash of insight. Just a wary sense of caution that he didn't want to be the man who pushed Michael Rutherford too far on a topic that clearly made him furious.

I'll ask Caroline what she thinks when I get home. She has such a unique way of looking at the world—perhaps to her the answer will be 'obvious'.

The introduction of his wife into his thoughts proved a complete distraction and a flood of familiar anxiety crept into his chest. He returned to the dais. "How much longer?"

"I am nearly done, Mr. Blackwell," Mr. Antonelli replied. "We will have the first pieces done in two or three days and can complete the order by the end of the week."

"Is anything amiss?" Michael asked.

"No. Not at all." Ashe picked a small invisible piece of lint off of Michael's sleeve. "I wanted to make sure you were bearing up."

"It's a fitting, Ashe. I'll survive." Michael shrugged carefully back into his coat, clenching his jaw to keep from betraying how much the movement pained him. "Although, I have my doubts about escaping unscathed for the next favor I must ask of you."

Ashe smiled. "I'd leap in with a quick speech about how I can't imagine anything worse for you than this, but from the terror in your eyes, I'm curious to hear what you're dreading asking me."

Michael crossed his arms slowly, a man bracing for battle. "We need to make one more stop after this and—I need you to help me. However, if you make one single sly comment," Michael took a deep breath before continuing, "I'll grind a very different lesson into your skull and we'll call it even."

Ashe nodded solemnly, the mischief in his eyes impossible to hide. "You're on."

* * *

Mrs. Dorsett walked into the sitting room and carelessly set a large box on the table. "This came for you." She turned and left the room without waiting for Grace's reply, forcing a small sigh out of her mistress.

What did I ever do to deserve you, Mrs. Dorsett?

Curiosity overcame her frustration at the woman's lack of manners and she approached the box with the anticipation of a child at Christmas. She retrieved a small, attached card from the top and read the note.

For Miss G. Porter—

Because.

M. Rutherford.

"Because? Only because?" she asked. "What an odd thing to say!"

Grace untied the ribbon and lifted off the lid only to drop it on the floor from nerveless fingers as pure shock overtook her. It was a gown out of a dream and for reasons she couldn't fathom, it was lying in a box with her name on it, apparently sent from a man who should know nothing of her dreams.

But there it was—a silk ball gown the color of sky blue with delicate glass beadwork that made it shimmer as if the fabric were covered in diamonds. Her fingers trembled as she reached out to lift it free from the box, her eyes misting with unshed tears at the weight and beauty of it. Silver braid at the neckline and sleeves were the only other adornment and she gasped at the perfection of the design.

"It must have cost a fortune!" she whispered as she carefully folded the dress to replace it.

Sterling came into the room without preamble. "Mrs. Dorsett said you'd gotten a rather mysterious box."

"I did but I don't think I can accept it. It's from Mr. Rutherford." She lifted the gown up for him to see. "It's far too fine and expensive!"

Sterling shook his head slowly. "It's perfect. You'll wear it to Bascombe's."

"I can't!" Grace dropped the dress again. "Mr. Rutherford is in no position to be buying me dresses and I can't believe you don't see that!"

Sterling walked over to retrieve the card that had come with it, reading it quickly. He tossed the card back onto the table. "I see that the dress is lovely.

That the man clearly means to ensure that your bully of a brother doesn't bring you in a burlap bag after I made a point of letting him know you didn't have anything to wear. *And* I see that our soldier is doing very well in this world, no matter how he wishes to portray himself as a humble commoner."

Grace held her breath. "Sterling. We can afford to politely decline this extravagant gift. Mrs. Ambley's shop has several good dresses. Our finances are—"

"About to improve." Sterling said firmly. "I consider this a small advance on the good fortune about to come our way!"

"Good fortune? In what guise?"

"That's none of your concern, but Rutherford is important to me, Grace. See that you make the most of this."

"I don't understand. You've always made it clear that I'm not made for the marriage markets and I've accepted it. What am I making the most of? You insist he comes to dinner and then you practically toss him out the door. One moment you're barely civil to him and the next you're encouraging me to—"

"God, woman! Why do you look so worried?"

"You. I don't recognize you. Not since Mr. Rutherford's arrival."

Sterling ground his teeth together and she saw the danger signs too late as his temper flared. He took a step toward her and caught hold of her upper arms to give her a firm shake. "We have business, Mr. Rutherford and I. I don't have to explain my every action to you. I don't have to tell you anything. It has nothing to do with you except that our dear Mr. Rutherford seems to enjoy your presence and if he is entranced by your charms, then he is less likely to cause me trouble."

"What trouble—"

He shoved her away from him, his expression one of disgust. "This is your chance, Grace. This is your one chance to repay me for everything that I've done for you. For the life I've given you, for the house I've provided and the care. The clothes on your back and every scrap on your plate has been at offered at my expense these last few years."

She rubbed her arms, wincing at the bruises blooming there. But she nodded, as if it made perfect sense that he was angry; as if everything he'd said made sense.

Sterling looked at her suddenly contrite. "I'm sorry. If you knew—you would beg to help me in my cause. Please, Grace. Just be a good girl and help your brother. All you have to do is smile sweetly at the man. Can you do that for me?"

She nodded, studying the carpet at her feet to ward off tears.

He touched her elbow gently. "I am not asking you to do anything inappropriate or unseemly. Write him a thank you note for the dress and invite him to the horse fair on Wednesday morning."

"Of course." *I'll write and tell him you're insane.*

"Show me the note before you send it, sister."

Grace's eyes widened in horror at the sensation that Sterling had overheard her thoughts, but she did her best to recover her composure before she lifted her chin. "Naturally."

He left the room as abruptly as he'd entered it and Grace's knees gave out. She slid down to sit on the floor, waiting until the pounding in her chest subsided to a gallop. It was a tangle that time wasn't resolving. One of the ball gown's sleeves trailed over the table's edge and glittered in the light. Grace stared at it, the perfect dress from a wonderful man. *I should be giddy with joy that this is happening. I have met a man and even if it is only a polite illusion, he is being kind.*

Whatever trouble is coming, I'll have to discover a way to shield Mr. Rutherford as he protected me and keep Sterling at bay.

CHAPTER TEN

Michael leaned against a wrought-iron railing beneath the shadows of an oak tree, hidden from the night watchmen. He had Grace's invitation burning in his pocket and despite the simple words, a hundred readings had only added to the mystery.

The street lamps were making a valiant effort to cut through the darkness but the fog defeated them easily. Michael shifted his stance subtly to assist the circulation in his legs. It was an old trick that allowed him to stay in one position for long periods without losing sensation in his extremities. He'd seen a soldier cut down when he couldn't move quickly enough after sitting too still in a covered position for several hours. It was a lesson he'd never forgotten but one that he'd applied with his own lethality.

It was an old assassin's trick.

He was drawn back to Porter's house on Baker Street, a moth to the flame. He told himself that it was a good thing to keep an eye on his enemy but it was Grace he couldn't stop thinking about. The note had been in her hand, the neat and metered art of a woman's handwriting. He'd studied it for its beauty alone for a long time, mesmerized by the notion that he had something tangible that was unique to her. He liked the tightness of her letters and the flourish of her loops and embellishments.

Except that the note itself reflected almost nothing of the woman he'd met.

It was a gracious expression of thanks for the dress he'd bought her and then an unexpected invitation to accompany her and Sterling to a horse fair. Every word was polite and precise.

Not Grace.

He dictated it and stood over her while she wrote it.

I would stake my life on it.

Michael let out a long slow breath, quietly sorting out the emotions that assaulted his senses. It was a small matter; a handwritten invitation. Sterling's involvement would be a natural thing and the bile that rose in Michael's throat was an overreaction at best. It would be a minor irritation if it were only a brother's dictation of an innocuous message.

But it was the Jackal, standing over Grace.

Michael closed his eyes to try to push the image away. After all, he had no right to feel possessive or even protective. But he did. He felt immensely protective. It was in his nature and he'd long ago accepted it. When the Jaded had met in that dungeon, it was Michael who had vowed to get them through it but also to protect them for the rest of their days. He felt he owed them no less. After all, when it came to India, Michael was the closest to the ideal villain that the natives wished to destroy and when the raj had taken them, a part of Michael would always believe that he was the prime target of the madman's sweep.

And so he'd shadowed them all, appointing himself as an unofficial guardian of sorts and doing his best to keep them from harm when enemies began to emerge from the shadows. Every turn in the game had frustrated him more until Michael knew the danger wasn't in losing the battle, but losing himself along the way.

And now there was Grace.

Grace who didn't believe that her brother was cruel; Grace who was kept to the house and ran secret errands; Grace who bullied him into carriages and was so unaware of her own bewitching beauty and charm that it warmed his blood and robbed him of his intellect.

Buying the dress had felt like an act of defiance. He'd nearly convinced himself that the impulse was purely a jab at Sterling's pride and nothing more. Michael had clung to that conviction to brave Ashe's sly looks and insinuating comments as he stood in the dressmaker's and made his choice. It was a robin egg blue that reminded him of Spring—and Grace Porter's eyes.

Michael shifted his weight again and gained a better view of one of the last lit windows in an otherwise dark house. From the lace curtains and a hanging nosegay of dried flowers below the eaves, he suspected it was Grace's room.

What is she doing up there so late at night when everyone else has long since retired to bed?

Another light appeared briefly in a window on the second floor. The unsteady path of it betrayed that it was a handheld lantern before he detected Sterling's silhouette in the frame.

Old instincts set off a familiar patter in his head.

Light's good even if the fog doesn't give much beyond the street corner. Steady enough. Wind's calm. Adjust for the angle of the window and the curtains. One shot. Not at the shadow but at the figure casting the shadow. One could even risk drawing him in with a noise to get him to step up to the glass and draw the drapery back a little further. He would press his forehead against the cool surface to gain a better view…

One shot through the eye and done.

Not that Michael had a rifle with him. And certainly not the Sharps rifle he'd bonded with in frightening speed. Old habits simply died harder than expected.

Damn it.

He raked a hand through his hair, cursing the common thug that still thought in terms of murder. The Jaded were relying on that very thug for justice and to bring an end to the tangle that threatened their fragile peace.

His humanity was something he'd fought so hard to regain and where the others had hated the black of that dungeon, Michael had embraced it for the restoration and salvation that suffering offered him. For a few weeks and months after their escape, he'd hoped to be a man transformed who could bury the demons of his past. But with the first strike against the Jaded, Michael's dreams had died.

Without a second's hesitation, he'd resumed the mantle of a warrior and accepted his fate. He'd known for a long time that if a confrontation were to come, it would be his duty to shield the others from the worst. Once the men began succumbing to the natural allure of the fairer sex and finding their wives, Michael had become even more resolute.

There would be no salvation for Michael Rutherford.

The light extinguished on the second floor and Grace's window was once again the only sign of life in the house, a faint beacon that drew him away from the grim twist of his thoughts.

Whatever kept her up, he hoped it was pleasant. Tomorrow, he would see her at the horse fair and attempt to better understand Sterling's game.

And do his best to keep his balance and—his distance.

✳ ✳ ✳

"Do you ride, Miss Porter?" Michael asked.

She shook her head. "No. I'm not…one for riding. I think I'm too soft hearted for the enterprise and a bit too short to enjoy being that far off the ground."

"Soft hearted?"

"It's true," Sterling said. "Grace cries every time she sees a man with a horse whip—mind you, *holding* it, not necessarily using it. A sweet fault but it does make riding around the streets of London with her an emotional affair I like to avoid at all costs."

Michael kept his eyes on the large roan being taken out for another turn in the auction stall and deliberately concentrated on not turning and striking Sterling in the face. "I share her loathing of cruelty, Mr. Porter. I admire her sentimentality."

"Do me a great favor, Mr. Rutherford." Sterling stepped back from the railing. "I see a gentleman I wish to talk to. Would you keep my sister company as I attend to this business?"

The request surprised him, but he nodded his assent. "Of course."

Sterling moved away, leaving him alone with Grace in the midst of the milling crowd of horse traders. Michael watched him go for a moment, suspicious at this sudden cavalier hand-off of his only sister's care.

But Sterling disappeared from sight and then there was only Grace to consider.

Let's see if my talent for small talk has improved.

"I've always had an admiration for horses," he started tentatively. "Perhaps that's why I avoided the cavalry. I couldn't imagine torturing some noble beast by asking it to haul me around on its back. Can you see it? Anything less than a destrier and I look like a man sitting on a Shetland pony."

When she didn't answer him, he looked down to see if he'd lost her. Her eyes were downcast but he immediately suspected that it was not out of maidenly shyness as her expression was one of rapt fascination. Although, he wasn't sure what it was about the ground that had captured her attention so completely.

"Miss Porter?"

"Yes."

"May I ask what you're studying down there?"

She looked up quickly, her cheeks flooding with pink. "I don't wish to say."

He nodded. "I see. That is your prerogative, naturally, to keep your thoughts to yourself but…I will admit that I'll have to assume you were thinking something dreadful about the state of my boots—or worse, the size of them. They are clumsy looking, aren't they?"

"Oh, no!" she said quickly, the color in face deepening. "That's not at all what I was thinking, Mr. Rutherford!"

"Well, then you'll have to confess. Surely you trust me to keep your confidences," he cajoled her gently. "After all, I *did* save your life."

She looked up at him and for the space of a single breath he wondered at the wisdom of pressing her. Her eyes shone with the intensity of her internal struggle to speak her mind and he nearly retracted the matter, about to babble something about his lack of conversation when she spoke. "My thoughts escaped the moment. I was listening. Truly I was but then I thought of the British army and all those feet marching all over the earth…and I was considering all the boot prints and then…yours next to another man's."

"Pardon?" he asked softly.

"You see, I read in a book once about a character who could tell all sorts of things about the villain he was tracking from one single foot print and— well, I was trying to see how such a thing were possible."

"What could he tell from a track?"

Grace smiled, warming to the subject. "Supposedly he knew how tall the man was, and that he had a limp and that he was left-handed! But," she eyed the ground again, "I'm at a loss and feeling a bit duped."

"You're clever to realize it," he said, glancing at the pattern of steps in the muck, including a few delicate imprints from Miss Grace Porter herself. "My father was a gameskeeper and he taught me to track everything, including men, but that bit about being left-handed is a bunch of codswollop, miss."

"What *can* you tell from a foot print?" she asked eagerly.

His breath caught in his throat. Why her questions and the keen sparkle in her blue eyes affected him; he had no idea. He only knew he'd answer any question she had and would have to fight the urge to make up fantastic lies if he didn't know the answers. He wanted to say anything and everything to keep her happy.

"A great deal sometimes. If someone is injured or limping, perhaps, but not which hand he prefers to use to pick up a tankard. You can tell if they're heavily laden or maybe just heavy…"

"What else?"

"You can tell if they're familiar with the terrain."

"How?"

Michael shifted back against the fence. "My father said it came down to a man's ability to see what others overlook. If at every moment, you are mindful of your surroundings then if there is a change, a broken branch, disturbed underbrush or wet leaves overturned amidst a dry bed; you are better prepared to see a trail or a sign."

"Mindful every minute," she said quietly. "It sounds exhausting."

"I read a penny dreadful," he began shyly. "Not that a lady like yourself would bother with those kinds of things, but…well, they are a bit habit forming and I pick them up occasionally." Michael cleared his throat. "Anyway, in this story, there was an island inhabited by centaurs who tracked their prey with scent alone. I thought it a terrible idea at first, since horses and men have a knack for using all their senses but as the tale unfolded, it was quite clever. Because they could *see* how a thing smelled, they could *feel* it on their skin and—"

He stopped, mortified at the tangent he'd gone off on. It felt inappropriate to tell her more. He'd forgotten how the story related the sensuality of the human animals and hinted about the symphony of pungent musk involved in their mating. Which was all well and good except he was suddenly wishing he'd brought up another example because even in the pungent and chaotic horse yard, he could smell lilacs from her skin and hair and she was provoking all his senses with a desire to lift her from the mud and hold her.

"Yes?" she asked, her face flushed.

"I…meant to say that it was…accurate in that when you are present and mindful, it overtakes all your senses. So, muddy footprints are merely the start of it—if you're tracking." A snake of heat unfurled up his spine. "Are you taking up hunting, Miss Porter?"

"No!" She replied quickly, averting her face to press her gloved fingers against her cheeks but then turned back to him in a blink, a woman recovered. "My thoughts are as scattered as leaves on a windy day. Sterling hates it. I am so comfortable with you, I forget myself. I ask all the wrong questions and say all the wrong things. In children, it's considered precocious if tolerated but as a grown woman, I should mind my tongue. Even the footprints, that wasn't what I meant to talk to you about at all! You distract me, Mr. Rutherford. It's…most unexpected."

Michael blinked. He loved her thoughts. They diverted and surprised him at every turn and he was mesmerized by the dance of her wit.

"And," she continued quickly, "You are not so tall."

"Pardon?" The comment caught him off guard as it related to almost nothing he could trace.

"I am scattered but I didn't want you to think I wasn't paying attention to what you said, Mr. Rutherford. You would look as noble on a horse as any man and while I agree that you may consider something more along the lines of a draft horse for your comfort, I don't agree that you would look foolish or that a horse would be unhappy to have a gentle and kind rider." She pressed her fingers against her cheeks and then smiled. "You, sir, are not so tall as you think."

His eyes widened, all his movement arrested in a single breath. "Am I not?"

Grace smiled. "Well, you are…tall, of course. And it is striking but I wonder if you are self-conscious of it and the characteristic is magnified in your mind."

God, she cut to the heart of things, didn't she? "Is it only in my mind then? The low ceilings and struggle to find a good pair of boots?"

Her eyes sparkled with mirth. "No. Which reminds me that under no circumstances should you ever cross my neighbor, Mrs. Goodman's threshold, sir. Her sitting room beams are so low that I've hit my head on her hanging lamps no less than three times."

"I'll make a note of it." He leaned back with a smile, and caught himself in the ridiculously relaxed motion of it. He was there to shadow Sterling and instead he'd been hanging on her every word. *Sterling! Where the*

hell did he get to? Michael turned as if a gun had gone off, instantly finding
Sterling in the small gathering across the yard. He appeared to be in
conversation over a pale grey gelding but Michael suddenly wasn't sure. *Could
it be a meeting with another assassin? Am I standing here like a fool while he
plots something?*

"Your brother's business looks serious," Michael stated. "I wonder
why he thinks to conduct it here."

"I don't know. We have no stables to fill." She shook her head slowly.
"I—cannot say for certain what his disposition is toward you, Mr. Rutherford.
Please don't think me disloyal to my brother but he's been acting strangely since
you arrived."

"I can imagine."

"Can you?" she asked, a genuine note of surprise on her face. "How?"

He'd overstepped. "I'm a ghost from the past. I can see how it would
make a man uneasy."

"So uneasy he's determined to drag you out for dinners and next a ball?
So uneasy that the sister he's long been too embarrassed to accompany outside
of his home is now worth showing off?"

"Grace!" Sterling interrupted them, calling across the paddock as he
began to make his way back to the pair. "What do you think of him?"

"Pardon?" Grace asked, a gloved hand covering her throat.

"The grey!" Sterling replied. "Whom else would I speak of?"

Miss Porter was openly flustered and Michael did his best to intervene.
"He looks solid enough from here. Are you truly in the market for a horse,
Porter?"

"Not at all." Sterling rebuttoned his coat. "But it is a good excuse to
get out on a beautiful day and take a stroll. I'm so glad you could join us,
Rutherford, though I wasn't sure you'd brave the outing."

"It was an invitation to a horse fair, Sterling, not a duel," Michael said.
"Courage may be a requirement but I was pleased to see Miss Porter again."

Damn. The truth of those last words made his throat feel tight. It *was* a pleasure to see her. Even with the strange distraction of Sterling's games and his dislike of feeling exposed in a public place, the world faded when Grace Porter began to speak. Attempting to predict what she would say was humbling, and he didn't try. He'd no sooner think to chart her thoughts than wager which way a swallow would turn.

"Did you thank Mr. Rutherford for the lovely gown, Grace?" Sterling asked her. "It was extremely generous of you, friend, and the nicest thing she's likely ever to possess."

Her face flushed pink. "I'm sure I meant to thank him again, Sterling."

"There's no need for that!" Michael said, displeased at the way that Sterling brought up the gift.

"Why so surly, old friend?" Sterling teased him easily, as relaxed as if they truly were old friends. "Grace isn't bothered by me. I have the advantage of being an older sibling in that she expects very little courtesy of me and is probably grateful that I torment her far less than I once did when we were children."

Grace turned away, her bonnet shielding her expression from view but Michael didn't need to see her unhappiness. His rage at Porter's bluntness required little fuel. "I've never heard a man boast about being a disappointment before. Your sister may not be bothered but I am." Michael held his place, daring Sterling to be the first to step back. "We are not children to forgive cruelty so easily."

Sterling smiled, before he stepped back with a mocking half-bow. "What a delight to see a man rise to her defense—and to be so generous with his opinions."

"Please!" Grace spoke out breaking the tension instantly. "Sterling isn't being cruel, he's being callus, Mr. Rutherford and since I agree that we are *not* children; I say you should both behave!" She smiled, gently touching Michael's elbow. "I've long since decided to accept my dear brother's wretched disposition and single-minded character in the hopes that it might improve my own to do so."

"I'm a fortunate man with a saint for a sister," Sterling proclaimed softly. "Envious, Rutherford?"

Michael's breath caught in his throat. It was worse than wrestling an eel. *God, he's slippery!* "Envious as any man would be," he conceded and was rewarded as some of the anxiety in Grace's eyes softened. "I apologize, Miss Porter, but I should be going. Thank you for including me in the day and for...the good company."

"You're welcome," Sterling replied, tucking his sister's hand into the crook of his arm. "We shall see you at Bascombe's then?"

"I've already given you my word."

Sterling shook his head in admiration. "A man of honor! So refreshing!"

Grace's cheeks flushed pink. "Of course he is a man of honor! Are you so surprised?"

Sterling shrugged his shoulders openly unapologetic. "I wasn't surprised. I meant to compliment the man."

Michael waved off the insult and touched his hat. "Until the ball, Miss Porter. Enjoy the rest of your morning."

He walked away before Sterling could add anything else to the exchange or draw him back into another round of verbal jousting. He circled the makeshift paddock and deliberately moved close enough to pass within arm's reach of the "gentleman" that Sterling had spent so much time talking to. He didn't stop and question him, but took a quick inventory of the horse trader. Michael was puzzled at the rough and frayed edges of the handler's coat, the dirt on his neck and the flat and crooked bent of his face after enduring more than a few fistfights in his lifetime.

For all his pretentions, not exactly a member of the Ton for Sterling to be so keen on spending time with the bloke...unless he's the most clever thug in disguise I've ever seen.

The handler spit on the ground laughing as a potential customer made a low offer and Michael subtly shook his head with a smile, dismissing the fantasy of Sterling openly meeting some assassin at a horse market.

Which meant the purpose of the outing still eluded him.

And the only thing he'd learned was that of all the women in the world, it turned out that Grace Porter was like a diamond in disguise.

"A successful morning," Sterling sighed as he settled into the carriage seat.

"Successful? In what way?" she asked. "You barely spent five minutes in his company and when you did rejoin us, it was…" Grace bit her lower lip. "You goad him into thinking he should come to my defense."

"Shouldn't he?" Sterling smoothed the cloth of his sleeve. "I *am* cruel to you, remember?"

Grace looked out the carriage window as she spoke. "I never forget it."

Sterling allowed her the pout. He stretched out his legs and tipped his head back, closing his eyes and effectively ignoring her completely. He had no intention of giving her any more insights into his plans. He was already regretting some of the unguarded comments he'd made.

His confidence in Grace's compliance wasn't absolute. But things were going so beautifully Sterling wasn't going to press his luck. Her ignorance was crucial and from where he'd stood, only added to her innocent appeal to Rutherford's inherently chivalrous nature. He'd never have guessed it looking at the hulk of a man that he would have as soft a nature as his addled sister. Sentiment was a mark of weakness and for now, it was the only clear advantage he would ever have with Rutherford.

The masks were off, even if neither of them had admitted it aloud.

But it was Grace that was holding Rutherford in check. Sterling was sure of it.

He'd watched them at the paddock. Rutherford so attentive, bending slightly to catch Grace's every word, smiling and nodding as if the woman were the cleverest creature ever born. Every instinct he'd had at that first dinner was cemented into fact.

Another week to the ball and Sterling would have the chance he'd dreamt of. He would publicly have one of the Jaded on a leash and have all the proof needed to demonstrate to his debtors that his schemes were finally coming to a head. Bascombe's folly would stand in even greater contrast to his own elegant patient plans and help him to put the minor setbacks he'd suffered into perspective.

Mine. Nearly mine now...

CHAPTER ELEVEN

Grace eyed the gown hanging on her wardrobe door. It sparkled in the afternoon light and scattered impossible miniature rainbows along the walls and floors. The morning's outing to the horse market had been surreal and her stomach hurt to think of the wasted chance for a private conversation with Michael. She'd meant to use whatever precious minutes she gained to warn him that Sterling was…

Her brow furrowed. Even now she didn't know what her brother intended. Something was wrong, that much was crystal clear. He wasn't going to his office regularly and his focus on every nuance of Mr. Rutherford's speeches and appearance made no sense to her. He'd emphasized his authority in urging her to be appealing and tightened his grip on control of the house. He'd repeatedly spoken of prizes and chances until Grace was convinced that some grand carnival had entered their lives. Sterling was like a manic matchmaker. But she couldn't see why after years of telling her that she was lucky to have her brother's protection to keep her from the workhouses, he was shoving her into Mr. Rutherford's path.

Worst of all, she was weakly allowing all of it.

Because being in Michael Rutherford's path was thrilling. God help her. The man's presence and quiet looks were enough to turn her knees to rubber and then, dear heaven! He listened so sweetly and attentively to her blathering on that she was struggling to remember why anything in the world mattered.

And then miracle of miracles! That was *her* story on centaurs he'd referenced—or rather a chapter from Mr. A.R. Crimson's "Isles of Thunder" series! He'd evoked a world that she'd created in secret and spoken of it with such intimate knowledge and even respect that she'd lost all feeling in her extremities. Fire and ice had tumbled over her skin in an excited rush and she'd very nearly clutched his arm and confessed all.

But fear of reproach and the consequences kept her in check. She wasn't ready to lose Michael Rutherford's approval. *Not just yet.*

Grace reached out to touch the gown's silver braiding and sighed. All those stories and she'd imagined seductions a dozen times. On the page, it was heated looks and the firm command of a man's hands; or something equally vague and sinful sounding. But this… This didn't match anything she'd written or read.

This was Michael Rutherford looking into her eyes and simply allowing her to be herself. Where Sterling would frown or say something cruel, Michael only encouraged and applauded her. He complimented her wit and entertained her odd opinions and god help her, he'd invaded more and more of her waking moments, commanding her senses and distracting her from the days ahead.

But then he'd gone even further. He'd defended her against Sterling. Against the verbal jabs she'd endured for so many years, she'd become numb to them.

"Ridiculous," she whispered. "All of it."

Grace turned on her heels and gathered her light coat and reticule. She hurried down to the ground floor as she pulled on her gloves. There was no hesitation in her step and when Mrs. Dorsett stepped out from the kitchens with unspoken questions in her eyes, Grace didn't blink.

"I have an errand to run, Mrs. Dorsett. I should be back before dinner but if I am late, please serve Sterling as he wishes." Grace retrieved her bonnet.

"And where am I to tell him you've gone?" Mrs. Dorsett demanded.

"Tell him the truth, Mrs. Dorsett." Grace finished tying the ribbon on her bonnet and rewarded the cook with a smile. "Tell him you have no idea."

She sailed out of the house with her head held high, a giddy schoolgirl escaping her governess.

And a tyrannical headmaster.

A large woman in a green work dress and a white apron cheerfully bustled forward, cheeks flushed from her labors. "How may I help you, miss? Is it a room you need, or a meal?"

"I've come to call on Mr. Rutherford. I understand he is in residence and I'm hoping…that he will see me."

"Oh!" The woman clasped her hands together, smiling. "Of course! I'm Mrs. Clay, owner and sole proprietor of the Grove. He only just returned, I believe, as Tally went up with a small tray. Not that he would ring for it! Dear man! It's only that I made some fresh lemon biscuits and our Mr. Rutherford has a weakness for them."

"Does he?" Grace swallowed at the familiarity toward *their* Mr. Rutherford, blinking at the tumble of information from the innkeeper regarding a tenant that she very openly adored. "Would you please tell him that Grace Porter has come to call?"

Mrs. Clay nodded, only to gently begin to corral Grace through the inn's ground floor. "Of course, my dear! I'll take you to the first floor parlor on the east side where you can have a lovely bit of conversation. There's a sitting area there and it is semi-private away from the rest of the inn. You understand, I wouldn't feel comfortable escorting you directly into his apartments. The Grove is a very respectable establishment."

"Oh, yes! I can wait in the common room if you—"

"What nonsense! A lady like yourself? Not that you wouldn't be safe as a church mouse in my dining room, Miss Porter! No rough trade allowed at the Grove. My husband, Mr. Clay, God rest his soul, always said that an inn worth its salt meant you could always forget to worry—just like home!" Mrs. Clay led the way past a large and cheerful Tudor style dining hall filled with guests where the smell of fresh bread and beef stew underlined her speech toward a separate entrance and stairway. "This way!"

Grace lifted her skirts as she climbed the stairway, marveling at the cozy inn's charms and how out of breath she was attempting to keep up with Mrs. Clay, a woman twice her age and girth. *I'm panting at the pace she's setting and I don't think she's drawn air between words! How remarkable!*

"So exciting! To have a lady call on Mr. Rutherford! It's a first!" Mrs. Clay announced as they reached the first floor landing and the parlor and private dining room she'd described. Diamond shaped panes revealed that there must be a tree-lined lane next to the Grove and the blossoms and greenery in the late afternoon sun gave the room a fairy-tale like cast. There was nothing ablaze in the large fireplace but the room retained a bit of warmth and Grace smiled at the bouquet of fresh lilacs atop a small table in the parlor's center. Two identical doors were visible on the opposite wall and Grace could see no other egress from this private end of the inn.

Mrs. Clay walked over to the fireplace. "If the room seems chilled, don't hesitate to pull the bell. My son, Tally, will come right away and see to things. He is such a dear boy! And growing so fast! He has a keen wit and a good way with our guests and long after I've departed, the Grove will stand in his care." She sighed. "I'm a very blessed woman."

Grace could only think to nod. Mrs. Clay was a genial font of enthusiastic information and after only a minute's acquaintance, she found herself bemused and envious that Mr. Rutherford had such a lively landlady. "You are indeed blessed, madam. Shall I…wait here then while you send word to Mr. Rutherford?"

Mrs. Clay smiled, wiping her hands on her apron. "Here, yes. Just there." She turned, surprising Grace at the development and walked toward the door on the right, knocking briskly. The portal opened to reveal Michael Rutherford in a white linen shirt open at his throat, his coat removed and his head bare—a man at home. Grace had to avert her gaze, a nervous smile blooming on her lips at Mrs. Clay's unorthodox approach to social matters.

"Mr. Rutherford," Mrs. Clay said. "Miss Grace Porter has come to call and I was sure you wouldn't mind if I brought her up. Shall I bring up another tray of lemon biscuits and tea for you and your guest?"

Shock on his face gave way to rote courtesy. "Mrs. Clay, I'll rely on your care."

"Aren't you a dear!" Mrs. Clay said beaming and then stepped back to bustle off, apparently determined to make a great show of the Grove's hospitality and assist her favorite tenant. "Back in a blink!"

He came out of his apartment, closing the solid oak door and Grace blushed. There was something strangely intimate in seeing him in this setting, in knowing that his most private sanctuary lay behind the door at his back. Mrs. Clay had insisted she wouldn't deliver Grace into his rooms but she'd certainly come close.

"Miss Porter? Is everything all right?" The bass of his voice was tempered with concern and something in her melted at his kindness.

"It's—well enough." She nervously twisted the ties on her reticule. "I'd have sent word to warn you of my visit but since I only just thought to come, it seems we are both surprised to see me here, Mr. Rutherford."

He studied her for a moment. "I'm guessing you must have had some reason to risk a call."

"A very good reason." She took one deep breath and then let it out slowly. "Which, as we speak, I am reordering and composing that reason inside my head so that when you hear it you won't think me any more scattered than you already must."

"I don't think you are scattered. I meant it when I said as much this morning. I like the way you think. But let me see if I can draw up some small talk to give you time to ease into whatever subject is troubling you." Michael gestured toward the pair of upholstered chairs set by the window. "Not my forté but I don't want to disappoint at my first attempt at playing host."

She laughed and took a seat. "No risk of that! And may I say that I find I don't fear breaking any of your chairs." She patted the solid cushion beneath her. "Yours is the more welcoming parlor, it appears."

"Or simply the sturdier of the two," he noted. He sat down across from her and Grace had to blink at the picture he unconsciously made of a large cat stretching out in the patterns of light from the window. He was truly handsome in a rugged way that ignited her imagination and awoke her senses. There was nothing affected in his manners, nothing practiced or polished. He was as different from her brother as the sun from the moon. "I know why you're here, Miss Porter."

"Do you?" she asked, a bolt of astonishment making her sit up a little straighter.

"I was a boorish brute today. Your brother's maneuvers are not very subtle and you wish to beg off of attending the ball. You'd begun to tell me at the horse market when your brother came over." He smoothed one hand down his shirt front. "I don't blame you for it, Miss Porter. While not either of our doing, I'm the first one to forgive you for expressing disgust or—"

"Oh!" Grace pressed a hand to her throat. "Your powers for clairvoyance fail you, sir."

"Then I…apologize," he spoke softly. "I'm trying to imagine what else would bring you to the Grove. Does Sterling know you're here?"

"No! I came," she began but then hesitated. "I came because…it's a tangle, isn't it?"

"Just start with one end of the string and let's see where it goes."

Grace steadied herself and decided that where logic failed, the heart would have to lead. "We *were* interrupted this morning, but you were about to tell me what is it between you and my brother."

"Was I?"

"Mr. Rutherford," Grace tapped her foot impatiently. "If you are trying to be evasive, it isn't working. If you know what it is that is pushing my brother to act so erratically, out with it."

"Here we are!" Mrs. Clay sang out, a large tray of baked goods and a teapot and cups providing an excuse for the intrusion. "As promised, lemon biscuits! And I added a few things to make more of an occasion of it, if no one objects to jam tarts and apple twists. I took the liberty of bringing cider as well."

Michael had to swallow relief at the timely interruption. He'd hoped to never have this conversation with Grace and felt like an idiot for not anticipating her questions. If small talk terrified him, lying had even less appeal. Especially to her...

"Thank you, Mrs. Clay. How kind of you," he said, standing to take the tray from her. "It's a feast."

"Not at all," Mrs. Clay demurred, relinquishing her burden. "I didn't want Miss Porter to think poorly of the Grove or our care for my fav—"

"Thank you, Mrs. Clay," he repeated quickly, cutting her off as kindly as he could. He gave her an apologetic look that he hoped would soften the blow. "I'll—serve Miss Porter and see to things."

To his relief, Mrs. Clay's surprise faded to understanding, although he would have gladly forgone the knowing wink she gave him as she retreated for the stairs. "Anything else, simply ring the bell, Mr. Rutherford."

As if that didn't look completely awkward, damn it!

"She likes you very much, doesn't she?" Grace noted with a sage smile.

"Yes." He set the tray down on a side table near the chairs. "Biscuit?"

Grace crossed her arms. "You're a lucky man to have such a sweet landlady and—"

"Please," he said, his throat closing a bit around the word. "It's..." He sank back down into his chair, aware that a gentleman did not just flop down while a lady stood presently, but helpless to stop the impulse. He was a man on the brink of defeat. "Do you remember how enthralled you were with the idea of appearing mysterious, Miss Porter?"

She nodded, retaking her own seat, instantly dismissing the breech of etiquette. "I still am."

"Well, I have always guarded the—details of my life. It is a habit curried over time and I cannot lie. The mere idea that you are here, that you might know how significant the Grove is, that this is—if not by blood, then by accident and choice, that this is my family and my home; it sets me back on my heels, Miss Porter."

"Why?" she whispered earnestly.

"You are sure that Sterling does not know you're here?" he asked.

She shook her head firmly. "I gave no indication of where I was going when I left the house. But," she tipped her head to one side as if to make a good study of him. "If you don't finish telling me why you are so disheartened to have the great secret of lemon-biscuit-wielding-landladies revealed, I might panic and strike you with that tray, Mr. Rutherford."

"I count myself warned, Miss Porter," he said, fighting the urge to laugh. "Let me clarify. It's disheartening to have anything of my life so easily discovered after—I thought myself very secure from casual scrutiny. No." Michael stopped himself. "It's more than that. I enjoyed the illusion of being an enigma."

She smiled back at him. "What person doesn't?"

"You'll keep my secrets then? As I've kept yours?"

She held out her hand solemnly. "I am not sure what critical knowledge I've uncovered, Mr. Rutherford, but I swear that whatever passes between us will forever remain a confidence."

He took her hand and savored the odd ritual. "As I am still at a loss about the events on Oxford Street, we are in agreement. Whatever passes between us will forever remain—in the strictest confidence."

She wore gloves while his hands were bare, but the elegant blades of her fingers and the sweet warmth of her touch began to ensnare his imagination and distract him from vows and promises.

"We are conspirators, Mr. Rutherford."

This time there was no stopping the laughter she provoked and he gave in to it—and to the ridiculous illogical reality that Grace Porter was perched across from him in the Grove holding his hand and keeping his secrets.

"Conspirators," he repeated when he could, reluctantly releasing his hold on her hand. "God help us."

"Mr. Rutherford," she said, straightening in her chair and then taking a lemon biscuit. "Tell me."

"Tell you?"

"What is it between you and Sterling?" she asked.

"Michael let out a long slow exhale before he answered her. "We met in Bengal. It wasn't the best of…circumstances. I meant what I said before. I think I am a ghost from his past that he would rather not encounter but also one he's been looking for, if that makes sense."

"It doesn't." She took a small bite from the biscuit. "Should I worry more, Mr. Rutherford? Is there something sinister in all of this?"

Lie. The truth gains you nothing, costs you her trust and puts you on the wrong side of the Jackal's sights. All the ground I've gained to get within striking distance of this man, all that we've lost, all the blood that's been spilt… Lie, Rutherford.

"Nothing sinister."

She looked into his eyes and Michael forced himself not to hold his breath until her shoulders finally relaxed and a small measure of relief flooded her countenance. "I should have known," she said with a sigh. "Sterling can be a bit…passionate and unpredictable. With all his posturing and the—strange turns of our recent outings, he seems to have pinned some great hope on you, sir, and I wished to state plainly that I wish nothing to do with it."

"Great hope? What great hope?"

She dropped her gaze to the half-eaten biscuit in her hand. "If it is his matchmaking you fear, I thought I would reassure you, Mr. Rutherford. I've set all that nonsense aside years ago when it was…made clear that I was not destined for marriage."

"Why in god's name not?" he blurted out.

"Pardon?" Grace blinked in surprise, looking up and nearly dropping her biscuit in the bargain.

"I meant to say, I don't understand what was made clear. You are young enough to marry and ridiculously…"

"I am ridiculous?" she asked.

"No! Not ridiculous! It's not my place to—" Michael pressed his lips together, his brow furrowing. "It's not my place to tell you how lovely you are. Hell, I'm sure there are a thousand social rules forbidding a man to start spouting off about how you look like a hint of heaven in this wretched world, Miss Porter, and how impossible that should be!"

"Oh!" Grace's surprise made her even more fetching as she innocently pressed her palm against her beating heart, inadvertently drawing his eyes to the lush firm curves of her body. "I'm—I've never had anyone say I was lovely."

"I don't believe that."

She straightened in her chair, a sparkling anger making her blue eyes snap with her displeasure. "I'm sure it isn't your intention to call me a liar, Mr. Rutherford!"

Michael bit the inside of his mouth to keep from smiling. He solemnly shook his head. "How many times can a man apologize for his lack of social graces?"

She pressed her lips together then lost the battle to smile at his odd question. "Seven."

"How many have I wasted so far?"

"I forgot to count."

"Then you must start at one," Michael said calmly, his confidence irrationally surging in her presence. "When I apologize, of course." The banter between them was intoxicating and he wasn't sure how a man ever navigated with any wisdom when a woman like Grace Porter was in his presence. She was mercurial but at the same time, always Grace.

"Didn't you just apologize?"

"No," he stated before retrieving a lemon biscuit. "I merely inquired as to how many times I might."

"True. But I should let you know that if you also apologize for telling me that I am lovely, I will be crushed, Mr. Rutherford."

"Your feelings are entirely safe on that account, Miss Porter. For I never said it."

"Didn't you?!" she asked with a breathless squeak that was extremely endearing and made Michael wish for everything he couldn't have.

"I said it wasn't *my place* to say it and then…I may have mentioned a rule about…angels on earth…" Michael sighed. "You are too clever for me, Miss Porter. I don't think I can keep up for fear of using up all my apologies in one sitting and then where will I be?"

She tipped her head to one side, a gesture he was becoming all too familiar with and Michael braced himself for the study. "As I've never gotten compliments," she paused, arching her eyebrows as if playfully waiting for his protest, then continued, "I cannot in good faith abandon the hint of one without a fight."

"It's not appropriate for me to pay you one, Miss Porter."

"True." Grace switched sides as if another angle would gain her a better advantage. "But if you could…"

"Then I would," he conceded. "I would say something unpracticed and rustic and you would have a new reason for being angry. And then I would quickly remind you that I'd saved your life to try to keep you from clouting me with that tray."

She sat back in her chair, a very sweet and impertinent grin on her lips. "Then I am satisfied."

God, I think I actually sailed through that! Hell, even Ashe couldn't have—

"And what of you, Mr. Rutherford? Are you sure it wasn't matchmaking you feared?" she asked.

"*I* am no suitor, Miss Porter, and would never presume—I never meant to encroach or disturb. I'm sure Sterling has no such designs and I should wish that you didn't feel the pressure of some giant fool holding your elbow and steering you to a course you didn't desire."

"You are not a giant fool!"

"I am a giant," he said, purposefully making her smile. "I'll concede that point but no other."

"I don't expect you to steer me at all! I believe we've already established that I am a force to be reckoned with, Mr. Rutherford."

"You are terrifying."

She clapped her hands, eyes bright with a fierce joy that made his chest ache. "I find I love being a terror, Mr. Rutherford!"

He finished his biscuit to avoid looking at her and began to pour the tea. "Power can be intoxicating."

"I shall strive not to become a bully, Mr. Rutherford, especially to you." She took the cup from his hand. Grace sipped her tea, then wrinkled her nose. "Oh! I think in her haste, Mrs. Clay may have..."

Michael quickly took a taste from his own cup and immediately grasped the problem. Hot water was good but without tea leaves in the lid's basket, it definitely lacked flavor. "Let's not mention it to her. She'd be mortified."

"Of course," Grace agreed quickly. "We are conspirators, remember? Here, pour the hot water back into the pot and I'll use my napkin to dry out the cups. Then we can say we never got to the tea and she will be relieved if she spots her mistake later."

"You've a gift for deception, Miss Porter." The heat that had been curling inside of him chilled. He was so blind when it came to her, so enthralled. She could easily have come at Sterling's bidding and in all their charming banter, how much had he given away?

She shrugged with a gentle laugh. "It is a survival skill, Mr. Rutherford, but a talent I hope I apply only for good."

"Was there—anything else? Any other reason you had for coming here that you've yet to say?" Michael asked.

"I…" Grace blinked in surprise as she finished drying the cups. "No. I suppose not."

He stood abruptly, wincing at his own rudeness. "You've risked too much of your reputation by coming here, Miss Porter. I shouldn't keep you."

"If I—" she started to speak and then stopped herself, standing as well and straightening her skirts. "Yes, I should be getting back before I am missed."

"I'll walk you down to—"

"No," she interrupted him gently but firmly. "If it's my reputation you wish to protect, then escorting me out to demonstrate that I was here, alone, in your company, would not be the most gallant gesture."

"Oh," Michael said, yielding to her better understanding of the subtle twists in social rules. "There is a separate entrance at this side of the building. If you'd prefer not to walk past the dining room again…at the bottom of the stairs just turn left."

"Thank you, Mr. Rutherford." Grace made her way to the top of the stairs and had taken two steps down before she hesitated. "My brother was right on one count."

"Which one?" Michael gripped the banister to hold himself in place.

She looked up at him from the steps and Michael's heart skipped a beat at the fetching image she presented. "The dress you bought me *is* the finest thing I am likely to ever possess and I…I wish I were strong enough to refuse it, but I find that I am a very ordinary person and very weak when it comes to you, Mr. Rutherford."

"What?" Confusion numbed him. *I make her weak?*

"But make no mistake. I will go to the ball at Bascombe's but I won't be accepting any more of my brother's invitations—or yours." She turned on her heels and was gone before he could summon an answer.

He acted without thinking and vaulted down the stairs, taking them four at a time and reaching her at the door to the inn before she could open it. "Miss Porter!"

"Yes, Mr. Rutherford?" she answered but did not turn her head so he found himself addressing the top of her bonnet.

Shit.

"I *do* think you're lovely," he blurted out and then went on in a rush, "You *are* terrifying and I find I'd much rather be bullied than lose your friendship and I hereby officially apologize for being a social idiot and ruining whatever it was…whatever magical thing that was…to share lemon biscuits and cups of hot water and feel…I'm out of words, Miss Porter."

Grace looked up her eyes shining with unshed tears. "One."

And he forgot every rule, every restraint and every thread of reason he'd ever known. He leaned forward and kissed her, the lightest brush of his lips to hers and for the space of a single breath, he at once savored the hot silk of her mouth but also waited for her retreat.

For Michael believed with every fiber of his being that ladies did not submit to the kisses of great brutish clods who towered over them and lumbered about fearful of breaking furniture or spoiling their toes. *God in His Grace, merciful—*

Grace didn't retreat.

Her hands reached up to frame his face and she deepened the kiss with an unpracticed sweetness that banished fear and inflamed his desires. She sighed in surrender and he experienced a madness that made the world fall away. Hunger gnawed at the edges of his heart and Michael almost cried out at the pain and the healing feast that was Grace Porter's mouth against him. He gently encircled her with his arms and lifted her against his chest. The pace of his kisses kept rhythm with his pounding heart, her lips parting and inviting a sensual exploration of his tongue—and he was ablaze with raw desire. There was no simmering build to warn him; no slow realization that there was even a line to cross. He was consumed with need and the line was long behind him and beyond his reckoning the instant he touched her.

Heat snaked up his spine and his body thrummed and vibrated with every breath, and Grace's arms were around his neck, leveraging her body against his, her responses so natural and unrestrained, he felt like a man clinging to heaven.

His body took the lead and muted the storm of his thoughts, silencing the whirlwind of protests and warnings raging in his mind with an electrical shimmer of sensation across his skin. Every nerve ending was stretched taut and he had the fleeting idea that this was what Lazarus might have felt. Kissing her was like being reborn, but also brought about the discovery that he'd been dead for a long time, shut away from the world.

His blood knew nothing of shame. Desire flowed down his spine, like hot sand pooling in his hips, and made his cock harden and swell. Grace arched her back and pulled his lower lip into her mouth, and sent another wicked dance of shuddering sparks through him. She was all woman, willing and warm and impossibly perfect against him…

Impossible. God, all of this…

Not private. Here. Not wise. Damn…

He'd have sold his soul to be able to claim that he'd ended it because of some gentlemanly streak of honor or that his reason had returned to proclaim that he was too good a man to ruin a woman in an entryway next to the coat closet and boot scrapers. But he'd have lost that wager for it was another agent entirely that restored order to the universe.

His savior was a young soul that Michael had long relied on.

The loud clatter of a dropped tray against the bottom step of the stairs had the effect of a cannon shot and Michael ended the kiss instantly and staggered back with a groan of frustration without dropping her.

Tally.

Michael looked over and Tally signed his unhappy dilemma. *I'd meant to bring the tea since mother was sure she'd forgotten it but—*Tally gestured to the destruction at his feet, his poor face as red as an apple. *I made a mess of everything, didn't I?*

Michael put Grace down, a thing of glass and priceless measure and turned to Tally. Michael spoke aloud so that Grace would understand the exchange as he used his hands to reply. "It's right as rain, Tally. I'll get it and if there's a mess, I made it. You're a good man."

Tally ducked his head with a shy smile and retreated back down the hallway, leaving them alone.

Michael let out a long slow breath and returned his attention to Grace. "Mrs. Clay's son, Tally. He's a deaf-mute but very clever and…" Michael's words trailed off and he braced himself to wait—for whatever tirade she would summon and that he had rightly earned. The damage was done and he didn't think a phrase of apology existed to make amends for what had occurred between them.

"Please," she whispered, stepping back on unsteady feet. He began to reach out to offer his hand but she waved it off, her cheeks blooming with pink and her eyes bright. "If you…have any regard for me, Mr. Rutherford, do *not* apologize."

Michael blinked. "No?" Guilt warred with the lingering effects of her kisses. "Isn't that—required?"

Something in her expression snagged at his memory of a breathless girl describing a carriage wheel passing in front of her face and Michael's throat tightened with emotion. He'd trespassed but apparently the lady was not as fragile as he'd feared.

Grace shook her head vehemently. "You only have six apologies left, Mr. Rutherford. Don't waste one on—" She pressed her fingers to her lips to cut off her own speech. "Good bye."

The door was open and she was gone before he could draw breath.

He leaned his head against the closed door and shut his eyes, and forced himself to let her go.

CHAPTER TWELVE

It was a battle of nerves Michael was already losing as he retied his cravat for the fourth time as he readied himself for Bascombe's ball. "I look like an actor."

Ashe grinned from his seat and took a sip of brandy from his glass. Michael had not invited his friend, but Ashe Blackwell had never needed a formal summons to call on the Grove. After all when had any of the Jaded ever waited for written words of welcome before dropping in on each other? "You look very elegant for a mountain troll."

"If you meant to either calm me or provide a rousing speech to inspire, I have to say you're failing miserably."

"Nonsense! I'm providing a distraction. Besides, the way you're fussing about over that one would think you had more at stake than a social outing to make mincemeat of a mortal enemy. Can it be that our Michael Rutherford is torturing his cravat because he is concerned about his appearance to the ladies in attendance?"

Michael turned away from the mirror and gifted Ashe with a look of deadly assessment. "Don't push me. Vanity is your cross to bear, not mine, and I'm in no mood to play. I hate social gatherings and this one has all the appeal of a flogging."

Ashe stood, his expression one of reconciliation. "And yet Galen still speaks gratefully of how you bravely entered all those salons as his emissary to find his Miss Moreland. You're a good man in any setting, Rutherford. And I can still come along if you'd like. Caroline will be glad to have a few hours without me and has already given her blessing."

"No, Ashe. Your heart is in the right place and don't take this the wrong way, but I don't trust you to keep your reserve. Sterling is bound to be there and you…have every right to call him out, Ashe, but—"

"But you'd rather I didn't spoil your very first formal ball by throttling the man until he's dead?" Ashe took another slow sip from his brandy.

"Don't joke. It's only my promise to you and the others that's keeping me from hanging myself with this damned cravat."

"You'll be fine. Keep the Jackal in your sights and pay a bit of attention to Miss Porter and you'll be fine."

Michael's spine stiffened of its own accord and Ashe's expression changed.

"Rutherford?" Ashe put his glass down. "It was a blind jab but *is* there truly something you'd like to tell an old friend?"

Michael retied his cravat for the fifth time and avoided meeting Ashe's gaze in the mirror. "No."

"I said nothing when we made that stop at the dressmakers, Michael. You wouldn't be the first man to lose his footing."

Hell, I've already lost my footing and insulted her beyond all reckoning.

Michael turned to face him. "I'm not losing anything. She is merely a means to an end and even so, I've been as clear as possible that I'm no proper suitor. Porter's sister has as much to do with me as the man in the moon and is kind only because she thinks I'm a friend to her brother." The lie tasted like wormwood but Michael wasn't about to admit his weakness for Grace aloud to Ashe.

"I see. Laid it all out did you? Declared your ineligibility?" Ashe pushed his hands away from the tie and took over as smoothly as any valet. "Rutherford, I can't help but get the feeling that as grounded as you are, you're a babe in arms when it comes to women."

"Don't be ridiculous."

"How many women have you bedded?"

"What the hell kind of question is that?"

Ashe stood back, surveying his handiwork. "There. Cravat tied. And it's a brilliant question."

"Dozens."

"Liar."

Michael's hands fisted in frustration. "I've bedded all that would have me! Satisfied?"

Ashe's gaze narrowed, his arms crossing. "Getting there." He went back to the small table and refilled his own glass but added another for Michael and splashed a healthy dose of brandy into it. "You and I, Rutherford, we are not as close as say, you might be with Rowan or even Darius."

He handed Michael the brandy and Michael took it gratefully. "I'm content with my place in the Jaded."

"You've kept your distance but at the same time, you're central to our little club, aren't you?" Ashe pressed on. "You're not even the oldest among us, but the unofficial leader and guardian all the same. We all respect you so much. You never broke in that hell hole and you took our beatings and stepped in front of the whip more times than I can count now."

"I'm a mountain troll, remember? We live for pain." Michael replied dryly than downed his brandy in one great gulp, savoring the burn down his throat and sweet heat of it in his stomach. "I don't want to talk about India, Ashe."

"That wasn't the topic at hand," Ashe said, returning to his chair and gesturing for Michael to take his own seat.

"I'll be late." Michael held his ground.

"Fashionably late is not late, Rutherford. Sit."

Damn it!

Michael begrudgingly sat down. "I'm sitting, Blackwell. Although, for the life of me, I can't see why! I am not discussing the intimate workings of my most private self and I'm amazed that you of all people aren't reminding me that this is not the time for diversions. It's about the Jackal."

Ashe nodded slowly. "Agreed. It was inappropriate to tease and I understand that your attentions to his sister are merely part of a ploy to stay close to the man. But, let's set aside the particulars, for the sake of debate."

"We're debating now?" Michael asked.

"Perhaps." Ashe leaned forward until his forearms rested on his knees. "I've gone over and over it in my mind, what you said at Antonelli's shop and if I'm to claim to be any kind of friend to you, then I can't let it go."

"I'm sorry, you've lost me. What was the topic again?"

"Women. You said you would never marry which wasn't a surprising claim from any bachelor but it was the next bit that snagged my attention. You said the reason was obvious."

"It is obvious!" Michael shifted uncomfortably in his chair. God, he hated this! He was as subject to human desire as the next man despite his denials. Kissing Grace had stripped him of his defenses and Michael Rutherford was not accustomed to feeling exposed and vulnerable. "Isn't it?"

Ashe shook his head. "Not to my eyes. Have you some malady?"

"No! Are you *blind*, man?"

Ashe said nothing and didn't move a muscle, patiently waiting for Michael to speak again.

"Blackwell, I can't believe I'm speaking of this. I'll indulge you *this* time and then I don't care if you're on your deathbed, we aren't speaking of this again."

"Agreed. Let's have it."

"I loathe you right now."

"Understood. Out with it."

"I'm…too tall," Michael said with a growl. "Is that obvious enough for you?"

Ashe narrowed his gaze, a man in enrapt concentration awaiting comprehension. "Not even vaguely."

"I'm…big." *Please God, let the ground open and swallow me whole.*

Ashe didn't move. "Women like tall men. It's a documented fact."

Michael stood, too uncomfortable with the subject to face the explanation head on, and began to pace. "Not in my experience they don't! And I'm not tall—I'm *too* tall! I was extremely shy as a youth and never really ventured out much but after I joined the Army—"

Ashe cleared his throat but didn't say anything as he pressed the fingers of one hand against his own lips. Still, Michael interpreted it as a good sign that he'd finally stuck a chord with Blackwell and that Ashe was struggling to take it all in. Michael went on, encouraged.

"On our first furlough, some older men, friends I'd made in the company took me to a whore house. It was to be great fun and I was…looking forward to…"

"Your first time?" Ashe supplied quietly.

Michael crossed his arms defensively, but kept pacing determined to get through the tale and get on with his life. "My first time."

"What young man doesn't?" Ashe said. "I'd normally insert a deliciously ribald tale about my own first encounter but I'd rather urge you to share yours."

"It was a disaster!" Michael bit off the last word. "Satisfied, Blackwell? We were sat upon a couch and instructed to select a partner and when I stood to go off with the brunette who'd caught my eye, she had a screeching fit! She—"

This time Ashe's demeanor was as solemn as a priest's as he patiently gave Michael the quiet he needed to get through his story.

"She said she wasn't about to have some giant bull of a man rearrange her innards and threaten her life. She didn't want to be split wide and bleed to death for the sake of a shagging. She begged for one of the other girls to take her place and when she looked at me—her eyes were wild with fear and dread. A practiced whore and she burst into tears at the threat of bedding me, Ashe." He shuddered. "I'll never forget it."

"God! What a mess!"

"The madam pushed another girl toward me, but I…left quickly and I never went back." Michael stopped pacing and turned to face his friend. "I'm not stupid. The others were always making crude jokes in the bath houses about how I'd be better suited to fucking horses or how any woman game enough to take me on had probably warmed up by riding a few fence posts. Clever, right?"

"How old were you?"

Michael shrugged. "Barely seventeen."

Ashe ran one hand through his golden hair and then stood. "Rutherford, do you trust me?"

Michael nodded. "Yes."

"In my notorious past, I became quite the expert on women and their pleasure, along with my own, of course. So, do you trust me on this subject above all others?" Ashe asked.

"Yes," Michael whispered.

"Your experience was unfortunate; that whore was imbalanced and," Ashe took a deep breath before continuing, "your friends in the military were idiots. Combined with your shy nature and avoidance of the matter, I can see how it has caused you to suffer from terrible misinformation and endure a lifetime of deprivation that I can't even begin to fathom."

"I hardly think I've—"

Ashe cut him off with a firm wave of his hand. "I will speak plainly. No doubt you are overtly blessed with a decidedly "large gift" to any woman lucky enough to ensnare you but let me assure you, it's not a cause for shame. I can refer you to any number of London whore houses in which they will likely have a celebration at the sight of you and you'll have dozens of lovely ladies clawing each other for a chance at you and a turn in your bed."

"That cannot be—"

"And not just whores, Rutherford, in case that mind of yours is ready to misunderstand me. *All* women are grateful for a well-applied and good-sized cock and while a virgin may take a few moments to get over her shock, that's where it's a gentleman's duty to ensure that he applies finesse and care to ease her anxiety. Anyone worth their salt knows that a woman's pleasure should be any lover's prime goal, since our own climaxes are so easy to come by." Ashe was warm to the subject now. "You should think of yourself as the envy of most men, Michael, and quite the object of desire for the weaker sex."

Michael had to blink in shock for a moment. "You *did* say you were going to speak plainly."

"There are no ladies present and after all the pain you've gone through, I owe you no less than the unvarnished truth. Look," Ashe straightened his shoulders, a man leaning into the task. "D has a rough translation of "The Perfumed Garden" and a few other exotic books and I'll ask him to loan them to you. If you don't believe me, perhaps an ancient text extolling the virtues of a cock that is three and a half hand-breadths in length and as shockingly wide will change your mind." Ashe went back to the side table and refilled their brandies. "They say it the measure of a meritorious man and the ecstasy such a man invokes in the woman he loves is as close as a human can come to paradise on earth."

"My god! Truly?"

Ashe turned back around and delivered the glass to Michael's hand. "Your soldier friends were jealous and took malicious fun in knocking you about, Rutherford. I imagine they all had thumb-size pricks and the intelligence of hedgehogs, stupid bastards!"

Michael took the drink but didn't sample it. "You're sure?"

"Of this and almost nothing else!" Ashe admitted with a smile. "Feel better, my meritorious friend? We'll put this Jackal business behind us and then you can set about to see for yourself how very wise and surprisingly insightful I am!"

Michael set his drink down, untouched. He had no desire to arrive at the ball with alcohol on his breath. Bad enough that he was now running late, but—Ashe's revelations made all of it worthwhile. Even if the man exaggerated his case, a faint glimmer of hope had come alive inside of him.

Perhaps not a freak, after all! Years lost to that one night's lingering effects and the hateful banter of men I barely knew… I was a fool.

"That may be, but I hope you'll keep my confidences, Blackwell."

"Your secrets are safe with me. This entertaining and informative conversation never happened." Ashe bowed his head. "Although, if I'm on my deathbed, it may make for a diverting laugh…"

"God help me," Michael sighed.

"Never invoke God when the Devil makes a better advisor," Ashe teased, moving to make his departure.

Michael couldn't help himself from laughing. Blackwell could charm hornets into thinking they were songbirds without even trying. "Go."

"I'll leave you to your evening and await a full accounting." Ashe opened the apartment door, adding, "You're sure you don't wish me to come along to—"

"Go! Enough!" Michael pushed his friend out and shut the door firmly behind him. Revelations or no about the nature of things between the sexes, he knew he was a man about to dance on a knife's edge. He would honor his commitment to the Jaded and ultimately see their enemy destroyed but more and more, he wanted to do all that he could to keep Grace from harm.

The worst lay ahead and his instincts were telling him that he would not only have the Jackal to fend off before long…but the Jaded as well.

CHAPTER THIRTEEN

"Stop fidgeting," Sterling chided her under his breath as he helped her climb down from the carriage. Grace cautiously alighted, mindful of her glittering gown's hem and the damp ground, ignoring her brother's scowls. She'd spent a sleepless night and then a long frenetic day in nervous anticipation of the evening's event and frankly, didn't trust herself not to trip on the steps or disintegrate into hysterics at the first mishap. Grace wasn't sure how any woman recovered from the fiery discovery of a particular man's kisses—and the certain knowledge that when it came to that man, she had no restraint or inhibitions whatsoever.

She'd told him he made her weak but she'd spent hours reliving his touch and the strength of her reaction had been so potent and empowering; Grace was convinced no opiate could have held more appeal.

Even so, she would betray nothing of herself to Sterling, fearful that whatever his intentions, he would think to misuse her passion for Mr. Rutherford. *He's misused me enough in whatever game he's trying to play.*

No, I shall enjoy tonight and be a proper lady—and reassure Mr. Rutherford and myself that I am capable of self-control.

She took her brother's arm as they followed several guests through the large open door into Mr. Rand Bascombe's grand London home. The house was finer than Grace had expected with ornately styled wrought-iron banisters setting off the main staircase centered in the foyer. It led up to the first floor landing where the reception line was greeting guests before they entered the salon.

She searched the guests on the stairs as they handed over their wraps and coats, wondering if Mr. Rutherford was already among them. She silently recited again the temperate greeting she'd been practicing for him.

'Good evening, Mr. Rutherford. How different you appear than when I saw you last at the horse fair!' There! That will serve to remind him of our conspiracy and impress him with my composure and indifference to—

"Grace?" Sterling squeezed her elbow. "Did you not hear what Lady Pringley said to you?"

"What?" Grace abruptly came round, blushing at her lapse of attention. "Oh, I'm so sorry, Your Ladyship! Was it a compliment or a question?"

Sterling's eyes flashed with suppressed fury before Lady Pringley replied, "What a cheeky thing, you are! It was neither."

"Her Ladyship was commenting that she had never seen you before and asked for your name," Sterling supplied, openly displeased.

"Grace Porter, Your Ladyship," Grace offered, adding a wobbly curtsey for good measure. "I was…distracted at the sights and guests' finery. It is my first ball and I meant no offense."

"May I present myself? I am Sterling Porter. A close associate of Mr. Bascombe's and assistant to Lord Waverly's man at the—"

"No," the older woman said with a sniff, cutting him off with disinterest as she turned back to address Grace directly. "Despite the fact that you are clearly too old to play the debutante, I hope you enjoy your evening, Miss Porter. I suspect your foray into society and our midst will be brief in light of your manners, but what a pretty thing you are! I have always been a great follower of fashion and had intended to compliment your gown."

"Th-thank you?" Grace wasn't sure whether to cry or laugh.

"You are most welcome," Lady Pringley pronounced before turning on her slippered heels and sailing up the grand staircase to cut to the head of the queue of guests and make her way inside the salon doors.

Grace smiled. "I nearly enjoyed that."

Sterling leaned in, his voice as cold as the hiss of a snake against the shell of her ear. "Goddamn it, Grace, that is precisely the sort of behavior you will forfeit instantly! Pay attention and keep your mouth shut for the remainder of the night or I will drag you out of here!"

She gripped her fan so tightly her knuckles turned white. Grace knew his anger was fueled by Lady Pringley's dismissal but she had no intention of giving him an excuse to ruin the evening; or denying herself the sight of Mr. Michael Rutherford in evening clothes. "As you wish."

She dutifully took his arm again and allowed him to escort her up the staircase toward their host and hostess.

"Ah, here is our host,

"Porter!" Mr. Rand Bascombe exclaimed. "I don't remember seeing your name on the guest list."

Grace nearly gasped at the icy loathing in the man's face and began to wonder if a retreat at Lady Pringley's insults might have been the wiser course. *What in the world are we doing here, Sterling?*

Sterling smiled unfazed. "I was sure your invitation was quite deliberate. What is the saying? Keep your friends close and your enemies closer?"

Rand smiled in return, without a trace of warmth. "Ah, yes! So right! How useful it is to be able to point you out to a few of our mutual acquaintances to make sure they have a face to go with the name. For I can assure you, you have been quite the subject of so many of my recent conversations."

"How appropriate," Sterling countered easily. "But let us talk later when you can tear yourself away from your wife's party. May I present my younger sister, Grace Porter?"

Rand gave her a cursory look but held out his hand as etiquette required. "A pleasure."

She took his hand and curtsied. "What a lovely home you have." *A safe enough comment, let's hope.*

"Yes." He turned to his wife and relinquished Grace's fingers. "May I introduce you to Mrs. Bascombe? Miss Grace Porter, my love."

"Porter?" Mrs. Bascombe's eyebrows arched and her look of assessment was far more thorough and judging than her husband's as she possessively seized Rand's arm. She was a handsome woman in her mid-forties, a well-preserved beauty though the effect was spoiled by her haughty expression. A tiara of small diamonds and seed pearls set off her dark hair and reminded Grace of a glittering spider on top of her head. "Ah, yes! My husband speaks so often of your brother, I couldn't resist meeting the infamous Sterling Porter but his sister as well? What an unexpected surprise!"

"Really?" Grace blurted out then pressed her lips together tightly. "I'll have to ask him how he earned his infamy when we get home."

Sterling cleared his throat. "Yes, later. Come, Grace. You don't want to miss the start of the dancing and we must find your Mr. Rutherford."

"Who?" Rand asked sharply.

"No one of your acquaintance, Bascombe. But a special guest I'm sure you'll thank me for including in the night's festivities." Sterling nodded in a mock bow and led Grace away from their hosts and into the salon.

She had no choice but to go with him into the crush and the noise. Once again, Grace was impressed by the rich details of the house. The room radiated wealth with its ornate marble floors and painted ceilings; gilt arches soared across the vaulted space and defied description. The writer her in her took note of every detail, greedily storing up each flash of color and striking chord of conversation. The furniture had been cleared from the large narrow salon; a theatre created for dancing filled with guests milling about in lively chatter awaiting the start of the music. The gallery above was lined with a narrow balcony and musician's loft, the curtains drawn back to reveal a small ensemble tuning up their instruments.

Within seconds, she knew that Michael was not there. He'd have stood out among any crowd and disappointment lashed at her frayed confidence. *I feel as welcome as a rag lady at a coronation—please, Michael. Do not let me face this alone!*

"Is that Sterling Porter, I spy?" a sultry voice carried over the din and Grace watched in astonishment as the most beautiful woman she had ever seen strolled toward them.

"Madame Pierre! I had hoped to find you here!" Sterling said, bowing at the waist, then taking the woman's gloved hand to kiss it. "You dull the company with your shining presence!"

Madame Orphée Pierre! Confined as I am, I know who she is!

The papers were full of scandalous references to the famed courtesan who was the current favorite of the Prince Regent and of her incomparable wit and sensuality. Grace watched in awe at the effects of the lady's irresistible charms. A bubble of overtly curious eavesdroppers formed around them and even the thin-lipped few who made a pretense of disapproval at Madame Pierre's appearance among their moral ranks craned their necks to get a better look. She was rumored to be a Creole and as exotic to the Ton as a bird of paradise. Her skin was the color of café au latté and her eyes were like emeralds. Her green emerald silk dress's décolletage bordered on indecent but it was the height of fashion. Around her neck, she wore what was unmistakably her latest gift from her royal lover, a choker of solid emeralds and diamonds that engulfed her delicate throat.

Grace couldn't determine what was more shocking; that the Madame Pierre she'd read of was standing within arm's reach or that the woman knew her brother so well. She tried not to gawk at Sterling's flowery speech and waited for an introduction or inclusion that never actually came. Instead she was a forgotten witness to their conversation.

"I see so little of you these days, Mr. Porter! You naughty man!"

"If only…I had the time I wished to attend more social functions, Madame Pierre. Alas, I am chained to my desk at the East India."

Her gaze narrowed but she kept smiling. "I would speak to you privately, sir."

"Of course! Of course!" Sterling quickly agreed, then drew her off to a corner for an intimate conversation abandoning his sister to stand alone near the ballroom's doorway.

She opened her mouth to protest but shut it quickly as nearby guests began to stare at her with speculation and open snicker at her predicament.

Please God...let Mr. Rutherford come as he's promised.

And before I burst into tears.

At the sight of Madame Pierre, Sterling was sure that it was another tangible sign that his luck had truly changed. He had been striving to cultivate his acquaintance with her for months and after a few overt mentions of a certain glittering property he was about to acquire, it appeared he finally had her full attention.

After all, despite his bravado with the East India, he was clever enough to engineer a secondary plan. He'd leveraged himself to the hilt and with the numerous broken promises he'd made, Sterling was sure it was to his advantage to have another investor who might make good on his debts and advance his cause.

He expected Grace to obediently wait for him and didn't care if she didn't. Madame Pierre was far more important at the moment than a spinster sister who was more trouble than she was worth.

"I had begun to suspect you were avoiding me, Mr. Porter," Orphée said. "You whet my interest and then I hear nothing from you..."

"I apologize. It's no small thing to offend a dear lady like yourself but neither is it a small thing to deliver something that a queen would dream of holding—and might go a lifetime without seeing anything remotely close to its like." He kept his voice low. "As I said before, you are not the only interested party and I have to be cautious. I don't want them to know that I'm considering other offers."

Orphée gasped, openly intrigued. "I have a fondness for...regal trinkets, Mr. Porter."

"And I have a fondness for rare beauty which has led to my current dilemma," he sighed. "If the others pay me, I will have no choice but to honor my agreement with them and hand it over—regretfully, of course."

She put a hand on his arm. "Accept no payment, Mr. Porter! Send me a note with the price that would ease your conscience and win me my prize. I will see to the rest."

"Thank you, Madame," he said, taking her hand to kiss it. "I am another willing slave to your charms."

She laughed, a pretty peal of music. "What a delightful thought! A stable of men to do my bidding! But as you know, my heart is secured for now so I will merely say, thank you."

She left him to head into the salon, the crowd parting in front of her as if she were a great ship cutting through a storm. He watched until her emerald swathed figure was lost in the crowd and then finally recalled his sister.

"I see you've obeyed me for once," he noted dryly as he returned to her side.

"I see you've forgotten that a woman cannot walk across a ball room unescorted without raising a few eyebrows," she responded pointedly looking in the direction that Madame Pierre had taken. "I'm trying to behave, sir."

Sterling had to bite his tongue, then smiled at the irony. He had in her in hand and just in time. Just in time to potentially not need her at all. Rutherford was a pawn he'd thought to require as leverage tonight to make his point, but now that he had two "queens" on the board, he felt untouchable.

Rutherford will give me what I want and I may commission his death for my own amusement...

CHAPTER FOURTEEN

Michael found her quickly, the robin's egg blue shimmer of her dress drawing his eyes. He was lamentably late and wary of the reception waiting for him but there was nothing to be done except to bravely waste his second official apology and pray things went smoothly.

Whispers coalesced around him as he moved through the crowd and Michael did his best to pretend he was deaf.

'My God, he's so tall!'

'A pretty brute, eh?'

'What a sight! Does anyone know him?'

'Look at that gentleman, my dear…what do you think? How tall is he?'

Michael's jaw tightened. He was shy of seven feet but just barely and he hated the gauntlet of stares and whispers. *Damn it, as if being tall were akin to having a horn growing out of your forehead!*

Apparently Bascombe had invited three times the number of guests his ballroom could comfortably hold and Michael was cursing the man within twenty steps of struggling not to step on anyone's toes and avoiding the shorter patrons' treacherous elbows or emphatic hand gestures. Ashe might want to wax poetic about his stature but he hadn't faced that particular danger to a man's vulnerable parts…

He was blocked for a few seconds behind a tight clutch of men in conversation too distracted to notice him.

"Their election will decide it and then it's to come to a civil war! Over the obvious immoralities of slavery as if they alone can—"

"It's a fight about their government's structure, Mr. Hodge! Their states apparently feel it's tyrannical to have their local laws dictated to them by a remote authority."

"There's an old story," another man said with a laugh. "Since when have the American Colonies ever enjoyed being subject to authority, Mr. Mitchell?"

"Sir Yeigh, you are too witty! I say we stay out of it when it comes, let them finish the nonsense in the course of a few weeks and enjoy better cotton prices!"

Michael cleared his throat and was rewarded by all three men turning to give him startled looks. "Coming through, gentlemen. Pardon me."

They parted and he began to celebrate that he was nearly halfway to his goal when a very different obstacle materialized in his path. Sterling stepped in front of him holding two filled punch glasses and then stopped.

"You look like a man facing a cannonade."

Michael didn't bother to deny the obvious. "Enjoying my discomfort, are you?"

Sterling smiled. "I might be. Only because it is astonishing to see a man of your strength and size so rattled by the sight of a few fluttering fans and silken skirts. It's a ballroom, Mr. Rutherford, not a battlefield."

"That depends on your vantage point, Mr. Porter," Michael said, straightening his shoulders and stiffening his spine. Hating Sterling was easy but keeping his guard up while Grace stood nearby, so lovely in her glittering gown with her shoulders bared was proving difficult. He wanted to follow the cat and mouse of Sterling's banter and hold his own. But the orchestra was beginning to tune up their instruments and an icy dread growing inside of his stomach presented a more immediate threat.

A footman came up to Sterling's elbow and whispered in his ear, ending momentarily, his pleasure at seeing Rutherford so off balance.

"If you'll excuse me, I've been called away," Sterling said without preamble and shoved the punch glasses into Michael's hands. "You don't mind keeping Grace company do you, Mr. Rutherford, while I pay my respects?"

What? It was an abrupt shift and an unexpected request. "I don't mind, Porter, and I'm not one to mince over etiquette but without a chaperone wouldn't you rather—"

"What could possibly be inappropriate in the favor? Especially since you are a *trusted* friend and associate, Mr. Rutherford, and a man who spent time with me in India, yes?"

Michael grit his teeth to keep a sarcastic snort from slipping past his lips. *Go on, Porter. Overestimate your power and see how far the game gets you.* "It's an odd habit you have of leaving your sister's care in my hands and wandering away."

"Nothing's odd in trusting my instincts. Besides," Sterling said as he adjusted his cuffs, " I doubt you'd harm her." Sterling shifted so that his back was to his sister, his voice lowering so that only Michael could hear him. "Even if you thought it would destroy me, Rutherford."

Sterling walked away before he could answer and Michael tracked his retreat until his gaze fell onto Grace who was looking at him with open relief and a familiar joy that made his chest ache. The crush faded and he swallowed the irony that a man who could follow a single sparrow through an oak forest could lose his way so quickly. Grace was in his sights and Michael sighed as her beauty inevitably blinded him to everything else.

※ ※ ※

The footman led Sterling upstairs away from the din of the party to Rand's private study and he went in alone. Five others were already waiting in the dim quiet where a single candelabra illuminated the space, and Rand Bascombe had notably given up the chair behind his desk to stand; a sign that even in his own home he wasn't the dominant force in the room.

Not in this gathering.

God help me, but this cliché of meeting in shadows is beginning to wear on my patience…

It was a dull room with one wall effectively lined with leather-bound books as if to clarify its purpose. Sterling sniffed at the notion that Bascombe could reel off three titles with his eyes closed if he were challenged to it. But his rival had openly campaigned for Sterling's destruction, and he knew better than to underestimate a wounded adversary.

The Jaded have taught me that, haven't they?

"Here he is, at last!" Bascombe said. "The source of so much misery!"

Sterling made a mock bow. "You're not blaming me for your recent misfortunes, are you Bascombe?" He straightened, putting his hands behind his back like a soldier facing a drum trial. "If I made a mistake it was in sharing my knowledge of the diamond with you far too early only to have you run off, half-cocked, to make a try for it yourself! It was mine! My scheme! You tried to make all of them believe that you were the mastermind to pull it off and it was your bungled hands that alerted the Jaded and drew this whole thing out!"

Bascombe's hands fisted at his side. "That's a lie!"

Hell, I should thank you, you fat prig, for distracting our associates for all that time! Bascombe's failure had been a small boon to him, drawing their attention away for a while and Sterling hadn't sat by idly.

"You tipped your hand too soon to his lady love and to Lord Winters and then you sailed off like an idiot to India despite every word of reason I offered." Sterling crossed his arms in front of him. "And how did that go again? Find anything interesting, old chap?"

Bascombe launched himself at Sterling's throat, his hands transfigured into claws, but strong hands restrained him and the calm icy voice of the man behind the desk ended it. "Both of you will sit, at once. We've lost control of the Company to the crown where India is concerned but don't make the mistake of thinking I'm not a power in my own right."

Rand's face was so red, Sterling wondered if the older man weren't about to keel over, but the man recovered. "I went into debt to chase that rock! At your urging, Porter, so how dare you look at me like some smug child and speak of my mistakes!"

Sterling shrugged as he sat down. "We are each responsible for our own choices."

Rand nearly jumped again, but this time a single hand on his shoulder was enough to remind him of the company he was keeping. "Well," Rand said, a slow cold smile creeping over his features, "that is true! *I* have repaid my debts to the Company and—" his eyes darted to the man behind the desk with eyes the color of frozen mud who barely blinked. "I remain grateful for that opportunity." Rand continued, turning his attention back to Sterling. "Whereas you, Mr. Porter, have yet to repay a single penny, is that not correct?"

Sterling had to swallow the cold dread that threatened to choke him. "Not *yet*. But unlike you, I accepted that after the raj fell nothing would be simple. I told you it wasn't there anymore. I was the one who made the connection to the Jaded and I've not wasted time and resources stomping around in a jungle nor will I be forced to marry some rich curdled old bitch to make good on my loans. *I* intend to deliver the diamond, Rand, single-handedly and without a nod to your hollow contributions."

"After all this time? After so many repetitions of that same promise?" Melrose said from his place leaning against the bookshelves. "You can still say those words and look us in the eyes?"

"How?" another man asked, as he refilled his glass from a small bar against the wall. "How are you going to do it single-handedly?" His words slurred from the whiskey's power but he was still steady on his feet.

Sterling pressed his lips together. He had no desire to tell them the particulars of his plan for at least two solid reasons. He didn't want Rand or any of them trying to intervene since they'd made it clear that they didn't trust his competence. And secondly, he was too close now. Tonight, he'd brought Rutherford as proof that he'd gained vantage into the Jaded's ranks but it was a move he regretted. Any of his compatriots could swoop in and spoil it or achieve the mystic diamond without involving Sterling and he may have tipped his own hand too far.

Damn it! If they'd given me the resources I demanded in the beginning, all this would be over! Instead I've been shoved aside and forced to beg and borrow at every turn; inventing ridiculous makeshift schemes to try to further my cause and break the Jaded without the others taking matters into their own hands.

"Well?" Rand asked, openly enjoying Sterling's discomfort. "Tell us, Sterling. Tell us how you only need a few more months and you'll have it this time. Tell us how you need "one more" small advance to seal the deal. I do so love a good fairy tale!"

"Feel free to fuck yourself, Bascombe." Sterling leaned forward and ignored everyone but the man behind the desk. "I have a very elegant solution underway. I don't think I'll say more except that *nothing* I've done has been wasted. I'll have it before the first day in July. The diamond is here, in London and I'm willing to stake all that I have on that."

"All?" The room fell silent and the flames on the candles danced from an unseen force.

Sterling began to pray as he hadn't in a long, long time. *Please dear God in Heaven. This time. This time let me win.*

"All that I have."

I may have staked my life on it.

And time was officially running out. He'd had enough of Bascombe's ridiculous party and the scrutiny of his peers. Sterling turned and left the room without a word, slamming the door behind him. Rutherford would be the work of another day. He would find his sister and drag her off the dance floor if need be, but the charade was over.

CHAPTER FIFTEEN

She was light in Michael's arms, but not insubstantial. Her smaller height was no true match for his, and yet she magically fit perfectly against him. Michael was able to place a hand between her shoulders at her back and to hold her without hunching over and as he accomplished the first few turns without incident, pride began to seep into him straightening his shoulders and allowing him to forget his fears.

Here was no porcelain doll! Grace Porter was warm and lively, her touch instantly reminding him that the current of desire that had nearly carried them away at the Grove was no dream. There'd been no reproach or mention of that embrace and Michael was grateful for the reprieve. He was determined to demonstrate restraint and prove that he could be a gentleman when he tried.

"Are you enjoying yourself?" he asked.

"Immensely!" she replied. "It is a night I will always remember as my first and likely last ball." There was no bitterness in her tone, only a matter-of-fact acceptance and joy in the moment.

"You are too confined to the house, Miss Porter."

"Oh, I get out." She gave him a secretive smile and evoked an English Mona Lisa. "I have my own unique methods for seeking escape. It's just that Sterling prefers me to run the household and he doesn't approve of ladies social clubs and the like."

"No?"

"My brother has a deep suspicion of them and swears that they are all essentially political and subversive."

"Are they?"

She laughed. "I wouldn't know! I'm not allowed to join any. But I don't think they are as dangerous as he imagines. Our neighbor three houses away, Mrs. Sieverding, is a member of one and it all looks rather innocent."

It was his turn to laugh. "But that would be the definition of a subversive group, wouldn't it? One that gives every appearance of innocence while they secretly plan to topple the government or assassinate every vicar in England? Can't you see it? Petticoats and petit fours as a cover for an elite team of female assassins?"

"Oh, yes. That's…true…" It was as if he'd flipped a switch and lost her. Wherever her thoughts had taken her, it was far away from his presence and Michael admired the phenomenon. Darius did the same sometimes when he was working on a vast problem. One minute he'd be making conversation and the next, mid-sentence, he was a man adrift.

She's a thinker, like Darius. God, she's so smart…but far prettier than Thorne when she's distracted.

She blinked suddenly as if recalling that she was in the midst of a waltz and that Michael was there. Her steps slowed and she would have stumbled if he didn't offer the steady frame of his arms for her to cling to. Michael eyed the other dancers who were less apt to slow their pace and decided that the best course of action was retreat. He gently escorted her off the floor and away from the swirling crowd. With her fingers tucked into the crook of his arm, he walked her out the French doors of the large salon out onto a narrow verandah overlooking the gardens. The spring night air was cool enough that balcony was empty ensuring their privacy. Michael chose to keep talking, as if nothing had happened. "Your brother is unworthy of you, Grace."

"Sterling would vehemently disagree, but I don't need rescue, sir."

His jaw clenched to bite off the argument that sprang to his lips. *Like hell, you don't!*

Another pair of dancers stepped out onto the verandah, openly clinging to each other and making Michael wonder if the punch were more potent than it appeared. Their privacy vanished and he regretted it deeply. "Miss Porter, if

it's not too forward, would you care to take a turn in the garden away from…"
He glanced over at the lovers, his own face growing hot. "The crowds. It seems
well-lit with Chinese lanterns and I confess, I might need some more fresh air
before attempting another life-threatening turn in that ballroom."

"How thoughtful!" she readily agreed and took his arm to walk down
the stone steps to the garden. "It is a crush, isn't it?" She stopped halfway
down, her movement abruptly coming to a halt. "If it's my life you're referring
to, I felt quite safe, Mr. Rutherford."

He smiled. "Perhaps I was thinking of the other dancers. My waltzing
skills are a bit erratic and there's no telling what weak soul I might have run
over in there."

She struck his arm playfully with her folded fan then laughed. "I have
always wanted to do that!"

"Hit me with a fan?" he asked.

"Not you! Anyone really…women do it all the time in dramatic fashion
from what I can gather and I read an article chiding ladies for getting a bit too
carried away with the use of their fans as weapons." She shrugged and resumed
their walk down the stairs to the symmetrical garden below. "It sounded
wickedly appealing."

You are wickedly appealing. His body tightened at her words and it
was Michael's turn to wrestle with his internal landscape. *This is ridiculous! I
have to be able to go more than two minutes without wishing to kiss this woman!*

"I can't see you causing real injury with a bit of folded fabric and
bamboo," he said.

"True," she echoed and then he lost her again.

He guided her down the gravel path lined with blooming French
lavender and patiently waited.

Her eyelashes fluttered and even by the pale light of the lanterns, he
could see the blush that crept up her neck. "I'm so sorry! I was daydreaming
again!"

"I'll forgive you only if you take a deep breath and without censure, tell me what you were thinking in that moment. All in one go."

"You're sure?" she asked, tipping her head to one side to study his offer. "All in one go?"

"Yes."

"I was thinking about fans as weapons and how men can put rapiers into their walking sticks and umbrella handles, but there is no feminine equivalent. And that it would be sinfully exciting to think of a stiletto built into the wooden handle of a lady's lace and feather fan and the very last place that anyone would ever think to look if they were disarming her." Grace released his arm and took a step back, a woman warily awaiting judgement. "Not...not that one would ever...do such a thing..."

"My god!"

Her eyes flooded with horror. "I was—jesting!"

"That was brilliant!" Michael exclaimed. "That popped into your head? Truly?"

She nodded slowly. "I did say that I was scattered, Mr. Rutherford. I'm afraid things tend to pop in my head quite often."

"So clever!" He held his arm back out. "What an original thinker you are, Miss Porter."

"You don't mind it?"

He shook his head firmly. "I find it very entertaining. I never know what you are going to say next and you never disappoint."

She was so still, her face tipped up toward him, eyes shining. "I could have said the same to you, Mr. Rutherford."

"I'm not entertaining," he asserted quietly.

"No, but you never disappoint, sir."

Michael fought to hold himself in check. "Would you—care to finish our turn about the garden?"

"Oh!" She smiled and recovered her composure, taking a small step forward to take his arm. "Lead on, Mr. Rutherford!"

The path wound to turn under a large oak tree before heading back toward the house and as they stepped into the dark shadows of the walled garden's end, Michael questioned his own sanity at proposing an "innocent walk" at night in Bascombe's little wilderness. They were too far from the house for his liking. "Perhaps we should head back before they send out a search party."

"We are a scandalous distance out," she said, apparently reading his mind. "But before we run in like guilty children, I have to tell you something, Mr. Rutherford."

"Yes?"

"I could be wrong, sir, but I have the distinct feeling that you are genuinely worried about me. You are so quick to come to my defense and I'm—humbled by it. But I don't wish to take advantage of any misplaced gallantry on your part." She reached up to nervously smooth back a curl from her face. "I'm not blind to the tensions between you and Sterling. I know he can be a difficult man but I can manage my own life."

"As you said, you don't need a rescue, Miss Porter," Michael said. "But that doesn't mean—"

"I don't wish to shock you, Mr. Rutherford, but I intend to live independently from Sterling and I have—plans to do exactly that."

"What?" Michael's amusement evaporated in a single breath. "What plans?" An irrational vision of Grace Porter having a clandestine lover ready to sweep her away from her brother's household stirred a dark weight in his chest—a possessive tiger stretching to life. "Grace." He took another deep breath and tried again. "Damn it."

"Sir?"

Michael moved fast, emotions outpacing all else, and he caught her upper arms in his hands, stepping close to look down into her startled eyes. "I shouldn't have cursed! If you only knew me...you'd know how out of character..." He softened his hold by an infinite degree but something in him refused to let go. "I'm a version of myself I have never known, Grace. If you

have—is there another man, Grace? I have no right to ask but I—you affect me.
You know you do. I demonstrated how much at the Grove but—I need to know.
Tell me, Grace. Tell me your plans."

Her eyelashes fluttered in shock but she didn't drop her gaze. "There is
no one and I…"

"Say it."

"I meant only that I've saved money of my own to leave my brother's
house. On my own, Mr. Rutherford." She tipped her head back a single inch,
innocently unaware of the inviting picture she created and the havoc she was
wreaking on his senses. "But I find that I want you to have every right to ask,
Mr. Rutherford, and that doesn't seem possible." She reached up to place one
hand against his chest, her fingers splayed against the rhythm of his heart. "I
want all my secrets to be yours to keep or betray, sir."

His hold on her was firm and commanding but not cruel. The heat of
her body, the scent of her hair and skin and the look of absolute rust and calm
nudged him over a line he had sworn to never again cross. It was sheer madness
not to release her, not to apologize or beg to reassure her that he would take
every secret she'd ever placed with him to his grave.

But Michael wasn't thinking anymore.

Relief that Grace Porter was free gave way to a raw desire to claim her,
to possess the right to protect her and hold her—to seize the chance to touch
what he could not keep. He lifted her up against his chest and off her feet,
lowering his lips to hers, hungry and eager to taste her mouth again. The
familiar and fiery assault of sensation drove him on as her lips parted eagerly,
matching his desires with a sigh and proving that the unpredictable Grace Porter
was always to be a surprise to him.

This was no echo of their first embrace but a moment unto itself as if he
had never kissed her before and as if this were the thousandth time he had held
her.

Her arms reached up to encircle his neck, leveraging herself against
him to demonstrate that she did indeed fit perfectly into his arms, the

disadvantage of her stature evaporating as her body pressed to his. He cradled her against this chest, then knelt down on one knee, unwilling to trust his balance as the world tipped one direction and then another; spinning at every touch. She tucked against him balanced on his thigh, the difference in their heights diminished and irrelevant, the sweet fire of her tongue against his in an erotic dance.

Grace sighed at the delights of kissing Mr. Rutherford, his mouth warm velvet against hers. It was intoxicating and she opened her mouth to taste more, inviting the touch of his tongue and boldly running the tip of her own tongue along his full lower lip. He moaned at its touch and deepened his kiss, his reaction a white hot passion that made her lose track of where her body ended and where his began.

She slid her fingers upward to touch his throat and then downward to trace the pulse of his heart. Her hand sought the bare skin at his chest, eager to press her fingertips. She had one fleeting thought that her boldness would disgust him but his responses quelled the notion instantly. This was a power Grace had never known. His touch commanded her but it was clear that she was the ruler of him in turn.

Michael came up for air only to renew a passionate assault on the delicate landscape that was Grace. It was like breathing lilacs and tasting spring. He trailed his mouth across her jaw to discover the shell of her ear. When she shivered and arched against him when he grazed the curve of its outer rim, he took it as an invitation and at the present moment, he was in no mood to refuse.

She sighed consent and wriggled with excitement at the attention of his lips and the gentle nips of his teeth to pull on her earlobes. She tipped her head to bare more of her neck and shoulders, beautiful feast of touch and taste that did nothing to diminish his hunger for her. Michael followed the lines of her throat to uncover every point that made Grace react and practically sing in his arms.

The lessons came quickly and Michael absorbed that every flash of pleasure she experienced was directly tied to his own body's demands, arcs of heat and a raw animalistic hunger for satisfaction unfurled inside him, as every touch built to hint at the release he knew was possible.

Her lips drew him back and his fingers splayed to cradle her head, to take all that she offered and possess this fiery gift of Grace's kisses. Her hair was silk in his hands and even as a part of him dryly noted that hairpins were falling and would be impossible to retrieve from the wet grass in a dark garden… Michael was wrestling with the very real danger that more than hairpins were about to fall.

"Grace," he lifted his head. "This. This cannot be the place or time for… I'm so weak when it comes to you, woman…" he let out a slow shuddering breath, "But even I…should know better. I care too much about you, Grace, to insult you within sight of a crowded ball and—"

"Unhand my sister!"

CHAPTER SIXTEEN

Damn it!

"You heard me! Unhand my sister, you vile excuse of a man!" Sterling shouted.

Michael lifted his head and surveyed the theatrical nightmare in all its full glory. He'd never heard footsteps on the gravel path approaching them, and it took one glance to ascertain that Sterling was standing on the opposite side of the lavender off the walkway and had strode on the wet grass to make a quieter approach.

Not that this detail made any difference now that Sterling's twisted displeasure and scathing judgment was conveniently illuminated by the hand lantern that Sterling so gallantly was holding aloft to make sure that his sister's state of dishevelment was impossible to hide.

He shifted to gently set her off of his knee, struggling to make sure he adjusted his evening coat before he stood up but the instant Grace gained her feet she moved toward Sterling, desperate to reach brother and make her case.

"It was an innocent kiss!" Grace cried out. "I…Mr. Rutherford…is very honorable and…he did nothing wrong! It was my fault! He wanted to…go back…but I…"

Michael winced. With her golden hair tumbling down her back and missing hairpins, lips swollen from his kisses and cheeks flushed—Michael was fairly certain that there wasn't a phrase of denial in existence to overcome the image of ruin she presented.

"Shut up, Grace!" Sterling barked.

"Don't speak to her like that again, Sterling," Michael warned him, a strange calm overtaking him. It was the Jackal's orchestrated performance but Michael knew his role.

"I'll speak to my slut of a sister however I wish! What kind of "innocent kiss" requires the darkest corner of the garden?" Sterling growled. "You were on the ground like animals!"

"Hardly," Michael muttered under his breath and did his best to gently pull Grace back against him, instinctively wanting to shield and protect her. "And lower your voice. I don't see the need to bring out the entire party for this, do you?"

Sterling glanced back at the house and Michael groaned at the realization that his words were apparently prophetic as the verandah was already lined with spectators ogling their gathering near the garden's farthest wall.

Shit!

Michael took a deep breath and tried another tact. "Sterling," he began, his voice low enough not to carry, "this is a private matter and I don't see how it aids anyone to ensure your sister's humiliation. I would not hurt her for the world and—"

"Come to my house tomorrow morning and we will settle this as gentlemen. Unless you are dishonorable cad and refuse to come to terms!" Sterling deliberately spoke with the projection and elocution of a stage actor and Michael came within two heartbeats of striking him for it.

"Terms?" Michael had the sinking feeling he'd stepped into a trap.

"You can't do this, Sterling!" Grace stepped away from Michael, recovering her voice. "It was my fault! He would have walked me back and—"

"That's enough, Grace." Sterling held up a hand to silence her and then grabbed her elbow to prepare to go. "Tomorrow, Rutherford."

"I won't marry him! You can't force me to marry someone because—"

Michael winced at the open declaration of her revulsion at marrying him but it was Sterling's bark that cut her off that sent him over the edge.

"Shut *up*, Grace!"

Michael gripped Sterling's coat front and lifted him off the ground so quickly that Sterling dropped the lantern at his feet, extinguishing the light and disappointing the crowd who'd been relishing the show. "I warned you not to speak to her like that again, Porter."

"No! Please!" Grace pleaded behind him then reached up to try to pull her brother back to earth. "It's not worth it and I'm—I beg you, Mr. Rutherford! Sterling's upset! I'm sure he didn't mean to be snide and horrible. It's sadly his...natural state..."

Michael smiled at the humor of her words and slowly set his nemesis back onto his feet. "I agree." He made a show of smoothing out the front of Sterling's jacket. "You're a lucky man, Porter."

Sterling's fury was palpable as he straightened his clothes and rewarded his sister with a searing look of animosity. "You'll never do that again, Rutherford."

Sterling outstretched one hand toward his sister. "Come, Grace. It's time to go home."

"Sterling, I—"

"Grace, come." Sterling's voice was taut with anger and echoed off the stone walls. "Or we can escalate this into a brawl and despite Mr. Rutherford's belief that he can bully his way out of this, I will have him subdued and arrested; and you will be carried out of here kicking and screaming. I'd prefer a quieter exit but at this moment, Grace Porter, I leave the choice in your hands."

Tears finally came and Grace meekly surrendered to take her brother's hand. She glanced back, a desperate look that gave way to her silently mouthing the words, '*I'm sorry.*'

Michael grimly folded his arms and watched as Grace was led out in disgrace.

It was the second time he was forced to let her go.

God, what a tangle! How will I ever explain it to the others without looking like a complete ass? Ashe will be like a terrier with a bone when he gets wind of this mess. Not only did I lose sight of Sterling in the first few minutes—

I'm fairly sure mauling Grace in the garden wasn't the best way to go unnoticed by Porter's cronies.

He waited until he was sure Porter had had ample time to make his escape and see Grace safely out and then squared his shoulders to face the gauntlet ahead. He strode out of the garden, up the steps of the verandah and past dozens of strangers whose eyes watched him with raw curiosity and blatant disapproval. Some of the men hissed at him in his wake and Michael fought not to roll his eyes.

He had trouble reconciling the impulsive and sweet fire of Grace in his arms and the condemnation that swirled around him as he progressed through the salon. Guests parted in front of him as if the very brush of his coat against them would contaminate and stain.

He wasn't nearly as embarrassed as he was angry; angry at himself for blindly putting Grace into such a horrible position, angry for forfeiting reason when the Jaded were counting on him most—and impossibly forgetting every vow he'd made to those men.

Grace.

I made her cry.

What kind of man does that?

Michael walked out of Bascombe's, his head held high.

Tomorrow would be soon enough to get a better grip on a deadly tiger's tail.

And forever yield the heaven of Grace's company to Providence. As far as Michael could see, Sterling may have done him a favor. She had every reason she needed to forbid him from entering into her company. The relationship between them was painfully and abruptly severed and now he could focus on his original mission without the complexities of Grace's direct involvement.

Sterling would pronounce him a villain and Grace would have to accept it.

And when her brother failed to come home from the East India one evening in the very near future, Michael would arrange for a fortune to fall into her grieving hands to allay the last breath of scandal she might endure.

I can do that much for her.

Even a demon can do that much.

✳ ✳ ✳

Grace fought to stop crying, fury and shame warring to break her spirit. "That was unnecessary, Sterling!"

He sat across from her in the carriage and for a moment, she didn't really recognize him. His lack of sympathy stung but the strange excitement in his eyes chilled her to the bone. "That was incredible! I couldn't have planned that better, if I say so myself! Not that I would have been so ham-fisted and blatant to instruct you to draw him out into a dark garden in the middle of a large ball and let him have his wicked way with you on the ground…" Sterling ran a hand through his hair and leaned back as if the weight of the world had left his shoulders. "Not as elegant as I'd hoped but there is more than one way to skin a cat!"

"Are you mad?" she whispered. "Can you hear yourself?"

"I knew he was taken with you. I knew it! How stupid of me to think it would take a bit of time for you to bring the man to a useful simmer!"

Grace gasped in shock. "What? I'm not boiling anyone alive, Sterling, and if you're insinuating otherwise, I hate to correct you but I did not seduce Mr. Rutherford!"

Sterling shrugged. "Of course you didn't! I doubt you would have the talent for it, which is why it is sheer luck that he fell on you anyway."

"He didn't—" Grace bit her tongue, amazed at the twists and turns of the conversation. She used the palm of her hand to wipe off her cheeks, determined to gain control of her emotions. "Sterling, please heed what I am about to tell you. *I. don't. care.*" She emphasized each word as if his comprehension were impaired. "I don't care that those people think I'm…"

"Fast? A slut? A rampant little whore?" Sterling provided with an unkind smile.

Grace took a deep breath before continuing. "Nothing irreparable happened in that garden that needed anything so ridiculously drastic as a threat of terms to Mr. Rutherford. It was a kiss and nothing more! I will never agree to marry Mr. Rutherford under these circumstances or any other of your imagination or manufacture!"

"You will do as I say."

She shook her head. "No, Sterling, I won't. Whatever madness has seized you has nothing to do with—"

He slapped her hard enough to throw her across the seat against the carriage's window frame and for a blazing moment, Grace forgot how to breathe as bright white pain ricocheted through her body. Her cheekbone throbbed with the force of a hammer's blow and shock alone kept her from crying out. The assault on her senses paled next to the crushing blow against her psyche.

Never. He never before…

"Your erratic manners cause me endless trouble, sister, and you'll rein yourself in or end up in bedlam," he said as calmly as if they'd been discussing the mild spring evening's weather. "I never asked your opinion on the matter and since I am your legal guardian and caretaker, you'll submit to my wishes or I'll finish beating you when we get home until you see reason."

Tears filled her eyes and spilled silently down her cheeks unheeded.

Sterling sat back, stretching his legs out in front of him. "Good. We are in accord at last, dear Grace. Now, be a good girl, sit quietly and let your brother think. There are preparations to be made and while others would rush the game, I am not a man without compassion."

She pressed one hand over her own mouth to keep a hysterical bubble of deranged laughter from slipping past her lips. *Compassion? God help me…what game are we playing?*

"Don't worry, sister. You'll make a beautiful bride."

CHAPTER SEVENTEEN

"You'll marry her."

Michael didn't move in his seat across from Sterling and held his silence for a moment. The man's study was a small room cluttered with a collection of exotic bits and pieces in a dark mash that made Michael miss the warmth and welcome of his friend Dr. West's library. He'd come early at Sterling's command, but Michael Rutherford had no intention of surrendering.

Not one blessed inch of ground.

At last, Michael summoned a reply. "No."

"What did you say?" Sterling asked, openly flabbergasted.

"I said, no. You see, there is a bit of a large hole in your net, Porter." Michael sighed. "You've misjudged my character."

"Have I?"

"I'm no gentleman to worry about my reputation, Sterling. I'm a common man and I have enough friends. What do I care if my name is struck off the invitation lists for the dry-chalk conversations of some crusted Duke's card party or a Dowager's childish birthday party for her dogs?" He wrinkled his nose at the notion. "I'd rather take a flogging."

"You compromised my sister!"

"I *kissed* your sister. Grace is...very lovely." Michael stiffened his spine unwilling to appear too engaged in the matter or share the truth of his affections with a man he hated. Any advantage the Jackal had sought to gain, Michael wanted to deny him. "I am willing to make an apology and offer what amends that Grace feels suitable but I'd say that should end it."

"You *ruined* her! You publicly *ruined* her!" Sterling's hands were splayed against his desk blotter, as if he were preparing to leap over its surface. "Are you saying you also care nothing for her reputation?"

Time to lie to your face, you blackguard.

Michael shrugged, taking on a nonchalance he hardly felt. "Grace made it clear in the garden that she has no interest in…traditional options," Michael said calmly. "Perhaps you weren't paying attention but before God and an entire balcony of people, she swore she wouldn't marry me."

"That is *not* her choice to make."

"Isn't it?" Michael asked. "Porter, our private business aside, if I thought for a moment that she was truly hurt by this or that I could amend the mistake by making a greater one, I wouldn't argue but—"

Sterling stood suddenly and rang a bell on his desk.

It was so shockingly unexpected and oddly formal that Michael had to catch his breath. *Am I about to be escorted out by an elusive footman he thinks he has on duty? Or the prune-faced housekeeper?*

Michael stood slowly, desiring to be on his feet just in case the door was about to burst open with several thugs wielding knives. Before he could think of a clever jest on the matter, the door slowly opened and Grace stood in the doorway to the small room.

The glittering vision of robin's egg blue had been replaced by grey muslin and black velvet trim but that wasn't the only drastic change. There was no sign of the spirited creature he'd held in his arms. Her head was bowed, her face averted from him with her shoulders hunched over as she meekly stepped inside and stood against the wall.

"Greet our guest, Grace." Sterling commanded softly.

Slowly, she lifted her face and Michael's heart stopped.

"Good morning, Mr. Rutherford." Her bottom lip was trembling with the effort it took her to keep her composure but it was the angry bruise across her cheek and the swollen ruin around her left eye that made his stomach churn with fury.

My God! He broke her! That son of a bitch!

"Go back to your room, Grace."

She curtsied, not even risking another glance at Michael, before she turned to leave closing the door behind her. Michael caught a glimpse of Mrs. Dorsett waiting in the hall and the entire horrifying picture dropped into place.

"Now, before you do something stupid, Rutherford and grab my shirt collar and start bellowing about how I treat my sister, I should remind you that under the law, I am well within my rights. While you…" Sterling's smile faded away. "You care nothing for your reputation, have proudly announced that you are no gentleman and that my sister's standing is hardly your concern."

Michael closed his eyes to try to absorb the white-hot rage that was exploding behind his eyelids. *Why? Why didn't I foresee this?*

And then it all came to him in a single flash of clarity.

There was no way on God's green earth that Grace Porter was going to remain under her brother's roof for a minute more than circumstances required and there was nothing he wouldn't hesitate to sacrifice to see to it. He would solve more than one problem by getting her clear of Sterling's reach and no matter how much she hated him for a forced marriage, it would be worth it.

Once he had Grace, she would be safe.

And Sterling will think he's got me in hand—right up until the moment he doesn't.

He opened his eyes and refocused on the man across the desk. Time slowed and Michael shook off every emotion that would hinder his ability to think. It was a shooter's trick and he invoked it with the ruthlessness of a mercenary.

"I'll marry her."

It was Sterling's turn to be surprised. "Without hearing my terms?"

"Your terms are irrelevant."

"Good!" Sterling gestured back toward the chair in front of the desk. "Sit down and we'll work out the details."

Michael didn't move a muscle.

"Or…" Sterling's brow furrowed, uncertainty filtering into his eyes. "Stand then."

Michael waited a man carved of granite.

"The only delay is the one needed to post the bans," Sterling said.

"Omit them. I'm sure you can obtain special dispensation considering recent events."

"And why are we suddenly in a hurry, Mr. Rutherford?" Sterling's gaze narrowed with suspicion. "Do you think you can throw me off by playing along?"

"Decide what you want, Porter. You demanded I marry her and I've agreed." Michael gave him a derisive look as if Sterling had pissed in his pants. "I begin to comprehend your weaknesses, Sterling."

The ploy worked.

Sterling stiffened as if his chair were electrified and the look of loathing he gifted Michael with was a balm to his soul. "I'll be in touch as soon as things are arranged. See that you don't leave Town in the next few days."

Michael didn't blink. "Anything else?"

"Until I contact you, I forbid you to so much as cross my doorstep since it is clear that you cannot be expected to control your animal passions when it comes to Grace and she behaves no better than a whore under your influence."

* * *

Sterling hummed to himself as he headed up the stairs to Grace's bedroom. His plan had worked so well he'd nearly overthrown his own success. He'd expected to have to make a vague threat of committing Grace to an asylum if Rutherford didn't come to heel, but apparently the sight of her black eye was all that was needed.

Sterling laughed, giddy with his impending triumph.

In recent months, he'd have pressed for the treasure instead of forcing Rutherford into a match first, but he was learning as he went. The Jaded were as skittish as colts and even harder to bridle. A ridiculous affection for Grace was all well and good, but Sterling didn't trust it.

He wanted Rutherford well and truly bound before he sprung the trap.

Only then would the giant fool see how he'd lost the high ground and forfeited his options. *Patience, old boy. This time. This time, I have him and well within my deadline to the others! Hell, there's even room to give the pair a few days to bond a bit and sample a little marital bliss...Which will make it all the more effective when I threaten to remove the ground beneath his feet!*

"Grace!" He knocked on her locked bedroom door. "It's settled! Rutherford's agreed and agreed to see to it soon." A strangled muffled cry was audible through the wooden door and Sterling smiled. "There, there! He's not so bad, is he?"

"Sterling, please!" Grace's voice was closer this time, just on the opposite side of the portal. "What can be gained by this? I'm begging you!"

He rolled his eyes and felt some of his joy fade. "I'll have no tears on the day. Cry now and then enough! For I swear, Grace, if you defy me and try to spoil this or throw a tantrum in front of the vicar—you'll spend the rest of your life in a madhouse sitting in your own filth! Do you hear me?"

He was rewarded with the sound of her tears and decided that that was as much agreement as the day required.

He passed Mrs. Dorsett on his way back down the stairs and stopped her briefly. "Keep her under lock and key, madam. I'll not have my sister slipping out to run any more errands. Is that understood?"

"Of course, Mr. Porter," the woman said, nodding.

"What a treasure you are!" Sterling clapped his hands together and continued on and never saw the pleased blush that crept up his housekeeper's face.

CHAPTER EIGHTEEN

"Rutherford, you came!" Darius Thorne stepped forward, relief evident on his face. "There was no real news after Bascombe's and you can't imagine how Ashe has been chomping at the bit!"

"I can imagine." Michael surveyed the gathering, surprised at the size of it. Josiah Hastings was having a small showing of two paintings for the Royal Society of the Arts and it was a milestone that their circle had long anticipated. Michael had naturally expected the Jaded and their wives to be there and then a few additional acquaintances of each but this… This was a large public gathering of apparently genteel art lovers and anyone curious as to what a blind man's painting would possibly look like. "I thought it was to be invitation only."

"It is quite a crowd, isn't it?"

"Yes. Though we need to find a private corner to talk. There's been…a bit of a development and I want to—"

Lord Winters walked up, unintentionally interrupting. "Thank God, you're alive!" Galen lowered his voice to add, "Not that I entertained speculation otherwise, but Ashe is a force."

Lady Winters laughed as she came around to take Galen's arm. "Mr. Rutherford, I *never* doubted your safety but it is a delight to see you again."

"You're too kind," Michael answered then nervously looked over the crowded gallery again. "I don't know why I thought it would be eight or so of us in a room."

"Eleanor would have preferred it in light of her nerves," Haley said in reference to Josiah's beautiful prim wife and reluctant model. "I'm afraid we overrode their simple plans for a quiet reveal. But Mr. Hastings work is too startling not to garner the public's attention and praise."

Darius sighed. "The press hasn't even gotten into it yet. I'd say the crush of curious onlookers will only get worse in a week or two after the Times publishes their critique. Isabel will regret missing the day."

"Where is she?" Michael asked bluntly. His urge to ascertain where everyone was and reaffirm that the Jaded and the women they loved were all secured was irrationally strong.

"With Caroline to entertain and distract her, though fatigue made it a wise choice. Rowan assures me it is a common complaint when…well, you know…" Darius finished awkwardly, shy to speak aloud of his wife's pregnancy but his eyes shone with pride and pleasure. "You wished to speak privately?"

"Yes."

Galen looked at his wife, "Would you excuse me for a moment, dearest?"

Haley pressed her lips together as if she would refuse but yielded after looking at Michael's face. "I'll go, but don't think you're not repeating every word to me later, Galen."

"Yes, dear. Every word." Galen kissed her hand and released her to retreat with the others to the emptier side of the room away from the portraits.

Michael shook his head. "So much for our secrets."

Darius smiled. "I think it's charming that you ever held the illusion that the women weren't keeping a close watch, Rutherford."

"All right, enough," Galen said. "We'd heard nothing of you for three days, although Rowan said he received a pithy note from you indicating that Bascombe's was nothing we'd hoped for."

Michael shook his head at the painful understatement. "No. It was *nothing* we'd hoped. Is Rowan coming?"

"Sadly, no," Darius answered. "He was called out with Gayle. Some rich client has fallen ill and as Rowan knows, disease and death don't often come at convenient times."

"And Ashe?" Michael pressed on.

"Running late but he should be here any moment." Galen crossed his arms. "But now that we know it's serious, you'd better tell us."

"How do you know it's serious?" Michael knew it was a waste of effort to delay the inevitable but he was in no hurry for the agonies ahead.

It was Darius who offered a reply. "Because you're taking a roll call like a headmaster before exams."

"Out with it," Galen said firmly. "Is it Bascombe? Did the fat old toad pop up to cause trouble the other night?"

"No, in fact, I never saw him which may have been a small blessing in disguise."

Darius reached up to adjust his wire-rimmed spectacles. "The paper made the gathering sound like a lively affair but of course, what we want to know is how Porter explained his insistence that you attend. Did he give nothing away?"

You mean, besides his sister? Michael cleared his throat. "Not really although there was certainly an unexpected...development, you could say."

"Finally! Progress?" Galen asked.

"I don't know if you would ever label it as "progress" but you'll find out soon enough." Michael took a deep breath to steady his nerves. "Things have taken a turn."

"Rutherford!" a voice called from across the room and their small circle instantly pivoted. "Fancy meeting you here!"

God, no! He wouldn't be this bold or this stupid—would he?

Michael had only a fraction of a second to give Darius and Galen a warning look, praying they'd take the hint and simply retreat while they still could. He stepped away from his friends hoping to redirect the Jackal from strolling into their midst. "It's a public showing and I didn't realize you were an art connoisseur, sir."

Sterling Porter smiled. "I heard from an associate of mine, a Lord Waverly that Lord Winters had been the prime supporter of the event and pressed the Royal Academy on Hastings behalf. It was a flimsy thread to follow, but I'd hoped to find you here. After all, Lord Winters is…rumored to be a dear friend of yours."

Galen held his place and Darius drifted back but didn't walk away. It was clear he wished to stay close but didn't want to get pulled in by this stranger.

"Introduce me to your friends, Rutherford."

"I'd rather not."

"God, what manners!" Sterling strolled around him as if he were no more than a potted plant in his way. "Then I shall ask for introductions myself." He shifted his hat and gloves to one hand. "Sterling Porter," he said with a half bow. "At your service."

Galen made a subtle signal to Thorne with his free hand behind his back and Darius applied himself to making a study of milling nearby as a disinterested by-stander. Michael shifted his own position to add to the distraction then watched in admiration as Galen pulled on an aristocratic air as smoothly as another man pulled on a cloak.

Galen dropped his chin an inch, adopting an expression of icy study. "Mr. Porter. I am Lord Winters. You'll forgive me but when you yelled across the room like that, I mistook you for a carter hawking his wares."

Sterling's façade of merriment cracked but he recovered quickly. "My enthusiasm overtook my better nature, Your Lordship. But was there not another gentleman? That one there?"

Galen's lip curled in distaste. "I don't know him really. Soliciting funds for a reformed college or something. A stupid project of an acquaintance of mine and one that I cannot endorse; education for women. Ridiculous!" Galen lied smoothly and deliberately turned his back toward Darius. "Why do you look familiar to me, Porter?"

Sterling's smile was as genuine as a crocodile's. "Do I? How fascinating!"

Galen narrowed his gaze, a ferocious and malicious intensity in his eyes. "Lord Waverly, did you say? You are not associated with Rand Bascombe, are you?"

"No. Not at all." It was Sterling's turn to lie and Michael had to hide his hands behind his back to disguise his growing anxiety.

"How lucky for you, Mr. Porter, that you are not." Galen tipped his head to one side, a dark raven staring at something shiny. "So oddly familiar..."

"I have that kind of face," Sterling said, openly enjoying the game.

Galen could hold his own in a dogfight but Michael knew that the only reason Sterling was there was to inflict as much damage as he could with as many of the Jaded in attendance as possible.

And there's no way Galen can anticipate the blow coming his way.

"I'll have you," Galen said with deadly calm. "These things take time but once I know your origins, I'll have you, won't I?"

"Lord Winters," Michael interrupted. "I've kept you too long."

"Yes!" Sterling chimed in. "I didn't mean to interrupt! Although as Lord Winters is obviously your esteemed friend he may be equally thrilled to hear my news. I came to tell you that I secured special dispensation."

Galen's brow furrowed. "Special dispensation?"

Sterling sobered. "No easy feat but I have a few connections of my own, Your Lordship." Sterling turned to Michael. "We can have the wedding a few days earlier than we'd thought."

"When?" Michael asked without looking at Galen.

"Say, tomorrow?"

Ashe Blackwell walked up, a striking lion-like figure in his olive silk jacket and gold waistcoat. "What happens tomorrow?"

"Ah, Mr. Blackwell! A moment of your time," Darius stepped in front of Ashe and blocked his approach. "Come, Blackwell, I wished to talk to you about funding our project and then perhaps we can pay our compliments to Mrs. Hastings."

Ashe gave Michael a sharp look, eyeing Sterling with a new curiosity but allowed himself to be shunted off to greet Eleanor.

Too close. That was too close for comfort.

"You didn't answer me, Rutherford." Sterling prodded him. "Will tomorrow be acceptable?"

"Wait," Galen said. "Who are we talking about marrying, Michael?"

"Mr. Rutherford wishes to marry my younger sister, Lord Winters," Sterling answered with a smug look at Michael. "And will do so tomorrow."

"W-what?!" Galen's shield of cold reserve evaporated instantly. "Like hell he will!"

Sterling's face tightened with fury but also with triumph, as the gallery began to quiet with whispers at Galen's outburst. "He is honor-bound to do so and practically begged me for her hand, Lord Winters. I assure you, Mr. Rutherford is a welcome addition to *my family*."

"He'd rather marry a muck-covered pit-bull bitch than any relation of yours, you—"

"Galen!" Michael cut him off, aware of several things at once; that Ashe was practically fighting Darius off to reach them as their words echoed off the walls, that the gallery crowd was enjoying a very different kind of display and that this, this would be the moment he could never take back.

He'd boasted like a fool to the Jackal that he had friends.

And now he would publicly lose them for the Jackal's amusement.

"Tomorrow cannot come quickly enough, Porter. Send a note to me with the time and details of the arrangements and I will be there." Michael kept his voice even and his tone level.

"I'll leave you to it, gentlemen," Sterling bowed again, "Until tomorrow, Rutherford." He left them, his feet nearly skipping out as he began to hum the wedding march on his way out of the gallery.

Damn.

"What the hell was—" Galen started, but Michael shook his head and turned away.

"Not here!"

"I disagree," Ashe reached them at last, with a very rumpled and breathless Darius on his heels. "*Here* is perfect!"

Lady Winters sailed up openly displeased at the ruckus. "No, Mr. Blackwell, it is most certainly *not* the place for whatever discussion you men are having! You are ruining Josiah's opening and Eleanor only just arrived to see all of you bashing about and making a scene!"

Darius glanced over and winced. "She looks crushed. Perhaps there's somewhere more quiet?"

Haley pointed imperiously toward a small door in the corner. "Go! It leads to the back hall and there is an empty storage room at the end of it. Or go to Rowan's brownstone since that seems to soothe, but out with all of you!"

They made it as far as the servant's back hall she'd directed them toward but no further before Ashe's impatience restarted the conversation.

"To hell with it! I'll send Eleanor a written apology and we'll all buy her flowers. I know I was late but someone tell me what nightmare I've strolled into or I'm going to start swinging at his head!" Ashe said as he turned to block their progress.

For a moment, no one spoke but it was Galen who cleared his throat and addressed Darius, and not Ashe. "Sorry for the cut direct, Thorne. I figured since we'd demonstrated our acting skills in front of Netherton, it might be rumored that you weren't my favorite person. And if Sterling couldn't quite place you, I didn't want to help him."

Darius shook his head. "It was brilliantly played. Clearly Porter knows of you, Ashe and Rowan. A dozen innocent scenarios outside of Bengal can explain the connection between all of us so I think he's still trying to piece it together. I hold to my instinct that Josiah and I are out of his sights."

"It doesn't matter!" Ashe broke in. "Why are you nattering about over which of us Sterling knows? Am I the only one who missed the explosion in there? That vile weasel thinks Michael is going to—" Ashe nearly choked on his revulsion before he could go on, "*Marry* his sister!"

"I am going to marry Grace Porter." Michael's words were delivered with quiet resolve. "Tomorrow."

Shock hit each of his friends and their responses were visceral and unmistakable. *Horror. Surprise. Disgust. Concern. Not exactly the joyful wishes or round of congratulations one could normally expect. Even in the midst of this madness, I never anticipated how much that would sting...*

"Why?" Galen asked.

"I didn't *encourage* you that night thinking you would set upon *his sister!*" Ashe ground out, his fury unconcealed. "Damn it! Are you mad?!"

Michael swallowed his anger, rounding on Ashe. "You watch your step, Blackwell. My life is mine and this—is *my life*! I've done the Jaded's bidding for a long time and given my share to our brotherhood. You all ignored me when it was your turn to wed and I advised caution, so you don't get to weigh in on my choice!"

"In all fairness," Darius said as he adjusted his glasses, "this seems very different. Grace Porter isn't just any woman. She is…"

"She is the woman I'm going to marry." Michael wasn't giving an inch.

"Why?" Galen asked again.

"I have my reasons."

Ashe shook his head in disbelief. "Then tell us. Tell me why you think that sharing wedding toasts with that despicable excuse for a human being and linking your name forever with his family is—even conceivable?"

"You have to trust me. If ever you trusted me, friends, I need you to trust me now. And I need you to stay back!" Michael crossed his arms. "I don't have to tell you anything, Ashe."

"Let's go to Rowan's." Galen offered. "My wife has the right of it. This isn't—"

"The rest of you can go and speak freely without my interference," Michael stepped back. "I have other matters to attend to."

He started back down the hall to the door of the gallery and hesitated with his hand on the latch. "And no, you're not invited to the wedding."

He closed the door behind him and was gone without a single protest from his friends.

∗ ∗ ∗

"Hellfire! That was…unexpected!" Dr. West raked his fingers through his brown curls. They'd landed at Rowan's after all, and Rowan had joined them in his study and endured the same rites of surprise and horror the rest of them had suffered as they recounted the day's revelations. "Sterling Porter, right in your midst—and Rutherford at his side?"

"We are betrayed," Ashe whispered distractedly holding an empty glass that he'd never remembered to fill. "And by the last man I'd ever expected."

"No. I won't believe that. Sterling may be preening in triumph but we know better than that. Michael is likely playing along in some scheme and couldn't reveal the details while the Jackal was present," Rowan countered.

Galen held up his hand. "The Jackal wasn't in that hallway and Rutherford was firm on the matter. If there were details to his plan, why not reveal them then?"

"We did promise to leave him alone to whatever scheme he devised," Darius added. "Something must have happened at Bascombe's. Has anyone seen her? Is she…beautiful?"

Ashe wasn't having it. "Damn it! She's probably as plain as mud and as horse-faced as her brother! There's nothing like the power of the first taste to make a man lose his mind and if I'd been thinking straight I wouldn't have said a word to nudge him down that path! Means to an end, he said! Bullshit!"

The others raised their eyebrows at the words "first taste" but said nothing of it. It seemed the lesser surprise of the day.

Darius walked over to grip his friend's arm. "You go too far! You're already close to saying too much and not being able to go back, friend. We don't know what he is facing and we cannot react like quarreling children!"

"I for one, don't believe that he intends to go through with it," Rowan said. "Michael has too much honor, too much respect for women to...marry this girl merely to use her as a pawn."

"A pawn," Darius repeated then he sat forward quickly. "Think of it like a chess game. This could all be some feint of Rutherford's! A ploy of sacrifice to draw the Jackal out from behind his castle."

"I hate chess," Ashe countered, his lips pressed into a thin line of disapproval.

Darius smiled. "That's because you always lose when we play." Darius sighed and softened his tone. "And you always lose because you're too impulsive."

Ashe let out a long slow breath and then scowled as he tried to take a sip from his empty glass. "Perhaps you're right."

Galen took a seat in the circle. "Chess. So what is his play? And what would be the next logical move for us?"

Darius's green eyes flashed with his thoughts and finally he spoke. "Let the Knight have his run. The Queen is either bait in the Jackal's gambit or..."

"Or?" Rowan asked.

"Or another deadly force on the board."

✳ ✳ ✳

Back at the Grove and in the sanctuary of his rooms, Michael poured himself a stiff drink. He wasn't usually a man to indulge in the afternoon but the last few days had pushed him hard. His worry over the social hurdles of attending Bascombe's felt trivial in retrospect. His attraction to Grace had been a heady distraction but he hadn't considered how dangerous it would be. Well, he might have accepted a threat to his own safety, but not Grace's.

Before Bascombe's it had been about shielding her from the damage he imagined inflicting on her brother. But it was Michael's touch that had brought her harm and that was a situation he must rectify before he could take another step toward the Jaded's aims.

My life has turned into a very bad penny novel.

Even so, a thread of anticipation cut through him like a hot wire and made him grimace at its power. Grace would be under his care and legally, his to possess. It was ridiculous to consider it. It was a marriage of convenience, only because her brother was conveniently mad enough to insist on it.

And Grace was openly adverse to it.

She will never forgive me for going along with her brother's wishes.

Damn it! I can't think of Grace's feelings or I'll throw myself out the window.

He went to the bell pull and yanked it hard, several times, not out of impatience but out of courtesy for Tally who could occasionally miss a tentative signal.

Within minutes, there was a knock on his door and Michael let Tally in. He waited until he knew his young friend was in position to look at his face directly as he spoke so that Tally could read his lips.

"You're getting taller," Michael told him.

Tally nodded and then signed his response. *'Not tall enough! Maggie thinks I'm a baby!'*

Michael smiled. The boy had shot up in height in the last few weeks and Michael suspected that Mrs. Clay had underestimated his age. Poor nutrition and a life on the streets could hold a child back, but Mrs. Clay's love and good cooking over the years was finally bearing fruit. Her blonde cherub was going to be a young man and nearly grown in another two or three years.

Where does the time go?

"Be patient, Tally." Michael shook himself out of his reverie. "I need my box, little brother. Can you fetch it for me without anyone seeing?"

Tally smiled. *'Of course! Mother's busy cheering the laundress with a cup of tea. Her husband is off drinking again.'*

Michael eyed his own room and decided that if he was bringing a bride home tomorrow he may as well ask. "Tears? Has Maggie been in to change the rooms yet?"

'Yes! I assisted her.' Tally's cheeks colored with his words. *'The linen basket is heavy and I like to be...helpful. She says I'm good company.'*

"Careful, little brother. Once you lose your heart, it's hard to get it back."

Tally nodded and ducked out, a shy smile his only answer to Michael's sage words of wisdom. Michael retrieved his drink from the mantle and then worked through the ritual of getting out his personal papers and reaching his desk. The methodical steps calmed him and by the time he had things laid out, there was a knock on the door heralding Tally's return.

"That was quick," he complimented the boy and took the padlocked box from Tally's hands.

'Anything else?' Tally signed.

"No, but tell your mother I'll be down later to speak to her privately." There was no way he was going to add to the shock of impending events without alerting Mrs. Clay to Grace's arrival. If possible, tomorrow he would limit the number of hysterical women in the Grove to one. Michael shuddered at the notion of even one...

'I'll tell her.' Tally hurried off and Michael closed his door, locking it behind him this time.

He carried the heavy wooden box, with its reinforced metal skin and thick iron strapping, to set it on the table by the fireplace. Michael dusted off the top of it and then unbuttoned the top of his shirt to more easily pull a silver chain from around his neck. A single key hang from the chain and Michael laid it on his palm. It was an ornate silver little thing that gave no hint of its match to the black and rusty lockbox on the table.

The idea behind the security of his diamonds was simple and fairly flawless. He'd given Tally the locked box early on asking him to hide it in the Grove, somewhere safe and secret that only Tally could access. Then Michael had kept the key around his neck at all times, never taking it off. So in reality, if he'd ever been pressed, he could honestly swear that he didn't know the actual location of his treasure.

And as Tally was a trustworthy boy, he'd never asked about the box's contents nor could he have opened it if he wanted to.

Michael inserted the key and turned it three times to the left to unlock the solid padlock, then set to work. Inside, the box was lined with worn brown velvet and contained several leather bags. Michael began to pull them out, then set the empty box on the floor. Each bag he emptied on the table, his brow furrowing in concentration. Large diamonds, cut and uncut, tumbled out onto the table's smooth surface from the first pouch and Michael sighed. He'd never really thoroughly culled through his portion of the jewels and when he'd initially needed money after their return to England, he'd sold six small gems and felt like King Midas. The profit had been insane and since he lived a fairly frugal existence, he'd never needed to sell any others and so had had no excuse to ask Tally for his box.

Even the entire quest for diamonds in disguise had never triggered the box's retrieval. *They're all diamonds—where's the disguise in that?*

But as tensions had ratcheted up with Sterling and as he was about to become a married man, it felt right to finally face his holdings; to reassure Grace that she would be provided for but also for his own peace of mind.

Michael emptied each pouch and dropped the leather pouches into the open box at his feet. The pile of diamonds was substantial and he let out a slow sigh before realizing that there was one more pouch left on the table. He picked it up and frowned at the size of the stone inside it.

God, that's a monster!

He dumped it out indelicately and then flinched at the sight of a dirty white rough stone the size of a large plum. It was the ugliest piece of quartz looking nonsense in the lot and he shook his head in pity as the lump of dull crystal landed like a plain cousin on top of all her glittering counterparts.

"I forgot this one..." he said aloud. Ashe had even made a joke at the time about what looked like a large piece of gravel when they were dividing up the gems by color and had offered him a choice of his sapphires to make up for the worthless thing. Michael had declined and made a joke about keeping the rock for luck if nothing else.

Luck, if nothing else.

Suddenly a new thought occurred to him and before logic overtook him, he swept all the other diamonds into the palm of his hand and funneled them into the lockbox's top. When the large ugly lump was alone on the table, Michael reached for the fireplace shovel and took aim. Just as he had at Ashe's, he swung decisively if a bit more cautiously as he feared Mrs. Clay's censure more than he did Godwin's.

He lifted the shovel's blade, expecting to see a similar pulverized show of crystalline snow and dropped the shovel on the floor in shock.

For the ugly dull and flawed exterior of the stone had indeed shattered but only to reveal an extraordinary diamond that had been inside the bland glass shell. The size of a small plum, organic in shape, it was flawlessly cut with facet after facet drawing out an inner fire and spectrum of color that defied description. By the firelight, it became a living thing, pulsing with glittering rainbows and refracting the light until Michael wasn't sure he hadn't been hypnotized staring at it and losing time...

After all this time, it was under my nose, exactly as Darius said it would be.

"I have it," he whispered. "I have the sacred treasure."

He sat back in his chair and absorbed the implications. His first impulse was to send word to the others immediately but something stopped him.

The diamond flashed and flared and Michael's breath caught in his throat.

Better to wait.

I may need all the leverage I can get and if Sterling fails to deliver Grace to the church...

Michael pushed the thought away and stood to begin pacing. The diamond changed nothing. He wanted to rescue Grace and secure her future before anything else happened. The Jaded would demand the stone be out of his hands for safekeeping but Michael's instincts jangled with alarm at the thought. It was a dangerous thing to possess and he wouldn't allow any of his friends to take on the risk. Not until he knew that he had control of things and had the Jackal in hand.

The diamond's colors winked again and Michael went back to kneel next to the table and begin to repack everything into the lockbox. "Sacred or no, I have a wedding to prepare for and Mrs. Clay to face, you troublesome rock."

He held it up to the light one last time and sighed.

Blood and tears, all our lives in the balance for something a man can hold in his hand. My God, it is *a penny novel!*

Let's just pray that I make a good ending.

CHAPTER NINETEEN

Grace studied the reflection of the woman in her vanity's mirror and marveled at the strangeness of the exercise. The bruising around her eye was nearly gone and powder had disguised the last signs of her brother's brutal hand. Her blonde hair was brushed to a sheen and the lady's maid that her brother had hired for the day had styled it into an ornate and flattering pile of curls and tiny braids that looped down to touch her ears.

Sterling hadn't trusted her to leave the house for anything as trivial as a shopping expedition so she was wearing her best day dress, a pale blue silk with an overlay of sheer muslin edged in lace. The plain bodice was buttoned up to her throat and the long sleeves puffed out to make her wrists seem even more delicate.

Grace pressed her lips together, trying to ward off her emotions. Pouting or railing against fate gained her nothing. Days locked in her room with only Mrs. Dorsett's icy silence bringing trays of food and drawing her bath. She'd already cried until she couldn't cry anymore and every argument and plea she made was useless and only strengthened her brother's case for her madness.

Bedlam.

It was like a cavern of terror opening up under her feet at the very word and Sterling had invoked the very thing she feared most. For had she not spent years with fantastical visions in her head and strange characters? Her writing was her sole comfort but also a source of anxiety. It was an abnormal pursuit for a woman and Grace knew it. She'd kept it secret from her family and particularly from Sterling not only to preserve her hopes for independence but also to preserve her very life. She wasn't sure but it was easy to say that the odd workings of her mind might border on madness and if Sterling desired to hurt her; would knowledge of her literary pursuits not arm him with the ultimate weapon?

She closed her eyes to banish the echoes of the imaginary cries of lunatics in chains that haunted her dreams and sighed. "It would be worse. God help me, no nightmare I can conjure would be worse than being trussed up and drug over the threshold of an asylum never to see the light of day again…"

Grace blinked and did her best to refocus on the pale woman's reflection in the mirror. The maid had left a small sprig of lavender and Queen Anne's lace on the table. She lifted it with trembling hands to pin it into her hair.

Michael Rutherford.

He was exactly the man she might have dreamed of marrying; if she'd permitted it. His kisses dizzied her but beyond that, his kindness overwrote a lifetime of being disregarded and ignored. The lure of his presence was irresistible and in better circumstances, she might not have fought the notion of becoming his wife.

But Sterling's hand in it tainted everything and there was nothing free or joyful in the ceremony ahead. Whatever his scheme involving Mr. Rutherford, she would be forced to play her part and quietly sacrifice every dream she had ever had of a life on her own as a writer.

Today, I marry. And then beg Michael to forgive me for being nothing he will want in a wife.

A knock on the door heralded the time and Grace retrieved the makeshift veil she'd made from the back of her chair. She tossed it over her head and spared one last look at the woman in the mirror.

She looks like a bride.

Or a ghost…

"Grace!" Her brother greeted her as he pushed through the door, unwilling to wait for her permission to enter. "We are waiting for you downstairs."

She stood slowly and smoothed out her skirts. "Then let us not make them wait any longer."

"That's a good girl!" he said and held out his arm to escort her out. "I knew you would come around, my dear. Of course, if you are thinking of some outburst or last minute scene, I won't hesitate to—"

"There's no need to threaten me again, brother." Grace took his arm and lifted the hem of her skirts as they began to head down the narrow stairs. "I may have my faults but a limited memory isn't one of them. There is not a word you've uttered in my lifetime that I don't recall and not an action that isn't carved into my heart."

"That's a good girl," he intoned again, the triumphant bite in his voice lessened.

Grace ignored him and the grating sound of his praise, as if she were a dog that had come to heel. They walked the rest of the way in silence, through the ground floor and out into the narrow garden she had worked so hard to make grand for her brother's pleasure.

The vicar was there by the small stone bench and alongside him...

Mr. Rutherford!

Every time Grace saw him, she was struck by his masculine beauty and imposing presence. Today, the impact was heightened. He wore a formal coat of dark grey and a snow-white linen shirt and cravat that set his coloring off to perfection. With his black hair streaked with white, he looked more like the Archangel Michael than her shy Mr. Rutherford. Her heart ached at the wretched position she'd put him in, honorably taking on a marriage against his will.

There was no music beyond the faint sounds of the city on the other side of the wall, no decorations beyond the spring blooms on the plants and trees in their haven and only Mrs. Dorsett and Sterling in attendance as the required witnesses.

Grace walked as steadily as she could to Mr. Rutherford's side and stepped into a strange dream where she recited her vows in a hollow voice devoid of feeling; where fear dominated so that she couldn't run away; and where the only thing that felt steady was Mr. Rutherford's arm.

"Congratulations!" the vicar said and Grace blinked in shock to realize it was over and she'd hardly been aware of any of it.

"Thank you," Mr. Rutherford replied and then guided her back inside to sign the license and paperwork for the registry. The vicar had apparently been informed ahead of time that there would be no lingering over the nuptials and he tacitly helped them hurry through the last of the process. Mr. Rutherford signed first, his hand steady and emphatic in the long strokes of his handwriting. He held the pen out to her and Grace's courage faltered. She took the pen and scrawled a name she hoped was her own, and then lost the battle against tears. "I'm…sorry…I just…"

"It's done," Sterling announced firmly. "For heaven's sake, stop that nonsense and—"

"There, there," Michael stepped in between them, retaking her arm and effectively cutting off Sterling's approach; his presence a shield from the others. "Cry if you wish, Grace. We're nearly there," he said softly for her ears alone.

"She is overcome, Father," Sterling offered to the vicar, even as he shot a disparaging look at the pair.

Father Parker nodded, overtly unsympathetic. "It is all too common, Mr. Rutherford. See that you don't take it to heart! Women's souls are simply weaker and tears a natural by-product of their delicate nature."

"Yes, thank you, Father. Why don't you show yourself out?" Michael told him without taking his eyes off of Grace.

Grace looked up, a faint smile crossing her lips at the delightful awkwardness of Mr. Rutherford tossing out a man of God on her behalf.

The vicar left in a huff and Sterling trailed after him, spewing apologies in the man's wake. And for a few precious moments, she had Mr. Rutherford to herself.

"Mr. Rutherford," she began unsteadily as she pulled the veil from her hair. "I…I don't know what to say except—"

"Grace," he interrupted her gently. "Let's get out of this house. Then we can say everything we need to and speak freely. What say you?"

She nodded, her throat closing with gratitude and relief.

"Are your bags packed?" he asked.

"By the front door."

"That is all I need to know."

Michael retrieved his hat and guided her out to the foyer. He opened the front door and called out to the waiting driver he'd hired as they stepped out onto the landing. "Come get these things if you would. We'll be leaving immediately."

Sterling was at the bottom of the steps after waving off the vicar and wheeled about in shock. "There's a cold luncheon waiting! And I had thought you'd want to have a chat before you…left with my sister, sir."

Grace's fingers tightened on Michael's arm, completely adverse to the notion of lingering for a single minute longer than necessary. Mr. Rutherford looked down into her eyes and she began to pray that he could read her thoughts.

He nodded and covered her hand with his, speaking again to her without regard to anyone else. "Grace. Will you go ahead for me? Will you wait for me at the Grove? Mrs. Clay is eager to make you comfortable and I—I don't know the way of it but if you need some time alone…"

She laughed, an odd hiccup of tears and mirth. She shook her head. She'd had endless days and nights alone but his thoughtfulness was unprecedented in her lifetime. "I'll go ahead to the Grove and make the best of it. Just please don't be too long. I-I don't know the way of it either, Mr. Rutherford, but I cannot go back inside this house. I can't."

"You never have to cross Sterling's door again. I swear it." He leaned forward and chastely kissed her cheek, then straightened, a man in command of his surroundings as he walked her down the steps. "Take her bags. The lady will be leaving now."

Sterling sputtered at the abrupt change to his envisioned plans but thanks to Mr. Rutherford's firm instructions, she was safely ensconced inside the cab and her luggage secured above before her brother could construct any delays.

Michael closed the carriage door and smiled encouragingly at her through the window. "Nearly there."

"Yes," she whispered. "Thank you."

Mr. Rutherford stepped back and the carriage pulled away at a good pace allowing her only one last glimpse of the house she'd shared with her brother for eight years and of Sterling standing on the top step to give the fleeting illusion that he was looming over Michael, like a dark bird of prey.

Sterling led him back into the house and up to his first floor study. The room was as depressingly appointed as Michael recalled from a few days ago and he fought the urge to sigh aloud. He wasn't sure he could stomach another lecture on his lack of honor or be taunted about Grace.

Then again, this might be the time for the conversation they'd been meant to have all along. Michael chose his position in the room and stood by the window next to the desk, bypassing the chairs and any hint that he would "sit like a good boy". He kept a clear path to the door whereas if Sterling chose to take his usual seat behind the desk, he would be hemmed in relinquishing the advantage of free movement.

Sterling sat at his desk and Michael averted his gaze out the window. "Why do I have the feeling you aren't about to offer your congratulations?"

"Tell me one thing, Rutherford. Tell me you don't already love my sister."

Michael turned around and leaned against the wall saying nothing.

"Never mind," Sterling waved off his own question. "It's obvious that you do. Why else would you have leapt to her defense at every turn? Why else would you have submitted to every ridiculous request I made of you? A ball? Really, Mr. Rutherford? I could have asked you to escort her to greased pig races and you'd have done it, wouldn't you?"

"I don't wish to be uncivil, but I hate you already so don't feel the need to try to spur me on." Michael deliberately held as still as a cobra about to strike, unnerving his new brother-in-law. "Make a point or stop talking, Porter."

Sterling smiled. "You're right. I've wasted enough time. What was it your secret little club calls me? The Jackal?"

He'd known. Of course, he'd known but hearing Sterling say it was still incredible. *My god, we are having that conversation, aren't we?*

"Yes. One of them wanted to call you something more illustrious but I thought a small carrion-feeding cowardly predator suited you better. But what can I do for you, Sterling?"

"You know what I'm after. It has never changed."

Michael's brow furrowed in confusion. "You never were clear. We've puzzled over it endlessly. Some nonsense about sacred treasure and threats but then you'd poison an innocent woman or set fire to a gambling hall..."

"I did not set that fire! You did! Don't deny it!" Sterling's fist pounded on his desk. "You meant to kill me!"

Michael shook his head. "Tell me, Sterling. How is it we are in this together?"

"We are in this because I was in that dungeon, too but not out of chance like the rest of you. I was after the sacred treasure all along and would have had it after I'd convinced the raj to let me go. I took note of the layout of his defenses and meant to return with a good mercenary fighting force to take the diamond by force since he didn't agree to my ruse of presenting the stone as a betrothal gift to one of Queen Victoria's daughters."

"What? You...tried to trade for...an English princess's hand in marriage?" Michael struggled to keep his composure. "I didn't realize you had that kind of royal influence or connections, Sterling."

"Shut up! He was mad enough to believe anything!"

"Except you, apparently, when you asked to waltz off with his favorite treasure..."

"I'd have had it if the Sepoy Rebellion hadn't broken out and delayed my progress!" Sterling leaned back in his chair. "By the time I'd convinced my superiors to fund another attempt once the natives were put down, the raj's madness led to his own destruction—and ultimately to your freedom."

"You never..." Michael took a deep breath. "You never told anyone that you'd met us down in that hole? You never sought to aid us while you were negotiating your own way out?"

It was Sterling's turn to shrug his shoulders. "Why would I? There was only one true treasure and I wasn't about to share the glory or the profit I'd worked so hard to uncover for myself."

"Have you no humanity?"

"Don't be so dramatic. You survived didn't you? Not that I ever expected it, otherwise I can assure you, I'd have paid closer attention to your names and asked a few more questions."

"How unlucky for you." Michael crossed his arms and casually shifted his weight to the balls of his feet. "Well, here is the message I'd have conveyed at the Thistle. Whatever it is you're after, the Jaded are in no position to give it to you and have no interest in your heathen treasure, sacred or otherwise. We're trying to get on with our lives and if you'd stop running a one man campaign of violence against us, we'd have a better chance at it."

Sterling's fury was a beautiful thing to behold. "One of you has it in his possession! Don't think to lie to me, Rutherford! You can't imagine what I've gone through and while it was necessary to take my time or wait for better opportunities to make my case, we are both running out of time."

"Running out of time? Why? Is this treasure's power waning?"

"Don't mock me! My superiors have accused me of creating the entire story as a scheme to bilk them out of their money." Sterling leaned forward on his elbows. "You think I'm dangerous, Rutherford? You have no idea what devils I have been forced to kneel before! I've promised them a mystic diamond and by god, I'll deliver it!"

"It's a diamond? *Mystic* diamond? What in the world are they going to do with it when they have it? Magic shows in Piccadilly Circus to entertain the crowds?"

"They'll buy it from me then gift it to the Crown! Of course, I've stipulated that I am credited with its discovery so I'll then be rewarded accordingly by Her Majesty."

"They'll deduct your debts, pay you a pittance, gift it the Crown and reward you with a handshake! After all this time, I doubt they'll be generous, Sterling. I don't remember a clerk ever being knighted on a lark."

"I'm not a *clerk* and I'm no fool! This is an opportunity for them to be an agent in the matter but if they seek to cheat me, I have already got a nice fat fish on the line who will pay handsomely to see a mystic diamond around the throat of his favorite mistress." Sterling smiled. "After all, if my prize can't land in the hands of a queen, then a prince's whore will do! It would serve them all right if I profited while they were forced to see the treasure they squandered around a courtesan's throat."

"That's brilliant," Michael said. "No offense, but I can see how your time is becoming constricted with two interested parties pressing you for delivery however I fail to see where your bad debts and magical promises affect me."

"Stop trying to play the child, Rutherford. The Jaded have my diamond and you are going to give it to me."

"Am I?"

"You are. Because you genuinely love Grace and the marriage is proof of it. After all, if you were pretending to care for Grace to get close to me, you'd have thumbed your nose at my weak threat of scandal and walked away." Sterling stood slowly. "But when you realized I might hurt her…"

Michael didn't bother denying it but waited patiently for the hammer to fall.

"I have the reins, Rutherford. But like any good trainer knows, I'm going to give you a run to stretch your legs and expend some of your energy galloping about before I really let you feel the bit and the whip."

Michael rolled his eyes. "I know I'm big enough to ride but I think you've stretched the comparison a bit too far, Porter. You don't have the whip-hand with me."

"I do. Enjoy your honeymoon, Mr. Rutherford. I am giving you seven days and seven nights as a wedding gift to my dear little sister."

"Seven days. That has a biblical ring to it."

Sterling didn't laugh at the jest. "On the eighth night, if you don't give me the diamond, I'll kill Grace and make it look like you did it."

"And why am I not simply stealing my bride away on the first boat to the Continent?" Michael asked.

"You don't think I've resources enough to follow your movements or track the ports? You don't think I'm a petty villain and wicked enough to strike out with vicious and wild abandon if I think you're trying to cross me? By all means, take her and run." Sterling leaned forward, his palms splayed against the desk's blotter. "And when you're gone, who will look out for your friends? Can you protect them all, Michael? Can you be everywhere at once? Care to gamble on whose throat I'll have slit or what building I might pay an arsonist to light?"

"I never thought I could hate you more than I already did."

"Noted. You're a soldier. I am betting that you would prefer to fight the battle you can see and the enemy you know than risk some unknown war where the front lines are invisible and more innocent lives are exposed." He gave Michael a smug smile. "Or am I wrong?"

"No."

"The diamond by midnight on Sunday next, Rutherford."

Michael nodded.

Sterling shook his head. "I need to hear you say it."

"You'll have it by midnight on Sunday next, Sterling, but not a moment sooner. And if you interfere before then or harm any of mine, then our agreement is forfeit."

Sterling clapped his hands together and smiled. "Agreed! Well, you must be off then! Enjoy your…reprieve."

Rutherford bowed quickly and retreated, remaining silent only with an act of iron will. He had the physical advantage, there was no denying it. But snapping the man's neck and getting arrested for murder wasn't how he intended to spend the remainder of his wedding day. He had seven days to find an answer before Sterling's threats would turn to deadly action.

And Grace was waiting for him.

CHAPTER TWENTY

The carriage arrived at the east side of the inn and Grace sat for a few extra moments to gather her courage. The last time she'd entered the Grove, she'd been a warmly welcomed caller but this time scandal had brought her to his doorstep. She dreaded the withdrawal of Mrs. Clay's kindness and the disapproving looks she would have to endure.

"I've your things delivered and their man's to take 'em up," the driver explained as he opened the carriage door. "Seems all set then, madam."

"Madam." Not a 'Miss' anymore...

Grace nodded and alighted, then had an anxious moment. "Your payment? I..."

"Ah, no! Don't trouble yerself! Your husband paid for everything and generously at that!" The driver touched his hat. "Though I meant to say that it's always good luck to deliver a bride to her happy home. I wish you joy, Mrs. Rutherford."

Your husband. She smiled even as her eyes filled with tears. "You are the first to do so. Thank you."

He climbed back up and drove off and Grace accepted that there was nothing to do but face the day. She went up the steps into the Grove, veil in hand, and walked into the small foyer only to find Mrs. Clay, her son and a few others in aprons and caps all awaiting her in an impromptu receiving line. The small staff had put matching flowers in their hair and caps and Tally was shyly holding a large bouquet of spring blooms.

Mrs. Clay bustled forward, the flower sprig in her own hair threatening to fall off her head at the speed of her approach. Without a word of warning, she swept Grace up into her arms and pressed her against her ample bosom. "There you are! A bride! Right here in the Grove and—what a blessing!"

"O-oh!" Grace answered shock making her eyes widen but the warmth of the landlady's hold was like a balm to her soul and Grace's hands reached up of their own accord to return a gentle echo of the embrace. "You are…too kind."

Mrs. Clay let go. "But I'm crushing you! What a bother!" The woman laughed as she wiped her hands down the front of her apron. "Welcome to the Grove, Mrs. Rutherford!"

"Thank you, Mrs. Clay. Thank you to—all of you. This is so much more than I expected," she said. "Or deserve."

"Nonsense! This is only the beginning and I don't mind saying, I've quite a lovely supper planned and Mrs. Watson outdid herself with a wedding cake to make angels applaud. She's a dear friend and owns the fancy bakery nearby." Mrs. Clay beamed as she spoke. "Come, let me introduce everyone so that when you the ring the bell, there is no chance of a stranger coming to your aid."

Grace nodded, unable to answer for the raw emotions crowding her heart.

The landlady gave staff members's name and added a complimentary quip or detail that made them all blush and smile at Grace. It was clear that Mrs. Clay mothered them all and that not a person in her employ didn't bask in it. It was a blur for Grace and while she recognized the tall blonde boy as Tally from her last visit when he handed over the bouquet, the rest would have to be repeated later. At the moment, it was all too much to take in.

"But, where is Mr. Rutherford?"

"He is—coming just behind in a separate carriage. My brother wished to share a toast with him but I was anxious…to be away and, I hope that doesn't sound terrible." Grace bit her lower lip.

"Not at all! Let's get you upstairs and settled. Jack, take up her things right away." Jack jumped to his duties with Tally behind him carrying two hatboxes and Mrs. Clay waved off the others. "Back to it, my dears. I'll lead Mrs. Rutherford up myself and then come down and lend a hand with the pies."

The maids and men dutifully scattered and Mrs. Clay led her up the stairs to the private first floor sitting room to linger while her trunks and boxes were tucked inside the room. The men retreated and Mrs. Clay waited at the doorway. "Here you are. Dear?"

Grace sat down on the chair by the unlit fireplace unsure of what to say.

Mrs. Clay's smile wavered and her brow furrowed with concern. "Are you all right? Is it nerves? Are you…why when I married Mr. Clay, God rest his soul; I hid in a wardrobe for hours! I was quite scared thanks to my mother's poorly worded advice about the wedding night and I was nearly prepared to spend the rest of my days in there with the coats and an old wool nightgown. Just me and the moths!"

Grace smiled since it was impossible not to. "Was Mr. Clay furious?"

"*My* Mr. Clay?! Never!" Mrs. Clay took the seat across from her as she laughed. "He pulled up a chair and sat near the door, talked about his dreams for the inn and spun such tales! I still think of the wonderful stories he told me that night…"

"I take it that you came out?" Grace asked softly.

"I did and never regretted it, I can tell you that!" Mrs. Clay sighed. "What pleasure that man gave me over the years!"

Grace gasped then gave in to her better humor. "Honestly, I wasn't—I'm not nervous." Even as she said the words, she realized they were far from the truth. She'd been dreading so much of the day, it had never occurred to her to dread the night. She'd expected things to unravel long before then…

But it was Mr. Rutherford, after all; Mr. Rutherford whose kisses invoked a fire in her that she'd never known and separated her from reason with a single touch; Mr. Rutherford who was kind and who had liberated her from her brother's prison.

Grace kept hold of her veil. "I want to wait for Mr. Rutherford."

"Oh! Of course!" Mrs. Clay stood up, and cheerfully retreated. "I'll leave you to it and if you need a thing, pull the bell."

"Yes, thank you, Mrs. Clay."

The quiet of the room enveloped her as the landlady's footsteps faded. To pass the time, she mentally inventoried what she'd carried from the house including a slightly uncomfortable sixpence the maid had put in her shoe for luck. The coin didn't feel particularly felicitous as it slid back and forth under the arch of her foot as she nervously shifted her ankle back and forth.

Who ever thought of a lucky coin? Other than the poor soul who might think any found wealth—even a penny—could change your fate? My sixpence could just as readily be cursed...

A story about a cursed piece of eight unwound slowly in her head though she shied away from drawing in obvious pirates and decided that the poor soul whose fate could be changed should be a self-righteous man with more money than heart. He would be cruel and greedy and find it in the mud a few feet away from some orphan child, its eyes sunken and little hands like a bird's claws. He would pick it up, flash the gold at the waif and pocket it with a smile—and unknowingly unleash a torrent of evil retribution on his own head that would make the plagues of Egypt look like a—

"Grace."

She jumped up with a startled cry as Mr. Rutherford spoke. She hadn't heard his footsteps but there he was, solid and substantial in his wedding finery standing a few feet away. "Mr. Rutherford!"

"Michael."

"Pardon?"

"It's a small thing, I know and selfish to ask, but if you would use my Christian name; if I could hear you say my name..."

"Michael." Grace put her fingertips to her lips. The name was hardly foreign but on her tongue it was as sweet and strange as any exotic spice.

He glanced over at his apartment's open door, ajar a few inches. "You didn't go in."

"I didn't know if you'd want me to. I thought I would give you the chance to choose."

"I thought I already had," Michael gestured back toward the pair of chairs near the fireplace. "Sit with me, then. Talk to me, Grace."

She sat back down and he joined her. Grace marveled that they were in the exact same position from her last visit to the Grove and at almost the same time of day—but nothing was the same. "Why aren't you furious? Sterling…bullied us both but it was my fault that you were in such a terrible position. You wanted to return to the house and I…I was the one who was weak and…" Grace's breath caught in her throat. "I wasn't thinking past the moment and I've robbed you of your life, Mr. Rutherford. How can you not be angry with me?"

"Michael," he supplied.

"If you aren't angry, I am." Grace sighed. "And you will be…

"I will?" He sat up a little straighter, a man bracing himself for the worst and Grace plunged ahead.

"I know I said once that I wished I was strong enough to refuse you…"

"And then you said I make you weak," he countered gently.

"I am *not* weak! And I am not some piece of chattel to be wed against my will! A lifetime of subjecting myself to my father's will and then my brother's and—I won't mince about and lose myself! Not even to you!"

"You mean especially to me?"

"I mean, not even to you, a man I have come to—care for deeply and so quickly it robs me of logic." Grace pressed a hand against her pounding heart. "It terrifies me how appealing you are, Mr. Rutherford! How—distracting! But I am not fit to be a wife, Mr. Rutherford! And if either you or my brother had bothered to ask, I'd have told you so and spared you the heartache! I'm— scattered and…"

"And you have plans," he finished for her.

"Didn't you?" she asked then winced at the harsh sound of the question in her ears.

He looked at her calmly, a man weathering the storm. "A few." He put his hands on his knees. "I'm not going to hold you against your will, Grace. I don't have any intentions of robbing you of your self-determination and you must know how much I admire your spirit. Then again, I should confess that if your brother hadn't demanded that I marry you—I might have resorted to kidnapping to get you out of his hands."

She gasped, heat flooding her cheeks. "How dramatic!"

He smiled. "It never fails to amaze me the things that delight you, Grace."

Tantalizing pleasure curled around her at his response and then something in her clamored in alarm. Because he wouldn't want to keep her once he knew the truth…and he deserved to know everything.

"I'm no wife," she said again, standing abruptly.

He stood more slowly, holding up his hands defensively as if he feared she was about to flee. "Because of your plans?" he asked.

She nodded. "I'm…" She looked up into Michael Rutherford's grey-blue eyes and then it all tumbled out in a desperate scattered rambling confession. "I'm a writer! I know it's a bit beyond the pale—I've never told anyone! Never. Not that anyone ever asked. But it's scandalous, isn't it? Because I *published* them! I…crossed some invisible line and if Sterling ever found out—not that it matters anymore if I'm out of his care. I always thought to go on my own steam. I have saved over three hundred pounds, you see, and—I can make my own way!"

"Grace—"

"What a terrible wife I'd make you! You see, I'm writing all the time. Well, whenever I can…but it's not a secret I could keep from a husband. You'd have found out eventually and I don't think I could compound my sins by ever lying to you. I don't cook, I clean well enough but beyond running a very small house and planting ornamental gardens, I'm hardly the wife you deserve, sir."

"Grace—" he tried again but she couldn't bear to hear him end it.

She bolted for the doorway to his apartment to grab her smallest valise, the one that held her papers and her life savings sewn into the lining. Grace seized the handle and stood only to freeze on the threshold.

She dropped the suitcase, her hands numb.

Michael came up slowly, unsure of what held her so still.

Grace began to walk, like a person sleepwalking toward the rough stone fireplace and Michael's gaze narrowed to study his room with new eyes. And then spotted the penny novels.

Damn it!

"I can explain!" he stepped forward. "I think I mentioned at the horse fair that I enjoy them. But if they offend, Grace, I will put them away. I know it's not the most respectable library for a home where a lady is present and…" Michael stopped himself as she reached the mantle and took down one of the serials he'd had bound together. "A favorite of mine, Grace, but not anything you'd ever…"

Oh, god. I'm losing my edge, aren't I? How didn't I piece this together before this moment?

"You're a writer."

"I'm a writer," she repeated breathlessly and pressed the bound serial to her chest like it was a holy tome.

"That's brilliant!" he said then watched the strange fierce pride in her eyes as she clutched the work of A.R. Crimson. "Grace? Are you…?"

"I told them I was a secretary and personal assistant to *the* Mr. A.R. Crimson and left a manuscript for their review. It was the worst kind of theatrical bravado but they believed me. I invented him. His entire portfolio and a few ridiculous letters he's supposedly dictated on travels in Spain to convince them. I've never been to Spain, sir. But I…never thought it would sell and—I can't give it up, Michael."

Michael ran a hand through his hair doing his best to absorb what she was saying. "You wrote *that*?"

She nodded. "It's...fanciful, I know. They're silly bits. Pirates and mermaids, centaurs and my favorite part, the floating cloud cities. Though I confess I added that part in at the last after I saw a man on a ladder painting a neighbor's house and started to think about ladders hanging down from the sky..."

Michael reached out to gently pull the book from her hands, turning it over as if it were made of glass. "You! *You* are A.R. Crimson? *You* wrote "The Black Staircase" and the "Isles of Thunder" series?"

She nodded solemnly. "I did."

"My God!" he spoke without thinking. "These stories are chilling and grim! But *you*! No offense, Grace, but you are the most cheerful person I have ever encountered. It doesn't seem possible." He turned the book over in his hands. "But all those clever things you say, so original and unexpected..."

"I won't give it up!"

Michael stared at her as if she'd grown horns. "I would never demand such a thing!"

It was Grace's turn to experience a shocked delay in comprehension. "'I would rather die than—what? What did you say?"

"It never occurred to me to ask you to cease writing! What kind of man do you think I am?" Michael asked.

"You're my husband... If it were improper before, it is most certainly more scandalous after I'm wed, is it not? For a married woman to pose as a man writing those kinds of books, it's unthinkable!"

He crossed his arms. "I don't see what difference it makes and frankly, since we are already up to our necks in scandal, I for one, can't see what you have to lose. I like—No! I love the notion that you keep your independence, Grace. You light up when you speak of your stories and I don't want to be the cause of seeing that end. I know marriage to me has destroyed much of your happiness but let me salvage what I can."

"Not destroyed!" she turned to him, touching his upper arm while her right hand still cradled "Isles of Thunder". "I was so fearful that you would seek to stop me or think less of me or—I dreaded disappointing you, Mr. Rutherford, more than I dreaded anything else in this world."

"Michael," he said again as he covered her hand with his and guided her to the large sofa in the middle of the room. "Grace, look again. I live in an inn. I have brought my bride to a very unconventional home. It is a small apartment of two rooms and we share our sitting room, dining room and the water closet with the other apartment on the same floor." Michael gestured around them, his tone changing. "But there is no cooking or cleaning to be done. Mrs. Clay and the staff would be mortified to think of you not pulling that bell and I should warn you that when the weather turns cool, Tally will make it his personal quest to keep this room so toasty you will never wear wool again."

"You make it sound so perfect," she smiled up at him.

"You'll write. You'll write to your heart's content and I will keep the world at bay. What say you?"

"I'm not sure what to say."

"There is a price for all of this, Grace. So you're wise not to jump quickly."

"What price?" she asked warily, the bright pink in her cheeks fading fast.

"You must vow to let me read all your new stories before you send them off to your publisher."

She laughed, the last tendril of fear in her eyes fading. "Consider it my wedding gift." She retrieved her valise and opened it to retrieve a few loose pages. "Here."

Michael took them and read quickly, secretly delighted beyond words at the notion that A.R. Crimson had handed him a hand-written excerpt of a story that no one else had seen.

"The opiate was derived from the blackest inky blood of the Kraken that swam in the deepest depths of icy ocean imaginable. It was rumored to first come to them as a "gift" from a sea witch to their King. No one was sure of its origins. But the residents of Atlantis had come to prize it above all other things.

One small dose transported the subject into a state of euphoria like no other, warming their skin and reminding them of what it had been to stand in the sun and walk as men—but the temporary side effects were a nightmare to behold! The black ink coursed through their veins and showed through the pale glove of their skin, pulsing in branches of gothic feathery dark veins across their bodies and proclaiming their immorality.

But the true horror was that over time, the addictive opium permanently stripped them of the white marble like beauty they possessed, a beauty that had inspired the Greeks and Romans to believe in Gods—and transformed them into tentacled monsters with gaping maws where their mouths had been and serpent shaped spines."

"Well?" Grace asked tentatively. "Grim enough for you?"

"It's the best present I have ever received." He handed the pages back to her. "Thank you, Grace." God, how had it come to this? He was married to a woman he'd already thought clever and beautiful but now, she was…so much more. Inside that golden head of hers were all the worlds he'd always escaped to; the epic stories that entertained and chilled. *His* Grace was the author he'd most admired.

And was still the woman whose beauty made his hands ache to touch her, to hold her and explore every inch of her body.

If Ashe's advice was true…

Michael shook himself to refocus on the moment at hand. It didn't matter. He wasn't going to impose himself on her, tonight or any night. "Welcome to your new home, Mrs. Rutherford."

Grace took in the room. Where the current fashion in décor was all patterns and contrasting textures with ornate useless objects, there was nothing in her new husband's rooms that didn't have a purpose or seem created for comfort. There wasn't a scrap of lace or feminine touches although she suspected that the flowers in a vase on the table by the windows were Mrs. Clay's influence. The furniture in the sitting area was oversized and upholstered in beautiful dark leather that looked worn yet butter-soft and obviously sturdy enough to allow Michael to relax as he wished. A beige and yellow thick oriental style rug lay in the room's center and the black walnut planked floors shone from years of wear and beeswax polish. She shyly noted that even his bed was larger to accommodate his height; the four-poster bed filled the entire alcove and jutted out two feet beyond.

The windows were diamond paned like the ones in the sitting room adding a certain charm as the oak trees outside filtered the light and gave his kingdom a magical touch. The noise of the city was muted and the haven of Mr. Rutherford's rooms had an appeal all their own.

Michael cleared his throat. "Here is the wardrobe. Mrs. Clay...took most of my clothes, well frankly, I don't know where she took them, but it seemed important that you have room to hang your things and to feel at home."

"You're very kind."

"Here is your private parlor, study and," his voice trailed off a bit as he pivoted in a circle without taking a single step. "Bedroom."

"Yes, I see." Grace nervously smoothed her palms on her skirts. "It's enchanting."

He gave her a wary look. "You're being generous but I'm grateful for the gesture, madam." Michael smiled and straightened his shoulders. "Are you hungry? I think Mrs. Clay will have dinner for us soon."

"To be honest, I don't think I can face all of them and a dinner...and cake and...I feel like a thief that's stolen into your life, Michael. And Mrs. Clay—she is so...kind." Grace twisted her hands, wishing she knew how to voice her fears. Everyone was being so accommodating and tender, she felt like she would fracture into a thousand pieces at the first touch. It was irrational but the new fierce happiness that had seized her was too raw and too impossible to absorb. "I'm sorry. It's a dream and I don't want to jostle myself awake and lose this. Can we stay here? Can we stop time?"

"Absolutely. Let's hide then, like the conspirators we are, for a while longer." Michael stood. "Stay here, settle in and unpack and I'll be back in a few minutes."

"What are you going to do?"

"Do you trust me, Grace?"

She nodded, unable to answer him as her emotions surged and her heart clamored to tell him the truth. *It's more than trust, Michael.*

My life is yours.

CHAPTER TWENTY-ONE

It decided to transform dinner into a decadent picnic as he returned with a tray piled high with a wedding feast for two. Mrs. Clay had even managed to make sure there was a healthy slice of wedding cake atop it all and Michael's brow furrowed as he balanced his burden and closed the apartment door behind him.

"Was she terribly disappointed?" Grace asked cautiously.

He shook his head as he triumphantly landed the tray on the small table in the sitting area. "Not even a smidge of a fuss, I swear it." He turned back and his chest tightened with the jolt of satisfaction at the sight of Grace Porter standing in the midst of his apartment still in her wedding finery.

Not Porter. She is Grace Rutherford from this day forward.

He prayed he looked more nonchalant than he felt. "I presented it as more of a romantic desire to spend time alone than…an aversion to hearing a dozens of speeches and impassioned toasts to our happiness."

She smiled. "Good. I, um, took the liberty of unpacking as you suggested and I have to agree that wherever your clothes have gone, Mr. Rutherford, you may need them if the weather changes."

He laughed. "They are a bell pull away, no fear!"

She moved to sit down and began to arrange their dinner. "I fear I've disrupted more than the arrangement of your wardrobe, Mr. Rutherford."

"Michael," he corrected her softly.

"Michael," she repeated it like a gentle caress and Michael's knees turned to rubber.

He conveniently sat down to hide his discomfort, assisting her as best he could by setting out the plates within his reach. "Would you like some wine, Grace?"

"Oh!" A flash of mischief sparkled in her eyes. "Sterling never allowed me wine." She pressed nervous fingers to her heart and Michael had to bite the inside of his cheek to keep from smiling at the fetching picture she made. "I would love to try it!"

My God! I'm...corrupting her....already....and I swear I don't feel even the vaguest twinge of remorse. I'm a horrible person.

"Then you should have a glass," he said with a confidence he didn't feel as he stood to go over to the side table where he had all his spirits. He chose a very small glass meant for sherry or port and delivered a sample of French Bordeaux to his bride. "It's not very sweet but the flavor is...very nice if you sip it slowly."

She sniffed it first, unsure of the contents, but merrily took a small taste.

Michael watched in fascination as his wife truly contemplated the liquid in her mouth, her expression mercurial with her internal assessments. At last, she smiled at him like a child at Christmas. "It was—vibrant!"

"Vibrant is good," he said.

The sun was setting and the spring night was cool with the apartment's windows slightly open for fresh air, and they both began to relax in each other's company. Before long, they were laughing and talking about nothing of Sterling or the shadows across the origins of their union. They ate until they were too full to even eye the scraps and Michael set the tray outside on the dining room table in the sitting room for Tally to collect later.

When he returned, she was sitting on the sofa with both of her feet tucked underneath her, like a Persian cat curled up atop the cushions of his sofa.

"What?" she asked self-consciously. "You are staring, Michael."

"Tell me a story, Grace."

"Really?" she asked.

He sat on the thick rug on the floor, resting an elbow on the cushions, to sit at her feet. "I can think of nothing I would like more."

"The power of a good story," she sighed remembering Mrs. Clay's tale and smiling. "I am Scheherazade."

"I wasn't going to kill you in the morning if you don't please me, Grace."

"Yes, but it does make it sound more thrilling."

"Then enchant me, wife. Enchant me and instead of saving a life, make mine worthwhile. I like that."

"Very well," she agreed, unconsciously relaxing her shoulders and taking on the timeless posture of a storyteller sitting by tribal fires. "Long ago, long before a time when life was measured by the heartless movement of clocks and the rush of machines and modern inventions, there was a young man who lived in a village on the edge of a vast wilderness…"

Michael leaned his head against a hand, giving in to the enchantment of Grace as she spun her tale. The story was wonderful but the glory of the woman telling it stole his breath away. Her hands gestured elegantly to emphasize the dramatic points as her words painted exotic landscapes transporting him to the world that existed only inside her mind.

Her voice rose and fell and characters wild and vivid took the stage as her eyes focused on a point far in the distance that only she could see. The room dimmed as time passed and Michael lit candles in the room and even started a fire without interrupting her, then took his seat to smile at the charming realization that when Grace was caught up in a story, he could probably set off a gun without notice.

"Down came the icy shards from the cave's ceiling, a crystal avalanche of death and—" Grace stopped suddenly, covering her face with the long blades of her fingers. "When did it get so late?"

"Is it?" he asked innocently, as if the changes to the room were not of his making. He shifted off the floor to sit next to her on the sofa. "I hadn't noticed."

"I can't believe this! I can't believe I'm rattling on about ice monsters and fire wizards and that *my husband* is allowing it!"

"Not allowing," he corrected. "Enjoying!"

He leaned forward to kiss her impulsively and the playfulness of the evening fell away. She tasted of wine and cherries, the hot silk of her lips and tongue intoxicating and Michael pulled her into his arms to drink in her kisses until his head was swimming with a desire that made the room spin.

There was no hesitation in her response and this time there was nothing to stop them. Not even his previous naïve illusion that he was not going to bed his wife.

Grace pushed against him and he instantly lifted his head to look into her eyes.

"H-how does this work?" she asked.

"How does it work in your stories?"

She blushed. "Michael, I don't think it's the same."

"Why not? I love your stories, Grace. Tell me. If we were in a story of your making, how would you want the tale of your wedding night to unfold?"

Grace's mouth fell open slightly as she absorbed the implications. *My story—he means to let me have all the power.* All his words praising her independence and her clever mind were more than words but coalesced in a gift that she'd never anticipated. *Mine. Mine to squander or mine to employ and discover what happiness might yet be possible.*

There had been so much about Michael that she had admired and so many of his qualities that she loved. But now, her breath caught and she swallowed as hard as she could because something inside of her broke free with a ragged cry of silent relief.

She did not love his qualities.

She loved *him.*

She loved *this man*—this man who listened to her stories and smiled at her odd speeches, defended her against Sterling and rescued her from a hollow life of lies; this man who was so generous and caring it defied belief. She had married a man she loved and the miracle of it set off a fire inside of her that left her speechless from its raw power and irresistible force.

"I…" Grace started unsteadily, and then decided to seize the moment. Happiness was something she'd been denied for a lifetime and she refused to allow fear to cheat her out of a moment of it. "I would start by telling my husband a story."

"Yes?"

"And then I would hope that he would see that I…am fearless." She took a deep breath. "I don't want to be a shy and retiring thing, fragile and ignored, like a porcelain figurine that he will admire but never touch."

He nodded, enrapt and she smiled, her frame infused with boldness as warm tendrils snaked out across her skin and awaking her senses.

"We would conspire together to create a little island of our own. A place where there would be no shame in finding pleasure or in…"

"Yes?" he asked, his voice low and level, his grey blue eyes alight with approval.

"In embracing as naked as natives?" she offered then covered her mouth with shocked fingers.

"I like this story, Grace." He smiled and then kissed her again to help her dismiss her nerves.

Michael reached up to pull the sprig of lavender and Queen Anne's lace from her hair, gently pulling out hair pins to free her hair at last, his hands fisting in the curls that fell down her back. Grace moaned, the simple act of loosing her braids transforming her into a pirate queen or a fiery sorceress or the wicked temptress seducing sailors in a storm. She was Grace no more.

She was *his*.

The ivory buttons of his shirt gave way beneath her fingers and she delighted at every discovery. Her burly husband wore a delicate silver chain and key underneath his clothes but before her imagination could catch at it, the impact of his bare skin beneath her fingertips diverted her mind. He had a few dark curls at the center of his chest but was very smooth, his flesh fever hot to her touch. His nipples were dark, almost brown, and every inch of him made her mouth water to taste and try.

Grace dropped her hands though when she spotted the last remnants of a pale purple and green bruise the size of a pie plate on his side. "The carriage…" she whispered.

"It's nothing," he bent over to kiss her behind her ear and Grace yielded to passion. Their clothes began to fall away and they were both smiling at the mutual puzzle of ties, hooks and buttons that thwarted their race to achieve access to the other.

Grace pushed his shirt from his shoulders and reached around to embrace him but was startled to feel the smoothness of his skin transform into a mottled and rough texture. Grace stepped back slightly, curiosity burning through the fog of her desires. "What is that?"

"Scars," he said simply, his attention to the tiny buttons running down the front of her dress unwavering. His fingertips brushed against the rise of her breasts through the thin silk of her chemise and Grace shivered with pleasure.

"How mysterious!" she sighed and leaned against him, arching her back to invite more of his touch.

"You can look at them later but at this moment, I'm wondering why women's clothes have so many buttons."

She laughed and kissed his throat, her tongue flicking out to tease his Adam's apple. "To torment our would-be seducers?"

He grunted. "It's working."

Grace's hands dropped to help him and within seconds divested herself of all of it, shamelessly allowing layers of petticoats and clothes to fall onto the floor around her feet. She untied the silk ribbons of her chemise and added it to the pile and then stepped free. Candles flickered as the cool spring air caressed her bare skin but Grace was warmed by the look in Michael's eyes.

She took a step forward and Michael simply stood in stunned silence, forgetting that the sofa was directly behind him. He was bare-chested but still in his trousers, though Grace knew that this last layer was soon to go. She began to tug at the button at his waist and he gently caught her wrist to stop her.

"I'm…big," he said cautiously.

She looked up into his face, puzzled at such an obvious proclamation. Even so, he released her hands and she ran her fingers lightly over the ridges of his chest and stomach, testing the firmness of his muscles and marveling at how merely touching the heated wall of a man's torso could send hundreds of fluttering butterflies loose in her chest. "You look like one of those statues in a museum," she whispered in awe. "It's like I have my very own…breathing sculpture to touch!"

Her hand slid down over the final barrier to touch him through the cloth of his trousers, orienting herself to the mysteries of male anatomy. Grace marveled at heat that almost burned her palm and something deep inside of her began to spasm at the promise of it; at the firm mass and power that moved underneath her touch.

His breath whistled through his teeth and she looked up to watch his face. "Am I…hurting you?"

"Not even close."

Grace smiled and returned her attention to the discovery at hand to free him, gasping at the reality of his flesh in her hands. Heavy against her touch, this part of him was velvet soft and paradoxically as hard as stone and nothing she'd imagined. Her cheeks flamed with heated embarrassment as her next thought was to comment that he was missing a bit of foliage and that she liked him much better than the odd little marble configurations she's only caught fleeting glimpses of in books. Her palms itched to touch all of him but she wasn't sure if he would appreciate such a brazen twist in the plot.

"Not made of stone," he said softly, gritting his teeth as he fought for control. "Careful, Grace. I'm—all too human and very much at your mercy."

With a smile she pushed him with a single fingertip against the center of his chest until the back of his legs bumped up against the sofa. *In my story, apparently the bed is too far away…*

He lost his balance willingly and seized her waist to pull her down with him to kiss her so thoroughly that she swore that the world fell away. Grace landed astride one of his thighs and the gentle pace of his kisses gave way to a possessive claim that made her moan into his mouth with a voracious madness of her own. Her arms encircled his neck and her breasts were pressed flat to his chest, their heartbeats matched in a mounting amorous duel.

Her sex was pressed against his naked thigh, the firm hard ridge of his leg the first touch of another to her most private and tender flesh. Grace bucked against the erotic sensation of friction and heat, squeezing her legs together to try to contain or capture the bewitching arcs of electricity that shot from between her hips and upward into her frame until she was sure that she would either shatter into a thousand pieces or end her existence.

Michael sensed the direction of her journey and did all he could to make sure his beloved girl didn't fall when her climax reached its zenith, closing his eyes to try to corral the lust coursing through his veins. Her sex was ripe satin and so wet on his thigh, he had to fight not to follow her down the path of carnal dreams.

She shuddered and fell against his chest, kissing him again, then pulling away breathlessly. "Oh, my!"

Not. Made. Of. Stone.

Michael gripped her hips and lifted her up easily, positioning her over him, holding her there for a second or two until she looked into his eyes, her own expression slightly dazed and she trembled with the after-effects of her first orgasm. "Grace."

She nodded, suddenly present and eager. "Yes."

Yes.

His cock jutted up and he fit himself inside of her, the large head pressing upward toward the glorious heat and saturated welcome of her body. She was so wet, so relaxed and open that he started to shake. This was the moment of truth and he did not want to hurt her.

But he no longer was sure he could stop if he did.

Slowly, ever so slowly, her inner channel stretched and shifted to accommodate him, and Grace threw her head back like an ancient priestess reveling in a voluptuous ritual of sacrifice. Without a single cry, her body accepted his and Michael almost wept in blessed relief. She was very tight but her channel was deep enough to take him inch by inch until he was buried to the hilt. "Mine," he whispered. "Oh, God, Grace, you are mine." He kissed her, and stroked the silken curtain of her hair that now shielded from the world. He studied her face to look for any sign of distress or regret but she was shameless and beautiful. The high color in her cheeks accented her exquisite face and she made a similar study of him.

"Am I bedded?"

He nodded slowly. They were locked together but he was anxious not to move, fearful that entry was one matter, and rampant jostling another game entirely. But his wife had other ideas.

"Grace, wait!"

"No. It's my story. And I wish to be wanton and wild—and never forget how this feels."

His hands had splayed across the soft rise of her belly, a sensual cage that held her hips in place. But now he freed her, to give her the freedom to move as she wished to accept the thrust of his hips or shy from him.

With her legs around his waist, she began to ride him from a slow cantor to a thundering gallop and Michael's mind slipped away to a world where there was nothing beyond the primal connection between them, beyond this woman and his need to possess her. The pert crests of her breasts rubbed against his chest with every thrust of his body into hers and he caught them in his hands, teasing the tips to roll them between his thumb and fingers, stroking and fondling the sweet weight of each against his palms.

Grace cried out as pleasure and pain mingled until there was only pleasure. The coil of need inside of her grew and pulled taut and she welcomed it with a shudder of anticipation. She had already tasted release and now with the resplendently firm flesh of her husband's body pressing up against her core, she could practically see the crest ahead. She was so close, it became less of a race and more of a supple fall into an erotic ocean. She drove herself up and onto him and the zenith broke over her, shuddering and bucking while Michael moaned his own release.

Something hot and wonderfully molten jetted inside of her and the muscles in her thighs tightened in response. *This! This was raw and real and...oh, god....how did I think to live? But I never knew what life was...*

It was several minutes before either one of them spoke and then Michael lifted her up, gently disengaging their bodies, only to carry her to the bed and hold her close. "There. Bedded."

"Pardon me," Grace climbed over him, deliberately making an effort to get a better view of his back. "I feel like Psyche so if you're hiding wings, I would like to know now, Michael."

"Not wings," he said with a sigh. "Scars."

Grace gasped as the candlelight in the room revealed not just a few raised lines across his back but dozens upon dozens of scarred stripes and deep wounds so layered she couldn't fathom their number or the agonies they represented.

"Are you disgusted, Grace?"

She shook her head. "No! They make you seem even more intriguing and very...virile. But are those—whip marks? Were you flogged?!"

He turned over to swiftly pull her back down onto the feather mattress and into his arms. "A story for another day, Mrs. Rutherford, but if it's any comfort, you did *not* marry a criminal."

"Well! There's a relief!" she said archly then kissed him on the tip of his nose.

He looked down at her as if she were the one wearing wings. "You never cease to amaze me, Grace. And I never meant to...press you for..." Michael sighed. "I was going to win you with a show of restraint, Grace."

"Oh," she said then laughed, nestling up against him, her palm pressed against his chest. "No offense, but I think my proposed version of events turned out far better, don't you?"

Once you lose your heart, it's hard to get it back.

CHAPTER TWENTY-TWO

"You found it, didn't you?" Josiah Hastings asked quietly and the Jaded all looked at Michael in stunned anticipation of his answer. "The diamond in disguise?"

"Yes." Michael kept his usual place by the window in Rowan's study. "I did, indeed."

"When?" Darius asked calmly.

Rowan sighed. "Thank God! Let's put it somewhere safe until this business is over."

"No." Michael crossed his arms, bracing for battle. "It's safe where it is and I'm not putting any of you in danger by burdening you with it at this point in the game."

Ashe leapt up from his chair. "To hell with the game! It's *not* a game! You're the one in the viper's nest, Rutherford!"

Galen cleared his throat. "I'm sure what Blackwell meant to say is, congratulations on your marriage, and we are all openly concerned about your continued well-being."

"I did not and I'm not congratulating the man on being half-witted enough to marry some—"

Darius also stood quickly to cut him off. "Ashe, you are letting your mouth run ahead of your manners! We have not met Mrs. Rutherford and there is no judgment to be made here."

"My home and this room have always been a sanctuary," Rowan said firmly. "And they will remain one so long as I have a say!"

Ashe swallowed hard and then let out a long slow breath. "I misspoke. I apologize."

Michael nodded his assent. "I take no offense considering Blackwell was once an expert on romantic impulses and half-witted choices, and while he was lucky enough to marry Caroline, there's not one of us that doesn't agree that landing on his feet with the love of his life was nothing short of a miracle." Michael smiled. "Apology accepted."

"When did he get so witty?" Ashe asked with a wry glance at Michael and retook his seat.

Darius laughed. "Rutherford was always clever but with the rest of us chattering away, when does a shy man get the opportunity to demonstrate it?"

"Marriage has brought out his sense of humor," Josiah Hastings noted from his favorite leather chair. "Bravo, Rutherford."

"Jests aside," Ashe readdressed the group, "I think you should reconsider the doctor's suggestion, Michael. Your bride is bound to get a little bored confined to a small apartment and women have a gift for going through a man's private things to amuse themselves. She'll find the diamond. And at the risk of starting another round of battles, that may be her true purpose in all of this."

The men grew quiet but Galen finally picked up the thread of the conversation. "It wouldn't be an unreasonable notion. You meant to use her to get closer to Sterling and he could have turned the tables on you. No longer any need for him to break in for a search, Rutherford, now that he has a potential agent in your home."

"Grace is not her brother's agent and has nothing to do with his schemes." Michael deliberately dropped his arms to avoid looking defensive. "She is innocent in all of this."

"You're sure?" Rowan asked gently.

"I am sure." Michael walked over to the bar set on the side table and poured himself and Ashe a drink. He delivered the glass to Ashe, as a small peace offering. "The diamond is safe. I've not abandoned my oaths and I know what I'm doing."

Ashe took the glass but the intensity in his eyes didn't soften. "Michael, every man thinks they know what they're doing but when it comes to a woman, when you're wrong, you'll be the last one to realize it."

"You doubt me, Blackwell?"

Ashe didn't answer him but sipped his drink without taking his eyes off of Michael.

Michael stiffened and returned to the window, looking out onto the moonlit gardens. "Nothing has changed."

"Nothing?" Josiah spoke quietly. "Can I mention the obvious danger? She is Sterling's sister and it's extremely possible that she would take her brother's side in whatever scheme he'd crafted. Your...romance has been a bit...convenient, wouldn't you say? And rather too sudden to suit."

Rowan put a hand on Michael's shoulder. "He's right. From an outsider's vantage point it would seem that Sterling insisted you attend that event and then apparently saw to it that you were caught in a compromising position; forcing you to marry his sister and drawing you into his web."

"Grace is innocent."

"As you keep telling us," Rowan replied. "Have you—married this girl in some grand deception?"

"I love her. There's no deception there."

"Love! Have you forgotten—"

"I've not forgotten, Ashe! Believe me when I tell you that my every waking moment is framed by my vow to you to see to the Jackal. And I will do what I must."

"When?"

"In seven days. I have seven days."

"And then what happens?"

Michael said nothing at first, and then turned his back on all of them.

It was Rowan who finally broke the silence. "And then all hell breaks loose."

Michael nodded and answered without turning around. "Gift me with these seven days. With this time with her…before all is lost. Sterling will get what he deserves and she'll never forgive me."

The men looked at each other, weighing out their brotherhood, their marrow-deep trust in Rutherford against their complete understanding that love could tip any scale and destroy any ties.

"We'll stay clear," Rowan spoke for all of them and Michael turned to leave without another word leaving his friends to an awkward silence that hung heavy in the air.

Galen stretched out his legs and finally risked conversation. "Well, that went better than we expected."

"What did we expect again?" Josiah asked. "Because I could have sworn that Rowan said something about a gentle intervention to make the man see reason…"

"He loves her," Rowan said. "Reason doesn't apply anymore. But it's Rutherford we're talking about and I believe him. He has something planned in a week and we must stand by him and wait."

Ashe put his head in his hands and groaned. "I hate waiting and I hate being the one to push so hard to steal another man's bliss." Ashe lifted his face and gave each of them a hard look. "But you have to ask yourselves, what would you give up for the woman you loved? Who would you betray if it came down to it?"

None of them answered him because the answer was too obvious and too painful.

Everything. Anyone. There was nothing and no one they wouldn't yield for the women they worshipped and adored. All bets were off.

And now their fates hung on the fragile hope that Michael Rutherford was somehow made of stronger stuff than the best man among them.

CHAPTER TWENTY-THREE

The ride to Oxford Street evoked memories of a different day but this time there was no need to shyly avoid his touch. The confines of the hackney carriage gave her a lovely excuse to lean against his arm and delight in his touch.

He trailed his fingers across her cheek and tipped her chin up for a kiss. He'd intended a chaste touch to simply calm his fidgeting wife and distract her from the appointment ahead. But when his unpredictable wife ran her hand down the line of his thigh and then slowly back up in a teasing assault on his control, Michael forfeited his plans.

He deepened the kiss and began to lift her up, voluminous skirts and all, onto his lap. Grace wriggled and sighed in compliance but then pushed against him, giggling as she pulled away. "Michael Rutherford! My bonnet is coming undone!"

He laughed. "Is that all?"

"It is enough to make me question my sanity in dragging you along," she said as her cheeks colored. Grace retied the wide satin ribbon underneath her chin to put a jaunty bow under her right ear. "You didn't need to accompany me, Michael." She pressed her fingers against her warm cheeks. "Not that I don't enjoy your distracting kisses."

"I'm sorry, Mrs. Rutherford but these streets are rife with pickpockets and I don't like the idea of you risking it alone. Not to mention the runaway carriages…"

"May I—do the talking, Michael? When we go up to meet with my editor, Mr. Pollson? Would it be untoward to ask such a thing? It's only that I know that it would be the natural course of things for him to assume you have a greater authority and I've fought so hard to—"

He kissed her, thoroughly enough to bring even more color to her cheeks and make her breath come quickly once he let her go. "I shall pretend to be mute if it pleases you. I confess, I am simply curious to catch a glimpse of the business of publishing. If pressed, I will assert your expertise and that is all I will say."

"No, but let's have our fun and omit introductions!" Grace offered with a mischievous grin. "He's a rough man but good hearted and I would love to keep him guessing."

"I'll play the intimidating tall gentleman at your back."

The stairway leading to Mr. Pollson's office was as dingy and narrow as always. The steps creaked with protest as Michael climbed them, his elbows and wide shoulders nearly blocking the passageway. Grace shyly held his hand as he walked behind her as proudly as a man walking a princess on a promenade. She knocked on the door to S&Y Publishers and entered the small office, stepping around the piles of papers on the floors by rote habit.

"Miss Porter! I'd hoped for you my month's end but this is a delightful...sur...prise..." Mr. Pollson's sharp powers of expression disappeared as Michael ducked under the doorframe. "Are we...delighted?"

"We are!" Grace beamed at his discomfort. "Mr. Crimson has experienced an unexpected burst of creative productivity," Grace began as if there was nothing out of the ordinary in a lady bringing along a nearly seven foot tall living fashion accessory on her errands. She held out her hand and Michael handed her the leather satchel with the pages they'd brought. "I have the newest in his brand new series, "The Fatal Storm"."

The title diverted her editor briefly and he took the bundled pages from her hand. "The Fatal Storm!" His eyes shifted over to Michael who was now studying the overflowing bookshelves of titles and odd stories. "Is *he*...pleased with it?"

"Mr. Crimson? I should say so! Would he have instructed me to come here post haste and demanded I do so without an appointment? Mr. Crimson's trust in your literary instincts is resolute."

Mr. Pollson's confusion was vastly entertaining but it was clear he didn't want to offend the massive tree of a man who was currently wrinkling his nose at a copy of a poetic ode to butterflies. "I…I take it our previous financial arrangement is still acceptable?"

The giant's head lifted and Mr. Pollson made a point of staying behind his desk. Grace smiled. "Your last payment was well-received."

Mr. Pollson's face sagged with visible relief. "Twenty, wasn't it? We'll do twenty again."

"No." Grace blinked fast. "You paid fifteen on my last call, sir. Not that I wish to be rude to correct you."

Michael stepped away from the bookcase and shifted to stand at her back. She could only imagine what his expression might be but the effect was magical on Mr. Pollson.

"I *meant* to pay twenty!" he said, then opened his desk drawer to pull out a few notes and an envelope. "Times are hard, of course, but a simple oversight like that can be corrected. Yes, an easy matter to make amends. Here!" He held out a brown envelope to her. "Twenty-five pounds! Five to make up for my clerical error in your last packet and twenty for the launch of "The Fatal Storm" and our assurance to Mr. Crimson that we will print all the future installments."

Grace took the packet, her fingers trembling. "Oh! How generous of you, Mr. Pollson!" She looked up at Michael. "Isn't that generous?"

Her groom was carved in granite and nonplussed. He shrugged his shoulders. "Is it?"

"It is!" Grace gave him a swift small kick to his shins and Michael smiled spoiling the effect but apparently her editor was not convinced.

"Twenty-five, then!" Mr. Pollson amended. "I will pay twenty five for each future installment but not a penny more!"

Grace wheeled back to Mr. Pollson with a gasp. "Twenty-five pounds? For each installment?"

"It is difficult times and sales lag in these hard times. Hard, *hard* times! You remind Mr. Crimson that times are *very* hard!" Mr. Pollson's eyes darted to Michael but he was doing his best to focus on Grace, perhaps hoping hers was the gentler voice of assent in the room. "But his pamphlets have been moving well and we will increase the number we produce."

Grace held out her hand to shake Mr. Pollson's, shocking him with the masculine gesture. "You have a deal, Mr. Pollson."

They retreated quickly but not quickly enough for Grace to stifle the giggles midway down the stairs. "Usually—I am so nervous in there I can barely breathe! But that, my dear Mr. Rutherford, was thrilling fun!"

"He's quite a badger of a man and his office smells like mushrooms," Michael observed. "But I'm going to agree. That was thrilling fun, Mrs. Rutherford."

"There's no doubt that he thinks that you are Mr. Crimson," she noted sagely, a mischievous smile crossing her features as they stepped out onto the sidewalk. "I knew he would! You certainly are mysterious enough, my handsome and *almost* mute husband."

"He can think whatever he likes. We know better."

"I love our conspiracies, Michael."

"As do I." He leaned down to speak softly into the shell of her ear, the bass of his voice sending a shiver of delight down her spine. "Shall we go back upstairs and see if he'll double it?"

Grace gasped and playfully punched him in the shoulder. "Michael! We are not thugs! Besides, if you give poor Mr. Pollson a heart attack, I will be hard pressed to find another publisher!"

He shook his head. "Hardly! What publisher in London wouldn't fall all over themselves to capture the newest works of the wicked Mr. A.R. Crimson?"

"You are prejudiced in my favor, husband."

"I should hope so."

He helped her alight back into the waiting hackney and the ride home to the Grove went quickly as her husband distracted and teased her senses. Michael was as gentlemanly as ever, but he could evoke her desires with a single light kiss on her bare throat and as she'd nearly begged him to throw her skirts over her head on their way to Oxford Street; it was her own restraint she didn't trust. She was reluctant to admit it, sure that it was a failing in her character, but if it hadn't been for the pre-set appointment with Mr. Pollson, she would have done her best to keep her husband abed for much of the day.

"If you don't stop doing that, I'm going to carry you upstairs over my shoulder and your afternoon will be wasted with a long series of hedonistic pursuits, Mrs. Rutherford."

Grace's eyes widened in shock, wondering if the wicked turn of her mind weren't audible. "If you are trying to intimidate me into submission, you're making a terrible mess of it." She flashed him an enticing grin. "I am spurred on to wicked disobedience in hope of his punishment."

"Very well!" He bent down and lifted her easily to balance her over his shoulder, eliciting peals of laughter from his bride. With one practical hand resting on the delicious curve of her bottom, he quickly mounted the stairs with his prize. "You are well and truly kidnapped!"

"Michael!" she pressed her hands against his back to push herself up but gave in to mirth. "It isn't a kidnapping!"

"Isn't it? Wait until I tell you what ransoms I'm going to demand in exchange for your release."

"Oh!" she squeaked and then relaxed in a playful feint. "How promising!"

He achieved their door, unlocked it and carried her inside, then turned to lock the portal behind him apparently fumbling with the mechanism and taking an inordinate amount of time to tease her with the delay. Grace lifted her head to protest and stiffened in surprise as she noticed a change in the room's layout.

"Michael! Put me down!"

"On the bed?" he asked innocently.

"Michael!"

He put her down very gently, then put his hands behind his back. "Do you like it then?"

Grace tried to answer him but couldn't. She walked forward in a daze, trailing her fingertips over the surface of a beautiful lady's writing desk and matching chair that had been delivered in their absence. The top was a splendid satin finish with inlaid woodwork in the shape of flowers and vines that trailed down to decorate the drawers and turned legs. The chair was upholstered in a rich yellow taffeta embroidered with golden stars and tiny silver crescents. Curved and delicate, everything about the pieces he'd selected brought a feminine touch into a room dominated by the stronger pieces that were his. A stack of fresh paper tied with gold ribbon sat atop a new leather-bound journal embossed with the gold letters, A.R.C. and a cut crystal writing tray glittered next to it. The main drawer pulled out as smoothly as velvet and revealed pens, small ink jars and a tiny gold key to allow her to keep her work secured if she wished.

Grace closed the drawer and turned back to look at him in amazement. "It's flawless and...I never dreamt of..."

"We can move it anywhere you wish. If the light doesn't suit there for working." Michael gestured to the last touch. "And Mrs. Clay suggested adding this shelf above the windows. For reference materials or...anything you'd like really."

It currently housed a blue glass vase with a small bouquet of spring flowers but her heart pounded at the possibilities. Her wonderful husband had gifted her with a little study all her own!

"But where is your desk?" she asked.

Michael pointed nonchalantly to the corner by the wardrobe where his desk was now housed. "I can work there just as easily if I need to or in the sitting room. I have a portable writing desk that a friend gave me. I'm no writer, Grace."

Grace's fingers touched her throat and she looked up at him through a shimmering curtain of unshed tears. "Michael."

His name.

Nothing more and it was the world at his feet. Michael rushed forward to pull Grace into his arms, bending over to lift her up against him and in three strides he'd achieved the bed.

She kissed the bare skin at his throat and pulled her hands through his hair to send chills down his back. He was instantly aware of every inch of his body and savored the moment when reason was tethered and desire took the reins.

Tears spilled down her cheeks and Michael kissed each one, his tongue darting out to drink in the salty sweetness of them. "Grace. If you cry, I'm not sure I can have my wicked way with you. It's very…disconcerting," he teased softly as he lowered her onto the bed.

"Shh! I'm happy! Now ravish me, Michael and allow your wife to have her own wicked way."

"I've never ravished anyone before," he whispered, nipping the juncture of her neck and shoulders the way he knew she loved. "If I tear your clothes off and then take my time, does it still count?"

She smiled and pushed away from him slightly, shifting up onto her knees next to him. "Let's omit the loss of a few buttons and the embarrassment of asking Mrs. Clay to help me repair my clothes, shall we?" Grace's hands moved quickly and with her eyes on his to measure his appreciation of her labors. The buttons gave way and Grace shrugged out of each layer, lingering when his eyes flashed with fascination and relishing the play of salacious need she alone was orchestrating.

The confidence in her eyes was an aphrodisiac more potent than any he knew.

Her chemise fell to pool around her and Michael's breath caught in his throat as his bare goddess lifted her arms to pose for his approval. The cool air across her skin made her nipples pebble hard and her skin was smooth as she innocently cavorted and turned to show off her curves and entice him with the seductive allure of her body. He reached out with his fingertips to trace the outline of her hips across to the indent of her waist and the exquisite firm set of her pert breasts.

His palm splayed across the soft rise of her belly above the triangle of silken dark curls that gleamed in the candlelight. Her inner thighs were already damp and a single trickle slipped down like honey and Michael's tongue darted out already anticipating the taste of her sex.

Grace reached for him and eagerly dispatched his clothes, caressing and stroking every inch of his flesh that was bared to her, hurrying him with the promise of her mouth and hands. God, she loved his physical form, every hard line and firm curve of his masculine beauty whet her appetite and made her crave him. The empty ache between her legs sharpened and she flushed at the strength of it.

There seemed nothing like the polite prose of romantic poetry in the insistent and unrelenting demands of her body for carnal satisfaction. There was nothing tepid or metered in the lust that whipped through her as she pushed his trousers down to free his growing sex into her hands. Lush and rampant, it did not feel ladylike to openly stare and admire it but Grace couldn't resist the impulse.

If it was devilry, she didn't care.

Without releasing him, she pushed him over onto the mattress and climbed atop him, her thighs spread across his hips. He wasn't yet fully aroused, but Grace stroked his phallus and guided him into her body where the searing coil of her desire begged for him; begged for him to overtake the emptiness and impale her core.

Michael held her hips to try to slow her descent as the grip of her tight wet channel squeezed and pulsed around his member forcing him to harden and swell, pushing up inside of her, filling her completely. Tighter and tighter their bodies meshed until he feared it was too much, that he would hurt her somehow with the length and girth of his searing cock.

But Grace dismissed his fears. She wrapped her legs around him and drove her ankles against his back, pressing him deeper and urging him to move against her. Michael withdrew as far as he could and then slowly drove back inside of her, nearly shuddering at the overwhelming feel of her body submitting to his. Again and again, he pulled out to tease her with the withdrawal of his body only to plunge inside, the speed of each thrust increasing until he'd forgotten everything beyond the woman in his arms and the tight fever-hot build of his own impending release.

He was trapped in a spiral of wanting; of anticipation and the selfish wish to make it last—to deprive himself of the zenith for a few moments more so that it would all last. But Grace was pushing him hard, moving with him and against him, crying out as she began to climax again and the spasms of her body as she came conquered his will. He couldn't hold anything back, his own orgasm tearing through his body and jetting out of him to mingle with hers. He had one last primal surge of pride at the idea that he could possess her so completely that her body would overflow with his release.

She was slow to return to her senses, clinging to Michael as he leveraged himself onto his elbows to make sure he wasn't crushing her. *As if he could, silly man!* Grace smiled up at the ceiling and kissed his chest, teasing the dark circle of one of his nipples and making him yelp in surprise.

"Woman!" Michael laughed. "You are incorrigible!"

"Kiss me," she commanded and he complied with the eager diligence of a man more than happy to oblige his new bride. When at last he lifted his head to allow her to catch her breath, Grace couldn't help but sigh in utter contentment.

"There. I am ravished."

"Mrs. Rutherford, you are indeed." He kissed her playfully on the forehead and they both lay back onto the bed laughing at the delights of the day.

CHAPTER TWENTY-FOUR

Sterling readjusted his coat front as he walked down the steps from the headquarters of the East India Trading Company. Lord Waverly's mood had been particularly arch and demanding today, grinding the hours into a long chain of slow minutes that drained a man of hope. The sun had set hours ago and his head ached with the reviews of tax codes and new tariffs the crown wished to see implemented on her rich holdings in India.

He looked forward to the quiet of his house. Since Grace's wedding two days ago, the house was already changed for the better. Mrs. Dorsett was all smiles as she regained control of the house and had resumed a more enthusiastic attitude in his bed—not that he hadn't enjoyed her without it. The woman had a gifted mouth and a fondness for his cock that had kept her on her knees and in his service for all their years together despite his sister's inconvenient arrival on his doorstep. The woman was plain but his sexual appetites were blind enough. Sterling's steps lightened as he contemplated ordering his proud housekeeper to bend over the dining room table while he—

"Porter!"

Sterling turned at the unfamiliar voice. A footman in a dark livery he knew all too well held up his hand and gestured toward a carriage that waited in the shadows of a nearby tree-lined lane.

Damn it. So much for their agreement to give a man time.

Sterling walked across to the black landau and dutifully climbed up into its interior to sit across from his longtime patron for a clandestine meeting. "It is nearly two weeks until July, sir," Sterling began calmly. "Has there been some change to our agreement?"

"I have always liked you, Porter. It makes no sense but it is actually true," the man answered without a trace of humor. "If we were honest, we would both have to admit that it is the only reason you're still living."

"Then I am again grateful for my charm."

A low gravel-filled sound like frozen metal chips sliding into a can made Sterling's skin crawl and he realized his patron was actually laughing.

"Oh, I don't find you charming! It is your ambition and drive I like."

Sterling swallowed hard. "Good. It is a trait I shall never relinquish."

"Porter," the man said. "The others are content to wait for you to fail yet again but I'm tired. I tired of all of it. You'll tell me *exactly* when you will bring me the diamond and you'll share *exactly* how you intend to manage it. Now, Porter. You'll tell me now."

"By the stroke of midnight in six days, yes, I shall have it in my hands by then. Within minutes of that instant, I will deliver it directly to you." Sterling wiped his palms on his pant legs. "Everything is set."

"How dramatic! The stroke of midnight on Sunday…" Gloved hands flexed atop his silver handled cane and drew Sterling's eye. "And the how?"

"I am making a trade for it."

"You mean to tell me that you think you have something equal to its worth to be bandying it about?" the man scoffed. "Or is that someone is stupid enough to trade away something priceless for what? For colored beads or a deed to a plot of land in Elysium?"

Sterling shook his head. "What I've given him is worthless but one man's trash is another man's…"

"Treasure," the man finished. "And why didn't the simple answer of proposing this worthless trade come to you sooner?"

Sterling shifted nervously on the cushioned seat. The shadows were playing wicked tricks on his eyes and he felt like he was having a private conference with Lucifer himself. "I cannot say but I'm glad that things are finally coming together as I'd promised you that they would. You'll see, sir. I am a man of my word."

His patron failed to answer him and an uncomfortable silence ate at Sterling's confidence.

"Everything is going according to plan," Sterling added.

"Yes, I'm sure it is."

"It is!" Sterling winced as the words left his lips. He sounded like a defensive child and he hated it.

There was another low chuckle from the other side of the carriage, a horrible sound that made Sterling's balls shrivel up against his thigh. "I don't care, Porter. You see, we met again, our friendly little circle and the sentiment was unanimous. It's been almost three years that you've strung us along, and while Bascombe was once your greatest supporter and advocate—well, we know how that has unfolded, don't we?"

"Rand Bascombe is an overstuffed—"

"Yes," the man cut him off, his voice calm and cruel. "Your love of Bascombe is understood. But let us get back to heart of the matter. We have all begun to suspect that there was never a diamond, a prophecy or any shred of truth to this business."

He held up a gloved hand before Sterling could reply and the snarling dragon figurine atop his cane gleamed dully. "So it's very simple, Mr. Porter. Deliver the diamond to us before the stroke of midnight Sunday, or we'll kill you."

"There's no need for threats."

"No, there isn't. You should believe that your death is possible without my having to spell it out like some common thug and don't think I'm not irritated that I'm required to be so blunt, Mr. Porter. But I want no mistakes and no claims of a misunderstanding. Deliver the diamond or face your death. Clear enough?"

Sterling nodded, his voice abandoning him completely.

"Good. Get out of my carriage."

Sterling opened the door and climbed down in an awkward descent with a mix of relief and humiliation. There would be no additional audiences and no more negotiations. The carriage pulled away and Sterling brushed off his coat, recovering his composure.

Six days.

And my life depends on Rutherford's attachment to my sister who he may already have strangled for rattling on about chestnuts and why fairies like cobwebs.

Damn it.

✳ ✳ ✳

A knock at the door interrupted her morning's progress on the chapter at hand and Grace set her pen down with a sigh. She went quickly to see if Mrs. Clay had come early but was greeted by Miss Maggie Beecham, the Grove's maid for the rooms and their neighbor on the floor.

"There's a man to see you, Mrs. Rutherford," Maggie said sweetly but then lowered her voice. "The one I'm under strict orders *not* to bring up to the east wing parlor or your door under any circumstances."

"Sterling? My brother is here?!" Grace's fingers flew to her throat.

"Bit of a cad, is he?" Maggie nodded sympathetically. "I thought he had the look."

"He is very much a cad," Grace agreed then stepped out from the doorway. "Maggie, Michael…Mr. Rutherford isn't home. Can you alert someone to keep an eye out? Just in case he is here to make trouble."

Maggie nodded. "Of course."

"Where is he?"

"I left him in the common room."

"Thank you, Maggie." Grace smoothed out her skirts and headed down quickly, dreading a confrontation in front of any of Mrs. Clay's lovely guests in the public room on the ground floor. She found him easily, sitting at a table by the nearest wall with a look of distaste on his face. The common room of an inn would be beneath him, she knew, and the sight of his grim discomfort made her smile.

"Sterling," she said quietly and sat down before he could make any grand show of false happiness at her arrival. "Why are you here?"

"Is that any way to greet your older brother? Has marriage to that brute of a giant soured you so quickly?" he asked.

"I don't mean to be rude. But in light of the way you've treated me, I fail to see why you'd be surprised."

"Grace," he sighed. "I was harsh, yes, but I had your best interests at heart and I do take some responsibility for the disaster at Bascombe's. I sheltered you too much and was too cautious about exposing you to the world. Your instincts were dulled by my mistakes and a villain like Rutherford was too clever not to sense it."

She gasped but bit her tongue to stop the reflexive defense of her husband's good name. Sterling was up to something and Grace kept her hands folded tightly in her lap. "Why are you here, Sterling?"

"I wished to see how you were faring. I couldn't sleep nights knowing you were miserable." Sterling leaned forward. "Is he mistreating you?"

"Of course not!" Grace's fingers clenched in frustration and she deliberately strived to take on an icy disinterested tone. "Mr. Rutherford's company is most congenial."

Sterling's eyebrows lifted and he glanced around the common room. "It would have to be. I feel no small amount of guilt to think that he has brought you here…as if this is any sort of home for a lady!"

She stood. "Thank you for coming, Sterling. As you can see I am neither mistreated nor miserable, but in fact very happy to be married and away from your brotherly care and concern. Now, I'll ask you to leave."

Sterling kept his seat, a slow smile creeping across his face. "This isn't your sitting room, Lady Rutherford. It's a public dining hall and a very common one at that! Do you seriously think to—"

"Get out, sir." Maggie Beecham came up behind him, hands on hips, her voice level but menacing. "Mrs. Rutherford's too sweet for the task but you get out of this very public dining hall or I'll start screeching like a hellcat and when my man comes over to inquire, I'll burst into tears and that, sir, will be the end of you!"

"W-what?" Sterling's confusion was paralyzing. Maggie was five feet of fiery indignation but she wasn't backing down. Sterling began to take note of all the large muscular patrons in the hall and slowly came to his feet. "I mean to leave as soon as I am done with this conversation, you insolent creature, so there is no need to…"

"Sterling, perhaps you should go." Grace added struggling not to smile as Maggie's color increased a telling degree.

"I've had enough of bullies to fill a hundred lifetimes." Maggie said calmly and then took a deep breath and let loose with a cry to make a banshee wince. "Aayaaa! Mrs. Clay! Mrs. Clay!"

The landlady was instantly on hand with a large handled broom in hand and Tally at her side. "What's that?"

Maggie lifted one hand and pointed it directly at Sterling's nose. "Rough trade, Mrs. Clay! He was horrible to Mrs. Rutherford and when I came to her defense, he…" Margaret Beecham's tears were astonishingly effective, "he called me…it's too cruel…"

Tally put two fingers in his mouth and whistled to conjure two large footmen who at the sight of Maggie's tears and a very red-faced man, launched into action at Tally's hand signal. Within seconds, Sterling's feet had left the floor as he was carried out with the added indignity of being hit with a broom by Mrs. Clay for good measure.

"Out!" Mrs. Clay huffed and lowered her weapon. "And don't you think to return!"

The room burst into applause and laughter as Mr. Sterling Porter was physically thrown from the Grove to land on his backside on the cobbled street.

Mrs. Clay shut the main doors firmly and reached up to tuck in a stray curl that had fallen onto her cheek. She beamed at all her guests. "Sorry for the disturbance. Thank you, dearies! Let's have a round of ale for any who'd care for it and for all of you, let's be extra kind to our Maggie for the next day or two, poor thing!"

There was more applause as everyone returned cheerfully to their business and Tally held out a handkerchief to comfort Maggie who had "miraculously" recovered enough to blush and converse silently with the blonde young man using her hands.

Grace covered her mouth with her fingers astonishment and shock taking over her senses. *My god! Sterling was thrown from the Grove! How— delightful!*

"Are you all right, Mrs. Rutherford?" Mrs. Clay asked her. "Was that man your brother?"

Grace nodded, swallowing a hiccup of nerves. "Yes. I'm afraid so."

"Well!" Mrs. Clay sighed. "My Mr. Clay always said, you can choose a fish at market but never the relatives across the table and one of those two things is bound to make a stink when you don't want them to!"

Grace smiled. "I think I'd have liked your Mr. Clay very much."

"And he you!" Mrs. Clay patted her hands. "Why don't you head back up to the peace and quiet of your rooms and I'll send up a special tray to make up for all this nonsense!"

"Yes, thank you." Grace retreated even as the round of complimentary ale was being served to the Grove's steady guests. Laughter echoed against the carved panel walls and her steps grew steadier as she went. There was magic to the inn that extended out from its owner as if every act of kindness and every stray soul she collected had only strengthened the spell. Mr. Crimson wrote of the dark seams of worlds unknown and grim acts that chilled his readers, but even her literary alter ego was inspired by the Grove.

It isn't just Michael's sanctuary anymore.

It's mine, too.

Michael came home his arms laden with packages. Ashe was no longer willing to act as his muse on shopping expeditions but Michael had found that he didn't need Blackwell's guidance. Grace was inspiration enough. He'd run a few important errands during the day, stopping at his lawyer's to make sure his will left everything in good order for his widow and leaving letters to each of the Jaded should the worst happen. Michael had always been a tactician and he refused to abandon his talents now.

But when he opened the door to their rooms, he found his wife with her head on her desk. "Grace? Are you unwell?"

She lifted tear-streaked cheeks to him and he dropped every package without a thought to rush to her side. Michael knelt down by the desk and anxiously took her in his arms, as he had in Bascombe's garden.

"What happened?"

She took one unsteady breath. "Sterling paid me a call." She reached up to pull the flat of her hand across her cheeks. "And I should say as quickly as I can, that I have no idea why I'm crying! Except that it was so horrible to see him here and—"

"Here?"

"Well, thanks to the staff, he only made it into the dining hall downstairs. Apparently you'd made it clear that he isn't a welcome caller," Grace said and reached up caress his face. "Thank you for that, Michael."

He shifted her to rest against his chest and sighed. "I didn't expect him to actually give his name…that was a long shot that paid off." He'd informed Mrs. Clay of the barest facts in the same sitting in which he'd given her the news of his impending wedding. He'd hinted at Sterling's villainy and his dear Mrs. Clay had filled in the rest, her protective ire fueling an immediate ban of Grace's brother from her doors. Whoever had let the man into the dining room, it wasn't Mrs. Clay.

Michael's eye caught sight of the heavily laden tray. "I take it from the presence of an entire ginger pudding on that tray that it didn't go well?"

"You can tell from a pudding?" she asked lifting her head from his shoulder.

"Mrs. Clay tends to express her concern with food and *that*," he nodded toward the small feast, "is a lot of concern for one very petite lady."

"It wasn't good," Grace sighed. "Sterling refused to leave when I asked him and Maggie intervened like a guardian angel. Although, perhaps not so angelic when she started screaming like a cat dipped in hot wax. Mrs. Clay struck him with a broom handle before two of the men tossed him out."

Michael used every trick he could think of not to laugh out loud. "Brilliant."

"It was exhilarating, but…"

"Why was Sterling here, Grace? What did he want to say to you?" he asked. "Or did Maggie send him running before he could spit it out?"

"He said he merely wanted to reassure himself that I wasn't miserable. My brother's usual dark choice of vocabulary hasn't lost its bite." She stroked his arms and shifted against him. "But he was fishing for something."

"Did he get what he wanted?"

"No!" She said, but her voice trembled. "I don't know! How could I possibly know what he's thinking? He's always been difficult to corner but I swear ever since he returned from India, it's like a demon took his place."

Michael lifted her back onto her chair, but held his place looking levelly into her eyes. "India changed so many."

"Tell me again that there is nothing—nothing else between you and Sterling that you haven't shared. I feel like I'm blind and there's a panther in the corner of the room. I can sense it there but every time I ask you, you tell me we're alone and that there's nothing!" She caught at his hands, and pressed them against her heart. "You would tell me, wouldn't you?"

"Grace. I would tell you. If I could."

"If you could?" She dropped his hands. "In the garden. Do you remember when you said you didn't know this version of yourself? As if I'd changed you…"

"You have."

"For the better?" Grace's hands dropped. "You've done so much to protect my independence and to—allow me to dream of embracing a better version of myself. But I want you to reassure me that you are better and that I've not somehow made your life worse or robbed you of—"

"Grace!" He pulled her into his arms. "My life was nothing. I'd have thrown it away, it held that much value to me…" And again, Michael had to stop as he'd gone far too close to admitting the worst. *Truth be told, I was in the process of laying it down when I met you, Grace. And I still will if it comes to it.* "None of it matters. I am better for knowing you. I'm sure of it."

"Sterling—"

"I don't want to talk about Sterling anymore. He's meddled and pushed for far too long and I won't give him any more of us. Not more than he's already taken."

"Michael, I know what he has taken from me. Tell me what he has taken from you."

Michael shook his head and led her toward the sofa where they could sit together to talk. "Not yet. Please, let me keep a few small mysteries for just a while longer."

"Mysteries?"

"Grace, I'm asking you to trust me. We are conspirators, are we not? My life is yours. And I won't keep secrets from you for much longer, I swear. But for now, if ever you cared for me or hold out any affection for my worthless carcass, I'm begging you to wait."

"Michael," she said carefully. "Do you…not know?"

"Know what?" he asked, instantly wary.

"That I love you. That it is not a question about holding affection for your carcass, which by the way, I don't believe is worthless! And that I…from the first moment I saw you, have been quite affected." She put her hands on either side of his face, cradling him. "I love you, Michael Rutherford, and I trust you without being asked."

For a moment, he couldn't breathe. *She loves me. Just like that.*

"Grace, I—should have said how I felt long before now. But I'm not gifted with a knack for prose and how do you tell your wife that you worship her, her every piece and part and mostly, her every unpredictable thought?"

She smiled. "Just so!" She kissed him on the cheek and stepped back, pressing her hands against her face to cool herself. "We mustn't start! Mrs. Clay will have noted your return and she'll be up any minute to make sure you're not starving."

He laughed and picked her up for a playful turn about the room before dutifully putting her back down on her feet. "Shall I tell her I intend to feast on my wife and live off your kisses for sustenance?"

Grace struck him on the shoulder, "No!"

"I've been spending my days at my sports club to give you privacy to work. Would you…like me to stay home tomorrow?"

She shook her head. "No. You cannot be tethered and I…I cannot think of wasting hours writing when you are close enough to kiss." She sighed. "Perhaps in time, do you think I'll grow used to you, Michael? Will I learn to think and work without being so distracted by the scent of your skin?"

"That must be true. Although," he kissed along the line of her shoulder, savoring the peak and then working his way to the sensitive valley where her neck rose in a proud and inviting column, "I won't rush to it. I like the idea of proving a distraction to my wife—that you might want me."

"Might?" She laughed, a sudden flurry of movement and pushed him back until she was proudly astride him on the couch, pinning him beneath her. "How can I relieve you of this doubt, husband?"

"You already have," he said as he looked into her eyes. "I want to protect you, Grace."

"You are the kindest, gentlest man in the world."

Michael closed his eyes. *No. Only in your eyes, Grace, and I will spend whatever time I have on this earth protecting the way you look at me.*

CHAPTER TWENTY-FIVE

"The next time my wife asks you to leave, may I suggest you obey her as quickly as you can?" Michael offered and then enjoyed the sight of Sterling nearly falling out of his chair in surprised terror. It had been frighteningly easy to get over the garden wall and enter Porter's house through the back door. But he was tired of ringing doorbells and pretending to follow the rules.

Time to make sure I've got the Jackal's complete attention and that he's not going to waste any of that fury on Grace or the Grove.

"How the hell did you get in my study?" Sterling asked, rage and fear making him sound weak.

Michael knew better. Sterling wasn't weak. He was unpredictable and dangerous.

"I walked in. Perhaps your housekeeper is too busy to answer the door?" Michael shrugged his shoulders. "I'm amazed you didn't expect me, Porter. After all, it's common courtesy to return a call, isn't it?"

"You rang the bell?" Porter was still struggling to accept Michael's silent entry into his study. "Return a call? Oh, that! As if you didn't have everything to do with the insulting mess of a—"

"You promised to leave us be." Michael leaned slowly against the window frame. "Don't push me, Sterling."

"I'll push where and when I wish." Sterling's shoulders relaxed as he warmed to the subject, sure of the solid ground beneath his feet. "Besides I said I wouldn't bother you. I never said I wouldn't drop in to make sure my sister was thriving in your loving hands."

"You upset her and the staff at the inn. I recall telling you that if you interfered or harmed any of mine before the deadline, all bets would be off." Michael crossed his ankles. "Or did that slip your mind?"

Sterling's lips pressed into a tight line. "I didn't think of it as interference. And the only one who was hurt was me!"

Michael smiled. "You look unbruised. Mind you don't drop in again, Sterling. I already loathe our deal. Don't give me a reason not to play along."

"Don't threaten me, Rutherford. I still have all the power and you know it." Sterling deliberately put his feet up on the corner of his desk. "Your presence here proves it! A little demonstration of how easily I can access my sister and you've come running to huff and puff and pound your chest to scare me off. You're the one who is frightened, Rutherford. It is you who has everything to lose."

Michael pushed away from the wall and took one step toward the desk. "Look at me, Sterling. What do you see?"

Sterling's brow furrowed in confusion. "Beyond a man outmatched by his betters?"

"Look again." Michael smiled slowly, deliberately summoning a demonic look to his eyes. It was a trick he'd once used to make a man piss himself with fear and he reveled in the slow crumbling of Sterling's confidence. "I meant to tell you but you were in such a hurry for the match, for the wedding, for any chance you could engineer to draw us closer to that moment when you could announce your intentions and crow like an idiot—I didn't want to spoil your fun."

"To tell me what?"

"Let's play a game first. Tell me what you know about me, Sterling."

"This is a pointless exercise! You were a soldier in the East India Trading Company's army. You live in an inn. You…"

Michael sighed. "You know nothing that I haven't told you, which means you don't know me at all."

"I know enough! I know you're one of the Jaded! I know you can get me that diamond and that you *will* get me that diamond by midnight on Sunday! You love Grace and unless any of that is untrue, I know everything I need to know!

"Oh, you're crafty! And yes, I will do what you ask to spare Grace's life and give you the diamond but I don't think you've really weighed it out, dear *brother*." Michael subtly shifted his weight to the balls of his feet. "May I say, with all due respect, you are a miserable tactician, Sterling."

"To hell with you!"

"Yes. You've already kicked open the door. The Jaded hate me for my betrayal of their interests to pursue this marriage. And once we make the exchange, my banishment will be permanent with no hope of forgiveness. I won't have a friend in the world."

"Good!" Sterling blurted out like a malicious child.

"Not good for you, Porter. You've made me deadlier than ever I was before and seen to it that I have nowhere to turn. And it gets worse."

"Worse? For you perhaps but I fail to see how your misery is any of my concern, Rutherford."

"Because you have a tiger by the tail, Porter." Michael put his hands on the edge of the desk, deliberately letting Sterling take in the disadvantages of his position in the room, how mismatched they were physically and how there was no chance of him reaching the doorway alive if Michael didn't want him to reach it. "I wasn't a soldier, Porter. I was a killer. I was the man the natives never saw and when my commanding officer pointed out a target that he wished removed, I *never* missed."

"Y-you exaggerate to—"

Michael shook his head. "I was the only man in that dungeon who deserved to be there. I'd have accepted my tortured end with a smile on my face but the innocence of the others—I couldn't live with another sacrifice for my sins. So I vowed to protect those men at any cost with my last breath. They inspired me to remake myself and when that wall broke away...*I lived for the Jaded.*"

Sterling opened his mouth but no sounds came out.

Michael continued. "Now thanks to you, I don't have their brotherhood and I'm deprived of that bond. But I have Grace." Michael stood up straight. "You mistook me for a man of honor and chivalry, Porter, and decided it was a weakness you could exploit. But those things died inside of me in India and the only thing I have left of my humanity is my love for Grace. I am honorable because Grace would have it so."

"The treasure..."

"I'll give you your diamond and when I walk away, you will be grateful, Porter, grateful because my lovely wife admires a man who keeps his word. But if you think to double back later and trouble me again, I want you to remember *exactly* what kind of man I am."

"Duly noted." Sterling folded his hands behind his back, as solemn as a priest.

Michael smiled. "Once you have the diamond, you'll have to let go of my tail, Porter, and then you're going to have to pray every day for Grace's continued health and happiness. Can you guess why?"

Sterling nodded. "I'm beginning to see the way of it."

"That's right. Because if *anything* ever happens to my beloved Grace, then my last tether to reason and the restrictions of a moral world are gone forever. Do you think one more soul's weight on my conscience will matter at the end of that day? Do you think I wouldn't kill you gleefully and laugh on my way to the gallows?"

"Aren't you afraid?" Sterling asked quietly, fear threading through his words. "That I'll take the diamond and kill you? If you're such a...threat?"

"Afraid? Aren't you afraid I'll leave detailed notes with evidence of who I'll be meeting and why so that the police are on your doorstep within hours of my death?" Michael crossed his arms. "We'll meet late Sunday at a place of my choosing. I'll send you word an hour before and you'll come to retrieve your treasure.   We shall both leave quite alive and unharmed.   For I have an appointment to keep later that night, Porter.   And if I miss it, how long will you last?"

"Unlike you," Sterling stiffened his spine.   "I am a man of my word. You give me what I want and no one will be harmed."

Michael sighed.   "You're a villain, Porter.   I never had any hope of Heaven, and Hell? Hell is familiar ground.   Threaten Grace after our deadline, or anyone I care to claim as family and your next lesson in tactics won't involve a polite outline of my skills or an explanation of my past."   Michael leaned in and lowered his voice to a whisper.   "You'll get to Hades in pieces, Porter."

CHAPTER TWENTY-SIX

Feint. Lunge. Strike. Feint. Lunge. Strike.

It was the fluid dance of man and sword that made Michael's muscles sing in protest as he repeated the forms over and over. He had no sparring partner and worked alone. Apparently even in his sports club, rumors of his blackened character still swirled around him and warned off any casual acquaintances. No gentleman would seek out friendship with a man with a damaged reputation—not without risk to his own good name. It was a rule Michael understood and he'd made no effort to breach the lines.

It's all over soon anyway. Why drag another soul into the mess or—

"Fighting ghosts?" Rowan asked, as he came up the outside walk alongside the workout room. The brick gym was open to the courtyard for air and a low wall with columns gave it an almost Spartan feel. "Or a better question, are you winning?"

Michael lowered the tip of his sword to the sawdust-covered ground and turned to wave at Rowan in greeting. "If I were losing, would I admit it?"

Rowan leaned through the opening and rested on his elbows. "Weeks ago, I'd have answered that without a thought. But now? You were always hard to read but lately you've made me feel like a seer trying to read owl feathers and pigeon bones."

"How do the signs look? Have I long to live, doctor?"

Rowan grimaced at the weak jest. "You're deliberately killing me. I take it your ribs have healed."

"Apparently so. I've always healed quickly and it's been nearly a month, Rowan."

"You say that as if it's an inordinate amount of time, Michael."

"I measure things in days and hours. Especially now." He grabbed a soft cloth to wipe down his blade, ignoring the fact that it was already gleaming. Dr. Rowan West had come for more than a check on his health and Michael simply waited.

"When do you intend to give him the diamond?"

And there it is. Not a long wait, after all.

"How did you know?"

"It was a guess, until just then." Rowan held up the note that Michael had sent him yesterday. "That and your final sounding note indicating that things were drawing to a close. It reads like a heartfelt farewell, Michael."

"I swore to keep you abreast of my progress and if I'm dead tomorrow night, you'd have enough to go on to get Grace out of the Grove."

"Get her out now and let's come up with a better plan together, all of us."

Michael shook his head. "None of the others trust me and they have good cause. I've married our arch enemy's sister and…I cannot make any more promises."

"Give us the diamond. Tell him you don't have it anymore."

A bitter laugh escaped Michael's lips. "And prolong the agony of his endless quest? Infuriate him past reason so that the next assault isn't even remotely defensible? Expect mercy from a petty-minded devil that has the conscience of a stone?"

"Rutherford—"

"I'm giving him the diamond in exchange for marrying Grace." Michael's tongue tasted bitter for the deception but there was no avoiding the lies. Sterling's inconsistent cruelties meant he couldn't rely on the Jackal making another misstep. He had to assume that the worst was not only possible but probable; that Sterling would make good on his threat and have Michael out of the way so that he could do as he wished to the others until they yielded the treasure into his hands.

The Jaded would have to accept betrayal.

"Ashe was right," Rowan whispered in horror. "He was sure you'd turned your back on us for…her."

"Grace never asked it of me. She doesn't know, Rowan." Michael kept his gaze steady. "It was love at first sight and it was the bargain I struck with Sterling to achieve her."

"And what of the prophecy?"

Michael closed his eyes. "There is nothing I'm not willing to give up to see to her safety."

"The retribution of the believers in that prophecy—"

"Will hopefully land on the ones who will have the diamond wrongfully. And if I have the chance, I'll make it clear that I alone betrayed you and gave up the treasure to the East India Trading Company's dogs. I can't think about that now."

"Because you love her."

"I love her."

"Then God help you, Michael, because the Jaded won't."

Rowan left without another word and Michael sat down on a wooden bench by the brick wall, poured a bucket of cold water over his head to clean off the sweat and let the rivulets of water trailing down his face hide his silent tears.

His hair was still damp as he walked back at dusk through the backstreets of London. His height and physical prowess gave him an untouchable air and he preferred to take the most direct, if not the wisest, paths through the city in his current mood. Michael pushed cold wet black and white curls back, cursing them for their refusal to stay out of his eyes. *I should ask Grace to cut my hair and be done with it.*

He pushed the notion off a bit, avoiding the dark idea that it would be like asking her for a trim before his burial. Not that he didn't have a slim hope of surviving but his odds were murky. Up until now, Sterling's every action had been edged in pettiness and small-minded villainy that Michael had laid his strategies against. He'd let his Sterling gloat and dance about with the "upper hand", then taunted, pushed and prodded whenever he could to make sure that Sterling's attention hadn't wavered and that the man's personal pride meant he wished to finish things alone. But if their upcoming grand finale had inspired him to bring in more muscle or heaven forbid, hire another thinker; Michael would be forced to improvise.

One thing was certain. Rowan's visit was the last. The Jaded would stay clear and spend tomorrow night cursing his name in the brownstone's study or holding Ashe down to keep him from hurting the furniture or himself in his rage.

There's a picture. Four men sitting on Ashe trussed up like a silk covered log while—

It was a combination of a single missed step and the sound of metal quietly kissing metal as a single blade was pulled from its sheath that alerted him. Instinct dictated that he jump out of the way or dart forward, but Michael knew that that would be a fatal error. So instead, he dropped and turned, shifting toward his attacker to eliminate the distance between them and spoil whatever form or fighting pattern they might have locked into their minds.

It was a solitary assailant wearing a workman's rough clothes but something in the smooth lines of the man's face belied the disguise. Broad shoulders and lean proportions gave away an athlete's strength and against anyone else, his killer would have possessed the greater size.

The knife was a curved blade but Michael absorbed its beauty only peripherally. His attacker hissed in surprise as his first strike was uselessly wide, cutting into Michael's coat. Before he could reset for another attempt, Michael decided he would risk that the weapon the man was holding was his only weapon.

Michael rolled into man's body, blocking the hand with the knife but failed to achieve an easy end to the fight. This was no common street thug. He moved with catlike grace and anticipated Michael's lunge intending to let him charge into the brick building's exterior.

But Michael was no mindless bull and surged against the wall with a purpose, using the firm surface to launch into a roll backward aiming at the man's shins. It was unconventional and far from graceful but Michael guessed that in a fight against gravity, it was better to imitate a badger than aim for something lofty like a jungle cat.

The man stumbled backward and this time, Michael caught the wrist of his knife hand in an iron hold as he tackled him to the alley's cobbled pavers. There wasn't time for finesse and he applied the only advantages he had—his height, size and brute strength.

The dry crunch of bones giving way made Michael wince but he didn't relent until the man's wrist flopped uselessly and the knife fell from his fingertips. A Hindustani curse about betrayers and demons was whispered into his ear and Michael froze. He lifted his head to get a better look and stared down into dark brown eyes as the entire attack took on a new light. Michael caught his breath and spoke as calmly as he could manage. "Tomorrow. *After* midnight. St. Martin's at Ludgate."

Michael hesitated. Once he let go and began to pull back, it was highly possible that the man would gift him with a different blade between his ribs but Michael trusted the icy look of comprehension reflecting back at him.

He doesn't like it but he'll be there.

He climbed off him slowly, giving himself the chance to change course if he needed to but his attacker didn't move.

"Don't come early," Michael added and held out a hand to help the man up.

The man's gaze narrowed but he finally nodded. Slowly, with his uninjured hand, he reached up and took the aid to find his feet.

"I'll come, Rutherford." His accent was flawless with traces of an Oxford education that reminded him of Darius. "What is the saying? Death keeps his appointments."

Michael bowed, without a trace of mockery in his expression. It was a strange gesture but something inside of him yielded to the impulse. He kept his eyes on his new "friend" and then retrieved the dagger from the filthy ground to hold it out, handle first.

The man's eyes widened but a look of respect replaced his shock. He took the knife slowly and sheathed it inside an ornate metal holder that hung at his side.

Michael looked down at the ruin of his coat and clothes from the muddy ground and began to brush off the worst of it. "My friend is a very good doctor if you'd like to…" his words trailed off as he realized he was now addressing thin air.

His "friend" was gone without a sound or sign of departure.

Michael smiled. It was his own favorite trick and he had to admire the other man's style. But his humor faded quickly as his fingers found the sharp rent in his coat and felt the small sting on the underside of his arm where he'd apparently been cut slightly.

"Damn it! That's a jacket, a coat, *and* a shirt ruined!" Michael frowned. The coat's tear he might have lied away but the ruin of his clothes and the bloodstains—his brow furrowed in displeasure and he looked up again for his assailant.

"Hey, Death!" he called out into the night. "I'll see you tomorrow night but you'd better compose a damn good apology for upsetting my wife, you bastard!"

Michael shook off the worst of the filth and hurried back onto his course home. As diverting as his encounter with "Death" had been, he knew he was running out of time.

Tomorrow night was the night of the deadline, and apparently all sides of the game now knew it. Every piece was in place and only the clock was moving inexorably forward to finish the game that Fate had started centuries ago. Michael wondered if whatever priest had scribbled down his fevered prophecy had ever imagined that it would all come down to the strange twists of a London night and the love of a woman.

He stepped out onto a wider lane, his steps quickening.

It was a full moon and Grace was waiting.

One last time.

Chapter

Twenty-seven

Grace awoke to a handwritten note from her husband propped up on his pillow. She pressed the folded paper to her cheeks with a blush recalling the night of passion they had shared. Her husband's tender pursuit of her pleasure had left her breathless and satiated. Her boldness in their love play shocked and delighted her as she discovered that he admired her every guise from shy to wanton.

Of all the lessons in her newly married bed, her husband's acceptance of her lustful impulses and shameless joy in his every touch was even now a miraculous surprise.

She rolled over onto her stomach and closed her eyes as the very thought of him awakened an inconvenient craving inside of her. *This is ridiculous!* Grace winced as a new warmth and familiar wetness spread out from between her thighs. Even the smell of his body on the bedding added to her dilemma and Grace sat up with an impatient sigh.

"This is ridiculous!"

She forced herself to climb out of the bed as efficiently as she could, doing her best to ignore the clamor of her imagination and her nethers. She was determined to dress and decided the unopened note would be her reward for demonstrating a touch of ladylike discipline.

Grace opened the wardrobe to whimsically retrieve his coat, frowning as she discovered the tear under one of the arms. Michael had made some offhand comment about cutting himself at his sports club during a fencing exercise but… *Did men fight in their street clothes?* It seemed impractical but then so much of the masculine world looked excessively impractical in her opinion.

Grace chose a dress that she knew Michael favored her in and made quick work of it. She wished to be presentable just in case the note was an invitation to go out or more possibly, if Mrs. Clay was about to come by at any moment with a tray.

She unfolded the paper and smiled at the familiar hand.

Grace—

Business calls me away for a day.

I will return tomorrow, my love.

No more secrets.

M.

Grace's brow furrowed as some of her contentment faded. "Not until tomorrow?" The tantalizing promise about secrets was mildly comforting but she felt like an orphaned child before Christmas. Patience was not one of her favorite virtues. She dressed to face the day and then decided to escape the silence of the room to head downstairs to the kitchens to find Mrs. Clay.

She used the back hallway to skirt the dining room and made her way toward the hypnotic smell of roasting venison and vegetables. Grace carefully peeked through the doorway before entering. Mrs. Clay clapped her hands as Maggie pulled out a tray of potato cakes from the oven.

"Perfect! Oh, my little bird, what a gift you have in the kitchen! And such a quick learner!" Mrs. Clay wiped her hands on her apron. "There, now…test the edges."

Grace began to retreat, unwilling to interrupt Margaret's well-earned praise but Mrs. Clay stopped her with a gentle hail. "Mrs. Rutherford! What fun!"

"I apologize for halting the lesson," she said and took a step back. "The cakes look delicious, Miss Beecham."

"Maggie," Mrs. Clay interjected, "I'll leave you to it and check back in a few minutes, dearest." She turned to Grace. "I want to indulge in a bit of conversation with my favorite new guest!"

Grace blushed, but found herself well in hand as Mrs. Clay directed her down a long hallway to an apartment she had never seen. It was Mrs. Clay's private rooms and residence tucked onto the back of the ground floor. The sitting room was a delightful clutter and every level space was covered with framed tintypes of what could only be Mr. Clay and Mrs. Clay in happier times along with their extended family. The most ornate frame sat atop her mantle and held the tintype of a very small golden hair boy with eyes so full of fright and hope that it made Grace's heart ache to see him.

Tally. Probably not long after she'd first taken him in.

"What a lovely room!" she exclaimed politely before taking the seat she was offered.

"It's a lovely apartment! I have my own sitting room and what Mr. Clay always called his study, though he did more smoking and napping in it than paperwork, I can assure you! Then there are four bedrooms! Four! There's two through there and two above via a darling spiral staircase from the study. Can you imagine it?" She sighed happily as she took a seat on a worn velvet upholstered chair embroidered with butterflies. "It juts out a bit and gobbled up some of the garden when Mr. Clay built it but we had plans for a large family when we first wed and there was no talking the man out of it!"

Grace bit her lower lip. "You didn't …have a large family?"

Mrs. Clay shook her head. "No. We weren't fortunate to be blessed with babies of our own, but," she gestured around the room to all the pictures, "as you can see, I have no shortage of family! The Grove blessed me with children, with friends and guests and most of the staff have been with me forever! And I have my son, Tally, and fond hopes for his future."

"He is so clever, Mrs. Clay, and such a kind boy."

"And what of you?" Mrs. Clay asked.

"Pardon?"

"It's not my place to poke about someone else's business but—have you family, Mrs. Rutherford? Beyond that scoundrel who came in and caused such a ruckus, I mean?"

"Oh," Grace sat up a little straighter. "I have…That is to say, my father owns a milling concern in a village in the north. I'm afraid he's long been disinterested in me and I suspected it was more thrilling for him to watch Sterling from afar after he'd flown the nest. I'm told I was a very disappointing child since my arrival heralded the loss of my poor mother." Grace took note of the horrified look of pity on her landlady's face and decided that a more cheerful tone was required. "But true happiness has found him, at last! He is remarried to a very elegant woman who plays the pianoforte. She was far too accomplished to need…me…so I came to London to run my brother's house."

"How old were you, lamb?"

"Seventeen," Grace said. "I learned a great deal from the experience, of course, and—Sterling is…well, you've met my brother." Grace sighed. "Have I fallen in your estimation, Mrs. Clay?"

Mrs. Clay stood abruptly and shocked Grace into mirroring the gesture. *She's throwing me out! A miller's daughter probably isn't what she had in mind for her beloved giant and—*

For the second time, Mrs. Clay clutched her in a hug that robbed her of all thought. This. This was a woman who loved without reserve.

"Poor lamb!" Mrs. Clay sobbed. "Just wanted a mother's love, all those years! Dried up old disinterested prune! I hope that new wife gives him dyspepsia and they both suffer boils!" Mrs. Clay released her with a shocked gasp. "Not that I generally curse the worst of them but, well, I speak what I think!"

Grace struggled not to giggle and failed. "I do love you, Mrs. Clay, and if I may speak candidly, I can't see how a mother could have given me more than you already have. You've been so…warm."

"Shows what you know!" Mrs. Clay retrieved a handkerchief and dabbed at her eyes. "Well, let's sit then. What a mess I've made of it already!"

"A mess of what?" Grace asked.

Mrs. Clay took a deep breath and plunged ahead. "I know it's still the honeymoon and I've no right to press! But I'm worried that if I wait too long, the chance will go. And my Mr. Clay, God rest his soul, always said that it was better to jump early than forget to jump at all!"

"Where are we jumping?"

Mrs. Clay folded her hands and straightened her shoulders. "Here's the way of it, Mrs. Rutherford. I'm surprised not to have seen a few friendly faces coming to call on you, what with Mr. Rutherford's circle of friends being so formidable. I've not met all the wives but the ones I know well, I know to expect their calls of welcome and naturally, their compliments and best wishes on your match."

Grace nodded. "It was a sudden match and Michael has said nothing of introductions."

"Yes! It is still the honeymoon, after all! But don't let him be selfish for too long, Mrs. Rutherford. You deserve to have lovely friends and I'm happy to help with any tea parties or gatherings you care to host!"

Grace's confidence faltered. Michael had many friends. She'd picked up on that much and on their married status. In the flurry of locked doors and fighting Sterling followed by the ecstasy of her marriage, she'd missed the step of social introductions. But there'd not been one note or letter expressing well wishes or congratulations addressed to him, much less to her.

Not one.

Perhaps they disapprove of his choice?

"Ah, I've worried you!" Mrs. Clay interrupted her thoughts. "And that wasn't where I meant to land at all!"

"Please go on, Mrs. Clay." Grace focused her attention back on the visit. "We were jumping?"

"You see, I know that when your friends, old and new, come to call they might question that you're…living in an inn."

"Oh! Will they?"

"Yes! And I know a young lady likes to be the mistress of her own house and…I respect that! I don't have a say, do I?" Mrs. Clay's cheeks reddened and her eyes gleamed with unshed tears. "But we love our Mr. Rutherford, you see. And Tally—he looks up to him like a father, if the truth be told! So let me say it in a rush and then I'll have spoken my piece!"

Grace nodded. "O-of course!"

"Maggie's happy to move into one of my empty bedrooms and well, she's practically mine, too, isn't she?" Mrs. Clay folded her hands. "I'm no gypsy fortune teller but I have a feeling in my bones about that girl and my dear Tally. The age difference can't be much and in a few years, it'll be no gap at all. She's an angel, that little bird and so fun! And," Mrs. Clay leaned in with a conspiratorially wink, "I think he's already lost his heart to her."

Grace nodded again, unsure of how anyone in the world ever managed to disagree with such a sweet and urgent soul. "Miss Beecham is very dear but why would she have to forfeit her apartment?"

"Because you are a proper married couple! I want to combine the two apartments to make a proper home for you, here at the Grove."

Grace blinked. "It is…already a proper home."

"Of course, there's all the amenities, yes? It is like having a little manor of your own, if you think of it properly. A kitchen downstairs with meals served and maids for the cleaning, laundry and even assistance with errands! Mind, I'm aware that not all homes include all the comings and goings of an inn and the problems that might entail." Mrs. Clay sat back against her chair's cushions. "Beyond the semi-private sitting room and dining room, two rooms are all you have now and, well, our Mr. Rutherford takes up a bit of space, but if you'll try, I know you can be happy here. If we combine the two flats, you'd have four rooms and we can build to suit. What say you?"

"I say that's far too generous!" Grace squeaked then did her best to regain her composure. "You should know that Michael has never said a word of going elsewhere—and I don't care what anyone says, Mrs. Clay. We will live here as long as you will allow it."

"Truly?" Mrs. Clay asked, her fingers pressed against her lips.

"Truly."

Mrs. Clay lost the battle to hold off her tears and Grace opened her arms without hesitation to embrace the dear woman. "There, there! I would never take your Mr. Rutherford away."

"Oh, what a relief! You can't imagine how worried I've been!" Mrs. Clay sighed. "Though I will hit your brother with a broom if he tries to cross my door again."

Grace smiled as they found their chairs again and began to laugh.

CHAPTER TWENTY-EIGHT

Waiting in the dark inside the old church, St. Martin's within Ludgate, his
nerves were already on edge when a shadow appeared on the wall inside the
nave. He'd lit only a few candles in the nave to use the light as a visual alarm
for his enemy's arrival. The narrow building and small space meant there would
be no ambushes. He'd chosen it deliberately as sacred ground to awe Sterling
and keep him off balance. After all, the best place to meet the Devil was the last
place you expected. The famous church was within sight of St. Paul's cathedral
and enough of a landmark to ward off any destructive impulses if Porter meant
to try his hand at arson.

Michael hoped it was also sacred enough to ward off any exotic third
parties who might follow him there and consider duplicating their work at the
Thistle to stop the exchange. Cultures ranged with vast differences but he was
gambling that the beauty of Christopher Wren's architecture was universal
enough to aid his plans.

Michael stepped out from the concealment of a prayer alcove only to
stop in shock when he recognized the man who defiantly stood in a battle-ready
stance on the worn flagstones in the aisle.

"Ashe! Get out of here!"

"Is that the extent of your friendly greeting, old friend?"

"How in god's name did you discover this meeting place?" But even as
he asked, the answer came to him. "Never mind. Rowan."

"In his defense, he didn't tell me. You shared the deadline with all of
us, remember?" Ashe held his place in the shadows. "Of all the Jaded, he's the
one we've always gone to for aid. I did press him but he honestly didn't know
where you meant to meet the Jackal for this travesty."

Michael sighed. "I told him once this was my favorite place. I thought he'd guessed..." He shook off his melancholy and refocused on the dire crisis at hand. "You followed me."

"I did." Ashe shrugged his shoulders. "Perhaps not as skillfully as you'd have done it—but obviously I managed well enough, didn't I? However did you get them to open it for you at this hour?"

"Damn it, Ashe. Go! Go before Sterling gets here!"

"Before he gets here and you give him the sacred treasure we've all risked our lives to keep safe?" Ashe's voice tightened into a deadly growl. "You care for your 'wife', Michael, and I am the last man to underestimate the power of a woman's hand in a man's life. But hear me. I can't stand aside while you reward that—Jackal! I won't meekly cower while he dances off with his prize and my son's life goes unavenged!"

"Ashe. I understand how you feel but there's more at stake than you know. He's threatened Grace if I don't give it to him and even if I don't trust the Jackal, I can't risk her."

"It's you who's not to be trusted, Michael. We could keep her safe. There's no need to do this."

"No. I've been through all that. We can't live our lives in prison, shut off and under guard. And what about the people we love beyond whatever walls we construct? Can you guarantee their safety? Family, friends or anyone foolish enough to be publicly associated with any of the Jaded? Sooner or later, your guard would drop and I don't know if you would want to live with the consequences, Ashe."

Ashe took a step to his left, leaning up against the end of one of the pews keeping his left arm behind his back. But there was nothing casual or relaxed in the set of his shoulders and Michael wasn't fooled.

"Rutherford, his threats are hollow. Sterling is playing you and so is your Grace. What man threatens the life of his sister? It's a ruse and a flimsy one. She's seduced you and you're not thinking straight."

"I'd say it's you who's off. Ashe, it's gone too far. The Jackal will be here any minute and I will do what I must whether you agree or not. You waste your time and mine."

Ashe raised his left arm and revealed the loaded pistol in his hand. He pointed it squarely at Michael's chest. "No. And don't ask me to trust you again. I did and there you stand, a traitor."

"Are you going to shoot me, Ashe?"

"I might."

Michael held his breath and weighed out his options. Unfortunately, allowing Ashe to kill him wasn't possible. "Higher."

"What?"

"Aim higher for my head or draw it to the right. You're going to hit me in a lung which is not the quick end I'd hope for, Ashe. For God sakes! Just three inches right or—"

Ashe's brow furrowed as his hand unsteadily and against his better judgment obeyed Rutherford's surprisingly calm commands. At the first sign of movement, Michael closed the gap between them with lightning speed to strike Ashe's wrist upward and twist Ashe's arm so that his friend either dropped the pistol or allowed his shoulder to become separated from his body.

As expected, Ashe surrendered his hold on the pistol's handle.

Michael drove his full weight into Ashe's frame and sent them both over the carved pew where Blackwell bore the brunt of their landing against the unforgiving flagstones. The air slammed out of his lungs and Ashe soundlessly opened his mouth in pain but Michael knew that even a semi-conscious Ashe Blackwell was not good.

"Sorry, friend." Michael sat up with his thighs astride Ashe's chest and punched him in the jaw with brutal economic force and efficiency. Michael pulled his fist back for a second strike if needed but Blackwell was no longer moving.

Michael quickly checked Ashe's pulse to reassure himself that he hadn't murdered him and then sighed.

Damn it, Ashe. I hope that didn't break that pretty jaw of yours.

He stood to retrieve the pistol and tucked it into his belt as he heard the doors to the church opening. He nudged Ashe's foot with his boot for effect and turned to make the best of it.

"My goodness! I seem to have missed all the excitement." Sterling came down the aisle breathlessly. "Is he dead?"

Michael shifted his feet with a shrug of his shoulders and stepped over Ashe's prone body. "Does it matter?"

Sterling warily took one small step back. "You really are a cold-hearted bastard."

"You didn't believe me when I told you as much?" Michael asked. "How stupid are you, Sterling?"

"No need for insults, old friend." Sterling almost snarled.

"I agree." Michael looked around the church, the candlelight barely illuminating the arches and columns but it was still enough to touch each surface with a flickering rosy tint that made it look alive.

Michael pulled the leather pouch from his coat pocket and emptied it onto the palm of his hand. Even in the dim glow of the sanctuary, the large diamond glittered and gleamed with an untold number of rainbows that beckoned the eye. He held it up so that Sterling could enjoy the sight of the play of beauty and power in his palm.

"My God!" Sterling exclaimed with a whisper. "After all this time...there it is."

Michael tucked it back into the leather pouch and returned it to his pocket nervously. "Wait, Sterling," he said. "Not so fast. Remember your promise. It ends here. No more blackmail. No further payments for our liberty. Grace is free and you will leave us alone."

"Yes! Yes! Damn it, hurry! It's nearly midnight and like you, I have an appointment of my own to keep this very night as well!"

"You swear to hold to your word?" Michael asked again.

"Yes!" Sterling held out his hand impatiently, the tip of his tongue darting out to touch his lips. His hunger for the diamond was palpable and Michael reluctantly put his hand back in his pocket to pull out the pouch.

His fingers fisted it for a few seconds and he ground his teeth together in frustration. There was no turning back now. Slowly, he forced his own hand to slowly open, his fingers releasing its prize. "Here, then."

Sterling snatched the pouch from his palm with an audible crow of triumph, then pressed it to his heart. "At last!"

Michael dropped his head and watched the man reluctantly through the veil of his black lashes.

Sterling jauntily tossed the bag in the air and caught it before quickly tucking it away into a deep inner waistcoat pocket. "See how easy that was? All this time and it's really mine!"

Michael narrowed his gaze, a man in no mood to be taunted. "Run, Sterling. Take your prize and run to claim your reward. But if you stand there much longer, I'm the one who might forget our agreement and snap your neck merely for the joy of hearing that sound."

Sterling gifted him with a foul gesture and turned on his heels to hurry from the church, his footsteps echoing off the ceiling and walls. Michael stood as still as a statue and waited.

He waited for silence to reclaim the room and cleanse any traces of Sterling's foul presence. He knelt to check on Ashe, reassured by his friend's even breathing.

And then stood back up to walk toward the doors and wait for Death to come.

CHAPTER TWENTY-NINE

"Nipson anomemata me monan opsin," Michael whispered to himself as he carried Ashe out of the church over his shoulder. "Heard that one, Blackwell?" he asked the unconscious man. "Darius taught me that from off of the font. It means, cleanse my sin and not my face only."

He shifted Ashe to get a better hold of him with a sigh. "Prophetic, don't you think?" Michael raised one of his hands and signaled the carriage he'd hired and had standing by one hundred yards from the church's doorway. "Good man!"

"What have you got there, sir?" the driver asked with a wary look at the body over his customer's shoulder.

"Bit too much gin! I'm sending him home to his wife who will make minced meat pies out of him. Unless you think it more merciful to leave him on a stranger's doorstep? Do you think they'd be more understanding?" Michael jested.

"Than his *wife*? No doubt of it, sir! Mine nearly skinned me whole last time I came home after a few too many," the driver shared laughing then leaned down. "Do you need a hand there, governor?"

"No," Michael smiled. "I'm big enough to manage and even if I dropped him, I don't see how he'd complain. But here, let's send him to a friend's for safekeeping." Michael handed up a card with an address written on it along with a generous payment for the fare and then got Ashe inside the cab as best he could. Michael tucked Ashe's coat around him and wasted one sentimental moment putting his hand over his friend's. "Good-bye, Ashe."

He closed the carriage door firmly and signaled the driver to go.

Michael adjusted his hat and sighed. It was a long walk home, but he desperately wanted to clear his head. Ashe would arrive at Rowan's and he knew that he and Gayle would make sure his head was bandaged and that Ashe was revived. He expected Blackwell to wake up with a headache cursing Michael's name but he would be alive and intact.

The only permanent damage was the destruction of Michael's happiness.

His thigh began to ache where he'd apparently hit the pew when he tackled Ashe and if he were honest, a dozen lingering pains began to knit together to eat at his senses. The cold damp night air made his ribs twinge unreasonably and Michael readjusted his own coat to ignore them. "A good night's sleep and all is cured," he said aloud.

It was something his father used to say and it was nonsense, of course. Michael was too exhausted to even pretend optimism. He limped all the way home to the Grove, his arms and legs felt sodden, his joints infused with lead.

The east entrance was a welcome sight and he entered as quietly as he could, not wanting to disturb the sleeping inhabitants of the inn. He climbed the stairs and unlocked the door to their rooms, then pressed his forehead against the heavy oak.

Home.

Waning moonlight through the windows revealed the details and delicate changes that Grace had already wrought. There were flowers on the mantle next to his penny novels and her desk arranged with the day's handwritten pages under a purple glass paperweight he'd bought for her. Her slippers were tucked neatly by the bedside and Grace—his breath caught in his throat at the sight of her, sleeping with her hair fanned out beneath her, one hand trailing over the bed's edge, as if she were drifting on a raft and trailing her fingers in the water.

My Lady of Shallot, weaving her stories through the day, confined to her rooms. Except I want to show you the world, Grace, not keep you from it. I

*want to lay it at your feet and take you anywhere your wonderful imagination
directs you to go.*

It was over.

He'd kept her safe but at a very high price.

Michael quietly approached the bed, kneeling next to it to trail his
fingers across her face. Her eyes fluttered open and even in the moonlight, he
could see how blue they were.

"Is it...late?"

He nodded. "Very." Without a word he began to uncover her,
unwrapping her like an ethereal present to bare her slowly to his touch.
Moonlight through the diamond paned windows caressed her skin and dusted
her beauty with its silver powers. She was a feast for his senses and he sat back
on his heels to take it all in.

His beautiful Grace.

Mine.

One last time.

Breathing in her skin, he leaned forward and began to sample every
surface, mapping each contour and savoring her responses to even this first
ghostly foray of his hands across her body. He kissed the arches of her feet and
made her giggle when he tried to nibble on her toes.

"Michael! I forbid you to suckle my toes!"

He shook his head, relinquishing her foot. "I'll yield the toes if you
submit to my next idea no matter what."

She looked at him, the last vestiges of sleep leaving her face, her eyes
alert and bright. "That's a vague premise."

"You said you trusted me, Grace."

"True," she said. "Very well, if my toes are to be left intact, then I am
your willing slave."

He smiled. "You are no one's slave, Grace Rutherford. But as my
mistress, let's see if we can't make you pleased at the bargain you've made."

He stood next to the bed and divested himself of his clothes, all the while relishing the sight of Grace naked and unashamed sprawled across the blankets. Once he was free of every stitch of his clothing, he climbed up on the bed to make a closer study of his enticing bride. He pushed her soft thighs apart and made a leisurely study of her sex, ignoring her half-hearted squeak of modesty.

"Shh. Remember the toes," he reminded her playfully and then positioned himself to kneel between her legs. Her sex was so pink and ripe, glistening with her arousal and the scent of it was musk sweet and compelling.

"Michael—"

He kissed her and effectively ended the discussion.

He licked the tight hot bud of her clit and explored the tender flesh around her channel with his fingers, circling the core of her need without pressing inside. Her thighs pressed against his ears but still he didn't relent. He shifted his hands away to hold her hips as she tried to buck and wiggle away from the relentless assault of his tongue. He teased a small ridge above her pearl and realized that whatever sensations it evoked were likely welcome as Grace began to keen in ecstasy. Her clit swelled against his mouth and he knew he had the way of it.

She came against his mouth in reckless spasms and he drank the dew of her body with the pride of a triumphant warrior conquering Aphrodite herself. *Mine, damn it!*

"Michael! That was—you have ruined me! I…" Grace pressed her hands against her eyes. "I have lost the ability to form sentences…I think…Can a climax injure a person's language skills?"

"It won't last," he said smiling as he shifted up to cover her body with his. "You do it to me all the time and *eventually* I always recover."

His cock leapt up to press against her thighs and Grace shifted to accommodate him, eagerly reaching for him to guide him toward the slippery taut entrance of her body. He fit perfectly inside her and her muscles immediately gripped the head of his erection as if her body's hunger were a separate being.

He dismissed the urge to drive into her and give in to the voracity of his appetite for her. He lingered there, notched up against her with the silken head working against the sensitive clit.

"Michael, please!"

He shook his head, a sadness seeping into his bones. He wouldn't rush it for any price. If this were the last time that she allowed him to touch her, to make love to her, to hold her; he would savor every moment.

He entered her so slowly he feared he would climax before he'd touched her deepest core. She fought the pace, desperately trying to urge him on, biting his shoulder in her frustration.

"There, there, dearest. Soon now…"

Too soon, he was there. Melded into her in an embrace that redefined his soul and then he had to move. He had to take her and all the divine pleasure that Grace's body alone could provide. But this was no frenzied rush to release. Even Grace had accepted the leisurely build that tugged him along on a relentless path. Each thrust was measured and complete, every turn of his rigid member inside her sheath was wrought with a raw tension that left him breathless.

At last, it was a fever that broke over him in waves. He came with her in a free fall of give and take, that made every movement a strange prayer, an homage to the unique beauty in his arms. She was all that he wanted. There would never be another to take her place and when the light of love in her eyes was dimmed to hatred, it would a mortal blow.

Even so, it didn't matter.

Loving her was all that was left to him. And he had no intentions of ceasing until the end; not until the very bitter end.

✳ ✳ ✳

Michael sipped his morning tea, savoring the quiet light in the private dining room outside their door. He'd slept in and found a note from his wife explaining that Maggie had offered to teach her to use her hands to talk more easily with Tally. She was downstairs enjoying her first lesson and would return with lemon biscuits later.

It was just like her, he thought, to be kind and make the effort for Tally. *And to remember the lemon biscuits.*

Michael heard them coming, not that they were attempting to be quiet. The door to the east entrance downstairs opened several times and by the sound of the number of men's boots coming up the stairs, they'd apparently decided to come *en masse.* Michael set his teacup down and kept his seat. "Gentlemen, good morning."

Ashe led the way with a very unhappy looking band of brothers behind him. Michael noted the bruised shadow on his chin and had to swallow hard at the raw relief at seeing Blackwell obviously on his feet and recovered.

"I was expecting you." He stood slowly, holding his hands up as if to demonstrate that he was unarmed. "Though a very tired and sore part of me was hoping to expect you later in the afternoon."

Rowan sighed. "Blackwell was sure it couldn't wait."

Ashe's temper flared. "It won't! The Jackal has the mystic diamond, thanks to your vile betrayal, and there's no time to waste!"

"We're going to go after it, Michael," Galen stated flatly. "Without your aid, obviously, but also we would hope, without your interference."

"I see." Michael nodded. "You've a plan already?"

"We do!" Ashe growled. "I still can't believe you've done this, Rutherford. But just in case you had the vague hope of ever crossing our doorsteps again, this circle is closed to you!"

"Blackwell," Darius's voice was calm. "We don't need to cover that ground."

"I understand," Michael said. "But here, before you gallop back down the stairs, ransack Sterling's home and Ashe ends up hurting himself, you might want this." Michael reached in his pocket and held out a leather pouch toward Rowan.

"What is it?" Rowan asked as he took the bag from Michael's hand.

"Open it." Michael sat back down and added more hot tea to his cup from the steaming pot on the tray.

"My God!" Ashe exclaimed as a diamond the size of a large plum came to fiery life in the palm of Rowan's hand. "Is that...? But how is that...possible?"

Michael added two lumps of sugar to his tea and milk as he spoke. "I've never had much talent with sleight of hand but I deliberately made sure the church wasn't well lit, so that might have helped. I had two leather pouches in my pocket last night. I showed Sterling the diamond, then appeared to have a change of heart so I could it back in my pocket."

"You gave him a different stone?"

Michael nodded. "A lovely hunk of diamond about the size of a peach pit but terribly flawed, I'm afraid." Michael looked up at them all. "It had to be a good size or he would have questioned it."

"You didn't give him the diamond?" Ashe repeated the question uselessly as he sat down in shock near the fireplace. "Why not tell me your intentions? Last night, you had every chance but you allowed me to believe the worst!"

"I had no choice," Michael confessed. "At any second, Sterling was going to be within earshot and one word to the contrary would have foiled everything."

"He wasn't in earshot when we spoke at the sports club or...you could have told us, Rutherford!" Rowan protested. "We'd have kept your secrets without risking your neck!"

Michael hesitated. "I needed Sterling to believe that he had me. I never knew exactly when things were going to come into play and I needed your reactions to be genuine and natural. If we appeared cozy or if there were signs of your support, he'd have become suspicious."

"Damn it!" Ashe ran a hand through his hair. "I'm a bit ashamed to realize my natural reaction was to behave like an ass."

"None of us have behaved well," Galen added. "For that, we're truly sorry, Michael."

"Wait," Josiah spoke up. "What about Sterling? Aren't we in the same bind again? Once he finds out that Michael didn't give him the right diamond, he's bound to be furious."

"He won't ever bother us again." Michael finished his tea and set the cup down. "I made sure of it."

"You made sure of it?" Galen asked. "What did you do, Michael?"

"Sterling borrowed money to finance his schemes and the promise of that diamond was his only collateral. He admitted more than he meant to about the pressure he was under and that he had his own deadline to meet." Michael leaned back in the chair as his friends began to settle into their own seats to hear the tale. "In fact, I think he meant to meet them after the exchange to deliver the gem into their hands."

"There's an awkward moment," Rowan noted.

"Exactly," Michael agreed. "Because once Sterling hands over that common rock to men who have waited impatiently for years for a stone without equal, they'll call in their debts and it won't be taken in coin. Sterling is gone, as surely as the sun rises, his body will never be recovered." A small ball of ice formed in his stomach as he spoke aware that he'd literally arranged for Sterling's demise and while he hadn't dirtied his own hands he knew it wouldn't make a difference to Grace.

"How do you know this? If he looked at it before his own meeting… How can you be so sure he won't double-back and demand the real treasure?"

"For several reasons. If he'd looked in the bag and discovered the switch, his rage would have brought him immediately to my door. It was a long sleepless night waiting but he never came." Michael ran a hand through his hair.

"And the men holding the Jackal's leash? Won't they think to come after us?" Darius asked.

"I don't expect them to. Yesterday, I had two notes delivered by courier in the city. I wrote an anonymous note to the secondary buyer he was lining up for the diamond warning them that Sterling was a con artist. The prince's mistress, Miss Pierre, wouldn't have taken the news lightly considering she'd already given him an advance payment. I told her that she was being swindled, that the East India Trading Company was being cheated and that if she received word of the diamond's availability, it would be a ruse. They won't be able to ignore her complaints."

"And the other note?"

"A bit riskier but I didn't want to leave any avenues open. I wrote to Lord Waverly via my lawyer that a certain man in his employ had been harassing me for some time now about imaginary treasures and demonic diamonds. I told him that I'd met Mr. Porter once in India while he was mumbling about mystic gems and that I had made a crude joke about possessing a treasure that I hide in my piss pot. Mr. Porter must have misunderstood me. I told Lord Waverly that as a simple soldier with a small pension, I would appreciate it if he would ask Mr. Sterling Porter to stop haranguing me or perhaps escort his man to an asylum."

"It's too ridiculous!"

"Exactly," Michael agreed. "Between their own doubts, Sterling's bluster, and my blatant misrepresentation of the facts, they will never ever look in the Jaded's direction again, god willing."

"When have the gods ever been willing?" Josiah asked.

"When the right hands have the diamond and have arranged to keep it safe. Prophecy respected, right, D?" Ashe teased with a wry grin.

"Not necessarily. You are all forgetting that extremely interested third party. The one who set fire to the Thistle and haunted every jewel cutter from London to Edinburgh," Darius replied. "If they believe that Michael gave Sterling and the East India what they were after, then we may be in even more danger than ever before."

Michael raised his hand. "No. I met one of their assassins accidentally after he tried to kill me and…" Michael shrugged his shoulders. "I invited him to meet me after midnight, after Sterling had left."

Shock in the room was almost universal. "You—*invited* a would-be assassin to meet you in a dark secluded location after midnight? Just in case, Sterling didn't kill you?" Ashe asked.

Michael smiled. "I wanted him to see that I still had the diamond; that it was still in my hands. He seemed satisfied with my vow to protect it with my life."

"My god, we're finally safe and out of it," Darius whispered. "Thanks to Rutherford!"

"The Jaded are safe," Michael stated flatly. "And my oath is fulfilled to Ashe to see to Sterling Porter. There is no way that Sterling survived to see the sun rise and if he did, then it's to beg for a quick end. The Jackal is finished and by the hands of the devils he served."

"But not your hands?" Grace asked from the top step where she stood frozen. "What do they call it when you watch someone walk to their doom and say nothing?"

CHAPTER THIRTY

"Grace."

"Who are these men?" she asked and stepped forward, her face pale. "Who are these men who all seem so calm and pleased to discuss my brother's demise, magical diamonds and jackals?"

Every man abruptly came to his feet and Michael knew every single one of them was wishing he was somewhere else...including himself.

Michael took one slow breath. "Gentlemen, I believe you haven't yet met my wife. Grace, these are my good friends—whose names escape me at the moment only because...I fear I might...be suffering a stroke."

In his worst nightmares, he was always on his knees initiating a confession to a very horrified Grace who was sobbing and unable to look at him. But in that nightmare, they had always been very much alone.

No, this is definitely worse.

None of the Jaded had recovered to speak yet and the delay was only a few heartbeats but to Michael it was an eternity falling away from his hands. He expected her to flee in tears, find Mrs. Clay and force him to begin a very long uphill siege. But once again, Grace's approach to her world had nothing to do with anyone's expectations.

"Eavesdropping," she began as she climbed the last step, "is a terrible thing and in books, I always found it a weak literary device for revealing someone's true nature. I always thought that if a person truly *knew* someone, they would hardly need to be reduced to standing on stair landings to realize that—" her voice broke and her eyes filled with unshed tears. "To realize that the man you love has married you only as part of some...twisted plot."

Ashe cleared his throat. "Madam, I grant you that circumstances are beyond strange but it's—"

Darius put a hand on his shoulder. "Perhaps we should go and leave Michael to explain things more clearly."

Grace folded her arms defiantly, apparently aware that she was in fact, blocking the only exit from the room as she stood squarely at the top of the stairs bottling them in. "Explanations are not part of my husband's skills," she said. "But how lucky for me to have the company of so many well-informed men. My brother—" Grace took a moment to steady her nerves. "My brother was unkind and often cruel but I never remember any word of a diamond. He did not speak of his time in India but I know he had vast hopes of advancing himself. He was ambitious and…"

"Grace," Michael began carefully. "He was more than ambitious. But we never sought him out. We're no gang of thugs. We were simply men who crossed his path once. Fate makes odd enemies sometimes and your brother was never willing to accept that he was alone in his quest for wealth and power. We never meant to interfere with his schemes. And if there had been any chance of him relenting and leaving us alone, all of us would have preferred it. I would have preferred it."

"Did you kill him, Michael?" she asked in a fearful whisper.

Michael shook his head slowly but he owed her the truth. He loved her too much to keep any more secrets. "I didn't but I knew he would be killed by others for his debts and lies and I did nothing to stop it."

She gasped and this time, Michael was sure she would run but the rapid rhythm of a new set of footsteps pounding up the stairs interrupted the scene. Tally slipped past her, his face set as he ignored everyone in the room but Michael to hand over a folded note. Michael took it from him but didn't open it. He held it out to Rowan. "It's addressed to you, Dr. West."

"Gayle's handwriting," Rowan opened the paper and read it immediately. Only Michael was close enough to realize that his breathing changed and that something very serious was underway. Rowan looked up at Ashe. "It's Caroline. Gayle sends word that she's in labor. It's time."

"It's too soon," Ashe said in a hoarse whisper. "Weeks yet, God's mercy!"

Rowan gripped him by the shoulders and forced him to look into his eyes. "All will be well, Ashe. But I need to leave now to attend her as quickly as I can."

"*We* will all go," Galen amended. "Blackwell cannot await the babe's arrival alone." The unspoken message was clear. *Ashe can't do this alone and if it ends badly, it would take all of them to prevent him from harming himself to follow his beloved Caroline to her grave.*

"Let's go then!"

"Ashe and Josiah are with me," Rowan calmly announced. "We'll see you at the house."

Michael stepped aside, agonized to be left behind but he couldn't see abandoning Grace, not when they had so much yet to say to each other. Grace deserved an opportunity to storm and rage and Michael wouldn't rob her of it.

But once again, the Jaded intervened.

"My name is Galen Hawke." Galen stepped forward to take Grace's arm, as if they'd decided to head out for a stroll in a park. "Come on, Mrs. Rutherford! You two can fight in the carriage."

"But, I—"

"You are one of us, by marriage, and as you'll soon learn, this is a circle that one does not simply step away from without very good cause," Galen explained as he propelled her quickly and carefully down the stairs. "Rowan is an excellent physician and we'll have to hurry but I feel compelled to say that your brother was the worst kind of man and while death gives many villains a certain saint-like aura, I fail to see it. Besides, *if* he's dead, it's through his own stupidity and criminal actions, wouldn't you agree?"

"Sterling…was hardly a criminal! He was…ruthless but…"

Michael was right behind them. "Lord Winters, I don't see how this is helping."

Galen ignored him. "The Jaded are cursed with misunderstandings early in our relationships, Mrs. Rutherford. I'm sure you'll sort Rutherford out but for the moment, we must attend to Ashe and offer him our compassion and prayers."

"The Jaded? I'm sorry, which of you is Ashe?"

Galen pointed. "That gentleman vaulting past Dr. Rowan West's waiting carriage there. The one who just commandeered that hackney and is even now shoving the driver aside. He is also probably about to whip those poor horses into a ridiculous and death-defying gallop through the streets of London…"

The hackney cab pulled away with a lurch and Grace's breath caught in her throat at the reckless speed of it. "I see. He is the father-to-be I take it?"

"Theo!" Rowan called up to his driver as he helped Josiah up into his carriage. "We're off to Blackwell's, as quick as you can, please."

Theo nodded, "Guessed as much!" As soon as Rowan's feet left the pavement, Theo snapped his whip. "Off then!"

Michael held out his hand to help her climb up into Lord Winter's waiting coach but Grace had a fleeting flash of stubborn rebellion. "I could wait here just as easily."

"Darius Thorne, madam." Darius stepped forward and held out his hand instead. "I don't think Michael would survive the worry that before we return you'd change your mind and decide to go without hearing him out." He moved his hand subtly forward. "And there's no time to delay. We are keeping the good doctor from his work and from Mrs. Blackwell's side."

Grace sighed, unwilling to cause any woman distress at such a time. "Very well." She took Darius's hand and made her way into the luxurious coach's interior. Darius and Michael joined her, as Lord Winters climbed up next to the driver to also take matters into his own hands.

She wasn't sure what to think or feel. She'd come back up those stairs so excited to demonstrate some of her new hand words to Michael only to be stopped in her tracks by the most unreal conversation she'd ever heard.

Jackals and diamonds! Sterling dead? Dealings with a prince's mistress and secret societies!? My brother? The man who never seem to have a blink of creative spark in his entire body but I'm now to accept that he is some sort of hidden mastermind or hardened criminal?

"What are you thinking, Grace?" Michael asked quietly, the gentle anxiety and open pain in his eyes making her chest ache.

Grace sat up, hating the surge of weakness that washed through her at the sight of her beloved husband. "I'm thinking that I don't even have my bonnet! I'm thinking that only an idiot allows herself to be kidnapped without a single word of protest and..." Her throat closed with raw emotion and she had to swallow hard to catch her breath. "I might yet hate you, Michael," she whispered.

"Hate me later, my love. Time enough to consign me to Hades but for this moment, be with me."

She closed her eyes and then opened them to watch the streets of London pass by the window. *Sterling might be dead and my beloved husband is somehow involved by his own admission... How could the man who made love to me so tenderly be a cold-blooded murderer? How is that possible?*

Lord Winters' words were echoing in her head. *'Your brother was the worst sort of man'. God, that sounds true, doesn't it? I thought him petty and horrible, cruel and unkind but...can his passing affect me so little? Is this grief that I feel, or guilt?*

One thing alone is certain. I've been kidnapped to attend the childbed vigil of a stranger by a collection of men I have never met along with a husband whose character I now can't fathom. If Mr. A. R. Crimson had written this, Mr. Pollson would throw it in my face and call it fantastical nonsense!

CHAPTER THIRTY-ONE

The logistics of hiring a wet nurse were a welcome, if temporary, distraction for Gayle. The drama that was unfolding in the bedroom upstairs was too much for her to manage alone. Isabel Thorne was staying by Caroline's side while Gayle hurried to attend to the task at hand. All she could do was hang on until Rowan arrived, praying that his presence would help and his experience bring Caroline back to health.

She knew better than to pray for miracles. Her training had been too thorough and the painful lessons on the limitations of medical skill and science were already absorbed. But if anyone could defy the odds and save Caroline's life again, it was Rowan.

Mrs. Clark knocked at the door. "I have Mrs. Sabrina Martin downstairs, Mrs. West."

"Very good." Gayle wasted no time, following the housekeeper down to the salon where the woman was waiting. It was bound to be an awkward and rushed appointment. Gayle knew the idealized requirements for a wet nurse and closed her eyes briefly before opening the door to summon her wits.

Robust.

Healthy.

Pink cheeks and bright eyes.

Not too pretty.

Broad at the hip and plentiful in the bosom.

Gayle turned the handle of the door and entered the room.

"Mrs. West?" the young woman spoke, rising quickly from her seat on the chair by the fireplace.

Gayle took it all in at once. The infant sleeping in the basket on the chair next to her, the pale cast to the woman's face and the hungry, haunted look in her eyes.

Fragile.

Underfed.

Ethereally beautiful.

Thin.

Gayle took another steadying breath and nodded. "Mrs. Martin. I've no time for polite exchanges or pleasantries and for that, I am genuinely sorry. The mistress of the house has given birth to twins and we were—unprepared. A challenge under the best of circumstances but I don't believe she has the constitution to sustain them both."

"I understand."

"Have you…the capacity to feed another infant? Or even two?" Gayle clasped her hands in front of her. "We'll supplement whatever you supply with a mixture of milk, sugar and other nutrients to accommodate both of the babies and I have every hope that Mrs. Blackwell will recover to…participate. But if she doesn't…"

"Yes. I know I'm slight," she answered, a modest blush creeping up her cheeks, "but my milk is very plentiful. I have my son here, and he thrives! I will wean him to ensure that my employer's babes are fed first. I have personal references. I am a moral woman, Mrs. West." Desperation colored her tone. "I don't drink spirits and have never partaken of—"

Gayle held up a hand to stop her. "Let's not speak of denying your own child nutrition, Mrs. Martin. But, what of your husband?"

The woman paused, her eyes dropping to study the patterned carpet at her feet, before looking up with a hollow gaze that betrayed her pain. "He died seven months ago. Paul was in a fire brigade and there was a factory blaze. It's the two of us, my son and I. I've no family."

Gayle believed her. It was enough. There was nothing brash or jarring in her appearance and demeanor to set off any misgivings. A chubby hand popped up from the confines of the basket and Mrs. Martin's attention was immediately diverted.

"May I?" Gayle asked.

"Y-yes, of course." The mother stepped away cautiously, and Gayle liked her all the more for the watchful eye she kept as Gayle retrieved the infant from his makeshift nest.

Gayle smiled at his clean sweet bright face and full pink cheeks. Here was the best assurance she could ever look for of Mrs. Martin's maternal care. "Hello, little man. He is a treasure, Mrs. Martin. What is his name?"

"Paul, for his father."

"What a quiet gentleman you are, Mr. Paul!"

"He is a very good boy, Mrs. West. He's no trouble! No trouble at all!" she said anxiously.

The baby cooed at Gayle and reached for her nose, making her smile. "Of course, he isn't." She handed him to his mother. "You are hired, Mrs. Martin."

"Oh!" She said softly, sitting with her babe as if the shock of the good news had robbed her of her ability to stand. "Thank God!"

Gayle walked over to the bell pull to summon Mrs. Clark, but at the first tug the housekeeper appeared in the doorway and betrayed that she'd been listening all along. Gayle didn't blame her for eavesdropping. The matter was too dire and too critical for discretion, and she knew that no lack of blood-ties would make the housekeeper's heart less involved. "Mrs. Clark, can you see Mrs. Martin to the room next to the nursery and make sure that she and Paul are comfortably settled?"

"Yes, Mrs. West."

"Mrs. Martin, Mr. Blackwell is the master of this house. I am merely a family friend and my husband, their friend and physician. But for now, Mrs. Clark will have your charge. Please use the servant's back stairs up to the nursery and be discreet to keep out of your new master's sight. Mrs. Blackwell is very ill and your presence will not give him comfort."

"I understand. Please—my greatest sympathies for—I pray, she recovers." Mrs. Martin stood with her basket and baby, readying to follow Mrs. Clark.

"As do we all, Mrs. Martin." Gayle squared her shoulders and turned her attention to the housekeeper. "Mrs. Clark, please see that Sabrina is fed wholesome meals with the freshest ingredients and plenty of meat. Nothing too spicy, but I will trust to your common sense in ensuring her best health in order to provide for the babies. We'll hire a nanny for days and another for nights as a precaution to see us through these first few weeks." Gayle looked at both women somberly. "You are the inner circle that will keep Ashe's newborn daughters alive. They will depend on you both for sustenance and care. Please. We must get them to nurse as quickly as possible. They are so small and fragile. Ring for me if their breathing seems labored or if there are any changes."

Sabrina instinctively kissed the soft head of her own child unconsciously grateful for his health and openly wishing the same for the infants she was about to encounter upstairs. "I won't sleep until we've gotten a first feeding, Mrs. West. I swear it."

Mrs. Clark's eyes filled with tears and she put a gentle hand on Sabrina's arm. "No, dear. You'll rest as you can! We'll get you some hearty soup and see to them together. They were sleeping like little angels and Daisy is guarding them like a bear. I know a trick with flannel and buttermilk to help them latch if anyone is struggling—"

"Ladies," Gayle interrupted gently. "I'll leave you to it. I need to get back upstairs to see to Caroline." She left the pair to make over their plans and bond on their way up to the nursery. By the looks of Mrs. Martin's worn shoes and thin coat, more than one life had been saved with her arrival.

But she couldn't celebrate that now.

For now, there was Caroline.

And Ashe, to manage when he returned. She knew the men were all together at Michael's—or she prayed that they were since that was where she'd sent one of two duplicate urgent notes.

Rowan, my love, hurry. I can't do this alone. I think the babes are safe but it's all so precarious!

"I'm here!" Ashe shouted as he burst through the front doors. "Godwin!" He saw her and stopped in his tracks. "Gayle. Tell me."

She took one deep breath to steady herself and immediately regretted the mistake. He interpreted the slight delay as a tragic hesitation on her part and she watched the color drain from his face as he began to stagger toward the stairs.

"Ashe! Twins!"

"What?" he froze.

"You have twin daughters and Caroline is upstairs resting. I am concerned for—"

The transformation happened so quickly she couldn't register it before he'd run past her up the staircase, taking the risers three at a time.

"Ashe, wait!" But no power could slow him and Gayle yielded for a moment, sinking down onto the step to put her face in her hands. But the weakness passed quickly. There was a patient to attend to and Gayle accepted her duties, as a physician and a friend. She would have to shield Ashe if she must and see to Caroline's comfort. Her foot touched the ninth riser on her ascent when the front doors burst open again and the welcome chaos of juggled coats and hurried greetings filled the foyer as Michael, Galen, Josiah and a woman she didn't recognize stepped inside, along with—

"Rowan!"

He pulled her into his arms, and Gayle experienced a rush of warm calm. Michael caught her eye over Rowan's shoulder as he nodded briefly and it was understood that introductions would wait.

"I'm here, dearest." He stepped back, reading her instantly. "Where's Ashe?"

"I'm afraid he's already bolted upstairs to be with her. I didn't have the heart or the strength to prevent him from reaching Caroline."

"No one does, dearest. Let's go upstairs and see to her together."

"Yes." She briefed him quietly as they went up the stairs. "We were visiting when the first labor pains began and I started to make preparations. Mrs. Clark and the others were champions and I think I washed and sterilized everything but the walls as we went along. As you know, we both guessed that we had another four to six weeks. All the experience I have told me that there was no need to hurry and that first babies can take hours and hours, but by the time I set pen to paper to summon you for what I believed would be a long and strenuous labor—the crisis was upon me and I've had no experience with…"

Rowan smiled. "Twins?"

She crossed her arms. "I'm already nervous, Rowan. Don't mock me."

"Twins are nothing to discount for the danger and complications they can present. I'm glad you sent for me, despite all your confident boasting that you could manage without me." He shifted his bag to his other hand to reach for her and pull her close. "Did you send for a wet nurse?"

"All hired and in attendance."

"That's my girl." Rowan kissed her, a quick but thorough kiss that altered the color in his wife's cheeks and reassured her of his affections. "You've a deft hand at these things, Gayle. There's not a physician in England who can match your instincts."

"The babies are so tiny, Rowan, but outwardly perfect."

"And their lungs?"

"Remarkably clear, and the heartbeats are very strong."

"We're a few weeks early but that's not to say they won't thrive." Rowan took one deep breath and then asked the harder question. "Caroline?"

"It's what you'd feared. The blood loss was substantial. I stopped the worst of the hemorrhaging but I couldn't stop it entirely. She needs surgery, but in my opinion she's too weak to survive it. I don't like her color. Rowan, I'm afraid she's failing."

"Blood loss," he repeated the words, thinking aloud. "How's her temperature?"

"It's higher than I'd like, but she swears she's cold."

"I'll examine her. We can speculate on this stair landing until dawn and accomplish nothing." He took her by the hand and they both headed down the hallway where the future of Ashe's happiness once again hung by a thread.

CHAPTER THIRTY-TWO

It was a very odd introduction to his friends. While they waited in the library together for news, Grace began to gain a better appreciation of the circle that Lord Winters had spoken of. Runners were sent to courier word to Mr. Hasting's wife and to Lady Winters. Mrs. Isabel Thorne was already upstairs in attendance to her friend Caroline and Mr. Godwin, the butler, shared that Darius and his wife were in residence as guests of the Blackwells.

Grace pressed her fingertips to her temples to push back a headache. It was a great deal of information to take in at once. The "Gayle" whose note had sent Tally into action turned out to be Dr. Rowan West's wife and a professional nurse or midwife of some sort. Mrs. West's rare standing as both a wife and a woman with a profession of her own gave Grace a bit of hope and insight; insight into Michael's acceptance of her desire to earn money of her own with her writing and hope that his sentiments might be genuine on the subject and not a facet of his deception.

Rowan came back down to talk to the men and Michael reluctantly retreated with the others for a private conference regarding Mrs. Blackwell's status, but not before he asked, "Will you wait for me, Grace?"

She nodded but did not answer him, making an effort to suddenly study the buttons on his waistcoat. *If I speak to you, it will be hard to hang onto this fury,* she told herself. *And it doesn't seem right to be anything but furious at a man who marries you because...*

"I'll be back in a few minutes." He retreated with the others and the ornate solid door to the library closed behind him.

Her brow furrowed and she pinched the bridge of her nose. *Truth be told, I don't know why he married me anymore, do I?*

The house was too quiet for her comfort and Grace dreaded the notion that the silence of the grave had already contaminated what was probably once a joyous home. She wondered about the babies and prayed that Mr. Ashe Blackwell would find it in his heart not to blame his daughters if the worst came to pass. Grace knew from her own childhood that a father who cared only enough to educate and ignore you was almost as bad as none at all.

There was a gentle knock at the door and a pale young woman stepped inside with hair so blonde it was white. Grace had the fleeting impression of a lovely phantom before she approached, substantial and living, in a periwinkle silk day dress edged in ivory lace. The woman shyly extended her hand. "I am Isabel Thorne and I'm…so sorry."

"Sorry?" Grace's fingers fluttered nervously at her throat. "Is it bad news about Mrs. Blackwell? Oh, God…"

"No!" Isabel quickly interrupted her. "She lives and while she is still very weak, Rowan is confident that she will make a full recovery." Isabel smiled. "Gayle was a wonder and saved her life. Her husband gives her full credit though I suspect he also had a hand in the reversal."

Grace nodded, relief shivering down her spine. "Thank goodness! I know it seems strange to be so overcome since I've never met her but…their faces when they heard she was in distress—I will never forget the look of heartbreak in Michael's eyes." Grace bit her lower lip and did her best to bring her mind back to the present. "I should have introduced myself. I'm Grace Rutherford. But you seem to have known that. Why were you apologizing to me?"

Isabel sighed and gestured elegantly toward a pair of chairs by a reading table. "Please let me explain."

Grace sat down as primly as she could. Isabel Thorne looked like a creature carved from bone china who even pregnant had the kind of innate confidence and beauty that made Grace acutely aware of her rustic background. Grace only hoped she didn't have a smudge on her own nose from leaning against the windows in the carriage. "Mrs. Thorne, you're a stranger to me. I can't think of a trespass that requires an apology that wouldn't also require…a prior meeting?"

Isabel smiled but her eyes were sad. "I wish that were true. Darius made a point of finding me upstairs after you arrived. You see, there was a terrible misunderstanding."

"Go on."

"When we heard of your impending marriage to Mr. Rutherford, the circumstances were less than ideal."

Grace's cheeks flooded with color. "Mr. Rutherford acted to shield me from scandal but I can assure you that he did *nothing* wrong that night at the ball! My brother was so convinced otherwise that there was no arguing with him and—I'm…" Grace put her cool hands up to her face. "Well, to be honest, now I'm not sure what happened but I was glad to be quit of my brother's house and no matter what lies were told to me, the truth is Michael saved my life when he married me." Grace's eyes widened in shock as she heard herself and she almost squeaked in misery.

Isabel shook her head and reached out with a comforting hand to pull Grace's hands into hers. "No! I am the *last* woman in England to raise an eyebrow over the threat of scandal! My own downfall was gleeful fodder for so many but I have no regrets. Love conquers all."

"I'm not sure that's true but I'm happy for you, Mrs. Thorne."

"Let me begin again." Isabel released her hands and nervously pushed back a stray curl from her cheek. "The men have a friendship and a bond, but so do the wives of the Jaded."

"The Jaded?" Grace asked.

"It's a terrible name for their little club started in jest and not very apt. We've campaigned them to change it but I confess, it's grown on us."

"Us," Grace echoed doing her best to follow the tangled threads of the conversation.

"The wives. I was the newest addition to the feminine inner circle, until you," Isabel said. "And you should have received the same warm welcome that we all did and that is why I'm apologizing."

"Oh!" Grace exclaimed. "Please don't."

Eyes the color of white opals shimmered with unshed tears. "I must. It was deliberate, the way we refused to call on you! Well, Caroline couldn't of course, being confined but we closed ranks against you so quickly. I think of it now and I shudder!"

"B-because you thought I'd been ruined?" Grace asked. "Isn't that understandable?"

"Because we were certain that you were conspiring with your brother and that you intended to hurt Michael," Isabel said.

Grace caught her breath. "I would never hurt Michael."

"After everything that Sterling Porter has done, we didn't think it beneath him to use a woman as bait—even his own sister." Isabel shifted in her chair, uncomfortable with the subject. "We thought the worst of you. We thought you were cruelly toying with Michael's affections to strike against him and we feared that Michael's honor was forfeit if he were the one playing some kind of game in which he would marry you for a tactical advantage."

"Did he?" Grace asked, an edge of desperation in her voice.

"Absolutely not!" Isabel shook her head firmly. "No. Gayle had it directly from Rowan's own lips that when he begged Michael to see reason, Michael refused. He refused because he said he loved you. When the Jaded told him that they would cut him off, when they accused him of being a traitor and turning against them, he stood fast—because he loved you! They are like brothers, Mrs. Rutherford. But he endured having every one of their doors closed to him for the love of a woman; for the younger sister of their sworn enemy."

"For me," Grace echoed softly. "It makes no sense!" Grace took a slow deep breath and then another. "Mrs. Thorne," she began slowly. "I am still not sure what Sterling…what he was, what he did. What I overheard this afternoon, it shook me to my core! My brother? A villain? A killer? It's a bad dream."

"You poor thing!"

Grace made a quick gesture as if to wave off any pity. "What I need now is for you to tell me everything you know about the diamond, the Jackal and the Jaded. Please."

Isabel smiled and in the quiet of Caroline Blackwell's library, she began to lay out a tale worthy of Mr. A.R. Crimson, patiently pausing for questions and working with Grace to slowly lay out the pieces of the vast puzzle of the Jaded's journey.

Until at last, Mrs. Grace Rutherford understood the game.

And where she would stand.

Michael sat with the others in the music salon where they'd finally heard the good news from Rowan and nearly collapsed in relief. Ashe had yet to make an appearance but it was understood that he would not be leaving his wife's side until his fears were completely assuaged. The rest was a blurred discussion of Darius's progress with Bellewood University's establishment and all the possibilities that life now offered them free of the Jackal. They toasted Ashe's beautiful daughters and Rowan assured them that they were tiny mirrors of each other and as identical as buttons.

"God, they'll have the running of him!" Josiah said. "*Two* daughters! He doesn't stand a chance!"

Michael stood at the first pause in the conversation. "Gentlemen, I have to return to the library and see if it's possible to…speak to my wife."

"Shall we go with you?" Galen offered. "To help plead your case?"

"Very amusing," Michael tried to smile. "No, this is something I will have to face alone."

Darius walked him to the salon door. "Give her time. It's a jolt to lose a brother."

"And what kind of jolt is it to find out that your new husband was practically a bystander to your brother's death?" Michael squared his shoulders before putting his hand on the doorknob. "She hates me, Darius."

"You are a very hard man to hate, Rutherford," Darius said as solemnly as a priest. "Take heart."

Michael opened the door and left his friends to their conversations.

He began to walk down the stairs and came to an awkward halt as Grace met him on her way up the same staircase. "Were you…coming up to…?"

"There is poetic balance in speaking to you here, don't you think?" she asked him calmly.

"In Ashe's home?"

"On stairs," she amended. "If I hadn't lingered on that landing today, I wonder what I would have missed."

Michael grimaced. "Why don't we go back down to the library and speak privately?"

She shook her head. "No. There is a wicked part of me that is enjoying how very awkward and miserable you look up there."

"Damn it," he muttered and deliberately walked to be three steps below her to level out their heights a touch and spare her neck from craning up at him. "You cannot be enjoying any part of this, Grace. I don't believe you."

"Nothing sinister, Michael. That is what you said to me; that there was nothing sinister in the business you had with my brother."

He nodded. "I lied."

"Why?"

"To protect you from the worst of it and as I'm being mortally honest from here forward, to make sure that you didn't warn your brother that I was aware of his villainy. It was like waltzing with the woman of my dreams with a viper at my feet, Grace."

"I never liked him, Michael. But that is a very horrible thing to admit…" she whispered. "I dreamt of a life free from him but I never wished him dead."

"I know." He ran a hand through his hair, his nerves getting the better of him. "I want to say I'm sorry but—I'm not sorry. I'm not sorry for stealing a taste of a happiness I'd long ago hardened my heart to ignore. But you, Grace, you are impossible to ignore."

"You, sir, are very talented when it comes to distracting me with sweet words and—"

"I love you, Grace." He bowed his head. "I wanted to say it one last time before you end this."

"Have you nothing else to say in your defense?"

"Other than the fact that your brother would have traded your life for a diamond? That he threatened to murder you and frame me for it if I didn't give him what he wanted? Or do you want me to try to go further back? As if his sins against all of us even after he abandoned us to die in a Bengal dungeon, his attempted murder and amoral disregard for the lives of innocents makes any difference to the ultimate truth that I was willing to do *anything* it took to keep you safe and to protect the people I love?"

"Anything?"

He nodded miserably. "I loved you enough to even see if there was a compromise to be made with a man who has actively tried to kill my friends and myself over the last few years. If there'd been even a glimmer of humanity in that man, I'd have laid down my own life before I'd have allowed him to lose his. I'd have found a path or forced an alliance because sparing his life might have meant that you wouldn't hate me."

"Do I hate you?" she asked, her eyes widening.

"You must," he said quickly but then a strange flicker of doubt came to life inside of him. "Don't you?"

She climbed one step and opened her arms, leaning forward to allow him to lift her into his arms. "I said I might but apparently, I cannot hate a man that I am in love with. It is a contrary but a terrible truth that I will live with for the rest of my life, Michael."

"You love me."

She nodded, tears shimmering like diamonds trailing down her cheeks. "I love you, Michael Rutherford."

He kissed her with a thorough sweetness that made everything inside of him break loose in a torrent of relief and joy. Her feet left the stairs and she clung to his neck as he held her fast, both of them desperate to relish their happiness and banish the last of fear.

He couldn't have saved Sterling, even if he'd wanted to. And he couldn't have handed over the diamond without risking the lives of his friends and their families. He'd forfeited almost everything and braced himself for the worst—and learned a valuable new lesson in the strategies of the heart.

Sometimes, a soldier has to accept defeat in order to achieve victory, and Grace was his reward.

Epilogue

"I still can't fathom it." Michael crossed his arms. "All of that misery and effort for what is ultimately a rock."

The diamond in question sat in the middle of the table between all of them, glittering with a brilliance that defied description.

"It's hardly a rock," Galen corrected him carefully. "And if so many believe it has magical properties as that prophesy claimed…"

"Bosh!" Rowan sputtered. "It's no more magical than a tea cup."

"Don't be so quick to judge," Ashe said, the solemn timber of his voice silencing them all for a moment. "Don't mock magic you yourself have benefitted from, Dr. West."

"I?" Rowan asked.

"All of you," Ashe said. "Ever since we walked out of that hell hole, the cards have generally fallen in our favor. Rowan came into that inheritance that allowed him to take over his father's practice and fund his clinic. Galen's investments paid off beyond his wildest dreams and he was able to restore his family's estate even before he came to the title. The few gems we did sell went for more than we'd expected and then good fortune touched us all. Darius will have his academic career. And look at me. Against all odds, I have my Caroline and two absolutely perfect angels who I intend to spend every spare moment spoiling until there is no chance of any man ever measuring up to their dear handsome father."

"He's a willing slave to them already," Josiah sighed.

Darius laughed. "It is a condition I'm eager to share in a few months."

"And what of you, Michael?" Ashe asked. "Aren't you curious how this sacred treasure in your possession extended to all of us, but not to you?"

Rutherford smiled. "And that's where you'd be wrong. *If* it's the source of our good fortunes, then I know exactly why my friends were included in its blessings."

"Do tell," Galen set down his glass of lemonade.

"Because we are all bound by brotherhood and I'd made a vow to leave none of you behind, to share whatever I had and to do everything in my power and possession to protect you if I could. I'd sworn an oath as we were leaving that dungeon. I think that chunk of rock was in my pocket when I said it out loud."

"My God! I remember that!" Darius exclaimed. "It was all chaos and noise but I remember you mumbling something about getting us out before you'd take a single breath of free air—and I thought you a little mad for it."

"So I think I blessed the Jaded without knowing it, and since we never broke the circle that connected us..."

"The spell was never broken?" Rowan finished. "But what of your fortunes, Michael?"

"I never cared for coin," Michael confessed. "On the ship, my greatest fears were finding a place to feel safe and belong, to achieve some sense of normal or family; and of course, to make sure I was in a position to uphold my oath to my friends."

"The Grove," Josiah said with a smile. "I brought you to the Grove!"

"Mrs. Clay and the Grove provided a home I'd only dreamt of and gave me everything I needed to heal." Michael's smile broadened. "Apparently, the raj's magic bauble recognizes the needs of a simple man."

"And now?" Josiah asked.

"Even with Grace, it's an extension of that first wish. She's family and my future. She makes any room a sweeter sanctuary and since we've added a door to adjoin both of the apartments, it's all the room we need. My Grace has no encumbrance of housework or duties, the largest desk I could find in all of London and..."

"And you," Galen finished the sentiment. "You are quite the unique and modern couple, Rutherford."

"So what now?" Darius pressed, shifting in his chair. "Don't forget the prophecy. So long as the East India Trading Company doesn't have it, then we are by default the foreign hands that hold it without ill intent that the ancient text referred to. If we keep it, we're safe but we have to keep it hidden away for all time."

Rowan ran a hand through his hair. "As a man of science, I'm still having trouble taking this all in."

The diamond's fire gleamed more brightly and each man did his best to convince himself it was a trick of the light.

"We keep it then." Michael stood from his chair and lifted his glass, and the others immediately followed suit. In an echo of mythical round tables and magical oaths in their country's past, every member of the Jaded raised his glass as they closed ranks. And as they spoke; their eyes were on each other and not the glittering stone between them. "Gentlemen!"

"To the continued haven and survival of the Weary and the Wicked!" Galen said.

"The Wanton and the Wandering," Ashe continued.

"And the Unwanted," Josiah whispered.

Their glasses touched and in unison they finished it.

"To the Jaded!"

fin

POSEIDON'S CURSE
OR
THE FATAL STORM
✩
A PENNY DREADFUL BY

A.R. CRIMSON
PRESENTED BY S&Y PUBLISHING
LONDON

CHAPTER ONE

An Ill Fated Voyage

The list of British ships that fought bravely against Napoleon is well known and celebrated by the people of Britain (as they should be, Dear Reader). But one ship in Her Majesty's Service is never spoken of; for its fate during the great Battle of the Nile of 1798 is unknown and her service has been largely stricken from the history books. At one time, she was officially listed as "lost in battle" but even that record has since vanished. Some say her captain must have turned traitor and run from the fray to disappear at such a critical moment; but no witness can say—for none have ever been found.

So here, Dear Reader, on these pages, allow me to tell you the final tale of the HMS *Fatal* and to reveal its true and unbelievable destiny. Read on, if you dare, and judge if her captain and crew be traitors or ultimately, heroes.

Captain Hiram Jack Martin, or Captain Hack Martin, as he known to his men is a striking figure, tall and sound with eyes as fierce as the seas. He is uncommonly tall and imposing. A fair leader who relies on his brave and moral example, the discipline of his officers and a generous spirit to earn the respect of his sailors and crew; it is war that binds them fast. The Mediterranean theater had encompassed a great naval campaign that summer between the English and French fleets and that now famous final battle in August loomed.

The *Fatal* was to bring up the rear of the English line of ships and support the *Justice*. In tandem with the fleet and under the command of the revered Admiral Nelson, Captain Martin is confident of ultimate victory. The crew is anxious to see battle again if only to end the gnawing toll on their nerves as they wait. Little do they know, they have a different battle ahead and an enemy unknown to them.

The sun sets in a ring of red and the sea turns to molten copper. It is a sign of foreboding for a superstitious traveler and portends blood to come. But Captain Martin laughs when his first mate, George Parsons, says as much. 'You're an old woman, George!' he teases. But the laughter dies quickly when the men on the ship slowly come to the realization that they cannot see the *Justice* or the line and a fog the color of pale mold is heading toward them with an uncanny speed—though the wind blows in the opposite direction.

Cries of alarm go up and within minutes, the ship is readied as if for battle. The wind changes, and changes again and something in his gut warns him that he spoke too soon and will owe his best friend an apology before the night is out. They were to sail toward Aboukir Bay with shallow shoals and challenging confines to take on the French directly but something tells him that they are now heading out to sea. He has navigated every form of weather known to man and with a sailor's understanding of wind and waves it is hard to shake his confidence. But he is shaken now.

CHAPTER TWO

A Storm for the Ages

For the space of several moments, too long to be dismissed as a figment of imagination, the wind stopped. It did not slow or lessen, it stopped. Grown men who had faced cannon fire and fought into the teeth of Napoleon Bonaparte's navy grew pale and one old salt began to cry. He couldn't be blamed for it and no one within hearing felt anything beyond a jealous wish that they weren't too frozen to weep as well.

Then the wind comes again with a hurricane force from above that presses the ship downward and lowers its keel so quickly that men stumble to clutch at the ropes and rails to prevent themselves from falling into the sea. Discipline takes over and they respond to the barked orders of the officers to save the ship. The wind lashes across the decks and the sails and the canvas begins to shred. Proud squares become strips of cloth that flutter like the mockery of a May Day celebration and the sky blackens but it doesn't rain.

The odd fog is gone but when Captain Hack Martin strides over to the wheel and looks up, his heart stops. The stars are gone and an umbrella of green fire arches over the tips of the masts encircling the ship like a mad sorcerer's cloak. Few have seen St. Elmo's fire but this—this is different. This fire burns. Men throw buckets of water onto the flames with no effect.

They cannot see another ship to signal their distress and Captain Martin fears that if the entire British Royal Navy is facing the same demons then all is lost. Green lightning sears the ship, the officers command the panic as best as they can and then the world fails to make sense when the ocean beneath the ship turns to glass but the waves encircling them churn and chop in a whirlpool that is higher than the rails on the decking. The HMS *Fatal* is trapped in a bowl of watery violence and then the main mast implodes. Hack took the wheel only to have it snap into a hundred pieces in his hand. The wood of the ship is brittle; the very structure they live and fight on begins to crumble beneath their feet. The *Fatal* is doomed.

Men below decks drown but the crew that have the means leap into the ocean to cling to what debris they can until the ship is gone beneath them. Gone as if it never existed and never sailed above but has always been a denizen of the depths. Wooden planks that should have held them aloft, abandoned them eager to disintegrate and sink along with the remainder of the *Fatal*.

Then the entire sea is the enemy. George Parsons calls out to Hack as the sea begins to eat the men. As if the waves became giant's hands with claws, men are gripped from below and overtaken by water than now has will. Man after man disappears in a malicious dance of magical seas and George screams before he meets his fate.

Captain Martin looks up to the sky, robbed even of the sight of the heavens to make his final plea or prayers, there is only a blanket of green flames and the vicious riptide of serpent shaped waves that surge up to consume him as well.

CHAPTER THREE

To Drown Alone

Hack holds his breath until he cannot. Invisible forces pull him downward and the pressure against his body is nearly unbearable. At last his lungs surrendered even when his will had not. Seawater flooded his lungs and darkness rules him as life slips away.

Captain Martin awakes and not to the bright glow of his heavenly reward but to the cold damp of a dim cavern with walls of rough stone and coral and door of bars formed from iron. The entire room looks as if it were quarried from a reef on the ocean's floor. He sits up from a pallet of rags and seaweed, sore and miserable but alive. He is alone.

He calls out for the guard and is rewarded quickly. Two men, half-naked of solid muscle necks as thick as bulls wearing nothing but what looked to his eyes like ancient Greek costumes unlock the bars and hold out the most savage looking weapons he has ever seen. It is a blade that curves and along the inside edge are shark's teeth edged in steel. It is not a rapier for graceful combat but a razor-sharp collection of aggressive cutting edges that promises pain to any adversary.

'Come, Human!'

He eyes them again convinced of their humanity but unsure enough not to argue. He complies without wasting words. Captain Martin is taken up through a palace the grandeur of which grows with each level they gain. But there is something otherworldly about the marble columns and ancient mosaics. Gemstones are set into the walls for effect, the floors are inlaid with mother of pearl and sea glass twisted like sea weed create sconces and vast lanterns that hang above to make his eyes widen. For the flames are green inside the sconces—green like the fire that overtook the *Fatal*.

At last, they reach a pair of doors large enough to herald an interior to shame the halls of Windsor. Captain Martin is pushed inside to a golden domed throne room filled with courtiers, all in similar Greek costumes that do nothing to hide their physical beauty. Each member is striking in his or her own way and he is amazed to think of such an assembly, all perfect and preening, now offended by his rougher appearance in their pristine midst.

He does not stumble as he approaches the dais and the throne. The massive throne glows and pulses faintly with the same green fire contained inside the sculpted sea glass that fans out in the shape of giant seashell but the woman perched atop it is not overshadowed by its beauty.

Venus would be vain enough to gnash her teeth at the woman there in a gown of gold with hair like mahogany wood. Her eyes flash like emeralds and she is too lovely for further description. Each time he looks at her, he is dazzled. But for now, curiosity and fear override appreciation.

'What is this place?' he asks without ceremony.

The courtiers gasp at his cheekiness but the woman only smiles. "This is Atlantis and I am its Queen. I am Queen Arête.'

CHAPTER FOUR
Atlantis Holds Court

His brow furrowed and he almost laughed at the ridiculous proclamation. Almost. For had he not been taken by the sea? Even so it is the nature of men to doubt. 'Atlantis is a myth. A child's tale of nonsense that only drunks repeat when the voyage is too long or they have a convenient map to sell.'

'Myth?' She waved a scepter toward the dome's peak above them and Captain Martin nearly fell to the marble floor as solid gold became as transparent as glass to reveal not sky but ocean. Ocean as he had never seen it because it was above him, with life teeming across the view, and the outline of a moon once familiar wavered distorted by the depths of the sea.

Martin turned to leave unwilling to accept what his eyes could not deny but the guards cut off his retreat. Their blades gleamed and reflected in the light, no mercy in their eyes. 'Poseidon will have your bones to atone for this trespass against the Queen! How dare you turn your back on Her Glorious Presence, human scum!'

They drag him back before the throne, this time to press him down against his will onto his knees on the steps of the dais.

'Hold! What is your name, man?'

'Captain Hiram Martin.'

She smiles. 'I shall make you my guest, Captain. It is a good omen. I always select one slave to act as my personal attendant for the Festival and while many find the position challenging, I like the look of you. I expect to enjoy our time together, Captain.'

'I am no slave.'

'Are you not?' Queen Arête waves her hand and at the far end of the room a rag-tag group of men, the crew they plucked from the sea, are brought in wearing chains around their necks and shackles on their feet. 'Behold! Your crew, yes?'

'Yes.' For there is George and his officers, several of the sailors and the crew he is bound to by honor and experience. These are brothers in arms and it is clear that their lives hang in the balance.

'What say you now?'

'If you spare my men—'

'We are not in a negotiation, Captain. These men will serve Atlantis in different ways and it is for us to determine their fate and their treatment. Not you. But of course, if you resist, we are less inclined to be kind.' She stood and Hack sees that resistance gains nothing where extending his life may allow him to extend the lives of others. If not directly—then by stealth. He nods to give himself time to think and plot a way out.

'I am your slave.' The words taste like bile in his mouth for he is proud but he holds to hope. And what are words? What are their weight or measure when a man kneels before the Queen of a mythical kingdom while sharks swim overhead?

Queen Arête smiles and gestures toward the floor next to her throne where he is to sit. Hack has never known surrender in battle or in life but he surrenders now. He sits like a dog next to her and his education begins.

As his crew is brought forward and examined by the courtiers who begin to divide them into seven groups, the Queen begins to explain the rituals ahead. The Festival of the Tides will last for seven nights, beginning tonight.

'We will blend the strengths of your crew to make each team as viable as possible but the first team, traditionally, is the strongest for we hope for the blessing of a successful hunt.'

'Hunt?'

She shrugs her shoulders, bored with teaching already.

'Prepare for the first excursion!' She stands and points to George who is glaring at all of them defiantly. 'That one! Put him in the lead!'

She turns back to Hack. 'Come. I want you to wear something better suited for the occasion.'

He is forced to follow her but looks to George and the others before they are hauled out, blades at their backs. He waves what he hopes is encouragement to his friend and then retreats with his new mistress.

'What is the Festival of Tides? Was mine the only ship you took? And what excursion is it that they prepare for?'

She ignores him and he is led to a room with a giant bath at its center. To his humiliation, she takes a seat as other servants, human like him but with hollow eyes come into the room. She claps her hands together and points at Hack. 'Bathe him.'

It is a wicked thing but he is stripped of his clothes before her. Too proud to cover himself he stands as if it doesn't grind at him to be treated thusly. The attendants push and pull him into the water and then bathe him while Queen Arête's gaze never wavers.

'I am pleased with your height and your form, Captain,' she teases. 'And now I am also pleased with the way you smell.'

Capt. Hiram is spared only because the Queen of Atlantis is taken with him. She feeds him and clothes him, like a pampered pet and as the night unfolds he is not adverse to her touch before a gong sounds and she leads him back to the public rooms of the palace.

'You will have your answers, Captain. Soon now.'

CHAPTER FIVE

A Deadly Harvest

The first Ritual is that night and Hack is given a new view of the city of Atlantis as they move out toward a temple where the Queen tells him that the Atlantians hold sacred. Sorcery holds the city to the ocean floor and every house and palace is interconnected with the ocean just outside its windows. The view out every window reminds him that there is no escape.

Finally they reach a long hall that has the look of a temple to him (though without any sign of which god they might be pleading to). Carved sea serpents wrap around every marble column and surface and Captain Martin eyes them without admiration. Their beauty is too terrifying. The courtiers in their best finery line along the temple's walls and their expressions convey delight, anticipation, and anxiety at the Queen's arrival though they ignore the human consort at her heels. Green fire danced atop an altar at the far end of the room with a huge portal behind it circled by a single sea serpent frozen in stone in the act of consuming his own tail.

A few members of the crew were already there, still chained together but their clothes had been changed. Hack winces to think that they too endured a bath like animals for the amusement of nearby courtiers. But unlike his clothes of silk and luxury, his men are swathed in leather pants and wide belts with the look of gladiators.

George's look is solemn. They cannot talk. Not without risking the wrath of their hosts but there is something in his eyes. They have told him something of the ordeal ahead and his expression reflects a dark fear and knowledge that cannot be forgotten.

It is time.

'For as long as we can remember, the Elixir is life! Immortality is ours and the gift of Poseidon ours for the taking!' Queen Arête addressed the room. 'Let the Harvest begin!'

His men are pushed toward the door and the carved stone portals slide back to reveal ocean, held in place as if by glass they cannot be seen.

Beyond is a dim natural rock tunnel that leads . . . Hack knows not where.

As the chains from their feet are removed, the crewmen are armed with strange weapons, long tubes of glass tipped with a twisted dagger…like a giant syringe or siphon but the black wrapped handles and echoes of a pikes make his skin crawl.

'Tell me.' Hack hisses in the Queen's ear.

'They will face the Kraken.'

'To kill it?'

'NO!' She stares at him in horror. 'It is the last of its kind! But we need the Elixir for the kingdom. The blood of the Kraken has power that you cannot imagine. We *must* have it and the Festival is the only time it can be harvested.'

'Why not send your own men to this task?'

She laughs cruelly. 'Why risk the worthy and lovely life of our own when your crew are at hand?'

Armed guards stand by the portal should any man lose his courage and refuse the task.

Drums pound and the men are shoved forward with their unwieldy weapons, and a black cloth is wrapped over their mouths and noses. As a gong sounds and the Atlantian priests begin to mumble and chant, the crew is pushed through the portal and into the water.

It is shock at first as they fight instinctively against the water and the terror of drowning and then more surprise as each man realizes that the cloth transforms water to air. They swim now, their feet lifted from the rocks and turn down the passage that is their only choice.

Each disappears from sight.

Hack waits and then a sound unlike any is heard. A roar that makes the temple walls rattle and the sea serpents on the columns vibrate. A trick of the light makes their stone eyes gleam and some of the courtiers burst into applause. Some murmur to each other in anxious hope of the Elixir but the cry at the end of the passage changes and deepens and the seawater they can see through the portal changes color.

Tendrils of red snake out from the dark until the water is red with blood and unrecognizable. It is too much blood for Hack to hope. None of the crew return.

The Atlantians are disappointed. The Queen shrugs. 'There are six nights left. It is rare to have success on the first night but there is time yet. Come, human. Let us be back to my bedroom and see if we cannot alleviate my mood.'

Captain Martin is trapped in a nightmare that repeats nightly. More, more, and more of his crew are brought into the temple each night, more familiar faces, trembling and crying some of them, as they are armed and then fed to the Kraken. Then the Queen leads him back to her rooms where he is held in lustful thrall. She hypnotizes him with her every sigh and Captain Hack Martin begins to despair of his soul.

Until the worst—the fifth night. George's young son, a boy barely twelve is in their number and Hack has had all he can of restraint and threats. The petted and pampered captive rebels.

'No!'

He races forward to put himself in front of the others. 'I will go! I will get the Elixir for you, Queen Arête! Stand aside. You cannot send children in and expect them to accomplish a manly feat.'

Shouts of protest and a struggle with the guards heralds failure but the Queen holds up her hand and the din of a melee is instantly silenced. 'Time is short.' She nods consent. 'Get me my Elixir and earn My Mercy.'

CHAPTER SIX

Facing the Kraken

He takes a weapon from George's son and places the belt around his waist. He ignores the rumbles behind him and shifts the long spear's handle from one side to the other to try to learn the weight and working of it. It is heavier than it looks but he's glad. The density in his palms makes it real and settles his nerves. He will do this thing and face this monster. He will save the lives of the men he can and the son of his friend. He shakes off the guilt that the Queen's sorcery has held him in check until now. That pain is for another day.

He does not wait for the gong or allow them their barbaric rituals. The priests aren't even in place as he grabs a black cloth from the altar and ties it around his own mouth and nose. They don't push him through the portal.

Captain Hiram Jack Martin strides in on his own volition.

He knows he will not drown. He has seen the others and simply begins swimming down the dark passage away from the temple. He does not look back. He kicks with his legs and holds the glass spear out in front of him.

Once the tunnel turns and the lights of the temple no longer illuminate his path, he slows. He knows that if George had greater numbers and still did not triumph that he cannot blunder in.

He ignores his normal senses that urge him to stay to the floor and instead begins to swim along the ceiling of the tunnel, his internal compass broken. Like a human spider he makes his way underwater toward Death.

The Kraken sleeps. He cannot see its mass or fathom its true form. It is too horrible and he is not there to study it for scholars. The dark changes and there is a faint illumination from strange creatures that gather in pockets of the rock. Barnacles glow yellow and there is enough light to ensure that his nightmares will be complete. There is no other opening or entrance. How the beast was captured to live in the confines of its own filth, it's hard to say. 'It is a prisoner and a slave to them, like me.'

One great eye is closed and he swims above it to decide his strategy.

Dropped weapons litter the floor of the lair and a few stick out from its tentacles like bristles on a sea urchin. The other men had tried to draw the Kraken's blood from an outstretched arm perhaps to avoid teeth the size of elephant tusk that seeped tendrils of milky poison into the seawater it slept in. Its body reveals several wounds, none fatal, but Captain Martin decides to take his chances.

He floats down behind its head, the skin a putrid surface of mottled browns near a small tear edged in glowing crystal shards from the ceiling above where the monster must have thrashed during a previous battle. He reads it as a sign that when angered, the monster thinks nothing in its rage.

Instead of driving his weapon in, he slides the scalpel sharp tip just into the sore, slowly, deeply to allow the tool to do its work.

'Is there such a thing? A gentle wounding?'

Black blood as dark as the darkest onyx ink fills the large glass tube—and other details find their way into his notice as he fulfills his purpose. The creature's breathing is labored. The skin reminds him of a landscape of disease and death. When the vial was full, he pulls it out as cautiously as he can and the dagger end becomes a stopper. He swims back down the tunnel and steps into the temple chamber bearing his ebony prize.

'Your elixir, my Queen.' He offered it into her greedy hands and the drums in the temple and the gong sound with a cacophony of celebration. The priests hold it aloft and the Atlantians cheer. 'But where is my crew?'

She smiles enigmatically. 'They will serve us in another way. But you are my champion and tonight we will partake of our traditional feast! It must be held to strengthen us before the final Rites tomorrow night.'

CHAPTER SEVEN
A Feast of Suffering

She prepares him for the evening's revelries and shows him her private gardens. Everything in her touch and look enchants and the horror of the Kraken fades in her presence as she bids him lay down with his head in her lap while she touches his face and weaves a tale. Queen Arête shares the story of the Elixir with her beloved captive.

'Immortality has long been the quest of the rulers and priests of Atlantis. Their
every thought and effort was shaded by their insatiable desire to live beyond all
other races and transcend the clutches of death. Men looked to Atlantis as a
shining City State without equal and their fame spread throughout the known
lands.'

'But the Gods of Olympus were disgusted by their arrogance and their pride and
decided to test their metal.'

'One day, an emissary of the sacred temple of Poseidon was sent to ask why the
Atlantians should live when others died and why they would deserve such a
Divine Gift. The King of Atlantis answered with a sneer that they received no
"gifts" but would earn the achievement of immortality on their own merit with
brilliant science and superior technology. He boasted that the world of men
would kneel in awe to them and the humblest Atlantian would surpass the
distant and dusty splendor of the gods.'

'What of your Patron Deity? What of Poseidon?' the emissary asked. 'Surely
you do not think to scoff at his powers!'

'The King laughed. "Poseidon should be pleased that his children have grown
so clever that we need not bow and scrape to every tide for our prosperity! And
if he is pouting at our glory, there are plenty of ignorant fishermen left in the
world to assuage the hurt.'

'And so the fate of Atlantis was sealed.'

'A gift was presented to the King of Atlantis at the next Rites of Tides. It was an
opiate derived from the blackest inky blood of the Kraken that swam in the
deepest depths of icy ocean imaginable. No one was sure of its origins. But a
gold embossed note explained that it was the gift of immortality from the gods
themselves in tribute to the worthy people of our kingdom. One small dose
transported the subject into a state of euphoria like no other, warming their skin
and reminding them of what it had been to stand in the sun and walk as men—
As the delight faded, their beauties returned to former glories, their bodies
refreshed and rejuvenated and they failed to fear!'

'Very quickly, we came to prize it above all other things.'

'It is addictive then?' he asks.

The Queen shrugs her shoulders unconcerned. 'It is terrible to feel the change come over us but we cannot resist the Elixir now. It is the only thing that sustains us and after all, we always return to our natural state.'

A chill creeps up his skin but he ignores it.

A gong sounds. 'Come, it is time for the Feast of Tides to celebrate your successful harvest of the Elixir.' She leads him from the idyllic garden with its glass walls and the ocean pressing in on all sides. 'They will sing your praises for a long time to come, Captain.'

Into the Throne Room, he follows her as if in a dream. The dome is once more solid gold and the courtiers all shine with an ethereal beauty that makes him wonder if any mortal would not mistake them for gods. A long table has been set up and already the feast is underway.

He is given a place of honor next to Queen Arête. Hack tastes the wine and the smell of the dishes is enticing but then the lids come off of the giant platters and as the revelers cheer the work of their kitchens.

And Captain Martin catches a glimpse of Hell.

The feast is comprised of his crew…all the men he thought to have saved. They are laid out in various forms and pieces on platters. Next to a great bowl filled with the eyes of his men, plates of hands and feet in jellied sauces, filets and pastries, even puddings of their sweet breads, he spies George's boy roasted whole atop a gold ornate stand. His cooked body is artfully arranged as if he were peacefully asleep but the nearest courtier has already cut open his belly to reveal a seafood stuffing that steams in the night air. New drink is brought out in sea glass pitchers and Hack recognizes human blood pouring out into the goblets of the guests.

The room spins and he stumbles from the table.

He hears laughter and then comes back to himself in the bed of the Queen. She tries to comfort her fevered captain, kissing him and casting an erotic spell that he slips into, grateful for the escape from the madness and horrors in the royal throne room. Aware that it is no escape at all but a dark fall into bedlam.

'You killed my crew.'

'Shh! They served their purpose. Tomorrow is the last night of the festival. You'll see. You'll see the Change and why we must have the Elixir.' She strokes his hair as if her words alone are enough.

And Hack tries not to hear the faint sound of cutlery and laughter from the throne room below them.

CHAPTER EIGHT
Poseidon's Revenge

He awakes alone just before the last night's ritual.

He can hear them downstairs and races to the throne room. The Elixir his crew died trying to get and that he alone retrieved is brought in, a giant marble bowl holds it on a dais in the center of the floor and every citizen lines up to take their portion and imbibes. He watches from a narrow alcove behind Queen Arête's throne.

At first it is like any bacchanalian orgy as the courtiers cavort and dance to celebrate the blinding beauty and pleasure the Elixir brings. Without hesitation they sample each other's forms, openly fornicating in a frenzy that exhausted the watcher, the tangle of bodies becoming unrecognizable.

And then it all changes.

His Queen is the most beautiful of all, laughing at her ecstasy and shamelessly dancing naked atop the dais for all to desire.

And then her beauty alters, her pale skin darkens and she transforms.

Around the room, all of them begin to cry out with a new tenor. They begin to writhe and twist, scream and screech. Yet even then, the sexual undercurrent only strengthens and Hack fights the vomit rising up in his throat as monsters pump and play at a mockery of love.

They are a nightmare to behold! The black ink coursed through their veins and showed through the pale glove of their skin, pulsing in branches of gothic feathery dark veins across their bodies and proclaiming their immorality.

For the true horror that our Captain could only guess at was that over time, the addictive opium permanently strips them of the white marble like beauty they once possessed. Lost now is a beauty that had inspired the Greeks and Romans to believe in Gods—and left them as tentacled monsters with gaping maws where their mouths had been and serpent shaped spines.

'Am I not beautiful to you, Captain Martin?' She hissed and undulated toward him, a trail of putrid slime in her wake. 'For you are beautiful to me and now that I have a man worthy of the Festival, you will repeat your bravery every year and bring us what we need…and I will reward you in my bed, my dearest pet. Does this not please you?'

CHAPTER NINE
The Fatal Storm

He races from her, from all of them. He races down the dreaded paths to the temple to escape sea monsters in pursuit. Captain Martin grabs one of the guard's weapons from the wall and a black cloth around his face. He is into the tunnel. This time there is no care. Death whispers in his ear and Hack is set on his course. He swims into the darkness and then toward the great beast, so deadly and so powerful…imprisoned in this hole.

He swims into its gaping mouth, narrowly missing its teeth and clutching his blades allows himself to become a meal that the Kraken will quickly regret. He cuts and slashes, twists and turns, a sharp whirling dervish that damages the monster with a dozen mortal wounds from within. He fights, the black cloth now converting blood to air and in the tight confines of the Kraken's guts, he conquers the wet until the cries and screams of the Kraken make him deaf. The Kraken dies and as the cave and tunnel turn black with its blood and the Elixir dies with it, the screams of Atlantis echo through the underwater city. For the Kraken was the last and Immortality, even as twisted monsters, is a prize they were unwilling to yield.

Captain Martin's fate? Who can say? Did they retrieve him from his gory prison of a rotting Kraken and tear him into pieces for a feast of their own? Or did they toss him back into the dungeons of Atlantis to cling to the narrow hope that if another Kraken were found, they would have their champion at the ready? And how would they keep such a champion alive? Would they use the last of their stores of Elixir? Would they extend his life and transform him against his will into the monsters he feared?

Believe me not? At your own peril, you must each decide what you will hold to when the storms come. Think your civilization divine? Think that you are above the gods? Hold fast, readers.

And who is it that can relay all this tale and convey the secrets of the HMS *Fatal?* Who is it that can testify to the truth of it or swear to seeing Captain Martin breathe his last in the arms of the ocean's Queen Arête when his body finally gave out and the icy touch of her love could not save him?

Perhaps only the Queen herself, mortal reader.

Beware. And Voyage safely.

The End

A Last Note to Readers

Still reading? Well here's your treat. I put my hidden notes where only you would find them. Where do I start? So many wonderful emails and questions have come my way as this series unfolded, so I'll try to hit a few fun tidbits and behind-the-scenes facts for my Super Readers. After all, I'm going to assume it's only my die-hard Jaded Fans that are venturing this far and that everyone else closed the book after the words "The End".

Truthfully, it was my first editor in the series, Kate Seaver, who pushed the jewels to the forefront (and into the titles!) and made me rework the plots around them. The thought was that readers are mostly women and women like jewels. I couldn't really argue since I'm a bit of a magpie and have a frightening penchant for anything shiny (this includes glass and plastic…I have no ability to discriminate between real gems and the sparkly fake stuff apparently and take equal delight in either one!) Even so, at first, I was a very reluctant player as I looked at the synopsis for the first book, REVENGE WEARS RUBIES, so I rebelliously decided that if there were going to be jewels I would take it to the next level. The gems became a thriller style sub-plot that I stubbornly carried forward…and here we are!

Okay, let's work backwards. Yes, Michael joined the military when he was fourteen and the British Army took boys as young as twelve at that time, bless their hearts. He was far too poor to have purchased a commission and I loved the idea of him existing in a twilight of rank as a bodyguard and personal attendant to his "betters". Michael's polish inevitably would have come from his association with more educated men and the necessities of becoming familiar with a gentleman's routines as he served and guarded them. He taught himself to read using penny novels and to this very day, refuses to give them up. (Especially now that his beloved Grace supplies him with all the stories he could ever hope for!)

To my military buffs, I am fully aware that snipers are a more modern convention of war and something the British would never have admitted deploying in the 19th century. I understand that an American Sharps rifle in the hands of a British shooter in 1857 would have been as rare as a butterfly on a battlefield. But for the sake of fiction, I pushed the envelope so that my beloved Michael could take on the full weight of war and because I find long-range snipers enigmatic, compelling and they fire up my imagination. Blame me. Not Ian. He gave me fabulous information that I then chose to ignore.

I never fully explained the madness of the raj or why he literally collected foreigners but honestly, why try? Explaining the rationale of a madman is a bit beyond me and I think life is full of lovely unanswered questions. Bottom Line: He was not right in the head and as the British culture/presence became a new reality in his twisted domain, he saw others turning their relationships with the British Crown into political advantages. But why be a servant to the British? Why not just "own" a few and have them on hand? I'm sure he thought to demonstrate his genius and power that he could pluck these white men off their feet and keep them without fear of retaliation… And then the rebellion hit, and his guests were even more "valuable" (although that value would have increased if he'd bothered to tell anyone outside of his palace that he had them.) And then he forgot he had them. Because his dinner was cold. Or his favorite peacock died. I'll let you paint in the rest of that grim tale.

And yes, my husband recently "gifted" me with a space of my own to write, so when it came to Grace, I couldn't think of anything she would appreciate more from the man of her dreams.

Lots of villains, so little time! I know I don't always kill the bad guys, but again, I think it makes for a more real and compelling read when things aren't too neatly tied up in a bow. Did you need to "see" Sterling's end? Trust me.

He's not coming back. Ever. And if they find pieces of him in the Thames at some point (highly unlikely), I doubt he would be recognizable. (Forensic sciences being what they were in 1860…) He is dead like the monster under the mountain in your favorite childhood books and if I edited out the scene where he bites it that was an artistic choice. Penny Dreadfuls are lovely reading and crime books thrill, but for this story, I didn't think it was a good call to have a gruesome scene where a bad man begs for his life and fails to convince the powers-that-be that his life is worth more than a flawed rock in a leather pouch. Not near the end of the story, and not so close to the drama of Caroline and Ashe.

And yes, if you really were paying attention there were ultimately six villains in that dark little club to mirror my six lovely heroes…and no, I never named them all. A writer has to save a little something for a rainy day.

Josiah Hastings is suffering from a delightful version of macular degeneration of my own making with a dash of cataracts and floaters to make it interesting. While I appreciate the notes begging me to give him only cataracts and send him off to France for surgery; Mr. Hastings declined to travel abroad to submit to the procedure. (Stubborn things, men, don't you agree?) Eleanor remains his source of beauty in the world and he has a few more paintings yet before the shadows win. But Josiah isn't afraid of the dark, and I know my readers understand that with his prim and lovely lady at his side, his future is very bright.

Gayle continues to study medicine and thrive under her husband's tutelage and while it was a work of fiction, I will respectfully not be giving her access to a formal education or licensing to honor the women who truly were first and fought that fight. Rowan is a progressive thinker but still a man of his age, so he has clearly encouraged her in the areas of midwifery and women's health but probably still engages in rousing arguments about how she doesn't need to treat the rougher elements in his weekly clinics.

Caroline's dreams of a university for women is part of a future series if you ask this writer. Bellewood College has a place in my heart and I love the idea of a series of books based on the women who will cross through those doors and turns of their lives and loves. (Besides a selfish wish to catch a glimpse of Darius Thorne the professor and his wife Isabel…and friends…and…)

How close did I come to killing Caroline? Close. I think a previous editor had a heart attack when I mentioned the option and I was talked out of it. It is a convention of our genre that main characters seem immortal—but every time I watch Downton Abbey, or any great romantic and dramatic series on television, I'm jealous at their knack for ending a character's life to wring more emotion from their audience. So apparently, I'm a wicked person. Please don't send me hate mail. I did NOT kill Caroline and Ashe's happiness remains intact.

Although, somebody out there admit it! If I'd done it and snuffed her, it would have made for an amazingly emotional ending and potentially…a great set-up for another story…Seriously. No hate mail, friends.

And finally, we're down to Galen's tale. After all this time, I'm not sure if I have any secrets left except to say that Herbert wasn't really intended to have a happy ending of his own until a reader sent me an email that was so kind and gracious, I decided to make her an opera singer and the rest, as they say, is history. Thank you, Betsy!

And yes, just in case no one was paying attention…there were a couple of fun new secondary characters in this last book and I for one would LOVE to see their stories. Anyone? Sabrina Martin is lovely, don't you think? I find something about beautiful widows very appealing and I think she deserves a fairy-tale of her own. And what about "Death"? Nothing like a tall, dark and handsome, English-educated, foreign assassin to make a future woman's day…I do enjoy bad boys.

If I missed anything, send me a note and I'll do my best to get you an answer. I won't promise that it will be a good answer, but I will promise to do my utmost.

Again, thank you, Dear Readers!

The Jaded will miss you…

Made in the USA
Lexington, KY
29 May 2014